SHAMAN OF SOULS

Scars of the Necromancer Book One:

Shaman of Souls

R. M. Wilshusen

Sidhe Publishing LLC

Sidhe Publishing LLC

Print ISBN: 978-1-7370165-0-2
E-book ISBN: 978-1-7370165-1-9

Library of Congress Control Number: 2021907401

CONTENTS

1: The Outcasts   1

2: The Seeker   20

3: The Soldier   29

4: The Outcasts   45

5: The Seeker   63

6: The Outcasts   77

7: The Soldier   97

8: The Seeker   109

9: The Outcasts   126

10: The Soldier   144

11: The Seeker   155

12: The Outcasts   166

13: The Soldier   186

14: The Seeker   201

15: The Outcasts   210

16: The Soldier   220

17: The Fallen   245

18: The Citadel   248

19: The Outcasts   264

20: The Soldier   285

21: The Citadel   291

22: The Outcasts   299

23: The Soldier   315

24: The Citadel   329

25: The Outcasts   350

26: The Soldier   361

27: The Citadel   375

28: The Outcasts   385

29: The Soldier   397

30: The Outcasts   409

31: The Citadel   426

32: The Soldier   444

33: The Outcasts   453

34: The Citadel   460

35: The Soldier   472

36: The Outcasts   484

37: The Citadel   491

38: The Soldier   502

39: The Outcasts   511

40: The Citadel   518

41: The Soldier   528

42: The Outcasts   533

43: The Citadel   542

44: The Soldier   547

45: The Apprentice   558

46: The Outcasts   566

47: The Citadel   583

48: The Soldier   597

49: The King   601

50: The Shaman   606

THE OUTCASTS

Criske Val-Zhang let out a yawn as he pulled on his boots, making sure that they were securely on his feet by stamping some feeling into his toes. Even though it was early summer, the nights were far too cold for his comfort. "I hate patrol day," he mumbled to no one in particular. Regardless of his own feelings, he stood, ensuring his uniform was in order, his thick truncheon and knife in his belt. He tossed on his cloak and flipped the hood up to hide his ears.

Despite how much he hated patrol day, he couldn't afford to miss the extra coin.

Shuffling over to the end of the barracks, he ran his finger down the long wooden board near the entrance to check the sheet that listed who his patrol partner would be for the day. After finding his own name, he scanned over to the person next to him. "Henrik…Ihvihlan?" Criske tried to wrap his mouth around the name, fighting the fog of in his mind.

"Oh. A Dwarf. Great." He had never worked with this particular Dwarf before. Most of the Dwarves he met were silent, brooding types. They said nothing to him while on patrol. They were too busy scanning the crowds like bloodhounds trying to sniff out a blood trail. No doubt about it, this was going to be a long shift. Especially since he had a double today.

"Ah! Greetings, *Khlanro*. I see you are already set to go this morning!" Criske jumped and turned, a hand reflexively going to his knife. He slowly eased his hand off the hilt when he saw the speaker. Facing him was a rather unusual Dwarf. His face was clean-shaven, his long and curly black hair plaited in a braid that hung partway down his back. He was rather tall for his race, just over five feet, though he was still around half a foot shorter than your average female Elf. His chocolate-brown eyes were bright with excitement and far too much enthusiasm for this early hour. He stepped forward, extending an arm that was covered in scars and muscle. Whoever this was, he had clearly been well fed when he was younger.

"I am Henrik Ihvihlan. I will be your patrol partner for today."

Criske extended his thin, comparatively delicate hand and grasped Henrik's. "Criske Val-Zhang. Pleasure," he said cautiously. "You ever done a morning patrol?"

Henrik nodded, staring at Criske's face with an air of detached curiosity. Then his face lit up in recognition. "Ah. So you are the Half-Elf in our unit!"

Criske yanked his hand out of Henrik's. "What's it to you?" he asked coolly.

"I heard that you were quite the patrolman. I was hoping I could pick up some pointers from you. I am rather new to the city." Henrik raised his hands in a mollifying gesture. "I meant no disrespect."

The Half-Elf looked at his new partner, unsure how to process the statement, before finally saying, "Alright. Let's go. We can't afford to be late to the merchant's district. There's always activity going on there."

With a swish, Henrik put his cloak on in one smooth motion. It had multiple stains and had clearly seen wear and tear. New to the city he might be, but whoever Henrik was, he wasn't unaccustomed to harsh weather and long travel. Not a bad trait for a fellow Guardian to have.

"Are you one of those already-trained guys?" Criske asked as they headed out of the barracks. The sun was already rapidly starting its climb, the very top of the celestial disk braving the horizon and entering a new day.

Henrik laughed. "Yes. I am. Though that isn't uncommon in my *Khlanriir*, for those of us who join. We can't afford to let down the Trifecta."

"How were your marks for basic training?" Criske asked. It was time for an honesty check. If his partner was going to hang him out to dry, he'd prefer to know now, instead of when he was stuck with a knife in his back.

"My marks were relatively high. Though, I heard a rather terrifying girl from the Human Territories surpassed everyone with relative ease. I had hoped to score higher, but that just means I'll have to put in more work than the rest of them when I'm on actual duty." He clapped Criske on the shoulder. "That is why I need to learn from my betters, no?"

Criske felt the knot in his stomach ease slightly. This one was kind of stiff, but at least he seemed more levelheaded than most. Regardless, he would have to do. The walk through the Guardian headquarters didn't take Criske long. "Headquarters," in reality, was a rather glorified term for the squat buildings made of stone and mortar, the slate shingles beaten down by weather and time. Even though they were the international guards of the Trifecta, the three nations preferred to spend most of their money on the fortresses of their actual homeland.

Henrik appeared to take a deep interest in his surroundings, staring at the stonework and cobblestone pathways. "Not bad," he mused. "Not Dwarven made, of course. But I must say that Humans have always done a great job with what they have."

Criske couldn't help smiling at the comment. "You an expert on architecture?"

Henrik shook his head. "Far from it. More like an enthusiast. It takes a lifetime to be considered an expert mason or architect. I actually—" Henrik faltered in embarrassment. "I was actually an archaeologist before I joined."

Archaeology was a subsection of history that involved gritty labor, little glory, and a lot of plinking away at rocks, from what Criske knew.

And that was not very much. Unsure what to say, he decided to let the statement lie with a noncommittal nod. "C'mon. It's going to be packed if we don't hurry up."

Trifectus' markets were always jammed in the early rush. Too many merchants, too few spots. It was a surefire recipe for trouble.

Passing through the open gates of the headquarters, the pair entered the city proper. Most merchants who weren't farm laborers, smiths, or bakers had yet to open shop. There wasn't much point until the later morning when most of the merchants had finished setting up for a day of dealing. As it stood, the narrow streets were empty, save for the occasional beggar to whom Criske tossed a coin or two. He came across a particularly old man with a dirty face and wild hair sticking out every which way.

"Hey, you still alive, you bag of bones?" Criske said with a wave.

The old man blinked awake, smiling when he saw Criske's face. He spoke with a gruff and strained voice, like a man who had spent most of his life shouting. "I dunno some days, Half. My joints creak and groan like an ol' ship's. Warnin' you: word is there are a few jewelry merchants down there today. I'm bettin' that a few will try and lighten their load."

Criske nodded and bade the man goodbye after handing him a chunk of bread from his lunch ration. He hurried through the streets, dipping into the still-dark back alleys he had memorized since he had started patrolling the city two years ago. Henrik, looking confused, followed him. "Is that man reliable?"

Criske nodded. "Yeah. Old man Ranth is a good one to lean on. No one pays much attention to a blind guy. Seem to forget he has ears. Follow me. It's about to get very loud."

Sure enough, Criske could already hear the cacophony of the merchant quarter up ahead, even though it was still a city block away. When they rounded onto one of the merchant streets, Henrik let out an impressed whistle. "That…is quite a *Bazariliiq*."

Criske nodded. "Yeah. Now keep your eyes peeled. There are going to be a few cutpurses here—guaranteed. If you see anything, let me know, but do it quietly. Last thing we want is to have them make a run for it, yeah?"

"Understood, *Khlanro*."

Criske adopted what he called his "scanning stance." To the common observer, he was just perusing the stalls, taking a gander at the morning's river fish, wheat crops, trinkets, and the like. In reality, he was using his peripheral vision to spot any sly hands or weird movements. It was a trick that had kept him alive over the years: keeping his head down and senses sharp.

Henrik had a very different tactic. The Dwarf would often stop and strike up conversation with the merchants, asking them how their travels were, how business was lately, and comment on particular histories. But every so often, Criske could see Henrik's occasional tilt of the head, as if he were listening for trouble.

It wasn't long before he found it.

A rather greasy-looking fellow tried to snag a low-hanging pheasant from a merchant while Henrik's back was turned. The Dwarf's truncheon came down with a solid thwack just inches above the would-be thief's fingertips. Henrik turned to the man and gave him a small smile. "Hold, my dear man." He pointed to another pheasant just above the one the man was going to steal. "You should consider this one instead. It has a little less meat on it, but the stock it would make would be fantastic." Henrik turned to the merchant, a portly Human huntsman. "Wouldn't you agree, *Siirnah*?"

The merchant looked at the pheasant for a moment. "Ah yes. I do believe it would. And the price is almost half."

"Forget it," growled the other man, sulking off and vanishing into the crowd.

Criske walked over and looked at the pheasant. He pointed to the knotted strings that held their limp feet to the stall. "You mind?" he asked the merchant. The man gave him an impartial shrug. Criske quickly took down the pheasants and tied them back up with a constrictor knot. "There. They won't be able to snatch off you so quickly."

The merchant looked at the knots and thanked them. The two Guardians returned to their patrolling. The hours passed by slowly and were relatively uneventful in Criske's eyes. Henrik's approach was a good one, he decided. A little haphazard and random, but he had an advantage that Criske did not: size. Even though Criske was taller, Henrik's broad shoulders, straight back, and demeanor seemed to dissuade crime by his mere presence. It made it all the easier for Criske to seemingly vanish into the shadows and wait.

He didn't have to wait long. "Stop, thief!"

Criske whipped around to see a man taking off and then disappearing into the crowd. Henrik was trying to muscle his way through the surrounding people but wasn't making much progress. Criske turned to see a nearby building. Without hesitation, he threw himself at the walls and began to climb, scrambling quickly up the stone and mortar with the tiny handholds that presented themselves to him. In a matter of moments, he was on the roof, the sprawling city laid out before him in all its vastness. He hurried to the edge of the building where he could see the street and the running thief, and followed, easily maintaining his balance, occasionally making a steady leap from building to building. After about a block, the thief ducked into a nearby alley to catch his breath.

"Got you," Criske muttered. He dropped down from the roof, using a brief cling to the edge to lessen the impact of his descent, then rolling to absorb the impact. He stood up in front of the thief, blocking the only exit out of the alley. The thief turned and his eyes widened in horror.

"What? But…how…"

Criske looked at the man's arms carefully for any kind of knife before he got closer. He had heard stories about guards or watchmen who didn't bother to check and, all too often, paid for it dearly later. A cornered person who was desperate would fight for all they were worth. When no knife or shiv was forthcoming, Criske calmly walked closer to the man, making sure to speak clearly. "Release the goods that you stole. Place them on the ground. Lay down any weapons you have. Resisting arrest will result in increased jail time. You don't want to do that. It's nasty in there."

The man took a step back, and Criske saw his hand instinctively go toward his back pocket. It was the only warning Criske had, but he leaned back just in time to avoid getting slashed across the face. The man started swinging at him wildly with the knife. "You're not taking me!" he screamed, his eyes wild. "I need to feed my family, damn it! I'm not going to let them starve!"

Criske dodged the knife again, watching the thrust go by him. He responded with a kick that landed solidly on the man's stomach. The thief fell backward and landed with a grunt, the air rushing out of him. He rolled on the ground with a groan. Next to him, Criske saw the stolen objects: two loaves of bakery bread and what looked like some kind of cheese, all wrapped in cloth. Upon closer inspection, he saw that the man he was talking to wasn't really so much a man as he was a young adult, maybe just two years older than himself. The Half-Elf sighed and knelt down next to the hacking, wheezing thief. "Hey. I get it. You're desperate. You can't stand the thought of seeing them hungry. You can't bear to think of their faces when there's no food on the table."

"What would you—" The young man turned and froze as he got a closer look at Criske. "Oh…Great Answers…you're a Half."

The young Guardian sucked in a breath. "That's right," he said, resigned.

The two of them stared at each other for a moment, a mutual understanding gradually forming in their eyes. The thief lowered his gaze. "So…what happens now?" he mumbled. "You haul me away to the stocks? Nail my ear to a post?"

Criske heard the sound of heavy, rapid footfalls behind him. He turned to see Henrik rounding the corner, his truncheon drawn, clearly ready for a fight. "Hey, turns out he wasn't a thief!" Criske called. He subtly pulled a few coins from his own purse and held them up. "He just couldn't get the merchant accept his payment and panicked when the guy started screaming."

Henrik looked up at the sky and let out a groan. "Of course. Of course!" he said. "*Khlaniik* forbid we catch a real criminal! I was looking forward to an actual fight for once!"

"Perish the thought," Criske said with a small grin. He turned back to the young man, pocketing the rest of his coins once more. "I'll just take your payment back to the merchant. You hurry along home, yeah?"

The young man looked at Criske in relief. "Who are you?" he asked.

Criske held out a hand and hauled the young man to his feet. "Criske Val-Zhang." He jerked a thumb at the heavily breathing Dwarf behind him. "That's Henrik, my patrol partner. We're Guardians of the Trifecta."

He leaned in and whispered quietly to the young man, "Do not let the normal Watch catch you. They'll likely shake you down. Out of this alley, I'd stick to the less beaten paths, yeah?"

The young man nodded. "I won't forget this, Val-Zhang," he said. He quickly hurried past Criske and Henrik, then disappeared out of sight and around the corner.

Henrik walked up to Criske. "You ran on the rooftops…" he said. "Yeah."

"I trust you do know that's illegal?"

"Sure do."

Henrik stared at Criske for a moment, looking him up and down, like he was a sculpture in some kind of museum. Then, he smiled, patting him on the shoulder. "Good man," he said. "We need to show those city Watch men how to really get things done, no? Come, let us go give the money to the merchant before they lose all hope of us returning." Despite being the constant flow of traffic, Henrik led the way back to the merchant's without fault. They returned to the baker, paying him his due.

The rest of the trading rush hour occurred without incident, and it wasn't long before the sun had carried itself into the late morning. It was fortunate it was still early summer. The press of people so close together, all moving and screaming as they shifted, was creating a terrible smell Criske doubted would be improved by hotter weather, even though he had no personal experience with Trifectus in the hotter months.

Soon, though, it was time for them to leave the merchant quarter and move on to patrol other neighborhoods, making sure that they were clearly visible to all passersby. Most would scarcely nod, though a few people Criske saw on a regular basis would give him a casual wave.

Henrik, it turned out, was actually good company. He possessed knowledge that Criske had no real use for, but it passed the time all the same. Henrik began to point out how certain buildings had likely been built at different stages of the city's development, identifying what kind of craftsman had worked on each. "See that one?" Henrik said, pointing to a building with worn-down stone walls covered in peeling lime plaster. "That's classic stationary Human Territories architecture. Probably one of the older buildings in the city."

"You think?" Criske said, feigning interest.

Henrik nodded. "Oh yes! Judging by the state of the stones, I'd say that the buildings in this area would predate the forming of the Trifecta." He looked at the street with an evaluating stare. "Hmm…" he glanced around some more, squinting at a few buildings until something caught his eye. "Ah! Yes, look!" he pointed up to a nearby archway made of stone that marked the entrance to the outer neighborhoods of the city. "That is where the old gate stood, before they expanded the city after Taron Idolon's reign. This means, naturally, that we're standing in front of buildings that have been here for just over three hundred years!"

Criske couldn't help smiling a little. "Really?" he asked. "All that information from an arch and some plaster? Truly incredible."

Henrik nodded, not catching his partner's apathetic tone. "Yes, I believe so. Then again, it is unsurprising. The three nations have been trading here long before it became Trifectus. It made it ideal for…" He paused for a moment, turning to look at Criske. "You don't…particularly…care, do you?"

The Half-Elf shrugged. "Never really had a reason to," he said. "More focused on other things. But, hey, at least your education shows?"

Henrik looked slightly put out, and he hung his head. After a pang of guilt, Criske patted him on the shoulder. "Don't look so glum, yeah? Tell you what, we'll split a pint after patrol and you can explain all about this stuff."

Henrik brightened instantly. "Truly?"

"Sure," Criske said with a smile. That pint was going to be entirely necessary to get through the explanations. "I mean, I've never been one for history, but no shame in learning new things, yeah?"

Henrik nodded enthusiastically. "Right you are! History is critical to understanding who we are today, though that doesn't always make it easy. After Idolon's reign three hundred years ago, much of the Territories' valuable early history has been lost, though the Nomadic peoples probably still have some tales. The validity of those, unfortunately, is much debated." Henrik's explanation continued, detailing the merits of oral tradition versus its drawbacks as Criske continued to scan the area. Finally, he saw an excellent opportunity to interrupt his partner.

"Look, that alleyway," he said, pointing. "We can cut through there to get to the rest of our route," he said.

Henrik stopped talking for a moment. "Right. Let us go, though, are you sure this route is entirely…" Henrik froze. He sniffed twice and drew not his truncheon but his sword. His expression became serious. Criske felt his stomach reflexively tighten. "Something's not right in the air, *Khlanro*," Henrik whispered. "Can you feel it?"

Criske looked around but didn't see anyone on the street. Strangely enough, though, he did feel a strange presence. There was a chill in the air that didn't make a bit of sense in the summer sun. He didn't draw his weapon, but he put a hand on his sword hilt. "Steady there," Criske said quietly. "Don't want to cause a panic if anyone comes near. We'll play this easy for now."

Henrik nodded and left his weapon sheathed, but his hand never left the grip. "Follow my lead," Henrik said. Criske looked at the Dwarf. All of the previous levity was gone from his face. Henrik's face was almost expressionless, save for his eyebrows, which creased slightly downward. He walked in front of Criske. As they got closer to the alleyway, the chill in the air deepened until it went from feeling slightly unusual to unnatural.

Henrik carefully placed himself at the edge of the alleyway, his back against the wall. He looked over and made a series of hand signals Criske remembered from training: *Watch my back. I'm taking point.*

Criske nodded. Henrik eased around the corner and started down the alleyway. Criske fell into a steady backpedal behind him, looking out for any sign of movement in the alley entrance way. The chill in the air intensified as the walls loomed overhead, and the shadows lengthened as the sun became hidden. Henrik stopped suddenly, causing Criske to bump into him.

"*Khlaniik* preserve us," Henrik said softly.

Criske turned around and saw the body of an Elven woman lying motionless on the ground. Her lips were blackened, eyes open and lifeless, and her limbs splayed out at odd angles.

Henrik muttered a short prayer in his native tongue. Criske opted for a much simpler set of words: "Damn it. I really hate patrol day."

THE SEEKER

The line of merchant carts outside the city of Trifectus seemed to stretch on for forever. The sun had risen at least two hours ago, and people were already complaining to guards about how late they were to market, shouting about their wares. Some just set up right outside the city walls next to the sprawling Kendross River that cut through the center of the city, hawking their products the best they could. Several fights had already broken out among the tired and frustrated caravans, but there was no way to get the participants inside the city to jail them, so the guards improvised by tying them to some nearby trees.

In the midst of the chaos, there was one particular individual who, unlike everyone around him, wished to be unseen and unheard.

He buried himself deeper into the stack of straw he had camouflaged himself into on the back of a merchant's cart, whispering almost silently to himself, "Come on...please..."

Finally, the cart started to move. As it bumped and rolled over the rough cobblestones, Xeile exhaled in relief. He was lucky. Now to see if he could push his luck just a little bit more. The cart continued to travel, Xeile wrapped in darkness, the cold seeping into his bones. Even in the summer air, he could feel the chill pulsating up his toes to his calves. He grabbed his piece of worn leather and bit down on it as the searing cold continued to surge up his body.

But he couldn't cry out. Not now. He was so close. Eventually, the wave passed and he forced his jaw apart, the tears rolling silently down his face. He opened his mouth to make sure his ragged breathing didn't attract too much attention, but the dust and debris of the hay made him long for water, something he hadn't been able to risk for...what was it now? A day? He forgot the last time he could walk around out in the sun without fear. It was hard to tell time by only seeing the moon.

Eventually, the cart came to rest, and Xeile froze. He heard the owner of the cart, a man he had learned was called "Manni," and his partner, a sharp woman named "Hess," talking about the troubles at the gate.

"Damn grays think they own the place, requiring a license to visit the city out of the blue," Manni grumbled. "Whatever happened to an honest living? I'm trying ta sell hay and crops, not a cart of jewels!"

"You can thank the double murder for that," Hess said wearily. "Damn swine making life harder for the rest of us. Just wish they'd hurry up and catch 'em."

"Give 'em a piece of my mind, I would," Manni agreed savagely. "Two girls killed. Just ain't right."

Xeile recoiled inwardly at the thought. A double murder? The thought made his stomach heave. If there was a double murder…security would have increased monumentally around the city.

And if there was an unsolved double murder, dangerous enough to warrant stopping merchants from coming or going, that would mean he would come for sure.

Kelt McNair would be here, and Xeile had to face him.

A sense of dreadful anticipation hit Xeile's body. "Stop shaking," he whispered to himself, trying to steady the tremors running up and down his body. "Stop shaking, you have a job to do."

He waited and waited in the hay, picking up the muffled voices of the guards, then the smell and sounds of the cart hitting the cobblestones. Every dip made his teeth rattle. Finally, the motion ceased, but he was careful not to move until Manni and Hess were long gone, likely to the town tax master and then dinner after paying their dues. He could hear no other movement from outside his refuge. It was now or never.

Xeile extracted himself from the pile slowly, stiff after hiding in one spot for most of the day, rolling out of the cart and hitting the ground with a soft thump. Rapidly taking in his surroundings, Xeile saw that he was in a series of low-slung stables, and it was just heading toward evening. A nearby horse huffed as it munched on oats in its stall. The dimming light cast everything into a series of long shadows, giving them a gaunt, stretched appearance.

Xeile silently walked over to the horses' water barrel. The horse continued to munch away without alarm, so Xeile scooped water out of the barrel with his thin, unsteady hands and took a drink. The water was rather disgusting, and probably unsafe for Humans to drink, but at the moment, he couldn't bring himself to care. The liquid slid down his throat, and he let out a sigh of relief. "Thank you," he whispered to the horse.

The creature let out a small snort, as if to show just how little it cared, then resumed eating.

Turning his attention away from the stables, Xeile looked for something to obscure his features from passersby. His black hair, long, curly, and matted from lack of care; pale gray-tinged skin; and black eyes were sure to draw more attention than he was looking for. After a rapid glance around, he found an old blanket hanging from a hook, likely meant to cover the back of a horse during colder months. Xeile grabbed it, slinging it around himself like a cloak. He found a piece of rope that would serve him as a belt well enough. Using an old knife, one of his few possessions, Xeile made several slits in the fabric, feeding the rope through the cloth until he had improvised a deep hood.

He put his new creation on, flipped up the makeshift hood, and with a deep breath, stepped out into the streets of Trifectus.

He was probably on the outskirts of town, given that no one seemed to be around. It was an awkward time of day. People had just finished returning home to their evening meal, and it was still too early for the frequent tavern-goers to make their usual rounds. Xeile felt the unusual texture of the cobblestones beneath his threadbare boots and grimaced. It was his first encounter with a city, and not even five minutes in, he wanted to be out in a field somewhere. The buildings all felt too close together, too cramped, compared to the yurts back home.

And the floating parade of spirits certainly wasn't helping either.

Their translucent bodies milled about, il-luminated by the glow of the orange and red streaks lancing across the sky. Some were more visible than others, which Xeile had long since grown accustomed to. The larger the strange glow in their chest, the easier they were for him to see. Those were the ones he had to look out for. They tended to notice him the most, try to talk to him. Well, *at* him. He'd figured he would see more spirits since there were so many more people in a city, but he didn't expect it to be this bad.

There were enough spirits that they were starting to block his view of the street ahead. He pushed through them, ignoring their faint whispers and mutterings. He couldn't afford to be distracted. He had to find a place to lay low long enough to get a little rest, and then he had to find Kelt.

A shudder ran through Xeile's body, and the cold flared up again. Xeile pulled out his piece of leather and clamped down on it, ducking into a nearby alley and sinking to the ground. He wrapped his arms around his legs and waited for the needling, bone-splitting chills to pass. Eventually, they did, but Xeile could feel that the constant cold was now reaching up to his ankles on a regular basis. His feet were numb to any feeling of touch.

The young man took the leather out of his mouth with a gasp that turned into a violent cough. When he drew back his hand, there was blood on it. It dripped down and pooled into his hands like a macabre water clock. He reached behind his cloak to the chain on his neck that contained the two possessions that had pushed him forward these few terrible months.

One was an amulet made of intricate steel. It wove a pattern of three pillars leaning against each other, all of which clasped a single cloudy piece of quartz. On the same chain, rubbing against it, was a highly polished ring made of wood. Xeile pressed the amulet against his head, closing his eyes and thinking of his mother's warm smile.

"No time like the present," he said quietly to himself, getting shakily to his feet. His blood dripped down from his palm and onto the earth. "I will forgive you, Kelt McNair," he said weakly, trying to find the motivation to keep walking forward. "Just you watch. Even if it's the last thing I do."

Xeile made a few small steps and then found his stride again as his body slowly uncoiled itself from the knives of pain it was all too occupied with lately. The spirits floated past him, looking dazed, confused, lost, and hopeless.

He wouldn't become one of them. He would leave no regrets that would make him cling to this world. As the remaining flecks of bloody phlegm started congealing on his fingers, his hands tightened into fists. He would find Kelt and forgive him.

He didn't have enough time left to get distracted.

THE SOLDIER

Kelt stared in bewilderment at the man before him. The sun shining through the window and hitting him in the face didn't help. Here was this bureaucratic oaf, with his perfect uniform, portly frame, balding head, and unsmiling face, demanding an answer. Truly, people's stupidity knew no bounds.

"I just started working a double murder case," Kelt explained slowly again. "I've been very busy, as you might imagine. Do you really think I can take the hours it would require from that, just to shuffle through all that paperwork again, Administrator?"

"So you have said." Administrator Poss adjusted his too-tight collar slightly. "However, you must select the apprentices to study under you, Kelt. It is standard procedure. Even for one as busy as yourself. I have compiled a list of candidates that we should—"

Kelt's chair scraped the floor loudly as he pushed back and stood up, leaning over the administrative stickler in front of him. "Look, I understand the requirements, but I—"

There was a knock on the office door. Kelt seized his chance for escape. "Enter," he called out.

The door swung open, and two younger boys stepped through. One of them was a clean-shaven, muscle-heavy Dwarf. His uniform was crisp, though straining across the shoulders. The other was a thin, angular boy with deep-brown eyes and startlingly blond hair. His sets of grays were the correct length but seemed far too baggy on him, even with the help of the standard-issue belt. He was younger, maybe seventeen at most, but his eyes had a ragged, world-weary quality that made Kelt feel slightly on edge. What united the two, however, was their youth. Elves and Humans aged at around the same rate, with Dwarves not reaching maturity until their late twenties. Both of them looked just under full adulthood, practically kids in Kelt's estimation. Kids...

"Ah yes!" he said, clapping his hands together, an idea formulating immediately. He turned to the older man. "These are the ones," he said. "Sharp as a honed knife, they are. Very qualified, I'm excited to work with them."

The old man turned to Kelt with a raised eyebrow. "Really, sir? May I ask their names?"

Kelt's momentary panic quickly vanished as the Dwarf stepped forward. "Patrolman, third class. Henrik Ihvihlan, *Taqraan*," he said with a salute. "I'm here to give my report."

The other boy gave a quick salute. "Criske Val-Zhang, sir," he said quietly. "Also reporting in."

Only years of discipline kept Kelt from reflexively staring at Criske with fascination. In all his years serving the Trifecta, he had never met a Half-Elf in an active-duty role. Most took up administration or serving labor, helping the Guardians indirectly, rather than risk combat.

No matter the reason Criske was here, Kelt was happy to see him. Kelt cheered internally, looking smugly at the older man. "Well, there you have it. Draw up the necessary paperwork, and I'll sign it by this evening. How does that sound?"

Administrator Poss turned to Kelt in a huff. "Very well. I expect them on my desk by the morning, sir." He pivoted out of the room and closed the door behind him with an authoritative clack.

There was a moment of awkward silence between the three of them. Finally, Criske turned and looked over his shoulder. "Wow. Who twisted his bowlines?" he muttered.

Henrik let out a reflexive snort, then, seeing Kelt's serious expression, immediately adopted a serious expression himself. "My apologies, *Taqraan*." Kelt noted the word for formal respect to an elder in Henrik's regrets. Probably someone who was used to manners, if not higher society. Possibly a servant of one of the Dwarven houses?

Kelt raised a hand. "No issue, lads. Please, at ease and take a seat."

Criske and Henrik both sat down opposite his desk and stared at him expectantly. Kelt took a deep breath. "Well, I called you both here today, and I'm fairly certain you know why. There have been two murders over the past two days, and you two happened upon one of the bodies."

He could see they hadn't expected the news of a double murder. Criske's face darkened in grim acceptance. Henrik's eyes showed alarm that then hardened into cool indignation. "Two?" Henrik repeated.

Kelt nodded. "That's right. Both Elven females, both middle-aged. Both of them dead without a single cut or broken bone. The one we found before your discovery was a sight. Her limbs were sprawled out, like she had just dropped to the ground without a struggle. I've just been assigned to work the case, and you two have been chosen to be my apprentices for the time being."

Criske recoiled backward. "Apprentices? Since when, sir?"

"Since just now," Kelt said, pointing at the door. "Hence why our fellow Guardian was paying us a visit. Now, I've read your report, but I'd like to hear it from your mouths. What happened?"

Criske took the lead, working through how they were on patrol when they stumbled across the victim earlier this morning. "It looked like frostbite on her lips," Criske finished.

Kelt raised an eyebrow. "Frostbite? In the middle of summer? Are you sure?"

Criske nodded. "Yes. My father has described it to me several times. It looks like it." Criske frowned. "The odd part is that if it was frostbite, it would normally be on her extremities. Fingers, toes, ears, and the like. How would it happen on her lips but not her nose too?"

He let out a sound of frustration, scratching his head.

"Nothing about that body made a damn bit of sense. No bruising, no signs of struggle, not a single entry or exit wound. No broken bones. Best I could see, no internal bleeding, signs of vomiting, or indicators of poisonous substances either."

"You could tell that?" Kelt asked skeptically.

Criske shrugged. "My father used to be a medic for the Army of the Human Territories. I know how to check for the obvious, at least. I'd have to get a closer look to be sure, though."

Henrik nodded in agreement. "It was most unusual, *Taqraan*. There was a very peculiar chill in the air. And I do not mean that in terms of doing a fright. I mean it was physically cold."

Criske looked at Henrik. "It's 'in terms of being frightening,' Henrik."

Henrik rolled his eyes. "Your language's conjugations are terrible. Too many little words."

More awkward silence settled down on them. Kelt let the silence stretch while he observed the boys to see how they would respond. Despite his glowing (and sudden) recommendation, he needed to know what he was actually working with in terms of patience and character, and a quiet place with some tension was sure to draw it out of them.

Henrik's eyes took small wanders around the room, though there wasn't much to look at in Kelt's office. Despite moving in a few months ago, Kelt clearly hadn't moved anything out of his personal chest since settling in. Those items all remained locked and bound in his personal storage chest. Instead, his room afforded him the highest luxuries someone in his position could be offered: a cot in the corner, a few shelves, a dresser for his uniforms, a simple four-legged table for a desk, and a small fireplace with a pot and kettle. The Dwarf was curious about his surroundings. Not a bad trait, but one that could get him in trouble later down the line. Criske's eyes, however, seemed intent on studying him. Not in a predatory way, just with a kind of detached calculation that Kelt had seen in few other people before. It was a practical sizing up of how strong Kelt would be, how quickly he could move, and how long his reach was. Kelt doubted Criske's estimations would be completely accurate, but that kind of habitual evaluation spoke of a harder life. He was probably used to more independence. Teamwork could wind up being an issue.

But neither of them said a word or prompted further action. They waited on him to speak. Patience, or at least the ability to not express discomfort, was something they already had. Kelt rapped his knuckles on his desk, finishing his evaluation. "Well, gentlemen, I think it's time we go take a look at our body."

"Time to see the stiff," Criske muttered, standing and stretching with a yawn. "Joy. I'm sure it smells fantastic after being out all night."

"Our team of inquisitor magicians will have kept the body preserved for us," Kelt assured him. A thought struck him. "Oh, I'm Inquisitor Kelt McNair, by the way. 'Sir' or 'Inquisitor McNair,' will be just fine."

Henrik's eyes widened. "Kelt McNair? *The* Kelt McNair?" He snapped to his feet and bowed. "Truly, it is an honor, sir."

Kelt let out an uncomfortable laugh. "I take it my reputation proceeds me. No need to extol. I just do my job."

Criske turned to Henrik, speaking casually, as if Kelt wasn't even present. "Is he a big deal or something?"

Henrik nodded. "Oh yes! He's a living legend. One of the best and most successful Spell Breakers in recent memory. He's the one they trusted to hunt down necromancers. He just stepped down from active Spell Breaking a few months ago—"

"I live a quieter life these days." Kelt sighed. "Let's go, gentleman."

The three of them left the office, which Kelt quickly locked. They hurried through the Guardian headquarters, Criske and Henrik keeping pace with him in silence until they exited the grounds. There were plenty of other Guardians already up and moving, talking quietly among themselves, going to the mess halls, and standing guard. The air was already somewhat humid, the dampness clinging to Kelt's skin, as it always did this far down south. He thought about his time up north and shook his head. It was far better than the biting cold up there, at least. Something immediately caught Kelt's eye: two soldiers of the Army of the Territories, dressed in their usual crimson-and-brown kit, a splash of color in a sea of gray, talking with another Guardian in hushed tones, likely about the murder cases.

Criske quietly sidled up to Kelt as they passed by the soldiers. "Shouldn't the Territories' Watch be handling this case instead of us?" Criske asked, as if the thought had just occurred to him. "Not to sound ungrateful for the experience, but I didn't think this was in our port."

Kelt nodded. "Generally, they would. But a double murder like this means all hands are called up. Besides, this one is particularly strange. No offense to the glorious Army of the Territories, but I don't think they'll have the expertise for this." Kelt looked at him with a raised eyebrow. "Why, you have better things to do, Patrolman?"

"No, sir," Criske said, though his voice indicated otherwise. "Just trying to figure out how my pay's affected by this."

"Do not worry," Henrik said, his tone grim. "I'm sure it will remain low, no matter how many hours we put in."

"'For the glory and peace of the Trifecta,'" Criske said heavily, quoting the start of the Guardian oath. "If you'll permit me, sir, I know a shortcut or two." Kelt nodded in approval. Criske took the lead, guiding them through a dizzying series of back alleys, fading in and out of the shadows cast by the buildings. Kelt noticed Criske rarely ever walked down the center of an alley, even if it was wide enough to comfortably do so, and he always looked down the alley, scanning side to side before fully committing to turning the corner. His movements had the paranoia of the chronically attacked that Kelt had seen in other cities. People with bent backs and downcast eyes. He made a mental note to investigate Criske's record later.

It didn't take long for them to reach the scene of the crime. Several soldiers were already there, casting wary glances back and forth, obscuring the site from curious onlookers. A violet glow lit up behind the soldiers, casting odd shadows in multiple directions. Kelt walked up to one of the soldiers. "Inquisitor McNair," he said, "I'm here to see the victim."

The soldier looked at him, unimpressed. "Sir, the army has already…" His eyes widened when he saw the patch just above Kelt's heart on his uniform: an equilateral triangle, snapped in two. "Oh…" He stepped aside. "F-Forgive me, Spell Breaker."

Kelt stepped through to see that several inquisitor magicians were there in meditative poses. Their violet auras were active, enshrouding the space, filtering the air. Careful not to touch any of them, Kelt gave a polite cough. "Inquisitor McNair, here to lead the case. Can I get a closer look at the victim?"

One of the magicians opened her eyes, and the rest soon followed suit, the violet lights bending a multitude of ways retracted into their eyes, giving their irises the unique lilac hue that set magicians apart. She bowed to him. "Ah, Kelt, I didn't think you would be here so soon," she said.

It took Kelt a moment to place her features. She was a female Elf, around seven and a half feet tall, with black hair and perfectly proportioned features. She was familiar, but her name refused to rise to the surface of his mind. "Sorry…" Kelt said slowly. "I'm afraid it's been a while, Inquisitor…"

"Kelt, it's me, Usumi? Usumi, the head magician of the Guardians of the Trifecta?" she reminded him gently. "You may have arrested some magicians with me once or twice?"

Kelt's eyebrows raised. "Ah. Right. Thought you were still studying shamans up north or something." Usumi was a legend in her own right.

Hailing from the Tropiciea Archipelago the Elves called home, she was already a capable warrior and magician when she joined the Guardians, but her magical talent was without equal, leading to her becoming the youngest head magician of the Guardians in history at just age twenty-nine. Chances were, if it was arcane, Usumi knew about it.

Usumi shook her head, her silken black hair swishing to and fro. "Oh no. I've been done with that for months. Kelt, my office is right next to yours."

"Oh," Kelt said, feeling his neck heat up. "Sorry about that. My plate has been filled with a lot lately…"

Usumi raised her hands, quelling his embarrassment. "No worries. Now, let's take a look at our unfortunate soul, hmm?"

The four of them quickly crowded around the body, and it didn't take Kelt long to realize that Criske had been spot on in his initial evaluation. There were no obvious signs of trauma other than the random patches of black on her lips and a few other parts of her body. No obvious signs of poison either. It was like she had just simply dropped dead. "Oh Trifecta,"

Kelt said with a sigh. He turned to Usumi. "Did you find anything else?"

Usumi shook her head. "No. No weapons, no blood, and no signs of magic, though I'll have to give the place a more thorough look over when I get the chance to be certain."

Henrik suddenly left the circle, his eye drawn to something on the wall. "Sir, ma'am," Henrik said. "Forgive me if I am out of place, but I believe I have found something of note."

Kelt, Usumi, and Criske gathered around the spot Henrik was indicating. "Can we get some light over here?" Kelt called over his shoulder. One of the Territories' men quickly handed him a lit candle. Kelt held the candle up to the spot and was surprised to see several deep gash marks in the wall, as if something had cut or gouged into the rock, leaving angular furrows that were several handspans in length.

"Hmm…potentially left by the murder weapon?" Usumi asked.

Henrik shook his head. "No, ma'am. No steel I know of can make a scratch like that in this kind of rock." He held out a hand to Kelt. "If I may, sir?"

Kelt handed him the candle, and Henrik put the light right next to the wall. "This stone is a red stone, commonly cut from the quarries they used from nearby around three hundred and fifty years ago. They floated them downriver, so it was an easy material to obtain. No weapon I know of, save a pick, can make that big a mark into the stone like that without leaving indicators of its presence. If it were a pick, or something similar…" Henrik lowered the candle down to the ground, kneeling down. "It should have left some dust or debris behind." They looked down at the cobble for some kind of red powder on the ground, but there was nothing.

"The fact that there is nothing leaves me with a few possible theories. One is that the stone came from the quarry like this when the original building was constructed, but if that were the case, we'd see far more erosion around the marks themselves."

Standing, Henrik handed the candle back to Kelt. "My second theory is that the stone was cut by some unnatural means, or shifted in some way."

"So, magic?" Kelt asked. Henrik nodded.

"Correct."

"Sharp eye, you two," Kelt said quietly. Henrik smiled, but Criske's eyes remained firmly fixed on Usumi, as if she were a wild animal that could attack at any moment. Kelt looked at Usumi. "Well? You know of any kinds of magic that can do something like this? I can think of a few, but they wouldn't be this precise."

Usumi frowned. "A few options come to mind, but I'd have to check my references, just to be sure."

"Well," Kelt said. "If you wouldn't mind checking on those, we'll keep combing over things here and visit soon. Late afternoon work for you?" Usumi confirmed, and left them. Kelt saw the tension slip out of Criske's shoulders, and he began to speak with Henrik as they looked up and down the alley for any further clues. Kelt spared another look at the corpse and noticed something on the back of her neck. There was a strange marking—no, a tattoo of three pillars leaning against each other, a symbol of the Trifecta.

Kelt let out a soft curse. This victim was one of their own. Whoever this murderer was, they could be targeting Guardians.

THE OUTCASTS

The search continued for most of the midday but turned up no new evidence, despite Henrik and Criske's meticulous comb-over. Kelt badly wanted to go examine the other body, but he had told Usumi they would meet up, and the last thing he wanted was to be late. Being head magician meant that Usumi was busy on a constant basis, and Kelt didn't know how much he could actually depend on her being there in the future of the investigation.

Henrik understood perfectly fine, but he looked at his fellow apprentice and saw that Criske appeared to be ill at ease. He wanted to say something, or at least ask what was wrong, but he didn't. Instead, Henrik turned his mental attention to the alleyway they had just left.

Those gouges made no sense at all from a masonry perspective, but what made even less sense was that there was no extra material on the ground at all. It was like someone had just scooped out pieces of the rock and stowed them away for later use. He didn't know much about magic, so perhaps it was possible. The chances of a murderer being so meticulous and controlling, so precise, was very small in the midst of their crime.

Henrik raised this concern to Criske, and Criske nodded in agreement. "Yeah. I got to thinking about that too. Look, that frostbite on the lips probably means that the woman got attacked while facing the murderer, right? But she got taken by sudden surprise, and died. No cutthroat's going to take the time to be neat about getting the job done. And it makes no sense they'd take a piece of rock afterward, to leave an obvious clue like that. If it were me, I'd want to sail my ass out of there as quickly as possible to avoid discovery."

"Do you think it'd be reasonable to think that their spell caused both of those events, the death and the gouges, at the same time?" Henrik asked.

Kelt cut into the conversation. "Entirely possible. That's the problem with magic: just about anything is possible if you train hard enough. Although the fact the killer could have attacked her from the front is a good point," he said with a grimace. "That'd mean they'd be so strong of a magician, they'd have killed her outright before she had a chance to do anything, except scream, maybe."

Criske shook his head. "No."

Kelt looked down at him with a raised eyebrow. "Excuse me?"

"No, sir," Criske added. "Look, Henrik, you said that place would normally have a lot of people in it, right? Living there or walking about?"

Henrik nodded. "Yes. Historically speaking, it's probably one of the busier main roads in the city."

"So the Watch would patrol it on a consistent basis?"

"Yes," Henrik said.

"So a woman lets out a bloodcurdling shriek or cry, and not one person hears it? I don't buy it."

"But you said the victim was likely facing the magician," Henrik pointed out.

"Why cry out in fear if it's someone you recognize?"

The thought made Henrik stop short. Murder of a friend? A fellow Guardian? The very notion was inconceivable. It refused to stay in his mind. "A traitor?" Henrik said softly. "*Khlaniik* watching us, it can't be."

Kelt put a hand on their shoulders. "Let's not rush to conclusions here. We don't even know if the magician had the victim facing them yet. And just because the victim could have recognized the attacker doesn't mean it was a fellow Guardian. The possibility of an unregistered magician is always on the table."

"What do you mean by 'unregistered'?" Criske asked.

"Every magician, or person capable of casting magic, has two things in common," Kelt explained calmly. "Violet eyes or eyes that are some shade of purple, and they must also have a license to use magic in any capacity while in the three lands of the Trifecta: the Human Territories, the Dwarfdom, and the Yi-Fe Douzhong. There are different levels of licenses that allow you to use magic in varying degrees. People like Usumi and Spell Breakers have the highest-level license, the open license. Most magicians, though, have a research license, which only allows for academic study. The Nomad shamans up north are the exception, but there are so few shamans these days that it's not an issue. They have their own subset of laws, at least, according to their peoples."

"So some magicians slip through the cracks, yeah?" Criske asked.

Kelt nodded. "It is very, very seldom that they do, as the violet eyes are there since birth, but it has happened on occasion. Most of the time, that lack of registration is accidental. But very occasionally, you get the people who don't register and then nurse their abilities in secret." Kelt's face darkened for a moment, and his neck tensed as if he were shoving bad memories back down into his chest where they belonged. "And those people are the ones that typically have Spell Breakers knocking at their door." They continued walking down the street, and heads turned their way.

Henrik wasn't terribly surprised. Kelt cut an intimidating figure, standing almost two full heads above Henrik and one above Criske. But more surprising than the height was his sheer strength. Cords of hard muscles, collections of minor scars, including a vicious one on the side of his throat that looked to be inflicted by a wild animal, gave him the appearance of a powerful mountain trapper who'd just happened to shove himself into a Guardian uniform. When they reached the main gate of headquarters, Kelt and his apprentices were let in without resistance.

Retracing the steps to Kelt's office, they stopped one door short down the hall, and Kelt knocked on the door. It took a moment, but there was the sound of a latch being undone, and it swung open, revealing a slightly worn-out Usumi. "Ah. I was wondering if you all would get here soon. Come in, come in. I'll get some tea started for us."

"Got any coffee?" Kelt asked.

Usumi nodded. "Of course. It's essential Spell Breaker kit, no?" She turned to Henrik and Criske with a warm smile. Henrik felt himself reflexively flush, with her flawless face so close. "Would you two like anything? Tea or water?"

Henrik brightened and returned the smile. "Ah, tea would be very nice, ma'am." He turned to Criske. "*Khlanro…*" His sentence drifted off as he saw Criske's expression. Criske's eyes were fixed on Usumi, like she was a snake that could strike at any moment. His body was leaned back like he was prepared to bolt out the door.

"No, thanks," Criske said quietly. "I'm fine."

Usumi nodded. "Very well. Two cups of tea and one of coffee, coming up. Please have a seat. I have plenty we will discuss, and I'm sure you all will have questions."

Henrik and the others took their seats by Usumi's fireplace as the water was set to heat up in the kettle. His gaze turned to the room around him. It was unlike Kelt's in most ways. Every wall seemed to have scroll racks, books, tomes, or other papers. Several small objects were hanging from the ceiling, and it took Henrik a moment to place the material and shapes. They were an entire flock of suspended paper cranes, lovingly folded with little wings and hung by strings to resemble the pattern of the creatures flying south for the winter. On the wall were several scrolls that hung open, rolling out to reveal Elvish characters in stylized, glossy black ink. Henrik read them and raised his eyes. "'Through rain, we… flourish'?" he asked.

Usumi looked up from preparing the teacups in front of her, and her smile widened. "You read High Elvish! Yes, you are correct, though there are many ways to translate the word '*feqi*.' Some would say it better means 'rise up' or 'sprout.'" Usumi hurried over and grabbed the heated kettle with a cloth, pouring water into the teapot before doing the same to a canister of coffee. "While this steeps," she said over her shoulder, "Tell me, did you find anything else at the crime location?"

"I did," Kelt said. "Our victim had a tattoo of the Trifecta on the back of her neck. So someone could be targeting Guardians, though I'll have to check the report on the other victim to be sure."

Usumi sighed. "That is most unfortunate. I was hoping you'd have found something more substantial, because I'm having difficulty on my end as well." She brought over a steaming cup of tea for Henrik and a coffee for Kelt, before sitting down with her own cups of tea and coffee. "I was initially looking through my magical theory books, trying to figure out where all the extra stone could have gone." She nodded at Henrik. "Apprentice Henrik's logic should be correct, even in the case of magic. There should have been some trace of magical disruption or some kind of physical evidence left behind. But there is none. So, I started looking for possible sources that could kill or cause physical damage to things without necessarily leaving much of a trail." Her face darkened. "Right now, the only thing I can think of is a spell that would absorb the evidence, cause it to stick like honey, or a malicious spirit."

"Honey?" Henrik asked. "That seems a little, forgive me for saying this, far-fetched, ma'am."

"A nasty ghost isn't a great lead to go off of either," Criske pointed out. "How would we actually check for something like that, anyway?"

Kelt gave Criske a withering look, and Criske sank down into his seat. "Just asking, sir," Criske mumbled.

Usumi nodded at both of them. "Yes, I agree with you both. However, there is one specific type of spirit that could cause this kind of damage: a wraith."

Henrik blinked without recognition, but he froze in fear when he saw Kelt's face drain of color. "You can't be serious," Kelt said, more to himself than to Usumi. "A wraith isn't exactly a quiet or clean killer, Usumi… Are you sure it isn't something else?"

"Fortunately, no, I'm not certain," Usumi said. "I'm going to keep checking and combing through my notes, but as it stands, it seems like the most plausible explanation, though the fact the victims have no major markings on them would mean that the wraith is being controlled, so that's a small blessing, if it comes to it."

Criske leaned forward in his seat. "Alright, time for me to admit it: I'm lost. What's a wraith, why's it bad, and what can we do to get more evidence for you…ma'am?" Henrik could see Criske forcing the respect out of his throat kicking and screaming as he looked at the head magician.

Usumi raised an eyebrow at Kelt. "Do you want to handle this explanation, or should I? You're more qualified than I am."

Kelt had just opened his mouth to speak when there was a knock at the door. Well, more like a pounding, in Henrik's opinion. "Enter," Usumi said.

The door swung open to show a Human girl with flowing brown hair tied back in a simple ponytail. Her complexion was fair, as if she saw little sunlight, her milky-white skin contrasting sharply with her eyes, dark-purple pools that almost blended in with her pupils. Her body was lean but strong, and her uniform impeccable. "I have the documents you wanted,

Master," she said. Her voice was surprisingly low with a kind of metallic quality behind it. Her words seemed to fill the entire room.

Usumi's eyes brightened, as though an idea came to her. "Well, you happened here just in time! Come in. We were just talking about some magic and need an explanation." She gave a polite gesture to the girl. "Gentlemen, this is my own apprentice, Glenna Nall. She's been studying with me the last few years since she joined the Guardians."

The men quickly introduced themselves. Henrik noticed that at the mention of Kelt's name, Glenna's eyes widened, then narrowed. Glenna entered the room, set the writings down on Usumi's desk, and then stood expectantly at attention, staring at a fixed point above the fireplace. "What do you need to know, Master?" Glenna asked.

"My friends need to know what a wraith is and what it does," Usumi said, nodding toward Criske. Criske looked like he'd sooner be friends with a dead rat, but said nothing in protest. "Maybe you could enlighten us?"

Glenna gave Usumi a smirk. "Of course, Master. That's not even a challenge. A wraith is a spirit or collection of spirits that has been artificially forced to take a physical form, usually by being bound to a spell caster. Their lack of an aura means they drain magic out of the air around them, and can drain the magic out of a person's aura, killing them on contact in almost an instant. Wraiths are hard to control, as most of them are spirits that are driven mad by the pain of being made physical. They tend to leave large paths of destruction and make a lot of terrible noises.

Necromancer-King Taron Idolon and the Remnant that hero-worshiped him after he died had a habit of using them." She looked at Criske expectantly. "Any other questions while I'm at it?"

Criske seemed deep in thought for a moment, then returned to the surface to ask another question. "This aura...thing you described...everyone's got one? Is it important?"

Glenna snorted. "Yeah, if that breaks, you're a dead man. Think of it like an eggshell around your body, and the yolk is the soul. One little crack, and *ta-da*, you're pretty much dead due to either wild magic exposure or your soul leaks out and your body crumples like a sack of potatoes."

Criske looked at Henrik, and Henrik saw the thought forming in Criske's eyes just as it came to his own mind. Henrik turned to Glenna. "Is it possible for a magician to break this…personal eggshell without a wraith?"

Usumi nodded, answering before Glenna had the chance. "Yes. Though it is incredibly difficult. In order to break someone's aura, it has to either absorb too much magical energy or lose what magical energy it has. It is incredibly difficult to overload an aura, but it has been done before. Most of the time, a magician wishing to do so will try to overload a very small spot on someone's aura, rather than charge the entire thing."

"Kind of like a shiv to the back," Criske said quietly. "Why slash the throat and get blood everywhere when you can just hit them once in the spine, yeah?" Kelt bit his lower lip but said nothing. Henrik could feel the awkwardness descend on the room like a cold wind. He drank his tea, both to stay warm and to avoid saying anything.

Glenna let out a small laugh, and Usumi shifted uncomfortably in her seat. "Yes…I suppose that's an apt comparison," the head magician said. Silence fell on them like a wet blanket, and they all stared at one another, waiting for someone to claw their way free.

Henrik cleared his throat before the silence stretched out for too long. "Regardless of the method," Henrik said slowly, "this individual would have to be highly trained, correct?"

Usumi nodded. "Yes. It would be inconceivable that someone would learn how to overload an aura without training."

Silence fell over the group as they contemplated this. Henrik looked at the people around him, wondering if an idea would fall into his head if he kept himself moving. Instead, he noticed that Glenna's eyes were firmly fixed on Kelt. Those violet eyes seemed to drill into him with an intensity Henrik couldn't place. Her expression was a carefully neutral mask. One that she had constructed.

Criske broke the silence by clapping his hands together and rubbing them back and forth. "So, we've kind of dead-ended ourselves with trying to figure out who the mystery magician is, yeah? What about the victims? I mean, both of them are Elves, both are female, both were walking through the city when attacked. That's got to narrow it down a little. Why not try it from that angle, see if there's any patterns or reasons there?"

Kelt nodded. "Not a bad notion." He looked at his two apprentices. "You two go to the library and see if you can't find any Elven Guardians who match our victims."

Henrik felt his heart rate speed up. The library. It was one of the few places in headquarters that the Guardians could really take pride in. He looked over at Criske, smiling, but then his smile faded when he saw Criske's expression. The Half-Elf didn't look annoyed or disinterested; he looked embarrassed. All he said was: "Yes, sir." Without another word, Criske rose and left the room, casting one more glance at Usumi, as if he was still expecting her to lunge at him. Henrik followed shortly after, bidding them all farewell with a salute.

He hurried out of the room and quickly caught up with Criske. "*Khlanro*," Henrik said. "Are you alright?"

"I'm fine."

"Are you sure—"

"I said I'm fine!"

Henrik recoiled. Criske's response was like hot iron. The Half-Elf saw his expression and sighed. "Sorry, Henrik. Sorry. It's not your fault, you didn't do anything. Just… let it be for now, yeah?"

Henrik put a hand on Criske's shoulder. "That's alright, *Khlanro*. I understand. If you ever decide you want to talk, I am here."

Criske nodded. "Thanks."

Henrik looked at the sun and groaned. "It is almost nightfall. We won't be able to go to the library right now. It will be closed, and I have night patrol tonight. *Khlaniik varaaq nahn…*"

"I have night patrol tonight too," Criske said, his voice lightening a little. "Looks like we're at it again."

Henrik's heart lifted at the prospect. "It would appear so."

They headed toward the armory to pick up their truncheons and swords, the setting sun causing a dazzling set of purple and red hues across the golden clouds. "Let's just hope we don't run across another stiff," Criske said with grim humor. "I'm not sure how much more work I can take."

"Forgive me if I don't say anything to that," Henrik said. "I'd rather not bring a *Mahnaraj* down upon us."

"A what?"

"It…is difficult to explain…" Henrik said, frowning and searching for the right words. "It is…you know, when you have…like, a horse, and you say the horse is fine…then the horse becomes not fine and dies."

"Oh! You mean a jinx?"

Henrik shook his head. "No, not quite. A *Mahnaraj* is…it isn't just because you said something. Normally it is because a *Khlaniik* decides to make it come true. So…it is like a punishment for asking to avoid a bad thing."

"Huh. You can get punished for asking to avoid something bad if you're a Dwarf?" Criske said. He shook his head. "Tough life, that. Seems a little unfair, if you ask me."

They entered the armory, checked out the weapons, belted them on to their waists and exited headquarters, torches in hand for later that evening, though they didn't need to light them quite yet.

Henrik thought for a moment, and an idea came out of his mouth before he could stop himself. "Is it any worse than someone getting punished just because they're a Half-Elf? That doesn't seem fair to me either." Criske came to a full stop. His expression changed multiple times within a few seconds before ultimately settling on an expression akin to shock. Henrik felt his stomach clench. "I…*Khlanro*…forgive me, that was insensitive—"

"You mean it…" Criske said softly. "You actually mean it…" Henrik didn't know how to respond, so he just stood in silence, the warmth of the sun on his back while his face started to feel the cool of evening. Criske took a few steps forward and punched him on the shoulder. "Come on, we can't jackdaw around here. We've got a patrol to do. No slacking on the job here. Don't know about you, but I can't afford to have my pay docked."

As he walked by, Henrik thought he could see the smallest of smiles on Criske's face.

THE SEEKER

It didn't take Xeile terribly long to find a good place to hide. There was a cellar in an abandoned storehouse that was unlocked but looked relatively unused. He doubted he could stay there all the time, but it wasn't a bad place to stay until nightfall, which would be the safest time for him to travel. Even though he could use larger crowds to take advantage of anonymity, his condition, skin, and eyes would probably make him stand out too much if there was just one overly curious person. And that would mean prison, and likely death, before he got the chance to see Kelt.

And he refused to die before he could see that man.

Fortunately, the cellar was blissfully quiet and free of anything spectral, so it allowed him to get an hour or two of light sleep. Most spirits, he noticed, would congregate around a place that was fairly significant to them. After a few hours, another wave of cold wracked his body, leaving him scraping the stone floor with his nails and biting down into his piece of leather as the agony of icy needles ran up from his legs toward his heart. Eventually, the wave passed, as they all did, with the numbing cold slightly higher than it was before.

"What are you?" Xeile whispered to the cold. "What do you even mean?"

There was no answer, only silence.

Xeile looked out of the cellar hatch and saw a pale beam of moonlight. He staggered to his feet. It was time for him to get moving anyway. After quietly padding up the stairs and shutting the door behind him, he walked out onto the streets, his beaten leather boots barely making a sound against the cobblestones. He wrapped his improvised cloak tightly around him, the hood drawn up.

The city, he discovered, was very different at night. The buildings that were once so different or unique now had a menacing uniformity to them, a featureless nature that was disorienting. There were very few signs of life, and every time there was, it seemed unnaturally loud. The city didn't completely go to rest like his home, where the only things that moved at night were the creatures of the wild. No, there were people out and about. A few patrolmen trudged along, holding torches and talking quietly to each other. Some people were spending the night at the local tavern or inn, where there was a lot of music and carousing. Xeile heard a drinking song start up from outside one building and couldn't help but smile and whisper along.

> *"Hey, ale man, hey, lager man,*
> *Why do you chip away at a rock?*
> *Hey, wine man, hey, stout man,*
> *Why do you not protect your flocks?*
> *I think that reason is quite clear,*
> *So go ahead, pass me that beer!"*

The story of the Drunkard Shepherd was always one of Xeile's favorites that his mother used to tell him, the story of a Dwarf who was absolutely terrible at managing his goats but accidentally became a legendary brew master by the end of the tale. She'd always turn it into a life lesson. *Just because one thing goes badly…* "Doesn't mean you can't make it into an opportunity," Xeile finished softly to himself. Careful not to draw attention to himself, Xeile slipped into the tavern.

Warmth immediately washed over him from a nearby roaring fire in a low trench that lit up the center of the tavern. Surrounding it was a series of tables where mugs of frothy alcohol were being passed back and forth, being raised and slung overhead, and cheers boomed forth. There was a small minstrel band in the corner playing for the occasional tip and leading the general merrymaking. Xeile sat himself down in the corner and turned his attention to the conversation he could hear nearby.

"So, you hear about them girls? Killed in a back alley?"

"Yeah. Two Elves. It's a shame, really."

"I heard they brought the grays onto the case."

"The Guardians? What good are they going to do?"

"Well…I heard they got Kelt McNair working on it."

Xeile felt a shiver run up his spine, and he leaned in closer to the voices. "Oh damn. Must be serious. I'm sure he'll sort it out. Rumor has it he's never had a case go south on him…yet."

Xeile jumped with a start as someone knocked on his table. "Sir, if you aren't gonna order something, you gotta leave."

Xeile turned to see an imperious-looking Elf looking down on him with intense brown eyes and shiny black hair. There was a frown on her face and a defensive posture to her stance.

Xeile raised a hand as if to ward her off. "Sorry… I… Here." He stood up and fished around in his pocket, pulling out a full Trifec coin. He handed it to her. "You never saw me," he said quietly.

Without another word and his head spinning with thoughts, he exited the tavern. The evening was rapidly starting to drop in temperature as Xeile staggered away from the tavern. There was double murder here, and Kelt McNair was definitely on the case. Kelt was here. Xeile could find him. For the first time in months, a faint sense of hope blossomed in his chest. What would he say when they met? Was Kelt still as strong as he was before? Would he even listen?

Xeile was so preoccupied with his thoughts that he almost didn't notice the floating spirit that was staring at him as he walked by. Other spirits, their near translucence glowing faintly in the night like little stars, drifted out of his way. Eventually, he felt the eyes on him as a reflexive shiver went up his spine. He turned around slowly to see an Elf woman staring down at him, a sad, desperate expression on her face. "Harvest…" she whispered. "Cold…"

The words made Xeile's skin crawl, just as a talking spirit always did. Xeile took a step backward. The spirit floated slightly forward. Xeile shook his head. "Sorry," he said with gritted teeth, his heart sinking. "I can't help you." He turned and started to walk away, though his heart was grinding against his mind. "You don't have time," Xeile whispered fiercely to himself. "Don't you dare. You don't have time."

His feet stopped. He turned around and looked at the spirit floating there. He felt his entire body give out a reflexive shudder and forced himself to stay put as he started to shake. Xeile let out a sigh of frustration. He slammed a clenched fist down on his leg. "Damn it!"

He walked back over to the spirit. "What's wrong?" Xeile asked. "Can you even understand me?"

The spirit was a woman who appeared to be in middle-age, clearly of striking beauty when she was alive. A green glow lit up her chest with a gentle light. She reached her slender, spectral fingers out to Xeile. "Harvest…" she whispered. "Harvest…"

"Harvest what?" Xeile asked, keeping his voice low. "A crop? Did you die during harvest? What's the matter?"

"Murder…"

The word was like a bucket of ice water on Xeile's mind. "What?" he hissed. The words of the man in the tavern flew back into his mind. "You… You're one of the victims…" The spirit said nothing but merely stared at him with concern. A thought occurred to Xeile.

He could help Kelt solve the case.

But how would he help Kelt without being seen? If he were caught by other Guardians, they'd kill him for sure. Xeile shook his head. It didn't matter if they killed him anymore, now that he knew Kelt was in Trifectus. Getting caught would probably be the quickest way to meet him. There was just one problem. He turned and looked at the spirit.

"If I don't help you," Xeile asked himself softly, "will I end up becoming like you?" He thought hard for a moment, searching his heart, as he had done so often recently. The cold pain had long ago stripped away anything that didn't matter. In that way, it was kind of refreshing, despite the agony he endured. He realized his answer. "Alright, come on. Follow me. We've got to figure out who you were and whatnot." Xeile started walking, and the spirit fell into an identical pace beside him, saying nothing, her expression unchanging. Unsure what to say, Xeile looked at her. "So…'harvest'…is a strange word for you to remember. Normally, spirits remember names or a goal they wanted to achieve. Do you remember anything about who you were? What you wanted to do?" The spirit looked at him but didn't show any emotional reaction.

Xeile swallowed a few times and decided to try a new approach. "Well…I mean… I have some things I want to do… My name is Xeile, and I want to find this guy…his name is Kelt McNair. I'm hoping I can find him soon, since I'm really sick. It's"—Xeile's voice dropped to a whisper—"my dying wish."

The words seemed to force silence down on him, leaving him walking in the night with the spirit. Xeile wasn't sure where he was supposed to go from this point. Kelt could conceivably be anywhere in the city, and Trifectus was a huge, sprawling place if what Xeile had seen from a distance was correct. The moon maintained its steady climb in the sky, and Xeile looked at it, trying to burn the image into his mind as much as possible. It was a beautiful silvery white, with dappled shades of gray, waxing toward a full moon. In fact, it was almost there. "I hope I get to see it," Xeile said hopefully. He looked at the spirit. "What about you, do you…or, I guess… did you like the moon?"

The spirit looked at the moon for a second, then looked back at Xeile, and there was a smile on its face. Xeile felt a thrill course through him. It wasn't much, but it was a start. He reached out and pointed toward the moon. "You know, my mother always said if you look closely, you could see the face of a horse imprinted on the moon, though the Elves apparently think that dragons come from the moon. I don't know much about dragons, but I don't think they'd pass up on a tasty horse, do you?" The spirit turned and her smile widened. Then her smile faded and shifted to an expression of panic.

"What's wrong?" Xeile asked gently.

Then, he heard the sound. It was a neigh: loud, powerful, angry, and close. Xeile whipped around to locate its source, and he didn't have to look hard. It would be impossible to miss the giant creature staring him down.

At first glance, it looked like a horse, with a massive, stocky body, roughly twenty hands tall, and hooves the size of dinner plates. However, its body had a kind of translucent quality to it, a black ominous mist seeming to roll off it. Its eyes were a bloody crimson. What was most strange, though, was the massive rack of antlers that sprang out from just behind its ears, coming out into a sprawling tangle of at least fifteen points, being five feet across. From each point hung a short string that had a skull, and each skull had eyes that glowed a different color. Tongues of black flame seemed to emerge from each point on the rack.

Xeile took a single step backward and immediately felt an incredible chill wash over him. It wasn't cold like the winter wind, or a splitting cold like one of his attacks. This was an instinctual cold. Right now, his entire body was screaming at him to run. The creature let out another loud neigh, one that made Xeile's ears ring, then started snorting and stamping the ground.

Xeile grabbed the spirit by the waist, picked her up, and took off running without another thought, his feet slapping softly against the cobblestone. The creature let out a bellow, and Xeile could hear the hoof beats behind him slamming into the ground like miniature earthquakes.

He would never beat a horse in a footrace when it came to speed. That left two options: face the monster or manage to evade it through agility. Xeile looked for a way out and found it in the form of an alleyway. He cut to the side, praying that it wasn't a dead end. He skidded around the corner, slamming his shoulder into the wall and taking off, the ghost still on his shoulder. The creature charged after him, rounding the corner, its horns crashing into the wall with a clatter. "What…*is*…this…thing?" Xeile asked himself between ragged breaths. He kept cutting through alleys, tight turns, and back loops, blindly trying to escape. The creature never seemed to tire, but Xeile felt that his lungs were on fire, his feet like lead.

Then, after one final sprint onto a wider street, the creature just stopped its pursuit. It halted, snorting at Xeile, stamping the ground. Suddenly, as if led on a bridle, it turned around and clopped away. Xeile doubled over and tried desperately not to lose what little water he had consumed, taking great, gulping breaths of air, dropping the spirit off his shoulder.

Then the thought occurred to him. How could he even touch the spirit to begin with? He looked at her, expecting to see fear. Instead, he saw the expression on her face was one of concern. "Harvest…" she said to him gently, reaching out to him. Xeile stepped back and held up a finger.

"I'll make it," Xeile said. "I'm a strong boy, you'll—"

The attack struck him. The lances of cold shot up from his leg and into his chest. Xeile fumbled around in his pocket for his leather and crammed it into his mouth as he let out a muffled scream, sinking to the ground and curling into a ball. There was nothing left of his mind but the animalistic desire to not be in pain, and the feeling of powerlessness that came with the ability to do nothing about it. Eventually, the attack passed, but Xeile could feel that the cold had risen from his ankles to about his mid-shin.

He hauled himself up off the ground, every joint protesting movement, every muscle resisting his wishes. He managed to stand by propping himself up against a wall and sucked in a few breaths of the now seemingly cold summer air, holding a shaky hand up in the moonlight. His skin was outlined in a strange flickering black light. Was that part of this disease? Was it another symptom of a flare-up? He dropped his hand, spitting out his leather into it. After tucking it into his pocket, he gradually started to turn his senses to the outside world.

He was visible from the current street, so he slowly pushed himself into a nearby shadow, inching along as quickly as his cramped legs would allow. At least this way, he couldn't be spotted in an instant. Then, he heard the steady tread of two pairs of feet and the voices of their owners.

"So, you think they'll get anywhere with those victims?"

"It is entirely possible. Although I'm not sure they'll be able to make much progress without any help, Master. Let's hope they get a good break while I work the magical angle."

"Wise observation, Glenna. Though you must learn to not make your distaste for Kelt so obvious. It was very disrespectful of you. Like him or not, he is good at what he does."

"I'll...try my best, Master."

"See that you do."

Xeile's entire body froze. No. There was no way. Xeile risked a peek around the corner, and there she was. Her hair was much longer than the last time he saw her, but those purple eyes and that confident stride were unmistakable. Xeile whipped back into his hiding place, sliding down the wall, panic and longing clutching his heart, squeezing it in a merciless vise. He reached down and grabbed his necklace, fiddling with the small wooden ring on it. "Glenna," he whispered to himself. "What are you doing here?"

The Outcasts

Criske continued his routine scan of the street, torch in hand. Henrik was treading lightly beside him, no doubt doing the same. It had been, by all accounts, a surprisingly peaceful night. There was little criminal activity in this region during the nighttime anyway. Most nighttime crime, Criske knew, would be down in the Riverside District, where the less fortunate dwelt. But they gave those areas to more experienced Guardians, fortunately. Criske knew he could handle that place, but he wasn't so sure about Henrik. The Dwarf was definitely athletic, and could probably take care of himself in a fight, but Criske doubted he had ever gotten into a scrap with someone who could care less what uniform was being worn. The waxing moon provided plenty of light, but Criske kept looking for any signs of disturbance. But even with his constant vigil, it was Henrik who stopped him first. "Listen," Henrik whispered. Criske focused his attention on the surrounding sounds. It didn't take him long to identify the source, or what it was. Blows, likely from fists.

"Come on," Criske said, taking off toward the sound. Henrik was right behind him, pulling his truncheon off his belt as they headed toward the shadowy alleyway the sounds were coming from.

They rounded the corner to see three larger men, all pounding away on a small, hunched figure. "Patrolman!" Henrik yelled. "Freeze."

The three figures looked up and turned to them. The leader, a taller Elf female, laughed. "Look at these little boys. We were just teaching this man his proper place. He decided to mouth off and take a swing at us." She turned to the figure on the ground. "Isn't that right?"

"Yes," came the muffled reply.

Criske felt rage crawl up from his toes and into his mind, clouding his thoughts. It took all his self-control not to run forward, sword swinging. Henrik stepped toward the figure. "Is that true, ma'am?" he asked quietly. "If so, then you will have no problem explaining this to the jailer as I draw up a report on your charge. Human Territories law thirty-four, section nine, under the Barony of Trilan: 'Thou shall not use excessive force in the vigor of self-defense unless under threat of imminent death.'"

The Elf laughed. "You can't prove anything. I'm hardly swinging at him now, am I?" Her friends laughed along, in high, lilting voices Criske wanted to silence with a punch to their throats.

Henrik sighed. "True." He stowed his truncheon away. Criske looked at him, his fury growing.

Henrik stepped forward, getting closer to the Elf. "I don't suppose you can prove anything either, if I claim all the injuries you receive here were on you and your compatriots when I arrived." His voice was still quiet, but Criske felt the hair on the back of his neck stand on end. His anger faded, replaced with concern.

"Henrik, we can't just go around smashing faces in," he said quietly. "No matter how much they deserve it."

Henrik looked at Criske and nodded slowly. "You speak the truth, *Khlanro*. But I still need to arrest them, if you'll assist me." He pulled the manacles off his belt. "There is enough evidence to at least bring them in." As he turned to the Elf, she brought a fist crashing down on Henrik's jaw. Henrik staggered backward for a moment.

Criske snapped. Without a second thought, he tackled the woman to the ground, pinning one of her arms in a very effective lock he had learned years ago at the cruel hands of others. "You're under arrest for assaulting an officer."

The other two friends started toward him, and Criske looked up at them. "Take one more step toward me, and I'll break every single one of you. How'd you feel about a scar or two on your face, eh?" Criske saw them freeze. He had to keep them from attacking. With Henrik stunned, it was one versus three, which was never a good matchup. No matter how strong the fighter, numbers had a nasty habit of winning out.

Henrik recovered enough to clap the manacles on the wrists of the Elf Criske had pinned. "We are only able to arrest her at this point. We don't have enough evidence for the others unless we get a confession." Henrik made sure to say it loud enough for the other two Elves to overhear.

The unrestrained Elves sprinted away from the alleyway without so much as a backwards glance. As much as Criske hated watching them run away, he told himself he'd have to settle with one. With Henrik securing the Elf, he walked over to the victim to assess the damage, and it didn't take him long to figure out the reason for the prolonged beating.

"Half-Elf," he said over his shoulder. "Add 'targeted assault' to her charges," he said. Upon closer inspection, the man's right eye was swollen shut, leaking a reflexive tear. Multiple bruises were already blossoming on his arms and legs. Criske knelt down next to the man, feeling his pulse at his neck. The heart was still beating strong. "Can you breathe?" he asked gently.

"Why do you care?" the Half-Elf snapped. He looked at Criske, and his one good eye widened. "Oh shit…you…"

"Yeah, yeah," Criske said with a wave. "Can you stand on your own, or you need a hand?"

The Half-Elf struggled to move, then let out an agonized cry. "Ah…my ribs, my ribs…"

"Easy now," Criske said. "I've got you." With a well-practiced motion, Criske hauled the man to his feet, putting one of the victim's arms around his shoulder. The four of them walked in silence, Henrik guiding the bound Elf, Criske escorting the injured Half-Elf.

It didn't take them long to reach the nearest prison. Trifectus was so large, it warranted having two. The guards of the Watch opened the door and recoiled in surprise. The officer on duty was a squat man, clean-shaven with an appearance remarkably similar to a bloodhound. He took one look at the Elf, then one at the Half-Elf. "Ah, damn it," he said. "Another one, eh? Drag 'er into cell six. I'll knock that sorry medic outta his bunk."

The Elf did not resist as Henrik pushed her toward the cell, though Criske couldn't blame her for the sudden meekness. It was hard to be disobedient when you could feel someone watching your every move. After quickly unlocking her manacles, Henrik pushed her inside her cell and slammed the door shut.

"I'll just walk free in the morning," the Elf said with a small grin. "Your little stunt didn't prove anything."

Henrik froze and turned around. Criske couldn't quite see Henrik's face, as his back was to the torchlight, casting his face into shadow.

But he heard his words. "My stunt proved you have no real friends. Consider this a life lesson."

The Elf's smile faded, replaced by a snarl of rage. She shouted a variety of insults, which Henrik ignored as he walked back to Criske. He raised an eyebrow at Criske and gestured to the Half-Elf. "Shouldn't we be tending to him?"

Criske snapped out of his trance, shaking his head. "Oh yeah. Come on, the jailer said he was getting the medic. He'll patch you up."

They went over to the medic's office, which was little more than a small room with a cot and a table with some materials for making medicine. There were some standard pieces Criske expected to see: a small fireplace for boiling water and cooking brews, a series of mortars and pestles for grinding herbs and other materials, and a set of wicked-looking instruments Criske knew the purpose of by sight alone: amputation. He suppressed a shudder and hoped he'd never have to see someone use those. Small bundles of dried plants hung from the ceiling, giving the room an earthy, slightly spicy scent.

"Onto the cot you go," Criske said, helping the Half-Elf settle down on its edge. Now in the light of the fire and several beeswax candles,

Criske could finally get a better look at the man's injuries. "Let's get that shirt off you," he said. "Can you raise your arms?"

The Half-Elf nodded and very slowly took off his shirt, revealing a collage of bruises, cuts, scrapes, and scars across his torso. Some of these injuries were old ones that were in the process of healing, but some were brand new. Angry burn marks riddled the man's arms, and he saw one scar that made the blood pound in his ears. Someone had taken a knife and carved the word "mongrel" into his flesh at some point.

"Alright," Criske said, "I'm going to do some basic examinations while we wait on that medic, alright? You tell me if any of these places I touch hurt." Criske ran through joint mobility, checking for any obviously broken limbs or bones. It quickly became evident that the man had several cracked ribs, a sprained shoulder, and bone bruising on his arms from when he had the good sense to protect his face. Moving quickly, Criske grabbed some nearby bandages off the shelf, along with several herbs. He stripped them of their leaves, seeds, and juices before grinding them into a paste in a mortar and pestle. He quickly gathered some of the paste and spread it across the series of minor cuts. "These will heal by themselves," Criske said, "but you need to make sure to keep them clean if you want to avoid pus and the like, yeah?"

The Half-Elf stared at him as if he were a strange ghost that had just materialized out of the wall, but nodded slowly in agreement anyway.

Next, Criske grabbed a piece of garlic from a braid that was hanging nearby, along with some poppy. With precise movements, he extracted liquid from the poppy, combining it with recently boiled water and crushed mint leaves, letting it steep and cool. While he waited, he crushed the garlic and smashed it into a fine paste. "Henrik," he said, "could you get the poppy water to our friend here?"

Henrik took the cooling contents of the small cauldron and poured it into a nearby ceramic mug, handing it to the Half-Elf, who silently took it without complaint. Criske reached into his own personal-effects pouch and pulled out a series of unusual instruments, including a needle and incredibly fine thread. Criske saw Henrik's expression turn into one of confusion, but he didn't say anything. Most Guardians didn't carry such things out into the field with them unless they were going on a very long-term mission where they wouldn't be in civilization for months. Fortunately for his Half-Elf patient, needle and thread could be used to mend more than just clothes. "Go ahead and finish that tea," Criske said. "It'll help with the pain." They waited quietly as the Half-Elf finished drinking the herbal concoction. After a minute or two, Criske scooped up half the garlic paste and put it into more heated water, swirling it around. "Rinse your mouth out with this," he said. "You've probably got some cuts in there that need cleaning." The Half-Elf looked at the liquid in the cup, then back up at Criske with some distrust. "Go on," Criske insisted. "We haven't got all night."

The Half-Elf took the mixture and rinsed out his mouth, wincing as he did so. Criske held out a hand to Henrik. "Bowl please." A moment later, a bowl was pressed into his hand, which Criske then had the Half-Elf spit in. Criske held the bowl under the light and examined its contents. It was bloody, but it wasn't particularly dark or a consistency that indicated a deeper injury than superficial cuts. He threw the liquid into the fire and set the bowl aside.

Now came the hard part. It didn't take him long to find the piece of leather the medic normally gave to soldiers with more severe injuries, riddled with deep teeth marks. "Bite into this," Criske said. "I'm going to be treating some of these larger cuts. It's going to be terrible. Henrik, I'm going to need some help here. Can you make sure our friend doesn't writhe around too much?"

Henrik hesitantly grabbed a hold of the Half-Elf, who now looked visibly panicked. Criske moved with efficiency, coating the needle and thread in some of the garlic mash and getting to work. The Half-Elf let out a reflexive cry of pain as the needle entered and exited his skin, but Henrik helped keep him still as Criske worked on gashes on the man's back, leg, and upper arm. In a matter of minutes, he was done. "Hard part over," Criske assured him with a pat on the shoulder. "Good man. Those will heal over time, but the thread will have to come out in about a week or so. The medic here will be able to do that for you, or you can go to Malron Val by the riverside. Get some rest for now."

The Half-Elf reached out and grasped Criske's arm in a viselike grip, fixing his non-swollen eye on him, as if trying to absorb every last detail of his face. "Thank you," he croaked. "Thank you so much."

Criske scratched the back of his head. "No problem. Just doing what I could. Lie down, get some rest. You'll need it to recover." He helped the man lie back on the cot, where he drifted off to sleep in seconds. Criske now turned his attention to his fellow patrolman.

Henrik had been bearing his injury without complaint, but Criske could see that a nasty gash had been opened along Henrik's hairline and was bleeding. "Are you alright?" Criske asked, tilting Henrik's head to examine the gash from multiple angles. "Light-headedness? Dizziness? Blurred vision?"

"No," Henrik said. "I managed to get away before most of the blow hit me. I think one of her nails managed to catch me."

What Criske saw didn't seem to dispute this. Despite being a long cut, it was still fairly shallow. After applying the herbal paste to the wound, it stopped bleeding entirely. He had Henrik do various movements and balance tests just in case, but it seemed Henrik had actually gotten lucky after all. Injuries to the head could take weeks to heal.

He had just finished up his examination of Henrik when the medic came into the room, slightly out of breath. "Sorry it took so long," he said, sucking in air. "Down in the barracks, there's a soldier with a bad fever that just did not want to break. What's the situation?"

"Assault case," Criske explained, jerking a thumb over at the Half-Elf. "You can check him if you want, but I've already patched him the best I could."

The medic went to the patient and gave him a look over. He nodded in approval. "Nice work. Seems you know your way around. What's the green paste on the cuts?"

"*Zhou Rang Bi*," Criske said. "Elvish recipe. Prevents inflaming and infection. They're shallow, but better safe than sorry, yeah."

The medic nodded and then grinned at him. "You sure you don't want my job? You'll be plenty busy."

"No, thanks," Criske said with a raised hand. "Kind of already took an oath and everything."

The medic exhaled with a melodramatic sigh. "Damn. Alright. I'll keep an eye on him for tonight and make sure nothing happens just in case, but you gentlemen should be good here."

Henrik and Criske quickly filled the jailer in on all of the details of the assault and left to resume their patrol. They traveled in quiet for a while before Henrik spoke. "Where did you learn the art of medicine?"

"I don't know about 'art,' but my father taught me a lot, and my mother knows plenty of home-based fixes," Criske said. "I just kind of picked it up as I went."

"I see," Henrik said. "You are most fortunate, then."

Criske let out a small laugh. "I don't know about that. Sometimes I wish I didn't know anything about it. People always come to you for help when they realize you can patch them up." The conversation faded again, but Criske could feel Henrik wanted to say something. Finally, he did find the words, and they weren't what Criske expected.

"I'm sorry."

"What?" Criske looked at him with a raised eyebrow. "What for?"

"I'm sorry that Half-Elves have to deal with this," Henrik said. His face was somber. "I'm sorry I had to drag that woman in on a technicality to actually help that man. If I were stronger, we could have gotten all three of them off the street." He looked at the ground, his hands clenched into fists. "I'm sorry I am too weak, *Khlanro*."

What was he supposed to say to that? Criske put a hand on Henrik's shoulder. "Don't apologize," he said. "We got one, which is better than none. We won't be able to catch everyone. It's just a fact of life. Be happy we were able to get one in the first place. And I don't think you're weak. You saw a fight where you were outmatched and went in anyway. That takes guts." Henrik nodded, but his expression told Criske the Dwarf didn't completely believe it.

It didn't take long for them to find their way back to their normal patrol route, which they completed without another major incident. On the way back to headquarters, their talk turned once more to the murder cases.

"Do you think it is possible that Kelt is right about there being an unregistered magician?" Henrik asked.

Criske shook his head. "No. I mean, we know they've got to be good at magic, right? But how could they get the training in secret? I doubt you can learn magic all by yourself without blowing something or someone up on accident. I think whoever did this is likely registered but trying to stay quiet for now. Keep from being too obvious, yeah?"

Henrik nodded. "I was thinking the same, though that lingering cold still doesn't make any sense to me. How could we still feel that, even though the magic was no longer being used? Once the magician was gone, the air should have warmed up immediately. It is summer, after all. Even if they were gone for only a few seconds, it should not have been that cold without any signs of frost or ice. You and I did not see any."

"Unless the magician was somewhere nearby when we found the body and still..." Criske's words trailed off as the realization struck him. He turned to Henrik, grabbing his arm. "You don't think they wanted us to find the body...do you?"

Henrik frowned as he considered the possibility. "If that is true...then they would have a vested interest in following what we're doing...including what we are doing now." The pair stopped and looked at each other for a moment before reflexively looking over their shoulders.

Criske saw the barest hint of movement in an alleyway.

"Come on!" he yelled at Henrik. The two of them took off after the figure. They wound up in the alley, and Criske was immediately struck by an incredible sensation of cold. It was actually enough to make his breath fog. The figure was limping down the alley as fast as he could.

"Freeze," Henrik commanded. His voice booked no room for argument.

The limping figure stopped and turned around. He was in a strange kind of hood that blocked his face from sight, but his boots were cracked and caked with dirt from either months of hard travel or neglect. Even with the cloak, it was hard to deny that he was incredibly thin, a thinness brought on by, in Criske's experience, a lack of proper meals.

"You're Guardians…" The figure started to shake. "Do you know Kelt McNair?"

"We do," Henrik said. "What is your business with him?"

"Tell him one of the victims keeps mentioning the word 'harvest.'"

Criske took a few steps forward. The figure took a few stumbling steps back. "How do you know what the victims are saying?" he challenged.

"Just trust me," the hooded creature insisted. "You can't see her, but I can. Please, tell Kelt."

"How about you tell him yourself when you come with us back to headquarters," Henrik said, stepping toward the figure.

"No," the male said immediately. "I can't go there. They'll kill me." Henrik was unfazed and kept walking forward, reaching for his manacles. The figure turned to try and run and let out an agonized cry, sinking to the ground with a moan. "Damn it… Not now…"

Criske immediately felt the temperature drop again. He hurried forward, reaching for the kneeling figure to offer assistance. "Don't," the figure gasped. "Don't. I'm sick—" Criske extended out a hand toward the man.

Criske's world immediately turned to frost, icy-hot pain flying up his arm, into his teeth, into his head. Suddenly, his limbs went weak and Criske fumbled backward. He tried to get his tongue to move, his chest to breathe, but they refused to function, as though they were new to the task of keeping him alive. His breath seemed to catch and freeze in his lungs, only to gradually be shoved out of his body to chill his throat. His ears rang, filling his world with senseless noise as his vision blurred and then turned black.

When Criske came to, Henrik was kneeling over him, supporting his head with one hand, his dark eyes lit with concern. "*Khlanro*, can you hear me?"

"Yeah." Criske's mouth felt dry, and his entire body was covered in sweat. "What happened? Did you get him?"

"No," Henrik said bitterly. "I'm not sure what kind of magic you got hit with, but after that, he took off running. It looks like he wasn't lying about being sick, though. He left a piece of leather behind that looked like it was covered in blood and bite marks."

"You should have gone after him," Criske said.

"And leave my *Khlanro*?" Henrik shook his head. "Not a chance. Can you stand?"

Criske got unsteadily to his feet, and Henrik looked back down the alleyway. "Even if we didn't catch him, we've got something out of it," Henrik reasoned. "Come on, we need to get you back to headquarters for an evaluation and some rest. And I think Kelt would like to know about our new suspect."

The Half-Elf gave him a shaky nod, and the two Guardians made slow progress back home, the moon illuminating their path away from the clawing shadows of narrow midnight streets.

THE SOLDIER

Kelt sighed as he rubbed his temples, staring at the piece of paperwork in front of him. "How can we be having this many problems with damn fish?" He looked over the request for additional reinforcements once more and signed off on it, moving to the next piece of paper in his pile. When he became an inquisitor, he was told he'd be in a role that required more signatures and seals, but he didn't think it'd be quite this bad.

He looked at the next two pieces side by side and smiled. It was Criske's and Henrik's official apprenticeship paperwork. Despite them being a random selection, they'd turned out well so far. Using his wax, Kelt happily pressed his seal of approval on the bottom of each of them next to his signature and moved on. His beeswax candles were starting to burn low. He'd have to put in a request to acquire more.

The next sheet was actually a letter, written in meticulous, flowing script. Kelt looked at it curiously before breaking the letter's seal and opening it up. Inside, orderly lines of text were crammed in tiny writing from one corner to the other. Kelt squinted at it, but the words seemed to blend together in the dim light. "Gah. That's waiting till morning," he said, setting the letter aside.

He let out a small sigh and leaned back in his chair, wincing at the stabbing pain in his shoulder. It still hadn't healed, even after a few months. "Damn it," he hissed. He flexed it a few times, hoping it would loosen itself, but there was little effect.

Maybe it was a good thing he had retired from Spell Breaking when he did. The work was less entertaining now, and he spent more time pushing paper than boundaries, but he managed to escape his Spell Breaking career with all four limbs, both eyes, and most of his health. That was a lot more than he could say for most his age.

So why was he so unsettled?

Kelt felt another wave of irrational emotions wash over him—the kind that only happened at night when he was alone with nothing to do but think. He pushed them back down. "Focus," he muttered to himself. "Focus. You have better things to do." He took a deep breath in, then exhaled, closing his eyes.

An image of a woman's face flashed across his mind's eye. Her black hair clung to her face in the middle of the rain, her bright-green eyes staring at him accusingly as she clutched a massive sword, resting it easily on one shoulder and maintaining its balance with one hand—

Kelt opened his eyes and took another deep breath. He looked down and realized he was shaking. Kelt clutched his left shoulder, squeezing it tight as he focused all his attention on the wood grain of his desk. Eventually, the tremors eased. "Damn it. Damn it all," he whispered. "Get out of my head."

There was a knock on his door, lifting him out of the fog of his own mind.

"Enter," he called, feeling some confusion. What would someone need him for this late at night? If it was an emergency, they would go to the Watch.

Henrik walked in, trying to push the door open with his foot and support an unsteady Criske at the same time. Kelt immediately went into action, holding the door for them as they stepped through. "I'd lock that," Criske said weakly. "We've got some news."

"I can see that," Kelt said, his tone dry. He shut the door behind them and dropped the dead bolt on it for good measure. "Any reason we have to be so secretive and paranoid?"

"Well, sir…" Henrik looked around as if the words had been dropped on the ground and required being picked up. Kelt held up a finger. He pulled a chair over for Criske and helped lower him into it. He couldn't see an exact reason why Criske wasn't able to walk under his own power, but the Half-Elf's skin had a nasty paleness to it and there was a sheen of sweat on his brow.

"Have you seen the medic?" Kelt asked.

"We just got back from seeing him," Criske said tiredly. "But there's nothing he can do, apparently. Called it something…"

"'Aura shock,'" Henrik finished for his friend. "The medic recommended rest and food, but we both agreed that this information could not afford to wait."

Kelt flinched in surprise. "What the blazes did you two get yourselves into?" Aura shock was a condition that occurred when a magician temporarily overloaded the amount of energy in someone else's aura, the invisible arcane eggshell that protected them from wild magic in the air. While it took a vast amount of energy or practice to break an aura, "shocking" one by suddenly increasing its energy could still completely incapacitate someone. It was a popular technique for Spell Breakers as a way to stop a rogue magician without killing them. It could be dealt with, but only after training, and few ever did. Getting blasted by energy wasn't a popular way to pass the time when swords could be swung much easier.

"We were on night patrol…and…" Criske winced, unable to speak anymore. "Oh…*Zhou mai fen na rang.*"

"Tea first," Kelt said. He walked over to his desk, opening a drawer to reveal a series of small ceramic jars with dry tea leaves inside. After sorting through them for a moment, Kelt found the one he was looking for. He poured the leaves into a cloth, tied it with string, and put a kettle on. When the water was steaming, he poured both of his apprentices cups, pressing one into Criske's hands. "Chamomile," he said. "It has a tendency to resettle your aura. You'll feel better."

Criske gave him a shaky nod and started taking small sips.

"Now, Henrik, start from the beginning of your patrol tonight and walk me through what happened," Kelt said, his voice calm.

Henrik took a deep breath and laid out the start of the night's events. Kelt could feel the disappointment radiating off of Henrik as he described the event with the Half-Elf, and then relayed what happened at the jail. Kelt looked over Henrik's injury and nodded to Criske with approval. "Good work," he said. "To the both of you."

"But two got away," Henrik said bitterly. "The cycle is just going to continue…"

Kelt put a hand on his shoulder. "I want you to pay close attention to me," he said. Henrik seemed to be staring at a point beyond Kelt. "Look at me," Kelt said firmly. Henrik looked at him, and Kelt saw frustration in his eyes. "You may think nothing changed, but for that one Half-Elf, you changed his entire world. You showed him that there are people who care, that there are some soldiers and officials who believe in something greater than themselves."

He grasped Henrik's other shoulder, kneeling down in front of him so that they were eye level.

"I don't expect you to understand everything you just did for that man, but I do want you to understand: you should hold your head high and be proud of the work you've done. You caught one of them, which is better than walking by and doing nothing. Even if you feel like you failed, you need to understand that a small victory is better than nothing. Being a Guardian isn't like a saga or a folktale. Not every story has a neat, happy ending. But we have to appreciate the successes we do have, or we may wind up eventually never doing any good at all. Understand, apprentice? If you do, say, 'I do.'"

"I do," Henrik said. Kelt saw the words sinking into him. Henrik had accepted the words, but it would take some time for him to fully realize what they meant. His expression said that he was trying hard to keep it in his mind, but he was grappling with some other experience that had told him otherwise.

"Alright," Kelt said. "Drink your tea and finish the rest of the story." Henrik sipped at his chamomile tea and relayed what happened after leaving the medic. The street, the darkened figure, the mention of the victim, the cold, and the fact he asked about Kelt by name. "He asked about you as soon as he found out we were Guardians," Henrik explained. "It was like he knew you. We thought it was suspicious and tried to bring him in, but he refused to cooperate. He seemed to think he'd be killed if he went into headquarters. I'm not sure why he was so panicked. Then, he kind of just fell to the ground. Criske went over to go help him, but a strange, flickering black seemed to kind of...explode out from him, knocking Criske out. I immediately went to help my *Khlanro*, but the figure got up and ran away. I couldn't follow him with Criske unresponsive on the ground..."

Kelt nodded. "You made a good call. You could have gotten lured into a trap or worse if you had given chase by yourself." His mind started going through possibilities. A blast backward like that definitely sounded like it could have been an aura shock, but the number of people capable of doing one was incredibly small. The issue with an aura shock was that it could easily backfire and incapacitate the one trying to use it. Spell Breakers would train for weeks and months before even trying to use it in a practice match.

"He told me to get away," Criske said. "He tried to warn me, as if he couldn't control it. He said he was sick…and he…acted like he was scared of himself."

"Do you believe him?" Kelt asked.

Criske nodded. "Yes. That's the strangest part in all this. I mean, he clearly sounded and looked sick, but absolutely didn't want our help. He wanted us to tell you that he could see the victim and she said something about 'harvest.' I don't understand why he'd want to communicate with us but then not actually meet with you."

Kelt could think of several reasons, but he needed more details if any of this was going to make sense. "Criske, could you describe the symptoms you felt when you were hit? Do you remember?"

Criske rapidly gulped down the hot tea and shuddered. "It was awful. So damn cold, I thought my eyes were going to freeze in their sockets. I couldn't breathe, like the air was stuck in my lungs, and forget about moving. It was like I had no energy at all."

Kelt's eyebrows knitted together in confusion. That didn't sound like an aura shock. The general lack of ability to function afterward and the symptoms Criske was displaying now certainly did, but the actual impact of the moment was very different. Most people explained it as a blinding heat, as if they were suddenly tossed into a fire, or as if they had somehow gotten struck by a lightning bolt and survived. A magician described it as "too much energy with nowhere to go." If he felt a cold…that meant…

"You are a lucky man," Kelt said quietly. "You should have died."

Criske looked at him, his eyes wide. "What? Are you saying that guy tried to off me?"

Kelt shook his head, his heart sinking as he came to a terrible realization. He sat down in his chair and put his head in his hands. "No. I think he was deliberately warning you…and trying to help me with this case because he killed one of the victims on accident."

"Accident?" Henrik asked. "Does that mean he's a magician who can't control himself?"

"Of sorts," Kelt said. He stood up and looked at Henrik. "Gentlemen, I hate to inform you of this, but from the sounds of it, the person you encountered has a broken aura."

Henrik frowned. "Wait, but you need an aura to live, yes?"

Kelt nodded. "Yes, you do." His voice became very quiet. "But I don't think the person you encountered is entirely alive."

Henrik blanched. "*Khlaniik vod taqarnah…* an undead? In this day and age? There hasn't been a true undead in Meraria since the reign of Taron Idolon."

Idolon. The word tripped a series of connections in the senior Guardian's mind, and all the pieces lined up to a terrible conclusion that filled him with rage. Kelt's fist came crashing down on his desk, causing everyone else to flinch and the nearby candle to sputter. "I worked for twenty-two years, and it still wasn't enough…"

Someone was targeting Guardians. An undead was roaming the streets of Trifectus, desperately trying to help Kelt catch a murdering, highly powerful magician. There was no question in his mind anymore.

The Idolon Remnant had returned, and they were out for blood.

He looked up at his apprentices, both of whom looked like they were preparing to bolt. Kelt forced his fist to relax. "My apologies," he muttered. "My temper got away from me."

He took a deep breath and drew himself up to his full height of six foot five inches, his blue eyes flashing with renewed energy. "We've got a lot to do. Henrik, I need you to grab Head Magician Usumi and her apprentice. I don't care that it's late. Tell her the coffee is on me."

Henrik snapped to attention for a brief salute and headed out the door. Kelt turned to Criske. "Val-Zhang," he said. Criske looked at him as if he really wanted to pay attention but the pain was making it difficult for him to focus. "I need you to rest for now." Criske opened his mouth to protest, and Kelt held up a finger. "For now. We can't afford to have you not at your best. You'll be following up possible leads on the clue our suspect gave us when you recover."

Kelt sighed. "And I think it's time I call on a few old friends of mine."

The Seeker

Xeile awoke with a gasp, clawing at the air to get away from something that didn't exist in actuality. His current reality gradually seeped into his senses. The rough stone floor underneath him, the shelves of the cellar just barely visible in the early-morning light through the cracks in the cellar door. Eventually, his heart settled back down. He looked up at the Elven woman floating above him who was looking back down at him with concern. He sat up. "Don't worry," he said, waving a hand at her. "I'm fine. Let's just focus on you for now, okay?"

In truth, he was far from fine. He could feel the cold in his kneecaps now, biting, chewing away at him, like he was candle wax around a lit wick. His head was throbbing, and exhaustion had settled deep in his bones from the events of the previous night. But he put on a brave face. It wouldn't do for him to complain about the pain he was in when the person in front of him was dead.

"You're hurt."

Xeile felt his stomach clench and a shiver run down his spine. He looked at the spirit in surprise. Every ghost he had ever encountered up to this point had a very narrow focus, their mind limited to the single goal that was binding them to this life. They seldom acknowledged anything, and whenever one did notice his presence, they thought he was someone from their past life. They never saw him as he was.

"You're hurt," the spirit repeated, floating closer to him, its eyes boring into his. Xeile felt himself become motionless in fear. "Who hurt you?"

"No one," Xeile whispered. "I'm just sick."

"Why haven't you gotten better?"

"I don't know," he answered. "I've been this way for months…ever since this changed color." He pulled the necklace out from under his shirt with stiff, uncooperative fingers. "My mother gave it to me before she died," Xeile said quietly. "It's all I have left of her." He waved a hand away.

"But I'm not what's important right now. We need to figure out how you died so I can tell Kelt."

The spirit, however, was not tolerating his attempts to turn the conversation away from himself. She reached out toward his necklace. "Harvest…" she said quietly. "It's just like his…"

Xeile got to his feet. He looked at the figure, eagerly seizing on the lead. "Harvest is a person?" he asked. "Was Harvest a person you knew well? Do you know where he lives?"

The Elf, for he had no other name to call her by, looked around at the cellar, as if struggling to see something. She clutched her chest, where her glowing shard pulsated with light. "Important to me…" she whispered. Xeile felt the temperature drop inside the cellar. "Why?" the spirit asked. "Why can't I remember?"

Xeile held out a mollifying hand. "Hey, hey. Relax. I'm here to help you figure this out, alright? But I can't do that if you're upset."

The spirit looked at him with pained eyes, but the temperature in the air returned to normal. "Why are you helping me?" she asked. "I'm not stupid. I know you're dying. Just like he was."

Xeile recoiled as if stung. He stared at the spirit, then at his own shaking hands, which he clenched into fists. He looked at the spirit. "I decided a long time ago," he explained, "that I would live what's left of my life without regrets. I don't think I could do that if I didn't help you. Helping people is what we're supposed to do. Even if the world is collapsing around you, even if there seems to be nothing good in this world, someone has to hold on to what makes life worth living, and it might as well be me, because if I don't, who will? I'm the only one who can see you right now, so I'm the only one who can help. If I don't help you, who will?"

The Elf stared at him for a long moment, her eyes becoming incredibly sad. "I have no right to ask anything of you in the final days of your life," she said quietly.

"Maybe not," Xeile said. "But I'm choosing to help you, so what does it matter?" He raised a hand up to her. "I promise you, we'll catch your killer, or I'll die trying. I want to give the last bit of my life to something greater than myself, so stop worrying, alright?"

The Elf reached out and her hand touched Xeile's. It was strangely solid to him. Was that a sign he was getting closer to death? Is that why she had so much more of a personality this morning? "Alright," she said.

There was a moment of silence as Xeile considered his next move. If Harvest was a person, that wasn't really much to go on. Moving around with the spirit seemed to help bring out more of her memories. He needed to go to places that would be likely to hold memories for her. An idea popped into his head. If he could find out where Elves lived, he may come across her old home, or perhaps even Harvest himself. He snapped his fingers and went to exit the cellar. "Better plan than none," he said with a small smile forming on his face.

He quickly looked outside the doors to see if anyone was coming. When he couldn't see anyone, he quietly lifted the cellar door and left the small hole he called his temporary home, shutting the door gently behind himself. The Elf just floated through the door and stared at him expectantly. Xeile raised a finger. "Well, first things first, we need to—"

His stomach let out a loud growl of protest.

Xeile sighed. "Apparently I need to get some food." The only question was, where to get it? He didn't want to risk a tavern or inn again. If someone stared at him too long, they might ask questions or draw attention to himself, with his ashen gray skin and his veins that were slowly blackening under his strange disease. No, it'd be far better if he could find some kind of open market where he could simply drop money onto a counter, grab some food, and leave without a word. Considering the size of the city, he wouldn't be surprised if there were several markets like that. The only question was where.

"Middle of the city…or close to it maybe?" he mumbled to himself.

With no better plan coming to mind, he started walking toward the center of the city, hoping that there would be some indicators he was heading in the right direction, the spirit floating behind him.

The city was slowly blooming to life, with the bakers and smiths being the first ones to rise so they could stoke the flames that powered their livelihoods. It wouldn't be long before the ringing of a hammer on hot metal would be resounding throughout the streets and the smell of baking bread filled the air. Xeile passed by one such blacksmith, a stout Dwarf with a white beard, who was commanding his two apprentices in the art of maintaining the fire.

Xeile felt his feet taking him over to watch them work before his mind could stop him. He stared at the coke and the anvil with longing. How long had it been since he had gotten to work metal? He tried to recall when that was, but his memory refused to cooperate. The Dwarf master looked up and saw him, then began striding over, his arms folded across his chest. His Territory came with a thick accent.

"You need things?"

Xeile quickly shook his head. "No, no. Sorry, just…looking. Sorry…" He went to shuffle away, but the Dwarf grabbed his hand.

"You sick? Come, sit. I feed. You too pale. Sit, sit."

"Oh, you don't have to… That's really…" Xeile's protests fell on deaf ears as the Dwarf sat Xeile down at a small workbench and gave him a small platter of bread and cheese. Even though the young man knew he should leave, the savory smell of the bread and the nutty scent of the cheese overpowered his thoughts. In that moment, all he could think of was how hungry he was. He quickly ate the cheese, manners far from the first thing on his mind, then consumed the bread. A mug of ale appeared before him, and he quaffed that down as well, setting the ceramic mug down with a clack.

He looked at the Dwarf and was not surprised to see the spirit floating behind him. Most Dwarves he met had spirits that followed them around, trying to get their attention without success. The few that actually could talk with the spirits that followed them were often a very unhappy lot.

Xeile pulled out one of his last few coins and went to hand it to the Dwarf. "Thank you," he said.

The Dwarf shook his head, raising his hands. "No, no take money. You bless house, *Khlaniik-Vahn?*"

Xeile frowned in confusion. "Bless?" He looked down at himself and realized that his mother's necklace was still showing. He quickly tucked it away and looked around at the smithy. He got up and walked over to it, placing his hand on one of the supporting beams of the building. "Um…. Hmm…" He had no idea what the Dwarf meant for him to do, but since he just fed him, Xeile figured he had to at least try something.

He leaned his head against the pillar and started whispering in what he hoped was a ritualistic manner. "Spirits that are here…um…please look after everyone in this place. They do really good work and could use your help on occasion, okay? They were really helpful to me, so if you could help me return the favor, I'd appreciate it."

It didn't take long for the spirit behind the Dwarf to respond to Xeile by getting close to him, muttering in Dwarvish. Soon, three other spirits appeared, likely the ones that were following the apprentices. Their words all became incoherent gibberish to Xeile, but he looked at the four of them and held up a finger. "Now, you be nice to them," Xeile said, not sure if his words were having any impact. "Got it? I don't want to hear about any possessions or malicious accidents." His finger brushed against one of the spirits, and he felt a tingle up his arm.

"Oops." He pulled his hand back. "Sorry about that."

When he looked at the Dwarf master, his eyes were the size of saucer plates. "Did I do okay?" Xeile asked. "I can…do another…blessing…if you'd like…"

The Dwarf pointed a finger at him awe and fear on his face,. "*Khlaniik-Raldem!*"

Xeile took one step back raising his hands. "Hey, hey, hey. No need to get emotional. Just trying to help."

The Dwarf looked at his apprentices, babbling to them rapidly in his native tongue. They stopped what they were doing and looked at Xeile in amazement. Xeile gave them a friendly wave and attempted a smile. The cold started to crawl up his spine, and he felt a surge of panic. "I have to leave now," Xeile explained urgently. The Dwarf looked at him in confusion. Xeile backed away with a wave. "I'm leaving. Thank yo—"

The cold slammed into his head like an ice pick, enveloping him with its biting malice. He felt like his eyelids were going to freeze shut. He couldn't afford to fall to the ground here. What if one of the Dwarves were to touch him and get hurt? So no matter the agony, he forced himself to stand, tears of silent pain rolling down his face.

The master Dwarf went pale, staring at him in amazement. He eventually sank to his knees. "*Khlaniik-Vahln,*" he whispered. Xeile looked around himself and noticed for the very first time that he was being surrounded by spirits. Dwarves, Elves, and Humans alike were drifting around him, staring at him with their different-colored eyes, their small shards of glowing light filling his vision with a kaleidoscope of color. Xeile tried to shove one of them away that was getting a little too close for comfort.

An immediate surge of warmth shot through his body, ripping away the pain in a sudden blaze that made his entire body tremble. There was a bang and a sound that reminded Xeile of the crackle of a wood fire. Soon, he saw a black layer of material form around his body, flickering and moving in little shards and pieces. He jerked his hand away from the spirit and looked at his hand in confusion.

He glanced at the Dwarf, unsure what to do. He shrugged and winced at the same time. "Oops?" he said hesitantly.

"Watch! Rogue magician, rogue magician!" someone screamed from behind him.

Xeile didn't bother to identify the source. He took off running. "Idiot," he growled at himself. "You should have just never accepted the food and run away immediately. What were you thinking?"

"What did you do?" the Elf spirit asked him with an edge of panic in her voice.

"I don't know!" Xeile cried. "I've never touched a spirit during an attack before! I didn't mean to do it, it was an accident!"

The two of them wove indiscriminately through the streets, slowing to a quick walk and weaving in and out of heavier crowds in an attempt to lose any potential pursuers. Eventually, Xeile felt his heart rate return to normal, and he turned his attention to his surroundings.

Wherever he was, he got the distinct feeling he didn't belong in this area. Most of the buildings were old and run down, with either shoddy homemade repairs or just open holes in the roofs. The river was snaking its way down a series of bridges below. Some of the few passersby had a distinctly Elven look to them, but lacked the necessary height or longer, angular ears. Half-Elves. No, this was distinctly not a place he should feel welcome.

"I need to get out of here," he muttered.

Then, he heard a high-pitched scream. Xeile whipped around, and his feet immediately carried him toward the source of the noise. "No!" screamed the voice. "No, no, no."

He rounded the corner to see a massive spectral frame looming over a very alive and terrified Elf. Its wicked horns were splayed out, and Xeile would recognize those massive hooves anywhere. "Hey!" Xeile screamed, jumping up and down, waving his arms. "Hey, ugly! I'm over here!"

The beast turned its head, its red eyes glowing dangerously, the skulls tied to its antlers rattling as it hit the wall. It stared at Xeile for a moment as if trying to identify him. Then, it let out a loud snort and angry neigh, stamping the ground in fury.

"I didn't think this one through," Xeile admitted to himself. He looked around for the nearest weapon he could find and saw a length of metal chain. He picked it up and started spinning it in what he hoped was an intimidating circle. "Get away from her," he said, wishing his voice didn't tremble so much. "Or I'll hit you."

The creature let out another snort and lowered its head, charging at Xeile with thunderous speed. He jumped to the side, throwing the chain, hoping it would hit the creature's eye. Instead, the chain wound up wrapping around on of the creature's antlers. "Damn it!" Xeile screamed. He felt his arm nearly get yanked out of its socket as he pulled, causing the creature to suddenly tilt to the side and smash into a nearby wall under the force of its own momentum, and letting out what he could only describe as a scream of protest. It righted itself and started tossing its head to and fro, trying to buck off the chain without success.

Luck was on Xeile's side as it thrashed about; he narrowly avoided getting slammed into the wall several times. No matter how terrifying this beast was, it was still a creature of instinct, and was trying to pull away from him rather than gore him with its horns. That instinct was probably the only thing keeping him alive.

Then, the creature suddenly stopped. Xeile felt a terrible cold wash over him. "Not now," he thought. The cold struck him without pause, eating away at his mind. Xeile tightened his grip around the chain as he fell to the ground, sinking to his knees, curling around the chain, protecting it with his body. Right now, he was the only defense that woman behind him had. Even if it was his last act, he couldn't leave her to die.

The black flickering around his body picked up again, but this time, it seemed to travel up the chain and slam into the creature, causing it to let out a neigh of pain. Pain? That's all he needed to make it not attack.

Xeile forced himself into a crawling position and started toward the creature. A wracking cough made him falter as flecks of blood splattered the cobblestones. "No," he said through gritted teeth. "I'm…going…to…stop… you…" Xeile said, his vision growing blurry, the monster becoming an indiscriminate mass. Another black flicker shot up the chain from his body, slamming into the creature. It tossed its head about and the chain finally fell free.

"No," Xeile said feebly, raising a hand to ward off the creature. "Go…away…"

"I've got you!"

Xeile felt a surge of strength suffuse his body. He looked up to identify the source of the voice and saw that the Elf spirit was standing beside him, touching his back with both hands. The glow in her chest was dimming. He yanked away from her. "No…" he said. "You'll hurt yourself." It took almost all his willpower for him to get to his feet; his entire world spun and twisted in strange ways, blurring in and out of existence. He leaned against the wall and tasted blood. He must have bitten his own cheek.

He looked at the monster before him. "C'mon, you bastard," he muttered. "I'm not dead yet."

The creature looked at him for a moment, and then, to Xeile's surprise, sank into the ground, disappearing out of sight. Xeile listened and waited for any signs of attack, but none were forthcoming.

With the imminent danger out of sight, he turned to the alive Elven woman. "Are you… okay?" he asked, trying to take deep breaths.

The Elf just stared at him, her eyes wide. "You…" she said. "You're the strange one from the tavern…"

"Are you okay?" Xeile repeated.

The Elf nodded, getting to her feet. "You don't look well… Can I—"

"Don't get any closer," Xeile warned her. The Elf froze in place. "If you see a Guardian, have them tell Kelt that Harvest is a person, and tell Glenna…" Xeile felt a lump form in his throat. "Tell Glenna…" He tried to force the words out, but he couldn't do it. He couldn't. The world heaved beneath his feet. He needed to get to a safe place to hide, to rest and recover. He turned and started shuffling away.

"Who are you?"

Xeile turned around to see the Elf that was looking at him with concern, her fists clenched at her side.

He let out a hacking cough, his blood splattering onto the cobbles, then wiped his mouth as clean as possible. He couldn't use his real name; the last thing he needed was the entire city hunting him down before he could meet Kelt and finish helping this spirit. But what could he use that would be hard to trace? The response came before he could really think it through. "Call me Exile," he said.

Without another word, he turned from the alley and limped away, wishing that the summer sun could put some warmth back into his body as the chill crept up to his thighs.

THE OUTCASTS

Criske stared in amazement at the Dwarf standing before him. "You're serious? No kidding?"

"No kidding," the Dwarf blacksmith urged him. His accent was so thick, the Half-Elf could barely understand the choppy words of Territory. "Every one of apprentices see."

"That's right, sir," said a Dwarf apprentice. "He just…summoned spirits out of thin air, made them appear in front of us for a few seconds. He was talking to 'em and everything. It was terrifying… He said he was making sure that they didn't hurt us or nothing, but I'm not so sure, with these murders and now this… It's just unnatural, it is."

"Well, rest assured we will look into it immediately," Henrik said, holding up a commanding hand. "We can't have a rogue magician running around town." He turned to Criske. "Let us go, *Khlanro*. We need to trace this lead down." Criske nodded, and the pair set off in the direction the witnesses last saw the figure running.

It had only been one day since Criske was aura shocked, but he had been fortunate enough to have made a quick recovery. No sooner had he been cleared to return to patrol duty and working Kelt's case than a lead had shown up on their doorstep in the form of a very breathless and panicked blacksmithing apprentice. A magician had apparently been walking by, a very sick-looking Human with dark hair and black eyes.

The Dwarven smith, believing him to be a specter or bringer of ill-omens, decided to feed and care for him in the hopes he wouldn't bring a curse down on the house. Instead, it turned out the man could talk with spirits, summon them, and command them. He apparently used his abilities briefly before fleeing the scene when someone tried to summon the Watch. Last they saw, he was heading toward the more crowded areas. He had been wearing a strange cloak, worn-out boots, and had black veins creeping up one side of his face.

"Just how sick is he?" Criske muttered. "It sounds like he's been poisoned."

He might have very well been, but Criske had never heard of a poison that created those kinds of symptoms. Did it have to do with his strange aura? This gap in his medical knowledge was quickly becoming a frustrating one he needed to fix. They started walking and an idea came to Criske. "Henrik, if you wanted to lose someone, or remain unnoticed so no one got a good look at you, where would you go?"

Henrik considered this for a moment. "Well…it would make more sense to go where there were very similar people to me. I would, for example, stand out like a second-century Dwarf piece in a crowd of fourth-century pieces if I were to try hiding among Elves. The crowd of people would do no good." He snapped his fingers several times, as if the sound were guiding his thoughts. "Ah! Maybe he went to an area where sick people would go unquestioned. Is there anywhere like that in the city?"

Criske thought for a moment, and then his heart skipped a beat. "No…" he whispered. "No. No. No." He grabbed Henrik's arm, pulling him along. "Come on! We have to get to the riverside!"

Criske picked up his pace, taking every shortcut he knew. It took all of his willpower not to break into a run or scale a rooftop for faster travel. If he did run into the person there, he would need Henrik's backup for sure. It was almost noon when they finally arrived at the riverside area, with its run-down buildings, its tenants gaunt-faced, looking at them initially with fear, then relaxing when they saw Criske.

"Hey, Val-Zhang!" one called out. "Here on leave?"

Criske turned to see one of the homeless Half-Elves, old man Willow, leaning casually against a wall, his weather-beaten face forming a smile, his gray hair twisted into braids. He and Criske had often chatted together, as Criske found him out and around the city when on patrol. Willow, as it turned out, was an excellent informant who responded well to money.

"No," Criske said. "Actually, I'm looking for someone."

Willow nodded. "Shady fellow? Sickly like?"

Criske nodded. "Yes… Seen him around here?"

Willow's eyes widened. "'Seen him? Damn, kid, I thought you knew already!"

"Knew what?"

"Your mother was attacked early this morning by some kind of…monster; bastard swooped in and saved her apparently—"

Criske didn't wait for Willow to finish his statement. He didn't wait for Henrik. His feet carried him, and he sprinted through the streets, weaving familiar paths until he crashed through the door to a ramshackle hut that was next to the river, right next to the city walls. There was a startled cry from a Human man who was sitting in the corner in an old rocking chair. His eyes were milky white, with a long beard that flowed in a white silvery ripple down his chest.

"*Who's there?*" he croaked. "I'll kill ya!"

"Grandfather," Criske said, slightly out of breath. "It's me."

The old man's face lit up at the sound of the voice. "Ah! Criske, you finally took a break from work! Come, come. Give an old man a hug, eh?" Criske stepped forward and wrapped his grandfather in a gentle embrace. The old man returned it for a moment, then they broke apart. "What brings you here?" he asked in a warbling tone. "I thought our rent wasn't due for a while yet…"

"I'm looking for Mother," Criske said. "Is she here?"

"*Kiresu?*"

Criske turned around to see his mother, staring at him in surprise. Her blue-black hair was tied back in a practical braid she used for when she wasn't at work. She was wearing a pair of work pants, and her blouse was tied at the waist with an elaborately woven ribbon, her one piece of fashion that she retained from her old life. Without hesitation, he walked over and enveloped her in a tight embrace. "Mama…I'm so sorry." He pulled back and looked her over, his neck having to crane up and down to take in her full seven feet. "Are you alright?"

His mother's face seemed to become distant and pained. "Yes. I am fine. But I don't think the person that helped me was… He was so sad, *Kiresu*."

"Did you tell the Watch what happened?" Criske asked.

His mother nodded. "Yes, but they turned me away. Said I was lying, looking to set them up to be robbed. They knew I lived riverside."

A cold anger settled into Criske's stomach. "Idiots," he growled. His fists clenched. "*Do they not realize what is going on?*"

"*Kiresu*, calm down," his mother chided. "I'll make tea for you and tell you about it, hmm? No running off. You never come home to eat. I never see you, and neither does your papa. You just work, work, work." She ruffled his already-messy blond hair. Criske glowered at her, but sat at the small, worn table and waited.

A few minutes passed when the door opened with several polite knocks on the frame.

"*Who's there?*" his grandfather screamed. "I'll kill ya!" Henrik gave the old man a confused look. "Um…I am sorry, *Khlanradan*. My name is Henrik. I am a Guardian of the Trifecta. I believe my patrol partner is…" Henrik's eyes fell upon Criske. "Ah! Criske. Perhaps you could explain…"

"He's a friend, Grandfather," Criske said. He felt his neck and face heating up. "My patrol partner."

"Eh?" his grandfather said. "Oh, he another one of them grays you work with?"

Criske fought the urge to crawl under a rock. "Yes. He's my patrol partner. Helping me out at work."

"Ah. Well…make sure he doesn't steal nothing."

The old man settled back into his rocker and drifted off to sleep. Criske waited for the condemning look, for the offended expression.

Instead, Henrik broke out into a broad, delighted smile. He stepped into the home, looking around at the building with a critical eye. Criske felt his stomach clench. He wanted to say something, but the words seemed to get stuck in his throat.

"I'm very surprised," Henrik finally said. "Whoever repaired this place did an excellent job. Good eye for woodworking. These houses were generally deliberately built with bad materials," he explained with an academic air. "But whoever did the repairs has managed to ensure structural integrity."

Criske felt his fear twist into confusion. What was Henrik going on about? His house was a disaster. There was a leak in one corner that was currently being taken care of with a pot underneath it. The central fireplace's stones were crumbling, and the roof cap was in a bad state of repair, causing the house to partially fill with smoke. All four of the beds for the house were crammed into the one bedroom that was off the main entrance. The door hinge was cracked and partially peeling off the rickety door, which badly needed to be fixed, but they couldn't afford to get it replaced by the smith. The floor was uneven and desperately needed to be broken up and redone, as it was full of cracks and splits.

But Henrik had already turned his attention from the building to his mother. "Ah! Who might you be?" he asked politely.

"I am Li Ren Zhang, but please call me Lira, I am *Kiresu*'s mama." Henrik bowed to her. "I am Henrik Ihvihlan. *Nin keru hao, Zhang-Riken.*"

Criske's mouth dropped open. How did a Dwarf know High Elvish? His mother looked like she had been hit over the head. "*Ni'er shuo Ryunato?*" she asked, asking him the question herself.

"*Yon dian'er,*" Henrik said with a small smile, professing only modest proficiency. "Though I am very bad at it. I much prefer Territory, if that is not too inconvenient, ma'am."

"No problem," Lira said. "Please sit, I make tea for you too. I was about to tell Kiresu what happened this morning."

Henrik happily took a seat across from Criske, continuing to stare at the building around him with a general sense of curiosity. Criske looked at him in a kind of shock. Henrik had mentioned he had done some academic study. Something about archaeology, and he had a weird fascination with buildings, but speaking High Elvish was another matter entirely. He wanted to ask but couldn't bring himself to. His mother quickly put two cups of tea in front of them before pulling up her own chair. "I was coming back from work," she said slowly. "But as I was walking, I got a terrible feeling that I was being watched. So, I tried to hurry home. I ducked down one of the alleys, hoping I would lose him, but I made mistake, and it was a… I could go no farther. There was a wall…a…a…" She let out a huff of air and waved one hand. "You know what I mean. Anyway, I turn around and there was a pair of big red eyes floating in front of me. I froze in place. I couldn't do anything. It was like a ghost had come to eat me…like a *ba-xi*."

"A wraith?" Henrik asked.

Lira nodded. "Yes, yes. Anyway, it drives me into corner. I think I'm going to die, but then, he showed up. He could have just run away. But no, he got its attention. Then…he fights it."

"He fought a ghost?" Henrik repeated. "How?"

She shook her head. "I don't know. He just…grabbed a chain and started throwing it. It grabbed on to the spirit. Then, he's surrounded by flickering black, and there's a terrible cracking sound. He fell to the ground in pain. The *ba-xi* threw off the chain, but he kept fighting. Another ghost touched him and he got to his feet. He touched it with that black, and the creature disappeared. He told me to tell someone with a hard name…um…Keleteru…"

"Kelt?" Criske asked quietly.

"Yes, yes," Lira said with a nod. "That name. Said to tell him 'Harvest is a person.' I ask around, but no one heard of Keleteru here, so I go to tell Watch, but they wouldn't help."

"Did he say anything else?" Henrik asked.

Lira thought for a moment, then nodded. "Oh yes. He mention name…'Glen-ha.' Then, call himself 'Exile.' He was very sick, but he wouldn't let me help at all!" She frowned, shaking her head. "Very sad. Looked like he was crying as he went away. Very hurt." There was a sound of boots at the door. Lira's face lit up with joy. "Ah! Papa's home!" she said.

Into the doorway stepped a man with pale-blue eyes and blond hair, a little shorter than average. He was thin but strong looking. His clothes were threadbare, but on his left breast, he wore a medal with pride. Criske had never seen him without it. It was the Injury in Valiance metal he had received from his time in the Army of the Territories almost two decades ago, for losing his hand in the middle of combat with a group of pirates.

"Ren," his grandfather said. "That you, boy?"

Ren Val smiled, the way he always did when he came home. "Sure is, Dad." He looked at Lira and then his eyes lit upon Criske. He laughed with delighted surprise. "Criske, you're home! Welcome back!" He hurried over and hugged his son in a tight embrace with his good arm before ruffling his hair. "Look at you! All sharp in your uniform."

"Dad," Criske said, ducking away from his father's affections. "Take it easy, will you? I can't stay for terribly long. Mother was attacked today."

Ren looked at Lira in horror. "Attacked? Attacked by who? Are you alright? You weren't hurt anywhere, were you?"

Lira shook her head. "I'm fine, Ren. Fine. Fine. And a person not attack me. It was a *ba-xi*. A man saved me, though."

Ren blinked uncomprehendingly at his wife. "A what now?"

"A wraith," Criske explained.

The color drained from Ren's face. "I thought wraiths existed only in the old sagas."

"Sadly, sir, she is probably correct. An individual has been attacking Elves recently, and the Guardians are trying to track him down."

Ren exhaled, running his hand through his hair. "Okay…anything else I should know about?"

"You don't have to worry," Henrik said in a reassuring tone. "Kelt McNair is working the case, and we've got a couple of leads we're working on."

Ren's eyes widened. "*McNair?* Heavens above, seas below, just how bad is this case?" He looked at the ceiling, and then froze as a thought occurred to him. "Wait…what do you mean, 'we'?"

Criske felt panic surge in his chest, but Henrik spoke before he could get a word in. "Your son and I are Kelt McNair's official apprentices now." He looked at Criske. "You didn't tell them?"

"No," Criske said through gritted teeth.

The effect on the room was immediate. Ren grabbed Criske's arm and squeezed. Not enough to hurt but enough to warrant his attention. "You're apprenticed…to the most insane Spell Breaker…in Guardian history… and you neglected to tell me…why?"

Criske swallowed hard. "Because I knew you'd be angry."

Ren sat down, staring at Criske so they were eye to eye. "I'm not angry, son. I'm concerned. I've gotten to work with McNair once. He was absolutely mad. He'd carve people to pieces without a second thought. He'd launch his own people out of a trebuchet if it meant catching a criminal."

Henrik frowned. "That doesn't sound like him at all. After Criske got attacked, he—"

"You were *attacked*?" Lira exclaimed. "What happened?"

Criske put his head in his hands, exhaling. He looked at Henrik. "You and I," he said slowly, "are going to have a nice long chat about learning to keep our mouths shut." He turned his attention to his family. "I wasn't attacked," he said slowly. "At least, not intentionally. He was a magician who didn't know how to control himself and was scared. I'm not dead, I've made a full recovery." He stood up. "With that said, Henrik and I need to go report back to Kelt and tell him what we've learned here."

He hugged his father and his mother. He knelt down in front of his grandfather.

"Grandfather," he said loudly. "I'm going."

"Alright," said the old man. "That gray didn't steal anything, did he?"

"No, Grandfather," Criske said with a sigh. "Henrik is very trustworthy."

"Good," the old man said. "Them grays need more people like that. Now get going, and don't get killed, ya hear? And come around for dinner! Your mother isn't as good a cook as you. I need a decent meal every once in a while."

"I heard that," Lira called from the other room, and Criske's grandfather grinned mischievously.

"Yes, sir," Criske said, smiling back. He exited the door and Henrik followed shortly behind.

He waited until they were about a block away before he rounded on Henrik. "What was that?"

"What do you mean?"

"Did you ever think that I might not tell them things for a reason?" Criske's voice was weary and cold.

Henrik's eyes fell. "I'm sorry, I did not realize—"

"No, you didn't," Criske said with a sigh. "You know how much they worried when I signed on because I'm a Half-Elf? My mother was fretting that I'd be dead in less than a week! Now they're going to be sitting there wondering if I'm ever going to come home alive. Every. Single. Night. Did you ever think I might be trying to keep them from panicking? Nope, you just had to spill everything you knew, didn't you?" Criske forced down the nausea in his stomach. Perhaps he needed to be told this lesson? "Maybe, just maybe, you'll think—"

"At least you have someone who will worry, *Khlanro*. Not all of us have that luxury." Henrik's expression was like an unreadable mask, his words like a slap across the face with a hot iron. Criske fell silent as the Dwarf walked ahead of him without another word, leaving him rooted in place.

Criske sighed and closed his eyes. "Shit."

He continued after his partner in silence. It was a long walk back to headquarters.

THE SOLDIER

Kelt looked at his workload and stood up from his desk, shaking his head. "I need to practice," he said. "I can't work like this." He had been doing nothing but paperwork the entire morning, and it had already nearly reached noon. The thought he'd have to spend another hour inside made him restless. He'd already signed and sealed the documents requesting Spell Breaker reinforcements, so what was the harm?

He quickly donned his practice gear, pulling on the partial plate with a familiarity born from years of practice, finishing with his helmet. He stepped out of his office, and a nearby Guardian froze, snapping to attention. "Sir!" he shouted. "Off on a Breaker, sir?"

Kelt laughed. "No, just practice. At ease, Guardian." He couldn't help but notice that the number of salutes he was getting had increased substantially, though it took him a moment to realize why. On his breastplate was an equilateral triangle with a break in it. *I'm going to have to request a new set,* he thought. *That life is behind me now.* The thought depressed him slightly. Even though he had chosen to stop being a Spell Breaker, this set of armor had been with him through so much, the thought of letting it go was like saying goodbye to an old friend.

He tried to clear his mind of such thoughts as he stepped onto the sandy practice field, but without much success.

It was fairly busy today. Several Elves were practicing their Grace Dances, while a few were engaged in War Dances, their fists and limbs colliding in brilliant flashes of movement. A group of Dwarves was practicing *Khlandraviirq,* going through various locks, grapples, and holds. Most, however, were practicing their sword work in a repetitive series of drills that were taught to them in basic training. As he walked by, he commented to one swordsman, "Hey, keep your elbows in, and that second cutback will get faster."

The swordsman, a younger Human of around twenty, looked for the source of the instruction. His eyes lit upon Kelt and widened immediately. "Gods above. Y-Yes, sir!"

"Good lad," Kelt said with an approving smile. "Show the sword you know how to handle it."

"Sir!"

Sure enough, the young man tucked in his elbows, and his speed increased considerably. Kelt walked away, feeling a lightness in his chest that took away a bit of the invisible weight on his shoulders. By the time he had reached a mannequin with a practice sword in hand, he felt much lighter on his feet.

After slowly warming up his body, he went into his forms. They were forms he had studied for years under teachers in the Elven lands, in the muggy air in his pursuit of mastering the art of the sword. The Dwarves, of course, had their own swordplay that he had studied later, but nothing made him feel as alive as the Nine Forms of the War Dance. He quickly made his way through the lower-level forms, going from one to another without stopping. Most people didn't realize how much of an endurance test it was to do them continuously. Then again, most practitioners didn't do the forms in half-plate either. By the time he had wrapped up the seventh form, he was covered in a sheen of sweat.

Kelt swung his sword again for the finishing blow. It swished through the air, hitting the practice mannequin's neck with a solid thump. It was a textbook kill. "Seventh form finished," he muttered. "On to eighth form: Dragon's Fangs."

He moved through the motions with ease, his sword weaving in an intricate pattern as he touched the tip of his sword into various targets, mostly where arteries or gaps in armor were located, before he finished with a powerful thrust into the throat, causing the dummy to reel backward from the force. Kelt pulled his sword back and flexed his neck. "Ninth form: Death's End."

He switched his grip, loosening it ever so slightly as he wove a strange series of movements around an imaginary opponent. Death's End was by far one of the most difficult forms in the Elvish War Dances. It was predicated on one premise: you couldn't touch your opponent except for one time. Everything else consisted of very close feints and apparent near misses meant to force an opening. As he reached the end of the form, Kelt moved in for the final blo—

In front of his eyes, a giant woman loomed before him, a sword swinging upward to cleave him in half—

Kelt froze and dodged out of the way, sweeping upward, nicking the mannequin's helmet with a clang. He regained his balance and exhaled. "Damn it," he whispered to himself. "Damn it to the deepest winters. You're stronger than this…you've faced worse…why is it bothering you now?"

The mannequin, of course, held no answers.

Kelt judged the sun's course and figured it was around noon by now. It was about time for Criske and Henrik to return from their regularly scheduled patrol. He made a mental note to request they get taken off the active patrol list until the case was solved. The lightness vanished, the familiar weight settling once again on his shoulders.

"Practicing your swing, sir?"

Kelt turned to see Glenna standing in front of him, her violet eyes fixed on his weapon. "Surprised you'd even bother at this point, considering how much real fighting you get in anyway." Her voice contained an unmistakable chill behind it, almost an accusation. "Would you prefer to spar with a partner, sir?"

He looked at her, with her folded arms and easy posture, leaning back on the heels of her feet. What rankled him most, though, was the look on her face, the indifference, as if she really didn't care if he wanted to spar with her or not. "Well, I wouldn't mind teaching you a thing or two, I suppose," Kelt said. "Grab a weapon. Let's see how you fare."

Glenna went over to the weapon rack and grabbed a practice sword of her own. Kelt had the advantage of reach by at least half an arm's length. He'd be at a distinct advantage to begin with. He raised his sword. "To disarm only," he declared. "I don't want Head Magician Usumi blasting me to the Dwarfdom because I hurt her apprentice."

"You don't have to worry about me," Glenna said. The indifference vanished from her face, replaced by calculative alertness. "I've had some very effective teachers." She raised her sword, keeping it between herself and Kelt as they circled each other. Kelt quickly evaluated her stance and posture. It was nothing short of exemplary. He moved forward and did a thrust to test the waters.

His blade was immediately knocked aside with so much force that if Kelt didn't have years of reflexes and training, it would have been flung out of his hand. He barely raised his sword to defend in time against a vicious slash from Glenna. She was fast. Faster than most fighters he had seen for one so young. Kelt returned her attacks with a counterblow that met nothing but air as Glenna seemed to slip away. They resumed circling each other.

"My teachers always held you in high esteem," Glenna said quietly. "So where is it?"

Kelt raised an eyebrow. "Where's what?" he asked.

"Where's your power?" Glenna lunged forward again, her blade slamming down on Kelt's with a loud crack. "Where's your fire?" Another blow that Kelt managed to deflect. "Where's that ferocity that allowed you to kill?" Her sword narrowly missed his left thigh. She looked at him, and Kelt saw fury behind her dark-purple eyes. "Where's your edge?" she challenged. "Did you leave it behind somewhere?" Kelt felt his temper rise slightly, but he forced it back down. "Up north, maybe?"

The words sent a chill down Kelt's spine. He backed away from Glenna, his eyes narrowing. "Up north?"

Glenna lunged forward again, her sword moving in an upward arc that Kelt dodged easily. He swung to retaliate, but his opponent ducked out of the way. She responded with a charge that made them clash against each other. Her face was just inches from his.

"I know what you did," Glenna snapped. "Can you sleep at night, or does it haunt you?"

Rage flooded Kelt's being. He shoved Glenna away, grabbing her uniform with one hand. Using his foot as a pivot point, he picked her up and flung her to the ground where she collided with the sand, the wind knocked out of her. He pointed his sword at her face, but her lips were twisted into a cold, cruel smile.

"Oh. Looks like I hit a sore spot. My apologies, sir."

Kelt looked at her, then evaluated himself. He was breathing hard, not from exertion but anger, and felt a deep, burning shame. He hauled Glenna to her feet and, without another word, put his practice sword on the rack and went to his office to clean up. His mind felt cloudy, unfocused. How could she know? There was no way she could. Kelt hadn't said a single word to anyone about his last mission as a Spell Breaker. Had she somehow learned about it? No, there was no way she could have. Everyone who'd gone on that assignment was sworn to absolute secrecy, or dead. It was likely she was just trying to unsettle him, and he had fallen for it.

"Get better control of yourself," he said to himself. He entered his office and took off his armor before using his washbasin to clean himself. He was in the middle of drying his face when there was a knock on the door.

"Enter," he said.

Criske and Henrik entered the office. There was tense air between them that neither seemed to want to acknowledge. "Good to see you two. Are you ready to follow up on some leads?"

"We've actually already gotten some…sir," Criske said. "The cloaked stranger apparently made another appearance."

Kelt dropped the towel next to his washbasin, pulling up a chair from behind his desk and bringing it around so he could sit closer to them. "Well, tell me what happened, then."

Criske quickly laid out everything he had seen and everyone he had talked to while on patrol that morning. Kelt listened in a detached manner, adding more facts and questions to his steadily growing mental list. He sighed. "So…if I'm understanding this correctly, this person…"

"Exile, sir."

"Right, this 'Exile' fought a ghost, interacted with spirits, coughed up blood, and told the person who was attacked to tell me that 'Harvest,' the clue he gave last time, 'was a person.' Am I getting all this correctly?"

"Well, sir…" Henrik swallowed a few times. "It…attacked Criske's mother. It makes me think that whoever is doing this knows we're on the case."

Kelt felt his heart sink when he saw Criske's face pale. "You think she was targeted…because of me?" Criske whispered. "It's my fault?"

"It isn't your fault," Kelt said firmly. "You weren't the one who told it to target your mother. That is the criminal's fault. It is entirely possible that they targeted your mother because you are working the case with me. But, it is also entirely possible that she was targeted because she was an Elf, and she just happened to be in the wrong place at the wrong time. Either way, we'll have to take your family into protective custody for the time being."

Criske put his head into his hands. "Dragons and phoenixes…" he said softly. "How am I going to explain this to them?"

"You're not," Kelt said. "I am. That's my job as lead inquisitor on the case. Now, did this 'Exile' say anything else, Henrik?"

Henrik thought for a moment and then nodded. "Yes. The witness, Lira, said that he mentioned 'Glen-ha.'"

"I think she meant 'Glenna,'" Criske said. "She's always had difficulty pronouncing two *n*'s that are next to each other."

Kelt stared at Criske for a long moment. "Are you sure?" he asked. "That's a pretty bold claim to make, and could make things very complicated."

Criske nodded.

Kelt stood. "Very well. Gentlemen, you two are going to talk to Glenna about any possible connection she may have to the suspect."

"What about you?" Henrik asked.

Kelt looked at the desk and was quiet for a long moment. "It looks like I'm going to be making an arrest," he said. "Let's just hope our suspect doesn't resist."

"I don't know why he would," Criske said. "The more we chase after him, the more he seems to be on our side, but we have no idea why." He shook his head. "Something just feels wrong about this, but I can't figure what it is. It's like we're going after the wrong person."

Kelt took a deep breath and buried his misgivings. "Regardless," he said, "We'll get our answers when we find him. Time to bring our Exile back to roost."

The Seeker

Xeile felt himself tilt sideways to lean against a wall, which he slid down. "Move," he muttered to himself. "You have to move. That creature could come back any minute." His legs refused to obey; the biting cold seemed to have robbed them of the ability to function. He looked at the Elf floating next to him. She was much more translucent than before, but she was gradually returning to normal opacity. "I'm sorry," he said quietly, which turned into a hacking cough. "Give me a moment, then we'll be back on the case."

"Don't worry about me," she said. "Worry about yourself!"

Xeile looked at her in amazement. Since when did ghosts show sympathy? Most of them thought only of themselves, focused on a singular task or thought. Why did it care about him suddenly? Unsure what to say, Xeile tried to move but found himself unable. "Just give me a moment," he said again, breaking into a cold sweat. "Just a moment." He fought the rising panic in his chest. How was he going to chase down that monster or help Kelt like this? "Come on, Xeile," he whispered to himself. "You can do this. Just stand…up!" It was quite possibly the greatest effort he had ever forced himself to make. But his legs held him as he clung to the wall for support.

"Alright," he panted. "Progress." He took a step, then another, slowly making his way down the streets, hobbling along as he limped out of the area by the river, with its broken-down houses and suspicious glares. After thirty minutes, his legs were trembling with exertion. How had he gotten so weak so quickly? Was it the encounter with the creature? He looked up and saw the sun was heading toward the horizon.

Beautiful streaks of purple and yellow were shooting across the sky, illuminating the clouds with a peaceful glow as the cool of a summer evening descended downward. It was breathtaking to see that small glimpse of the sky, and Xeile drank it in as much as he could. Who knew if he'd make it to the next sunrise?

The young man had only just been able to get away from the alleyway, with that Elf woman who seemed incredibly familiar to him, before collapsing. Fortunately, she didn't seem to have an interest in following him. Maybe she went to tell the Guardians like he had suggested. He released a breath and felt his stomach let out a pang of protest. How long had it been since he had eaten anything? Half a day? That bread and cheese from the Dwarf seemed like a century ago. Maybe that was a good thing. He wasn't sure he would be able to stomach any food at the moment anyway. Xeile limped along, continuing to lean on the wall for support. A wave of cold hit him. Xeile gasped. He didn't have his piece of leather anymore. He must have dropped it somewhere, so he bit down on the edge of his shirtsleeve, trying to muffle his pained groans. But, he didn't fall to the ground as it passed. He could still keep walking. "I have to…get to Kelt," he said to himself. "Even if they kill me…I don't have time to spare anymore." It was true. His feet were cracked and scabbed. His skin was the color of cold ash, with startling veins of black creeping up his chest and face. His rough hood and ratted, snarled length of unwashed hair could only hide so much. He would be discovered soon, whether he found Kelt or not.

He looked at the Elf ghost beside him. "I'm so sorry." Tears spilled down his face. "I couldn't finish helping you. I'm so sorry. Maybe what I give them will be enough… But I can't… I don't have any time…" His tongue felt like lead in his mouth, refusing to move to form words.

The Elf ghost's face fell, and she stared into the distance, as if coming to a decision. She turned around and reached her hands toward Xeile. "Tell them everything you know. You'll solve it. I know you will." Her hands grabbed Xeile's shoulders, and warmth flooded his body. The wracking pain in his legs receded.

"What are you doing?" Xeile asked. She continued to fade away, her silhouette growing weaker and her glow fainter. "No. Stop. Don't do this! I don't even know your name!" She kept her hands on his shoulders and looked him straight in the eye.

"I don't know it either anymore," she whispered. "But I do know that you can solve this. You're a good man, Xeile. You made me into a person again, even at the cost of your own life. I can pass knowing that my death will not go unanswered for as long as you're alive."

"No," Xeile whispered. "Please don't leave me. I don't want to be alone again."

"You won't be alone. There are others like me out there that will need your help. Now live, and go find them."

She gave him a small kiss on the forehead. Xeile felt a final burst of heat across his scalp, and there was a small cracking sound. Her glow vanished and her silhouette evaporated in the summer breeze.

Even with the newfound strength in his body, Xeile felt himself go weak at the knees and sink to the ground, the dirt and cobblestones digging into his legs. It was a strange sensation. He hadn't been able to feel in his ankles for so long that the discomfort almost went unnoticed. He held his head in his hands and cried over losing a person that was already dead, a person whose name he didn't even know. And somehow, those two facts made him feel even worse.

He didn't really know how long he had sat there, but when he had cried himself out, a new conviction roared to life in his chest like a wildfire. He had to find out who murdered her. He had to find Kelt. No matter the cost. Xeile went to get to his feet when he heard a voice that was vaguely familiar.

"Are you alright, young man?"

Xeile looked up and saw a violet-eyed Elf staring down at him. The concern on her face was clear. In one hand, she clutched a staff of some kind that looked as though it belonged to one of the northern Nomadic peoples. Eagles and animalistic imagery were carved into it with exquisite detail. At her side hung a simple short sword and a curved blade he couldn't identify, but despite that, she wore a gray uniform. A Guardian.

He reflexively backed away, scrambling to his feet, turning around so she couldn't see his face. "I'm fine," he said, his heart pounding. He steeled himself and slowly turned around. "You...wouldn't happen to know Kelt McNair, would you?"

The Elf's face paled in horror as she saw his face. "Black eyes," she whispered. "Your aura's completely broken... You shouldn't be alive unless...you're an undead..."

"Do you know Kelt McNair?" Xeile repeated, surprised at the force in his voice, considering the fear that was coursing through him.

The Elf's face fixed on him, becoming an unreadable, detached mask. "Most Guardians do. It is hard to forget a legendary fighter," she said, her tone very clipped. "What business do you have with him?"

"If you know where he is, you will take me to him," Xeile said, swallowing. "Or I'll…I might hurt more people on accident." He couldn't bring himself to make an actual threat, but what he said would probably come true. "I need to talk to him."

The woman's mask slipped for just a moment, and Xeile saw a flash of anger. "The only business Kelt would have with one of your kind," she said slowly, "is that he would kill you without a second glance."

Xeile took a deep, shuddering breath. "I know. But I have to let him know things about the double murder case before he kills me."

The Elf's mask slipped again. Confusion. "The murder case?"

"Yes. And"—Xeile grabbed the necklace around his neck—"I need to see Glenna…one last time."

The Elf's mask broke completely. Her anger straightened her spine to her full seven-foot height. "You will not be getting anywhere near my apprentice."

Xeile let out a weak laugh. "Little late for that," he said. "You two walked right by me a few nights ago." He stepped forward. "Please. Just take me to Kelt. I won't resist. I'll put the damn manacles on myself, if I have to."

"Or, I just kill you here and now," the Guardian said. She had a violet glow surrounding her that stretched out toward Xeile. He batted at it with his hand. Another wash of warmth flowed into his body, and the purple immediately retreated back to her body. She sank to one knee and groaned.

Xeile looked at his hand and then at her in horror. "Galloping horses, I'm so sorry! It was an accident! Are you o—"

He felt himself knocked off his feet by some kind of wind, landing hard enough on the ground to make his ears ring. Had he hit his head?

With a groan, he rolled to one side, trying to get to his feet. "Move and I'll blast you to pieces."

Xeile looked up at the voice, his heart filled with joy and dread. A Human girl, maybe a year or two older, stood over him, her body surrounded by a glowing dark-purple shroud. Her hair was longer than he remembered. She must have gotten over her habit of cutting it short. Her face was less lean too. Good, she was eating properly here. Her entire body was rigid, the muscles in her shoulders clear beneath her uniform. She hadn't missed a day of training either. And she was just as beautiful as she had been three years ago.

"Glenna," he said, a lump forming in his throat. "Good to see you again."

"Get on the ground," she snapped. "And don't move."

Xeile quickly got on his knees. "Alright, I'm on the ground," he said. "I can't believe it's really you. You don't look like you've changed that—"

"On the ground!" she shouted. "Lie on your stomach, hands behind your head."

A lance to the heart might have hurt him less than this. He felt his body starting to shake. She didn't recognize him. Of course she didn't recognize him. He was a physical wreck. "Gigi," he said quietly. "Gigi, it's me. Please."

The words were like a physical slap across the face. Glenna took two steps backward, and the dark shroud vanished. She looked down at him, her eyes wide. "Xeile?" she whispered.

Xeile smiled at her, his heart soaring. "Hey, Gigi. Sorry to drop in like this. Took me a while to get—" His body was wracked by a fit of coughing, and he felt the sticky flecks of blood on his hand and chin as he covered his mouth. "It took me a while to get here."

He fumbled for his necklace and held it up. "I know it's not made of gold and jewels like I promised…but I brought the ring for you…" He took the necklace off and undid the clasp, sliding the smooth wooden ring, holding it for a moment in his dirty, blood-flecked palm. He tossed it to her. She made no move to catch it as the wood clattered against the stone street. The sound was sharp and felt unnaturally loud as Glenna stood absolutely motionless.

"I…I don't know how much…longer I have to live, so I'm not expecting you to hold to our…" His heart felt like it was breaking under the weight of the words he forced out of his lips. "I'd understand if you don't want me anymore. No point in tying you down to a dead man walking. It wouldn't be fair to you."

Glenna picked up the ring and stared at it for a moment, as if it were a peculiar gemstone she had just unearthed. Without hesitation, she slid it onto her finger. "You idiot," she snapped. Tears formed in her eyes and started streaking down her face. "You damn idiot! I study for years. *Years*, just so I can protect you one day, and you have the audacity, the gall, to just allow me to *walk away* if I want?" Her fists clenched at her side. "Why? Why are you always like this? Why can't you be selfish just once?"

She started those strangled, repressed sobs she had whenever she was upset. It took every bit of Xeile's willpower not to immediately reach out and embrace her. He couldn't touch her. What if he hurt her, like he did that patrolman, or his teacher? What if he killed her, like he did that poor ghost? Instead, he tried to embrace her with words.

"I am being selfish," Xeile said quietly. "Because right now, I'm the happiest I've been in months, even though I have no right to be. Even though I'm ill, and probably never going to get better. Even though your master probably wants me dead right now. Even though I'm in pain and coughing up blood. I want to freeze time, in this moment, just so I can keep looking at you and remember there's a reason to keep living."

THE OUTCASTS

"Remind me again," Criske asked slowly. "Why we're doing this?"

"Head Magician Usumi told us to," Henrik said. "And orders are orders. Would you pass me that scroll, please?"

Criske obliged, picking up the hefty scroll, handing it to Henrik's outstretched hand. Henrik's hand closed around it without him looking up. "*Dahkiev, Khlanro.*"

"Don't mention it," Criske said with a nod. No sooner had they told Usumi about what they'd encountered on their patrol had she disappeared, taking her apprentice with her. She had assigned them to look through the Guardian records for any possible matches to one of the victims. Criske felt it was a useless long shot, but Henrik did make a good point. Even if this turned out to be a waste of time, he was getting paid either way. The hours were passing painfully slowly, with only Henrik's request for new material breaking the monotony. Criske's mind began to wander as he gazed at his surroundings.

Walls upon walls of books, scrolls, and manuscripts towered above him. The Grand Library was, at least by his estimation, the largest building in headquarters. An amalgamation of three hundred years of records, histories, and literature from the Trifecta's three nations made it almost unrivaled in sheer scope of content. Even without knowing how to read, Criske found it a fascinating place, with its many tomes bound in leather, the scrolls stacked high in their little cubbyholes, and its quiet atmosphere almost felt like a temple or shrine to knowledge, even though he had never stepped foot into a religious building. There were some places he didn't want to push his luck.

Almost as fascinating as the library was Henrik's attitude. He moved about with a sense of poise and authority here, clearly in his element. He could tell which books and scrolls might have the information he sought in just a matter of seconds, his eyes and fingers flicking across pages before a quick dismissal or continued reading.

Eventually, curiosity overcame Criske, and he glanced over Henrik's shoulder. To his surprise, the scroll was full of little bumps and nothing else. Henrik was running his fingers over it, moving down the page, a frown of concentration on his face.

"What's that?" he asked.

"Oh, this? It is a registry of Elven Guardians from about a decade ago."

"No, I mean…the bumps," he said. "Those don't look like any letters I've ever seen."

Henrik grinned. "Oh, these! They are the *Khlanratiiq*. It is the writing system of the Dwarfdom. In older days, before we journeyed to the world above, our *Khlaniik* developed a writing system that can be read in both light and in complete darkness, for when there was no light in a tunnel or mine. Of course, when it came to making it, they created divots in the rock, rather than bumps on a page, but the principle is the same." Criske thought for a moment, the gears in his mind turning. "Then…could this be adapted to Territory or Elvish?"

Henrik frowned, considering this. "Possibly. Territory would likely be possible. Elvish uses a system of *Ma-Tai-Rou*, and those wouldn't work very well unless you were to make the bumps in the form of the *Taizi Ru Ne*."

"So a blind person could read if you used this kind of system?"

Henrik's eyebrows rose and a smile formed on his face. "Oh yes, I suppose they could! A fantastic idea, in fact. Hmm…if only there was some way to test it…"

"Teach me to read and I'll test it."

Henrik looked up from his work and turned around. "You do not know how to read?"

Criske sighed. "I just asked you to teach me. What do you think?"

Henrik nodded. "Right. Right. My apologies. Come. We will learn Territory. Then you can help me tackle all of these records." He smiled at Criske excitedly. "Your world is about to become a much larger place, and I'm honored to be your guide, *Khlanro*."

The Half-Elf couldn't help but smile back. It was hard not to feel Henrik's enthusiasm. "Alright. Let's get started."

Monotony soon gave way to intense concentration and frustration as Criske set about the difficult task of becoming literate. There were so many letters, with big and small versions, some of which looked nothing alike. He kept mixing up a few letters, and they seemed to appear backward to him or try to float off the page. But, gradually, he managed to pick up a few words that would help him. He learned numbers, the word "Guardian," and the word "Elf." Armed with his rudimentary vocabulary and grit, he started helping Henrik by pulling documents ahead of time, creating a sizable pile on the desk where they were working.

Eventually, Henrik set the book he was reading down, rubbing his eyes. "I can't continue," he said. "My eyes feel like they are about to fall out. There has to be a faster way to do this."

Criske thought for a moment. "We've got too large of a group to search…" An idea came to him. "What if that guy Exile we encountered on patrol was actually right?"

Henrik looked at him with a raised eyebrow. "Pardon?"

"I mean, he gave us a name to look for. 'Harvest,' yeah?" Criske explained. "Wouldn't it be way easier to check for that single name than pawing through all of these documents, even if he was leading us on?"

Henrik looked up at Criske. "We could check the active-duty registry. Since our victims were alive until recently, it is highly probable Harvest is still alive and active as well." He snapped his fingers. "Good idea, *Khlanro*. Let us go inquire."

The pair shuffled to the Service Archives, which kept track of which Guardians were on active duty, retired, dead, or out on assignment. Most of the time, the nature of their field assignments wasn't made clear for security reasons, but it was better than sending a letter with sensitive information and not getting a response for months because they were out in the field.

The current keeper of the Service Archives was the same portly man they had first met in Kelt's office. He stared at them disinterestedly. "Can I help you?" His tone indicated he wanted to help them about as much as Criske wanted to walk through the Elvish areas in town.

"Yes, sir," Henrik said. "We are looking for the current status of a Guardian by the name 'Harvest.'"

The man nodded several times, smacking his lips in a way that made Criske twitch in annoyance. "Well, let me take a look for a moment." He turned around, almost with deliberately frustrating slowness, running his fingers along the scroll racks behind him. The Half-Elf was pretty certain he had seen his blind and arthritic grandfather move faster than this man.

Eventually, the man turned around and shook his head. "I'm afraid I cannot give you access to Harvest's record."

"What? Why?" Criske asked loudly. Henrik grabbed the Half-Elf and held up a finger. Criske clamped his mouth shut and stared in frustration at the wall of scrolls behind his partner.

"Well, simply put, you two do not have a high enough authority to view it," he said with a small smile. "It is apparently highly classified. As a matter of fact, I'm not sure there's a single Guardian here who could open it. Now, either request another name or go back to whatever you were doing."

Defeated, the two of them returned to the desk they were working at. Criske threw himself into one of the nearby chairs in a huff. "Stupid moron. We were so close to getting something," he hissed. "I hate people like him."

Henrik smiled. "On the contrary. We did get something useful."

"What's that?"

"We got proof that Harvest's name exists. Which means that the potentially dangerous man named Exile could actually be trying to help us."

"But he doesn't want to come to headquarters because he's…what, scared of what we'll do to him?" Criske asked, trying to work through it in his brain. "Why would he be…" He looked up at Henrik. "Do you think he's an unregistered magician? That would explain the fear. They'd try and execute him if he had harmed someone, wouldn't they?"

Henrik tapped his fingers rapidly on the desk, staring off into space for a moment. Then, he nodded. "It is possible. If they were to catch him. But, unless they killed him to stop an imminent threat on someone's life, there would have to be a trial to decide his fate, according to the law of the First Trifecta."

Criske frowned. "Does the fact it's the first one matter?"

Henrik nodded. "Absolutely. Three hundred years ago, in order to make sure that the Trifecta—which is to say, the alliance between the three nations—didn't become corrupted by future rulers and the Guardian's purpose twisted, the Guardians were assigned to follow the laws of the First Trifecta only. The First Trifecta's laws are few in number, but immutable."

"Immu—What now?"

"They cannot be altered."

Criske nodded in realization. "Oh. I get it. They made sure no one could shank each other in the back using the Guardians later on, yeah?"

"Precisely," Henrik said with a grin. "And all regulations concerning the proper use of magic were written down in the First Trifecta's laws. Anything added after it is just deciding how a certain kind of magic fits under the First Trifecta's law."

All of this talk of magic and legal work was starting to make his head spin. How could people like Usumi and Glenna keep track of things like this? Then, an idea came into Criske's head that spurred him to his feet. "Henrik, that's it!"

"What?"

"Usumi! She's head magician of the Guardians. Shouldn't she have the authority to look at Harvest's records? And Kelt could back her up. It is for an actual investigation. Between those two, they should have enough clout to look at it, yeah?"

Henrik stood up as well, and nodded. "Absolutely. We should go at once." He froze, as if a thought occurred to him. He turned to the tomes and scrolls scattered about his desk. "Maybe once we put all these back," he added.

The two of them worked in relative silence, Henrik moving much faster than Criske, on account of Criske having to struggle to read each piece before putting it away. Why did the words keep floating off the page? A prickle of envy struck him as he saw Henrik accomplishing the task so effortlessly. Perhaps it would come to him as easily with practice.

When they finally put away all of the reading materials, they exited the library, heading straight for Usumi's office. The sun had almost finished its arc, the red traveling across the sky, dyeing it hues of pink and purple that rippled and flowed like an astral sea. "You ever wonder why the sky changes color as the day goes on?" Criske asked.

Henrik frowned. "Hmm…there are many theories, but none of them have been proven. Most assume it has to do with the movement of the sun, but we haven't quite figured out the specific cause. At least, not yet. Why?"

Criske shook his head. "Just wondering. Reminds me of the ocean." The two of them kept walking, and it wasn't long before they had arrived at Usumi's office. Henrik knocked on the door and waited politely. There was no response, so Henrik tried again. Still nothing. Criske tried the door handle, but it refused to budge. "She must be out," he said. "Let's try Kelt's."

They didn't have any luck with his door either. As Criske rattled the handle to his door, a passerby looked over. "Trying to find Weapons Master McNair?" he asked. It was a Dwarf, very unlike Henrik. His head was shaved clean, save for the massive beard and mustache on his face. The beard was braided into elaborate patterns and knots. His squat frame came to just over four feet, with broad shoulders and powerful short legs, with dark eyes that reminded Criske of a blued steel resting above a bulbous nose.

"Yeah, you see him around...sir?" Criske asked as he noticed the Dwarf's rank of woodsman, the kind of Guardian who ensured that natural menaces and bandits alike stayed away from the fringe towns at the edge of civilization.

The Dwarf nodded, his bushy beard swaying with the movement. "Oh, aye, Master *Ilf.*

Marched out of his office in full kit. Met up and left with some other Spell Breakers a while ago. Looked like he was about to go make an arrest of someone. Face like a tombstone."

Henrik and Criske shared a look of concern. "You don't think he went after Exile, do you?" Henrik asked.

"I bet that's exactly what he did," Criske said. "We'd better talk to them as soon as they get back. Do you have patrol today?"

"No," Henrik said. "Do you?"

Criske shook his head. "No."

They looked at each other for a moment. Criske had been taking double patrol duties so frequently that the sudden opening of free time left him at a loss for what to do. Henrik, on the other hand, seemed to know instantly what he had on his agenda. He smiled at Criske. "You know, *Khlanro*, this would be the perfect time to get some combat practice in. Want to go spar?"

Criske looked at Henrik's forearms and shoulders that rippled with muscle under his uniform and silently hoped Henrik had good self-control in a fight. "Sure," he said. "Just don't rip me in half, yeah?"

Henrik laughed and clapped him on the shoulder. "I would never! Let us go!"

They headed out onto the practice field, its sandy lot with packed earth a familiar sight. Few people were actually practicing at the moment, as it was so late in the day. Criske quietly welcomed the privacy. He hated fighting in front of a lot of people. It tended to cause more problems later down the line.

"So, shall we practice barehanded, or with weapons?" Henrik asked.

"Either. I don't care," Criske replied, though that wasn't exactly the truth. Henrik would likely beat him in a barehanded fight, simply due to the fact he was likely stronger. But, he'd have to face stronger opponents eventually, so it would be good practice either way.

"Very well. We shall practice with weapons," Henrik said, rubbing his palms together excitedly. "I look forward to seeing your capabilities with a sword, *Khlanro*." Criske swallowed his trepidation as Henrik handed him a practice sword before taking a crouched stance. "Are you ready?" Henrik asked.

The Half-Elf had no sooner nodded when Henrik had darted forward with a thrust that nearly clipped Criske in the ribs. Only years of constant alertness and paranoia kept it from connecting with Criske as he twisted out of the way. He immediately responded by reflex, his leg spinning in a high arc as he jumped upward, colliding with Henrik's shoulder. On a normal person, it probably would have slammed into their ribs, sending them to the ground gasping for air. On Henrik, it hit his shoulder and sent him staggering sideways with a grunt.

"First form," Criske whispered to himself. "Dragon's Dawn."

His sword flashed in a powerful arc as he used his arm like a whip. The tip of the sword smacked Henrik's blade with an echoing crack. Henrik's block was solid, sending vibrations up Criske's arm and rattling his teeth.

Criske continued weaving around Henrik, going through the first, second, and third forms. Every thrust, cut, and sweep ended in Henrik blocking it before pushing his blade away. Several times, Henrik counterattacked, which gave Criske multiple brilliant marks he knew would become bruises. The Half-Elf felt his frustration mounting as his breathing became heavier.

"Damn it!" he yelled. He crouched down low and lunged forward in a thrust that on a normal person would have collided with their liver. On Henrik, it was going to connect with his chest. Henrik knocked the blow aside, Criske's blade sailing harmlessly past his target. At the last moment, Criske twisted at the hip, driving his elbow into Henrik's stomach.

The Dwarf went flying backward, rolling in the sand with a groan. Criske dropped his sword and immediately rushed to Henrik's side. "Henrik," he said. "Henrik, are you okay?"

Henrik looked at him as though he were very far away, then his eyes came back into focus. "*Khlanro*…what did you just hit me with?"

"My elbow."

"I'm sure you can aim well, but I don't think your elbow can hit me that hard. It was like getting hit with a *hahnniir*."

"A what?"

"War hammer," Henrik said, sucking in a strained breath. "You went under. I guess next time I should go over, yes?" He gave Criske a weak smile, but it did little to assuage the Half-Elf's fears.

"Alright, did you hit your head when you landed?"

That single question launched an entire on-the-spot exam. Fortunately, besides being winded, Henrik seemed to be in good shape. Admittedly, Criske was just as confused as Henrik. Sure, a blow with his elbow would have doubled him over, knocked the air out of him, maybe—but there was no way it would send him flying for two feet.

But he didn't have time to question it any further. A messenger page, a young boy in a gray uniform, tapped him on the shoulder. "Are you Mr. Val-Zhang?"

Criske looked at the boy and nodded. "Yeah. What's up?"

"Your master, Inquisitor McNair, made an arrest and wants to see you in his office."

Criske hauled Henrik to his feet, and they hurried off toward Kelt's office. Criske's mind was spinning with possibilities. Had he arrested Exile or someone else? Did he manage to catch the killer? They reached the door in a matter of minutes. Criske rapped twice.

"Val-Zhang and Ihvihlan reporting!" he called.

"Enter."

Henrik and Criske opened the door to see Kelt sitting in one of the chairs opposite his desk. His half-plate was splattered with blood, as were his gauntlets, which were on the floor next to him. His head was in his hands, his scarlet hair was in a disarray around his shoulders. Criske and Henrik immediately went over to him and knelt down in front of him.

"Sir, are you alright?" Henrik asked. "What happened?"

Kelt didn't speak for a long moment, but then finally started to explain. "Well, we found Exile. Usumi did, anyway. Her apprentice came and found us, and we went to go make the arrest."

"And?" Criske prompted gently.

Kelt sighed. "He didn't resist. At all. Because he was unconscious."

"What? Did Usumi knock him out?" Henrik asked.

"No. He was lying in a puddle of his own vomit and blood," Kelt said. "Glenna was in complete hysterics when we found him. Usumi looked like she had been aura shocked, and was in the process of trying to recover when we arrived. She said he tried to attack her, and she had to knock him out."

Criske nodded. That seemed reasonable enough to him.

Henrik frowned. "That doesn't seem right," he said. "From our encounter with him…you shouldn't be able to touch him at all without feeling extreme pain, or potentially dying. Not to discredit Head Magician Usumi's incredible skills, of course."

"That's just it," Kelt said quietly. "I'm not sure that Exile actually did assault Usumi. Normally, I'd disagree with you. But…if Glenna is telling me the truth, which I'm betting she is, then he was in no state to fight at all. Which means something else happened, and he hasn't told anyone his side of the story, because he's unconscious." He looked down at his half-plate. "I had to slide him onto a stretcher with a pole, and we carried him through the city." His face seemed to tighten around his eyes. "I've worked these kinds of cases for over twenty years. I've seen a lot of terrible, twisted magic I'd not care to describe. But that boy…"

Kelt's hands tightened into fists hard enough to turn his knuckles white. "I have no idea how he's alive," he said. "We took him to the medical bay for prisoners. You know what we saw when we cut off his clothes? Scars. All over his damn body. Something isn't adding up to him being the killer, but I have nothing to go off of besides instinct."

The three of them stood in silence for a moment. Henrik looked unsure about what to do. An idea came to Criske, who put the kettle over the coals for the tea he found tucked away on a shelf next to the hearth. After a few minutes, he pulled the kettle off the fire and poured each of them tea, handing one wordlessly to Henrik. Then, one to Kelt. After a few sips, Henrik finally found the words to speak.

"A teacher of mine once said that 'instinct was the guidance of our *Khlaniik*, because it sees things our eyes do not.' I think your instinct is trying to tell you much the same, sir. And if it helps, Criske and I found that the information he gave us may actually be accurate. There is a person known as 'Harvest' in the records, but Criske and I didn't have the authority to access it."

Kelt looked up, his eyes wide. "What? But that would mean he actually was trying to help... Usumi said he seemed desperate to find me...is that why, you think?"

"Possibly," Criske said. "But is no one else concerned that he supposedly got that information from a ghost?"

Henrik gave Criske a dismissive wave. "It isn't such a terrible thing," Henrik said. "Our priests communicate with *Khlaniik* all the time."

Kelt shook his head. "That's where you're wrong, Henrik. The priests of the Dwarfdom do 'communicate' with spirits. But those spirits aren't exactly responsive. From the sound of it, this spirit actually spoke with him in a conversational manner. If that's accurate, then there are only a handful of people who can pull that off. None of which are good."

"So, if he can talk with spirits…" Criske said slowly. "Isn't sticking him in a dungeon, where there are probably a lot of angry, unhappy spirits, a really bad idea?"

THE SOLDIER

Kelt rose from his seat immediately. "You two, with me," he said. Criske and Henrik fell in line behind him, trying to match his controlled, quick walk down a hallway and across the main grounds of headquarters. Exile should be fine for the moment, since he was being treated, but Val-Zhang was probably right about the danger of leaving him in a room full of angry spirits. And if Exile was somehow able to control spirits, the last thing they wanted was for him to be put in a dungeon where he could rapidly win them to his side.

As they walked into the medical bay, night had finally fallen. The rays of moonlight were drifting down through the shutters high in the ceiling. The night patrolmen were lighting their torches, and the servants were doing the same, filling the area with dim pools of light to illuminate pathways, casting multiple stretched shadows in various directions. There was a statue of the Trifecta's first head medic of the Guardians, the Dwarf Vahnkiir Tadiq, outside the medical bay doors. In the flickering light, his face cast an ominous glare down on the trio as they entered his former domain.

The medical bay, unlike other parts of headquarters, was continuously lit so the medical team could keep a close eye on the condition of their patients. There were several people in there with minor illnesses or broken bones, but Kelt ignored them as he hurried all the way to the back of the bay. Two wardens, distinguished by the shield badge sewn into their uniform, snapped to attention as they saw him.

"Breaker Kelt," one said quietly, an Elven male with emerald-green eyes. "The head medic is looking over the prisoner now."

Kelt nodded. "Excellent. My apprentices and I need to take a look for the investigation."

The warden stepped aside, his eyes staring at Kelt intensely. He put a hand on Kelt's shoulder. "A word of caution, sir: it's not going well right now."

The weapons master nodded, opening the door and stepping inside.

The first smell that hit Kelt was the scent of blood, heavy and metallic in the air. After that came the heady smell of herbal concoctions. Then, there was the strange smell that came before a heavy thunderstorm, the smell of magic. He stepped into the room, a large enough space to comfortably fit a team of medics, but not a breaker and his two apprentices along with them. Kelt flattened himself against the wall as the head medic's apprentices scurried about, grinding herbs, fetching bandages, all of them with looks of mild panic on their faces.

In the midst of the turmoil stood the head medic of the Guardians, an older Human woman with tanned skin and short graying hair that was tied back into a little knot on her head: Nedra Kellem. She was enveloped in a purple shroud, the color somewhat marred by blood and years of wear and tear. Her eyes were glowing violet as she held a small stone the same color as her eyes. The stone was emitting a high-pitched whining hum in response to its patient. As she ran the stone over the body lying on the table, the stone's hum vanished and the color changed to blue, then green, then yellow, then orange, then red before turning clear. "Oh damn it," she muttered. She turned to one of her apprentices. "He drained another one! Someone go get a few more magicians! I can't keep this up forever."

An apprentice immediately hurried off, shoving Henrik out of the way. Kelt knew they'd break into a run as soon as they got out the door. One did not want to run around the bay when there was the risk of being stabbed by a sharp instrument.

"Head medic," Kelt said as a greeting. He gave her a salute, but she didn't look up to acknowledge it. "What's his current condition?"

"Honestly, piss poor," the woman said, her frown deepening. "It's no wonder he's coughing up blood. The boy has the worst case of wild-magic poisoning I've ever seen."

"Wild magic?" Henrik asked.

"Wild magic is magic that is just in the air around us. Normally, our auras protect us from it, filter it out and make it safe to just live life," a male apprentice explained. "Occasionally, though, there are areas dense with wild magic, and it can make people with weaker auras sick for a while. Prolonged exposure causes all kinds of health problems. But this kid…" She shook her head. "It's not that his aura's weak. The thing's broken."

"*Broken?*" Kelt exclaimed. "He should be dead within a matter of minutes, then." Even an undead couldn't exist without a fully functioning aura. It was part of the reason undead were so tricky to make.

"I know," Nedra said. "That's what I can't figure out. How the hell has he survived so long, and how is he still surviving? Right now, these stones are the only thing that's helping."

She held up what seemed to be the piece of cloudy quartz in her hand. "I charge them with energy from my aura, and his body seems to absorb it and stabilize a little. I've been at that for hours, but his body just seems desperate for it."

"Can I help?"

The weapons master turned to see Criske looking at the head medic, brown eyes fixated on the rock in her palm. Nedra raised an eyebrow. "Lad, you have to be a magician to charge one of these."

Kelt saw Criske's fists tighten at his sides. "Can I at least try?" Criske asked quietly. "He saved my mother's life. I owe him."

She gave him a sympathetic look but handed over the crystal anyway. Criske took it and stared at her expectantly. "So…how do I work it?" Criske asked.

"You concentrate your mind," she said. "Imagine pouring your willpower into the crystal, filling it bit by bit until it can't contain anything else. Like pouring water into a bucket."

Criske nodded and Kelt saw him stare at the crystal. About a minute passed with Nedra working in silence, pouring energy into her own stone, Criske staring at his with intense concentration. Eventually he looked up, frustration flushing his face.

Henrik put a hand on his shoulder. "Did you know, *Khlanro*, about this type of rock? It is very unusual in structure, this crystal. When it breaks, it has a very angular structure, like a cube. *Khlannan* like myself call it *Waqiirnah* or 'Ordered Stones,' because we can take it out piece by piece."

Criske looked at Henrik and his frustration simmered down. "Piece by piece, yeah?" Criske said. "I wonder…"

The Half-Elf closed his eyes, and Kelt saw his shoulders relax, his jaw loosen. Nedra drained another stone over Exile and then looked up at Criske. "Alright, lad, I need that b—"

The stone let out a high-pitched keening sound, shooting from red to violet in a flash—the violet growing paler and paler until the stone was a thrumming, brilliant white, like a piece of iron that had been made too hot by a forge. Criske seemed to pale, but then Kelt could just barely make out the practically translucent white glimmer around his body.

Criske opened his eyes, and the shimmer vanished. He placed the stone over Xeile's still frame, ignoring Nedra's outstretched hand. The color slowly trickled out of the stone, going down through the colors until it turned clear. Kelt noticed that the stone lasted nearly twice as long as it had before.

He looked at Kelt, a triumphant smile on his face. "Kelt, I did it! I mean…I did it, sir," he added.

Kelt recoiled in shock. Criske's dark-brown eyes had turned a brilliant golden orange, and were rapidly lightening in color, as if someone were siphoning away pigment on the surface of water: rippling and trickling away until just the palest gray remained, so pale they were practically white. Then, the color rushed back in a dazzling array, going from blue to hazel, crimson to red, before returning to their usual dark brown. Criske's smile faded. "Sir?"

"Have you ever done that before, Val-Zhang?" Kelt asked.

"Sir, what's—"

"Answer my question," Kelt said firmly. "Have you ever done that before?" He stepped forward, looming over Criske, staring down at him, trying to discern the truth from the youth's features. The boy was definitely hiding something, judging by the sweat breaking out on his forehead and his eyes shifting back and forth. Eventually, he spoke in a small voice.

"No…not to a rock, at least…"

"You've done it on something else?" Nedra asked sharply.

Criske turned, his posture echoing his intent to bolt. "It was just one time! His heart had stopped and I panicked and…" His words faded off and he lowered his head. "He came back to life. I restarted his heart on accident…" He grabbed his head and was shaking. "Please," he whispered. "Please don't arrest me… My family can't afford it… They'll starve. I'm the only one who makes enough so they can eat."

Kelt sighed. "Lad, we're not going to arrest you."

Criske looked at Kelt, eyes rimmed with tears. "You're not?"

"No. You're going to stay here and help charge these stones for Nedra, for now. We'll address this later, but we need to get this boy stabilized. Henrik, you're with me. We're going to the library to get that damn record. I want to know if we need to arrest him when he wakes up."

Henrik snapped to attention. "Yes, sir!"

The two of them left Criske with the head medic, Kelt leading the way out of the bay. Eventually, when they got outside, Henrik finally spoke. "My *Khlanro* is an unregistered magician…" he said softly. He looked at Kelt, both mystified and panicked. "Are you going to lock him away?"

Kelt shook his head. "No. But you'd do best to keep quiet about it for now. Last thing we need is an investigation into my investigation, got it?"

The Dwarf nodded. "Understood."

They continued to walk, the night sky blooming out before them, the dazzling array of stars twinkling down. There wasn't a cloud in the sky, giving the waxing moon a feeling of unnatural closeness, their progress an eerie sensation of motionlessness. Kelt kept walking, so deep in thought, he didn't notice as he slammed into Usumi.

The head magician let out a grunt of pain. Kelt looked up at her. "Sorry, Usumi. How are you feeling? Better after some tea and a bit of rest?" Usumi was more trained than most to withstand an aura shock, but that didn't make the symptoms any less pleasant. Usumi gripped Kelt's arm.

"Kelt, I need your help."

"I'm kind of in the middle of—"

"Please. It's my apprentice. She apparently knows this Exile person from before she joined the Guardians."

The weapons master looked at the library with a sigh, then altered course toward Usumi's office. He turned to Henrik. "Go wait outside the bay and come get me if Exile's condition worsens." Henrik snapped briefly to attention before running off. Kelt turned back to the door. After a moment, he knocked on it and walked in.

Usumi's room was completely dark, save for the single lit fireplace, casting a faint flickering light over everything. Glenna was sitting in front of the fire, cross-legged, her hands resting in her lap in a pose of meditation, her waves of brown hair cascading down her back. Kelt stood there in silence for a moment, wondering how to initiate the conversation. Glenna soon took the problem out of his hands.

"What do you want, Kelt, sir?"

The words were like a verbal knife, slicing Kelt across the chest, filling him with a hot pain. "I want answers," he said evenly. "I was told you could give me some. I'll give you two options. You can tell me here, or I haul you away to a dungeon until you talk or the investigation's over. Your choice."

Glenna uncrossed her legs and flexed her neck, sitting casually in front of the fire, so seemingly unconcerned with his ultimatum. "Well, then, I guess I'd better talk," she said, the ice in her voice contrasting with the heat roaring in front of her. "Considering you aren't exactly known for negotiating with people before dragging them away."

Kelt swallowed twice to help contain the fire trying to rush up his chest and out of his mouth in the form of anger. "No, I'm not. But I'm trying to be better about it," he said.

"Bully for you," Glenna said bitterly. "A little late for that now. Where did you put him, the dungeon? So he could die in a cell before you toss him into a mass grave?"

Kelt took a step back under the weight of the words. He responded with a direct block. "No. He's in the medical bay. The head medic is doing everything she can to save his life. I even have my apprentice helping. Now, what is your connection with him?"

"We lived in the same village for around a year before I joined the Guardians," Glenna said.

"That's it? What was your relationship with him?"

Glenna went quiet for a moment, looking down at the ground. "You know, he really wanted to meet you. You were his hero."

Kelt frowned in confusion. He knew that Exile was trying to help him solve the case, or at least claimed he was, and wanted to know where he was, but "his hero"? That was an unexpected bit of information. "Well, we did meet, though, probably not the way either of us would have wanted. What village did you two live in?"

"A quiet one up north. Little place called Davadain. Ever heard of it?"

Kelt felt his blood go cold, but he managed to keep his voice level. "I have."

"Then you've probably heard the name Mathiene too, right?"

The weapons master felt like he had been dealt a hook straight to his liver, but Glenna wasn't finished. She let out a caustic laugh. "What am I saying, of course you've heard that name. You killed her."

Glenna stood up, walking over to Kelt, her face tilting up to look him in the eyes. "You just stabbed her through the heart and left her body lay. You couldn't even be bothered to bury her, right? No, you left her for my parents to bury."

The weapons master felt his fists clench and his jaw lock as he received the verbal uppercut. The fire was crawling out of his chest and up his tensed throat, threatening to escape. "What was your relationship?" he repeated.

"You just left," Glenna said, her dark-purple eyes drilling into him, the shadows from the fire making her appear gaunt and cruel. The cold fury behind them was unmistakable. "My parents went to check on him, and he had just disappeared. They looked for months to try and find him, with no luck. I thought you had killed him. But no, you just left him for dead too."

"*What are you talking about?*" Kelt shouted, his booming voice bouncing off the walls. "I've never met Exile before today!"

"No, you didn't!" Glenna spat. "Because you never even bothered to check Mathiene's house!"

A dark-purple glow started to fill the room, enveloping Glenna. There was a crackle of energy and the smell of a thunderstorm. The room was cast into strange, twisting shadows from the ethereal source of light. "You ruined his life, but you act like nothing's wrong, you don't even act fazed. You just packed up your belongings and retired from Spell Breaking, job well done! A shining career! Do you even have a conscience at this point, or did you leave that behind somewhere *for the sake of an assignment?*"

"I retired because of that damn mission!" Kelt burst out. "It's been months and I still can't function! I see her everywhere! Just because you can't see it doesn't mean I don't feel anything!" He channeled his rage by grabbing a nearby clay jar and throwing it against the wall. "I was under orders that I didn't want to take!"

"You are his godfather!" Glenna yelled. "*Do you realize that?*" Kelt froze, his rage stopped by confusion. "What?"

"You're his godfather! Mathiene named you his godfather, in case she couldn't raise him! She said you'd protect him no matter what! So much for that plan, *right*?" The weapons master took a step back. "Wait…that doesn't make any sense. She was executed for abandoning her post, defying orders, and high treason against the Trifecta…"

"And how long ago did she do that, I wonder?" Glenna asked, the glow intensifying. "Think about it, the math isn't that difficult."

"Roughly fifteen to sixteen years ago," Kelt murmured. He looked at Glenna. A terrible, horrifying revelation burst into his mind. "How old is Exile?" he asked her.

"He's seventeen now, and his name isn't 'Exile.' It's 'Xeile,'" Glenna said.

Kelt felt himself go weak at the knees. "She left because she was pregnant…" he whispered. "Oh, Great Answer…" He staggered back against the wall, sinking downward, holding his head in his hands. "No wonder he wants to find me. I killed his mother."

The Seeker

Warmth. It was the first thing Xeile was aware of as consciousness returned. A strange kind of all-encompassing warmth he hadn't felt in months. It seemed to come in tides, warm waves of the ocean washing over his body. He eventually had the strength to open his eyes. He was staring at a stone ceiling. It took his eyes a while to adjust to the light in the room, and there was the sound of a fireplace nearby, but most of the light came from candles. His other senses gradually came into focus, and he started noticing more details. There was a table underneath him, but he was lying on some kind of cloth or sheet. Then, he noticed he was bound at the ankles and wrists.

Fighting panic, he swallowed twice. He didn't want to speak, for fear of drawing attention to himself. He didn't think this was some kind of torture chamber. But he wasn't sure who was in the room with him. A familiar face came into his field of view.

It was a Half-Elf with brown eyes and blond hair. He was sweating profusely, as if he had been on a long run or spent the entire day in a smithy. His slightly angular features lit up with joy. "Nedra! We did it! He's awake!"

The response came from Xeile's lower right side, a woman. "Oh, thank the gods…I was afraid he wasn't going to make it."

"You're the patrolman…" Xeile croaked, his voice hoarse and scratchy. Suddenly, the need for water consumed all his thoughts. "Please… water…" A waterskin was pressed to his lips, and Xeile gulped down two swigs before it was taken away.

"Careful. Don't want you vomiting it all back up, yeah?" the Half-Elf said with a wry grin. "Welcome back to the land of the living, Exile."

"Where am I?" Xeile asked. His eyes widened as his memory flooded back. "The Elf… There was an Elf… I accidentally touched her… Is she okay?"

The Half-Elf's grin stayed. "Who, Usumi? She's fine, though feeling a little under the weather. Nothing a little tea and rest won't help. How are you feeling?"

"Warm…" Xeile said, shifting around uncomfortably against his bonds. "What did you do to me?"

"Poured energy back into your aura," the woman's voice said. "A lot of energy. It's a miracle you even survived. I don't know where you got your grit from, but if more people were as stubborn as you, I wouldn't be so busy."

"Where am I?" Xeile repeated.

"Guardian headquarters," the Half-Elf said. "Kelt came and got you with a Spell Breaking squad. They found you unconscious in the street." Dread shot through Xeile with icy needles. He started to struggle against his bonds. "No…please…please let me go," he said. His pulse began to race, blood pounding in his ears. He yanked against his restraints. "I can't be here," he said. "Please, let me go. I'm begging you."

"Hey, calm down," the Half-Elf said. "No one's going to hurt you here."

"You don't understand!" Xeile yelled. "They'll kill me! I need to get out of here before they find me!"

"Whoa, whoa, whoa, who's 'they'? I don't think 'they'll' stand much of a chance against an entire place full of Guardians."

"They are Guardians!" Xeile shouted. "They've been trying to kill me for months!"

"What? Why?"

"I don't know. I barely escaped my hometown alive. I've been running here ever since, trying to get to Kelt. He's the only one I can count on."

Xeile felt pressure on the table as the Half-Elf leaned on it, looking down at Xeile. "I won't let them touch you," he said quietly. "Neither will Henrik. He's the Dwarf that was with me. And he's probably the most justice-driven protector of the innocent I've ever seen. Right now, Kelt thinks you're the primary suspect behind the murders—"

"It wasn't me," Xeile said firmly. "I wasn't even in the city when they happened. I came across one of the victim's ghosts."

The Half-Elf nodded. "Okay. Do you have any way to prove that?" Xeile thought about how he entered the city, and his heart dropped.

"No. I crept into the city because I was afraid of being spotted." He smiled a little despite his situation. "My appearance isn't exactly subtle.

Coughing up blood everywhere, ashen skin, black eyes, I'm pretty sure the Watch would've arrested me on principle."

The Half-Elf quirked an eyebrow. "Fair, I suppose. But…if you didn't do it, then who did?"

"I don't know for sure," Xeile said. "I mean, that thing I stopped from killing that Elf woman could be it…but somehow, I don't think Kelt will buy the explanation that a giant horse spirit with antlers has been going around killing people."

The patrolman sucked a breath in through his teeth. "Yeah…might be a tough sell, that one."

A moment of silence fell between them.

"I'm Criske, by the way. I'd shake your hand…but I'd rather not risk it, if you don't mind."

Xeile nodded. "I'm Xeile. Xeile Taeris."

More silence fell between them, and Xeile's mind began to move to other things. Glenna… she had accepted the ring. Even though he was going to die, she had put it on without hesitation. A lump formed in his throat and his heart ached. He wanted nothing more than to see her right now, but asking for her might result in her getting in even more trouble, which was the last thing he wanted.

He tried to think about what had happened after she had put on the ring. The Elf, Usumi, had told Glenna to go fetch Spell Breakers. Xeile had tried to run after Glenna and had nearly made it out of the alley when Usumi had slammed him against the wall, probably hard enough to crack his ribs. After that, he had gotten an attack of cold and passed out.

Xeile wasn't sure how long he spent staring at the ceiling, staring at nothing, lying on that table. He was too busy deliberating about what way he'd be executed. He had just decided it would likely be by hanging when he heard the sound of the door open. Criske's pressure on the table disappeared. "Sir, he's awake!"

"Good."

Xeile felt both panic and peace at the sound of the other man's voice. It was rough and low, and didn't sound happy in the least. Pain and fear mixed together into a terrible cocktail in Xeile's stomach, making it twist and heave.

"Are you…Kelt McNair?" The question hung in the air for an eternity as the man surveyed Xeile for a moment, turning away for a second as a flicker of recognition passed across his features.

"I know you probably don't know who I am…but…" He struggled to find the words, and eventually they faded into silence.

"I know who you are," the man said. "You're Mathiene's son."

"Yes," Xeile whispered. "And you're the one who executed her."

The room went silent save for the crackling of the fire. Xeile couldn't even hear Criske breathing next to him. Slowly, Kelt's face came into view as he made his way into the light, shadows from the fireplace dancing across it.

His nose was slightly crooked, as if it had been broken at some point. There were multiple thin scars across his face, likely put there by some kind of very fine knife. Had he been tortured at some point? A thick scar ran down his jawline. His face was covered in stubble, and there were bags under his eyes from lack of sleep. The eyes were filled with an emotion Xeile couldn't place.

"I heard you were looking for me," Kelt said quietly. "Do you want revenge?"

Xeile shook his head. "No. I'm here to forgive you."

Kelt recoiled. "What?"

"I'm here to forgive you," Xeile repeated. He took a deep breath and continued speaking. "I forgive you for killing my mother, Kelt McNair."

"Why?" he asked, face scrunched in pain. "I wouldn't, if I were in your situation."

"I know," Xeile said quietly. "I could never beat you in a fight, you're an incredible swordsman. I can't get you locked away because you were under orders. I can't force you to feel any regret for what you've done. You beat me at every turn. But there's one way I can beat you, and you can't do a thing about it. I forgive you, Kelt McNair. I put what you've done behind me. I still have a lot of emotions about what you did, but I refuse to let it keep dragging me down for what little life I have left."

Xeile locked eyes with him. "You don't control me anymore, Kelt McNair, and you never will again."

Xeile felt lighter than he had in months. A sense of strength flowed into him, an inner iron seemed to fortify around his heart and lock into place. "So…are you going to kill me now? Or are you going to give me the courtesy of a trial first?"

Kelt took a step back, out of Xeile's view. He heard the sound of footsteps, the door opening, and then closing. "Well, then, trial it is," Xeile said in a horribly jovial voice that didn't feel like it belonged to him. "Hey, Criske, want to record my witness statement for me? I have a feeling I'm going to need one."

There was a moment of silence, and then a sigh. "Damn, and I thought I could be scrappy," Criske said. "I can't read or write well enough, but I'm betting someone around here could. Might take a while to get someone, considering most of them are probably asleep."

"Don't you worry, I'm not going anywhere." Xeile chuckled. "I have to make sure Kelt's able to catch this killer before he turns around and executes me."

"What did you do to warrant killing?" the head medic asked.

Xeile sighed. "According to the laws of the Trifecta, I'm not supposed to exist. I'm technically undead, after all."

THE OUTCASTS

Henrik stood outside the medical bay, waiting expectantly. He hadn't heard the conversation between Glenna and Kelt, but the muffled shouting voices were enough to give him a rising feeling of concern. After that, Kelt had headed straight to the bay, presumably to talk with Exile, telling Henrik to stand outside.

The Dwarf was still confused but was trying to take the opportunity to enjoy the evening. A pleasant summer breeze was circulating around headquarters, cooling his skin and bringing him some respite. His head hurt and his eyes ached from the effort of staying open, but he gritted his teeth and bore it. He'd had to deal with far worse pain in his training before he joined the Guardians; this was nothing by comparison.

To distract himself, he tried turning his attention to the statue before him. The Dwarf's face was severe looking, not exactly the expression Henrik would want to see when having a medic attend to his injuries.

"I wonder how many *Khlaniik* you had," he said softly to the statue. The statue continued to stare down in dour silence. Henrik chuckled to himself and turned his attention to the inscription that was written in Territory, Dwarvish, and High Elvish: *Unite to Heal the Pain of All Peoples.*

It was the code for every Guardian that became a medic. The phrase made him think of the gaunt faces of the Half-Elven streets he and Criske had traveled. Was every city like that to their Half-Elves? Possibly even worse? The thought made Henrik's fists tighten. How could the Trifecta just stand by and let that kind of treatment happen, let them starve like that? How could it see their suffering and treat it as a normality? The thought suddenly spurred him to think of poor Exile. The man was clearly injured, so desperate to help them, but he was being treated like a criminal. He'd even saved Criske's mother at the expense of his own well-being, even though he could have just run away, probably avoiding capture from the Guardians altogether. The thoughts swirled into a vortex, like a terrible autumn storm on the sea, a hurricane with one question at its eye.

What kind of order was he actually serving? "Well, someone's deep in thought."

The voice made Henrik jump and turn around. Glenna was strolling toward him, her hands in her pockets. "What're you thinking about?" she asked, eyes carefully trained on him.

"I am wondering how I am supposed to feel about Exile, among other things," Henrik said.

"His actual name is Xeile," Glenna said. She shook her head. "I can't believe he used the same name from when he played make-believe as a kid." She smiled. "He used to tell me all these stories, about how he would run into the woods, being a Guardian named Exile, and he'd fight off all these terrible wolves and creatures. Then, his mother would hunt him down and beat some sense into him for going missing without telling anyone where he was going."

"Xeile..." Henrik said softly. "What an unusual name..."

"And yours is much better?" She arched an eyebrow, lightening their conversation.

Henrik shook his head. "No, you misunderstand me. Names oftentimes have meanings, but it requires a great deal of effort to find them. That name is a very old one and likely belongs to one of the northern Nomadic tribes in the Territories. I just didn't expect him to have any Nomad heritage in him."

Glenna shrugged. "I don't know what to tell you there. I haven't known him his whole life. He never talks about his father, so I figured he didn't want to."

"Well, family matters are very difficult," he said quietly. "I can understand his hesitation to make mention of anything of that nature. Though…I am very surprised you actually know each other. The chances of that would be very small, especially considering the circumstances."

Glenna laughed. "Yes. Fate really did bring us together. My parents and I moved to Davadain to avoid causing any problems while I learned magic. It's a remote place, and we didn't have to worry about too many catastrophes as I learned. We heard rumors that a lady lived there and she could stop magic with a single touch. Turned out to be true. Xeile's mother could stop magic with a single finger. She became…my mentor while I practiced."

Henrik thought about this for a moment. If Xeile's mother could stop magic completely, that would be an incredible feat. But, how could one stop magic? Magic was just the alteration of the world by the use of your aura and mind. Nothing could just be created, at least as far as he knew. He turned his attention back to Glenna, who was still talking.

"I met Xeile because of his mother. He was…terrifying at first."

"How so?"

"He was so…*quiet*. First few times I met him, I didn't think he could actually speak. He would just sit and watch me work whenever he had some free time, which wasn't often. He worked with the village smith on a number of projects, but he'd weave baskets, set snares and traps, fish, cut wood, anything to help keep Davadain running. If anyone talked to him, he'd just stare until they finished saying something, then go do it."

Glenna shook her head. "Eventually, I got annoyed. I finally snapped at him, demanded to know what he was there for. He just looks at me and says, 'You. Your practice is beautiful.'"

She raised her head slightly. "I mean, I know my magic is skillful, but it still felt different when he said it. We got to know each other better ever since. I helped get him talking more, and he supported me in just about everything." She held a hand up, staring at it with a pained expression. Henrik saw a beautifully carved wooden ring on the finger meant for a wedding ring.

"You love him," he said.

Glenna looked at Henrik, her lips forming a very small smile. "I've always known what to do. I've always been the best. But now…" She lowered her hand, letting it fall limply to her side. "Now I don't know what to do to protect him."

Henrik tried his best to choose his words carefully. "My first suggestion is to try and cooperate as much as possible. Even if you and Kelt do not get along, the two of you working together are Xeile's best chance of survival. My second is that you make sure Xeile is as honest and cooperative as possible. If I were in his situation, I would feel very alone and trapped. You should make sure he feels like he can at least rely upon you."

Glenna digested these words in a long silence that was only occasionally broken by a grasshopper's cry. Then, she turned to Henrik. "You make it sound so easy. Where did you pick up that advice? Philosophy book?"

Henrik shook his head. "Real life. One does not survive the Dwarven courts without a careful eye toward a possible ally's needs and wants."

"Courts? You're a noble?"

Henrik looked at the ground and quelled the pain trying to resurface in his memory. "I was a servant of one," he said quietly.

The medical bay doors opened and Kelt emerged. His footsteps seemed so loud, an unwelcome intrusion on the quiet between Glenna and Henrik. He saw the pair standing in front of the statue and sighed. Henrik snapped to attention and gave him a salute. Glenna just looked at Kelt, gave him a small salute, and resumed staring at the statue. Kelt looked Henrik up and down. "You look almost dead on your feet, apprentice."

Henrik looked at Kelt's expression, his slumped shoulders, and the armor he was still wearing. "You appear to be in a similar state, sir."

Kelt nodded. "I am. But, the good news is, Exile's condition has stabilized for now, thanks to Val-Zhang and the head medic. So, I am going to propose we all get a few hours of sleep and pick up where we left off in the morning."

"Master McNair!"

Kelt and Henrik turned to see a warden walking over to Kelt, throwing him a salute. "We have the Half-Elf's family secured in their quarters and under watch." Henrik flinched but said nothing.

The weapons master let out a sigh of relief. "Well, that will make Criske's day," he said. "Thank you, warden. Return to your post."

"Sir," he said with another salute, running off.

Kelt looked between Henrik and Glenna. "Now, you both need to rest. We'll have a lot to do in the morning. Us three are going to meet at the library at sunup. Glenna, I'm counting on you to bring Usumi, and I'll need you when I talk to Exile."

"His name is 'Xeile,' sir," Henrik said.

Kelt looked at Henrik and blinked. "Oh. Well, I'll need you to talk to Xeile, then," he said to Glenna. "Can you do that? I'll need a statement from him. I know you don't like me, but it is for his sake."

Glenna locked eyes with Kelt and eventually nodded, the moments passing by with painful slowness. "Good," the weapons master said. "Now, both of you hurry off to your cots."

Kelt started walking away in the direction of the library. "What about you, sir?" Henrik asked, glancing over his shoulder to see where Kelt was going. "Aren't you going to get some sleep?"

"In a little bit," Kelt assured him. "I'm going to get some answers first." The two watched him go, then, without saying another word, parted ways. Glenna headed toward Usumi's office, and Henrik toward the barracks.

The Dwarf's head was spinning with a parade of details:

Exile's name was Xeile; he was from the north and his mother could completely stop magic.

Xeile was sick. Xeile wanted to help Kelt solve these murders. Xeile could see spirits.

Glenna loved Xeile, and Xeile apparently loved her in return. Xeile was a suspect in the case.

The killer was likely a spirit, from the sounds of what attacked Criske's mother.

Xeile could drive it off using some kind of dark power. He could communicate with spirits.

He was terrified of being trapped by the Guardians, convinced they would kill him.

But why?

Very few acts of magic were punishable by death. Most of the time, the local military would take care of a rogue magician in all but the most severe of cases. The only one the Guardians were called upon in particular to handle was…

Henrik came to a full stop halfway to the barracks as the thought struck him. He pivoted around and took off at a sprint toward the library, his feet slapping against the stone and grass as he flew through the night, using his memory as a guide. Unfortunately, the torches were interfering with his ability to see as well in the low-light spaces, like dazzling bright spots on his vision. He cursed his *Khlaniik* as he stumbled a few times, but kept going. He had to reach Kelt.

He managed to do so just before Kelt entered the library, vaulting up two steps at a time and grabbing Kelt by the elbow, gasping for breath and light-headed. Kelt stumbled slightly as he was yanked down by the sudden weight on his arm. He ripped his arm away from the intruder, turning to snap when he saw Henrik. "Steady there, lad. What's wrong?"

"He's a necromancer," Henrik wheezed between gulps of air. "Xeile is scared of Guardians because he's a necromancer."

16
THE SOLDIER

Kelt gawked at Henrik's face, lit dimly by flickering torchlight. Henrik's eyes were partially closed as if he were in pain. Maybe he was, considering how fast he had run here. Still, the idea that Exile—no, Xeile—was a necromancer was a troubling one.

"Henrik, lad," Kelt said slowly, quietly, in case someone around them was listening. "That's a very serious charge to level against someone, and the conditions to meet it are very specific, according to the law."

"That…is not the point…" Henrik said, his breathing slowly steadying, his hands on his knees. "How would he know what those conditions were? In most people's minds, interacting with the dead in any kind of way is necromancy. He can see and talk to spirits. He can even fight them, if he's telling the truth. If I knew nothing about Trifecta law…"

"I would think I've done something illegal and punishable by death," Kelt agreed.

"And he wants your help, because you're the most experienced person in fighting necromancy there is," Henrik continued. "He is scared of himself, maybe even wants you to kill him so he doesn't accidentally hurt anyone else. Xeile is trying to protect others…"

"By getting himself killed," Kelt finished softly. His fists clenched at his side. "That's why he never sought treatment for his illness… He wants to die so he doesn't hurt anyone else." He looked in the direction of the medical bay. Kelt turned and looked back at the library doors. "Thank you. I'll make sure to relay that to Usumi and bring it up with Glenna. Keep it quiet for now until we can confirm. Go get some sleep, Henrik."

Henrik gave him a nod and slowly walked off, too tired to even bother saluting.

Kelt turned back to the library doors and fought the urge to scream in frustration. Guilt was pouring through him like molten lead. Xeile forgave him, forgave him for killing her. Kelt tried to wrap his mind around it, but he just couldn't. What level of strength did it take for Xeile to do that? How could he possibly empathize with Kelt? Most days, Kelt couldn't even empathize with himself. Orders or no, something about that last assignment had just felt so…wrong. She was executed because she was called an immediate threat, a disaster waiting to happen, on top of being treasonous and abandoning her post. But that didn't make any sense. Why would she abandon her post for her pregnancy alone?

The Guardians rarely had women get pregnant while on duty, but it did happen on occasion. Most were allowed leave to go have the child and then return to duty—or they were given the option to leave their service early, and were honorably discharged for their time served. Why wouldn't Mathiene have taken either of those options? She didn't steal anything, otherwise Kelt and his squad would have been ordered to retrieve the item in question. She hadn't murdered anyone, despite rumors after her disappearance. That would have been added to her writ of execution, which Kelt had read countless times both before and after executing her. Treason and abandoning a post was definitely punishable by death, but that would require a trial and definite proof. The Trifecta wouldn't order the execution of someone just for wanting to raise their child. It wasn't like giving birth was treasonous.

The thought set off a chain reaction in Kelt's mind like an avalanche. One conclusion, then another, then another, until it was a terrible tide crashing down the mountain of his consciousness, slamming down into his stomach, making him nauseous under the impact.

The only reason she would run was because she wasn't supposed to have the child. And the only reason Xeile would run to him instead of anywhere else…why? Why? Why? Why would Mathiene make him Xeile's godfather? That was a Nomad tradition. Best he knew, she wasn't of Nomad blood. Was his father?

Kelt looked up and entered the library. He immediately strode over to the bored-looking attendant who was busy spinning a Trifec on the desk, watching the little coin twirl with a detached expression. Kelt put his hand on the table, startling the young man out of his stupor. "I need to know where all your documents related to Nomadic traditions of godparents are."

The words came out of his mouth before he could stop them. Then, he added on his original purpose. "Oh, and I need access to all service records, active and inactive, related to the name 'Harvest,' please."

The young attendant nodded. "R–right, sir…um…would you…uh…" He pointed at Kelt's chest with a shaky hand. "Would you like me to get you…something for that?"

Kelt looked down and realized he was still in his bloody armor. He sighed. "Right, sorry. Yes. That'd be excellent."

The attendant pointed to an eerily dark section of the library. "That section has everything we've got on Nomad religions. Maybe you'd want to start there while I get those records and some rags for your armor?"

The weapons master peered into the darkness and nodded. "Alright. Thank you." He walked down to the rather unlit corner carrying a lit beeswax candle in a little tray the attendant had provided.

The library was one of the places Kelt always felt changed the most between night and day at headquarters. It was inviting during the day, a place of peace and quietly buzzing with people craving new knowledge for personal and professional reasons. At night, the sudden silence became oppressive. Monuments of knowledge became expressionless walls looming too close for comfort. The normally wide and inviting desks acted like a tiny string of candlelit oases in a difficult sea of darkness. Kelt found the nearest oasis to the corner section and unbuckled his sword, propping it against the desk to reserve his spot, in case there were any other late-night scholars lurking about. Besides, if he was ambushed, his sword would be too long in a practical fight in these narrow passages.

Nevertheless, he kept his dagger. It never hurt to be prepared, after all. Kelt turned his attention to the sections, reading the labels carefully before extracting a few scrolls with odd titles such as *The Wind God's Mandate* and *The Greater Family*. He had no idea if those would have the information he wanted, but it was as good a place to start as any.

A pile of scrolls in one arm and fighting exhaustion, Kelt pulled out a chair with his free hand. He collapsed into it and began to read. Most of the works he went into were direct transcriptions of the Nomad's oral traditions.

Each tribe had different kinds of stories, different deities, and most frustrating of all, a kind of storytelling that was seldom explicit, being parabolic in nature. He would oftentimes find the term "godfather" or "godmother" mentioned in passing between a few characters or in a genealogy, but nothing about what they were actually supposed to do. "Come on," he growled. "There has to be something more specific…"

Eventually, his pile dwindled to just a few scrolls, so he went on the hunt for more. The less progress he made, the more frustrated he became. The candle he was using had burned about halfway down, and the attendant still hadn't returned. How long did it take to bring all the records for people named "Harvest"?

He shook his head and returned to the task at hand. After scanning a few more scrolls, he happened across a very interesting one. It was not a parable, nor a direct transcript, but a journal of a scholar named Falaran Xol. The writing was very neat and orderly. The fascinating part of his journal was that it wasn't based on date but on category. As a result, there were multiple entries on the same subjects scattered throughout the scrolls:

On the matter of religion:

These Nomadic peoples seem particularly obsessed with the concept of what they call the Gray Plains. It appears to be some kind of afterlife, though they treat it more as another plane of existence, a land where spirits dwell that the Nomads can interact with. Perhaps the proximity to the Khlaniik Mountains or an interaction with the commonplace Dwarven ancestor ghost worship at some point in time caused this unique belief to form.

On the matter of societal structure:

Like many Nomad tribes, this people group seems to place a great deal of importance on their hunters and their healers. The hunters are exceptional horsemen and archers, though they also hunt with another weapon fashioned of three stones tied together with ropes. It seems to excel in causing their prey to trip and fall. Slings are also very common weapons, particularly for non-militaristic daily use for the defending of their yaks, goats, and sheep.

Their women are incredibly utilitarian and seem to handle most matters of governance, as the men are too busy collecting resources to decide such matters. As a result, the men are only given positions of power by the vote of the women. The leader of the women is called the ulaan, and is part of a larger council of *elders. These are the people who handle the matter of naming children and the bestowing of the godparents.*

Kelt leaned in closer to the scroll, his heartbeat quickening.

On the matter of naming and family:

A child was born today and I was given unique access to their naming rituals. The ulaan *and elders took the child and, after ritually bathing it and placing it in a bed of moss, held it over a fire infused with herbs and spices for a brief amount of time. The elders then seemed to entreat the spirits of the Gray Plains to name and bless the child, to act as a protector, much like the Dwarves entreat their ancestors (Khlaniik) to do the same for their children.*

It is unique, however, that they seem to wish to bond the children to a spirit in the Gray Plains. Normally, they entreat an animal to do this, such as a wolf, bear, eagle, or another type of beast. Is this an early form of shamanism or animism? I must investigate further and keep a close eye upon the child, for I am concerned this may be a form of necromancy.

Kelt felt an unease crawl up his spine. All exhaustion vanished from him as his candle guttered low, the dim light valiantly fighting off the encroaching dark. He continued to read on.

On the matter of the small child:

They have decided to name the small boy "Taeris" after supposedly consulting their spirits. He seems to be relatively healthy, though his skin has a grayish pallor and his eyes are black as a starless midnight sky. I mentioned my concern to the ulaan, *and she assured me the boy would be well, as his godparents would look after him. I will keep a close eye upon the boy, because upon closer examination, he seems to be displaying symptoms of a weak aura that could lead to potential magic poisoning.*

On the matter of the small child, continued:

The boy is not doing well; he came down with a small fever and has cried constantly throughout the night. I am unable to stand idly by and record any longer. I must do whatever it takes to help. I refuse to let a child die and do nothing.

"No…" Kelt whispered to himself. "Please live, little laddie."

On the matter of Taeris, continued:

Through my limited knowledge of medicine, I have broken the poor child's fever and stabilized him. The temperature around the boy is a constant chill, which I have sought to rectify through several blankets. Fortunately, the ulaan *and elders have been nothing but supportive of my efforts. On the contrary, they seem suspiciously delighted. I will now sleep with my dagger in hand at night. I no longer feel safe among these people, though I cannot point out the precise reason why.*

On the matter of Taeris, continued:

I now know the true purpose of the ritual the tribe has placed upon the small boy. They were summoning the spirits in hopes that one would possess him, turning him into what we would call a shaman, one of the oldest forms of a magician in Merarian history, and one of the types of magicians that is a precursor to a necromancer. They gain the knowledge to cast magic by bonding with a spirit, using the memories of a past life to understand the world around them and manipulate it. This, of course, comes at the risk of the caster's sanity and well-being.

This can go no further. I must get word to the Guardians at once. Such a terrible ritual should not be inflicted upon one so small and innocent. I fear poor Taeris will not survive this terrible fate if he does not escape. So, I shall make haste. The child will either escape, or I shall die. There can be no other options.

May the Great Answer guide me to the Higher Truths.

Kelt found himself standing as he finished reading. He quickly rolled up the scroll, placing it on his chair. He grabbed the next one and splayed it out before him, his eyes chewing through the text with a ravenous hunger.

On the matter of Taeris, continued:

I have discovered the purpose of a godparent. The day before I planned to escape, I was approached by the ulaan, who at this point has seemed to notice my fear for the small boy. She and the elders have decided to name me a godparent. In this tribe, a godparent is not one who brings a child up in the ways of the tribe, should their parents pass. A godparent is to protect the child from the malicious spirits of the Gray Plains while encouraging good spirits to guide him. They are to play the role of a divine protector, ordained by a particular deity.

In the case of Taeris, he has been deemed a rather unique case. Apparently, no spirits have yet bonded with him. I have no idea how to protect him from anything like a spirit of malice. I am no magician or Spell Breaker. I can only hope his other godparents are more informed than I.

On the matter of Taeris, continued:

I have made my escape with the boy. I do not know what deity has appointed me to protect this child in their minds, but regardless, I seem to have been chosen to carry this burden. I have made considerable progress on my horse, the boy in tow. He seems to have taken a liking to me, which is a small blessing. I am just a scholar, and am ill-equipped for such a long or perilous journey. But I shall not give in.

Kelt nodded. "Steady on, man. Please tell me you got there." He kept reading.

On the matter of Taeris, continued:

They were wrong. A spirit did find Taeris. The tribe's warriors ambushed us about two weeks away from Tenorkiv. While they nearly killed me, Taeris seemed to glow black and, for lack of better terminology, drain the life out of them, the blackness like a terrible cloud of miasma, choking and strangling them, afflicting different parts of their body with what appeared to be frostbite. The blackness seemed to coalesce into a kind of beast with the giant antlers of a stag but the body of a horse. Then, with an earth-shaking cry, it turned back into a black mist.

I, of course, was terrified as the spirit disappeared back into the small child, turning his eyes black again, though Taeris seemed to settle back down once more and we continued on.

What kind of monster have I unwittingly unleashed upon the world?

As much as it pains me, I must surrender the baby over to the Guardians, though he will likely be killed. If only there were some way I could separate the creature from the small child! No, I cannot surrender him without at least trying to do so.

"No…" Kelt said. "Don't do it. The Guardians will kill you for necromancy charges…" Steeling his emotions, he kept going.

On the matter of Taeris, continued:

I have done it. The spirit was tied to the boy via some kind of strange thread, which I was able to make appear once I was placed in suitable peril from more of the Nomad tribe, who seems desperate to bring the boy back to their lands. But with this severance has come a terrible price. His aura has seemed to have broken, and is only sustainable by the use of energy transfer. I have managed to buy him time by draining and killing the Nomads who have continued to hunt us, but I do not know how long this will keep him alive. I pray it will be enough for me to find a Guardian. Surely they will know what to do.

Kelt felt his heart plummet. "No…no… no…"

On the matter of Taeris, continued:

Finally, an act of mercy! Though I can barely touch the child without suffering the pain of drainage myself, I seem to have found one who can handle him without repercussion. She is a fine Guardian, though she seems to have the sole task of hunting me down and killing me for crimes of necromancy.

"I told you," Kelt said viciously. "I told you." But…a single person? That didn't make sense. In cases of suspected necromancy, Spell Breakers always traveled in squads of four. One magician, one bowman, and two frontal attackers. How could they justify sending one person?

He kept reading, hoping for an answer.

She has allowed me to explain my situation and the reason for my criminal act, and is even kind enough to let me record this final entry, though she is watching me as I speak. I have her word that the child will remain safe with her, and that is all I can do for now. Though initially grieved, I am happy to see little Taeris in capable hands. His pallor has much improved since the severance from the creature, as long as his aura is sustained by energy.

She has decided to rename the boy, in an effort to better hide him from the Nomads who wish to reclaim him. After some discussion, we agreed that Xain is an acceptable name. In the language of his people, it means "severed."

Here I must end my entry and face my fate. I can only hope that the boy will live and thrive under these circumstances, though I fear for him later in life if he were to have children. It is likely that he will continue to be hunted, and I'm afraid his weakened aura will result in his offspring facing similarly problematic health conditions. I'll be sure to note this before I am brought to trial and executed.

Though I face death, I will hold my head high, for I have found my Great Answer for living, and that Answer is saving the life of a small boy named Xain Taeris. Long may he live, and may he be blessed by fate. Farewell.

Kelt looked at the ending in horror. He then immediately looked at the date on the outside of the scroll. It was in 294 A.T. Almost forty years ago. Long enough for Xain to grow up, long enough for him to meet a certain Guardian and have a child who also suffered cold spells and black eyes…a child he likely had no knowledge of, from the sound of it.

If Kelt was named as a godfather that meant Mathiene was counting on him to protect Xeile from malicious spirits. Spirits that were likely hunting him down, destroying anything in their path to get to him, like they did to Xain in the past. Not to mention that the Nomads were likely still trying to find Xain in order to create a shaman.

Or worse.

Kelt sat back down, his mind thinking over the victims of the murder. They definitely had the marks of frostbite that Faralan described. But why would the creature target those people specifically? And that creature was certainly nothing Kelt had ever heard of before. A beast that was a horse with antlers? It seemed so surreal. But, it was one of the leads he actually had to work with. He looked around to try and figure out where such a mythological creature would be mentioned, and where that might be in the library.

Where was that blasted attendant?

A wave of cold washed over him like a bitter winter wind. Kelt grabbed his sword and unsheathed it, holding up his candle in the other hand. "Hello?" he called. "Is anyone there?"

The cold intensified, and Kelt started to see his breath in a fog in the dim candlelight. "It's illegal to use magic in the library, whoever you are. I suggest you stop or face the consequences."

There was a huff of air, and a loud, animal snort to Kelt's left.

He turned, holding his candle upward. "Show yourself," he demanded in an authoritative voice. "Or I will be forced to take action."

Then he felt a vibration in his feet as a series of steps seemed to resonate through the floor. Whatever was in here, it wasn't a person, and it didn't seem to be a wraith either. The steps got louder, and then Kelt finally identified what they sounded like.

Hooves.

"Oh, damn it all," he said through gritted teeth. He started running for the door just as his desk was demolished, heaved into the wall, and shattered into splinters by some great unseen force. Kelt risked a quick glance behind himself to see a pair of ominous red eyes bearing down on him. There was a terrible neigh like a thunderclap as the being reoriented itself to head in his direction.

Kelt quickly burst out of the library, shouting at the top of his lungs: "*To arms! Wraith! To arms! Wraith! To arms!*" The nearby night patrolman froze for a moment, then, seeing Kelt running away from the library, scrambled for the nearby signaling horn in one of the watchtowers. Sure enough, the oak doors, installed nearly a hundred years ago onto the library, hand-carved by master Elven artisans, were blasted off their hinges by the malevolent force, slamming down the stairs with a loud crash. An angry neigh filled the grounds, sending chills down Kelt's spine. Whatever this wraith was, he had never seen its kind before. Wraiths did have some ability to interact with the physical world, but they never had this kind of strength, or this strange, practically invisible appearance.

He pivoted on one foot and held up his sword, looking at the pair of malevolent crimson eyes. "C'mon, you bastard!" Kelt said. "I didn't survive twenty-two years of active duty for nothing!"

An arrow flew out of nowhere and embedded itself in one of the eyes. The creature let out a strangled, pained cry, but the arrow fell out when it should have stuck. But there was no flesh to stick to. Suddenly, Henrik was at Kelt's side, a Dwarven bow in hand. "At the ready for your orders, sir," Henrik said.

A dagger flew from the night, passing the side of the creature. "Damn it, all!" Criske appeared out of the shadows from Kelt's other side, a fist full of knives in one hand, and one prepared in the other. "Sorry for the miss. What now?"

Kelt looked at the two of them, his brain and years of experience taking over. "Sound the alarm. Evacuate everyone out of the west side, send all available Spell Breakers back in and let's kill this thing!"

Henrik didn't hesitate. He reached behind his belt and pulled out something that made Kelt's eyes widen. It was a horn made of silver, reinforced with delicately carved bone, a single insignia burned onto its side.

The symbol of a hammer and pick linked by tongues of flame. The symbol of House Ihvihlic, the royal family of the Dwarfdom.

Henrik sucked in a breath and blew a string of notes Kelt had heard only twice in his life. The signal for mass evacuation, and the signal for an impending disaster.

It wasn't long before the watchtower signal blared too, and the whole world seemed to explode at once.

Doors were flung open, and soldiers scrambled for the exits, pouring out of entrances. Wardens immediately took up the post in the medical bay. Doors were barred shut in some areas. The few Spell Breakers who heard the alarm burst onto the grounds, weapons in hand: two Elven archers and a Dwarf wielding an arming sword and a shield.

Criske and Henrik were shouting directions in bellowing voices, clearing out the barracks with as much speed as they could.

Kelt, as senior officer, took command of the other Spell Breakers. "Circle and Snare!" Kelt yelled. "This one is wild!"

Circle and Snare was a commonly studied maneuver in Spell Breaking training. They'd surround and force the wraith to move in a general direction, mostly away from a certain target or group. The pair of eyes moved left, then right. Kelt wasn't sure what it was, but he managed to duck just in time to avoid a black tendril that shot out from the beast and slammed into the wall behind him hard enough to crack the stone.

"It's got range!" Kelt yelled. "Archers, get on—"

More tendrils shot out, piercing the two archers and the Dwarf immediately, punching through their armor like it was paper. There were brief explosions of color as their auras flared to life and then shattered.

"No!" Kelt screamed. But it was too late. Their lifeless bodies slumped to the ground like dolls. He looked at the creature in front of him. No wraith was capable of that.

"Hey! Horse monster!"

Kelt froze at the voice. The creature immediately whipped around. Kelt turned to see Xeile limping toward it with some kind of chain in one hand. "Get away from my godfather!" Xeile threw the chain, and it seemed to snag on something in midair. The creature roared in protest, trying to toss it off. Then, Kelt saw an explosion of black energy erupt from Xeile, shooting up the chain, slamming into the creature.

It was only visible for a few seconds. But the image burned itself into Kelt's mind. At first glance, it was a giant shadowy horse, but attached to its head was a massive rack of antlers, with skulls hanging from each of its tines, the sockets glowing different colors.

Xeile sent another shock of energy coursing through it. "Get. Away. From him," he commanded through gritted teeth. The creature didn't need telling twice. With a roar, the silhouette blurred and faded before seeming to melt through the ground and vanish into the night.

Xeile sank to his knees. The weapons master ran forward to catch him. "Don't." Xeile held up a hand. "It'll hurt you to touch me," he said in a weak voice. "Get away for now."

Kelt backpedaled a few steps before taking a knee. A few wardens rushed onto the scene, looking at the dead Spell Breakers on the ground. The wardens immediately rushed to seize Xeile. "Hold!" Kelt barked. The wardens backed away slowly. "You just saved my life," Kelt said quietly. "Why?"

"Because if I didn't, who would? I'm not going to stand by if someone's in trouble." A fit of violent coughing shook his body, and Kelt saw him double over. "I'm not going to die knowing I could have done something and didn't," he said with a strained breath.

"Get a stretcher!" Kelt yelled to the wardens. They ran off and Xeile looked up at Kelt. Kelt gasped. A black fog seemed to be running down Xeile's face, dripping from his eyes.

"I'm sorry…" he moaned. Xeile slumped to the side, falling to the ground.

Kelt darted forward, reaching for his godson before pulling back his hand. He couldn't touch him—not if he was still alive. But Xeile's words resounded in Kelt's mind.

I'm not going to stand by if someone's in trouble.

Kelt reached his hand forward and grabbed Xeile's shoulder.

There was no reaction. "No," Kelt said. "No. Don't do this to me." He seized Xeile with both hands, shaking him. "Come on, laddie." He held his hand to Xeile's neck to feel for a pulse. Nothing. He put his hand to Xeile's chest to feel for a heartbeat. Nothing.

The weapons master began rhythmically pumping Xeile's chest, occasionally breathing into his mouth, pinching off his nose. He continued working for upward of a minute, sweat starting to pour down his face from the exertion.

"No," he said. "Come on, stay with me, Xeile. I don't want to have killed you both, damn it!"

Xeile's hand shot up and grabbed Kelt's arm. "Stop."

Kelt immediately took his hands off Xeile. Sitting back in shock, he took a few deep breaths of air. "What… But your pulse… Your heartbeat…"

The young man sat up and looked at Kelt. "What? Oh…that happens sometimes, during a cold attack."

"*What?* That's not an attack, that's dying!" the Guardian yelled.

"Oh. Guess I've died a lot lately," Xeile said, his voice nonchalant, but his words were slurred.

"Though I've always come back or gotten through it. I really owe your Half-Elf friend. That stone he used worked wonders. I haven't felt this good in ages."

Kelt opened his mouth and then shut it again. Xeile looked up at the sky and smiled. "You know, the stars here are really beautiful." Exhaustion must have gotten to him because he lay back down on the ground. "I always wanted to see something incredible. All I had to do is look up…"

He shut his eyes and didn't move again.

The Fallen

In the dark of the night, a single spirit seemed to drift through the buildings it once called home. It nodded to a few of the spirits it recognized, but its memory was hazy. Why were all of them here again? Oh, that's right. They were supposed to be looking for something. What was it again? The spirit frowned, unsure of the answer. Then it came to them in a flash of brilliance, a burst of clarity, like a sunbeam piercing a clouded sky. Of course. They were looking for their brother-in-arms.

Renewed by the vigor of this purpose, the spirit continued its search. Where was he? They thought they had seen him around here somewhere…

The spirit continued to drift as people were running and shouting everywhere. Most looked confused. One of them, in blood-soaked armor, looked devastated. He was crying, holding on to someone, yelling at them to come back. Where did they go?

Two others were coming around the man. One was…a Dwarf? Yes, it must have been, though fairly tall for one. The other let out a string of terrible curses and was throwing something on the ground, pounding at the earth with his fists. The Dwarf was on his knees, bowing and praying to the person the man in armor was holding. Why?

Then, he heard a terrible scream. A woman? The spirit turned and looked at her. She had sunk to her knees, clutching her mouth, clearly upset. Why?

Whoever this person was, they must have been really important, the spirit noted. Curiosity piqued, it went over to take a look. The person being held was a young man, thin and pale. The spirit looked down and at him and frowned. He certainly didn't look like anything special. Then, the spirit spotted a glint near the boy's chest. A necklace?

The spirit peered closer and then recoiled in shock. It was a brother! But he needed help. He looked so broken.

The fog seemed to clear from the spirit's mind again as a promise it made a long time ago echoed throughout its mind:

When the light has faded, and wrong has won, when the enemy's victory anthem is sung,

I will become the light for the hopeless.

In times where all is lost and there is no recompense, I will be a Citadel,

The greatest and final defense.

The spirit reached down and put its hand on the young man. Then, another spirit came by and joined him. Then another, and then another, until eighteen spirits were gathered around, unified in their chant. The other people seemed to scatter away from him, pointing at them, but the spirits paid them no mind.

They had found their final brother. And they refused to let him die.

As they touched the young man, their memories returned. Their grievances, their betrayal, their rage. Their names.

Harvest Zhong—oh right, that was his name—had one final thought for the young man on the ground before he vanished.

You're our final and greatest defense, kid. Show them what you're made of, Citadel of the Dead.

18

THE CITADEL

Recovery, Xeile discovered, was neither a pleasant nor an easy process. He felt like he was gradually being filled with pain that spread all across his body until every single part of his skin itched and burned. It was like when he had fallen into poison ivy as a child. Then, his hearing returned with a painful ringing in his ears. A stabbing pain filled his eyes. His sense of taste, in particular, returned with a vengeance, filling his mouth with the metallic tang of blood and sour milk, making his stomach twist in response. Then, there was the sensation of his heartbeat, loud, clamorous, every beat felt like a colossal heave in his chest. Next, a massive strike on his chest, as if he had been hit by a sledge and then stuck with a hot branding iron.

Xeile let out a cry of agony, his back arching in protest against the torment.

Wait, he had a voice again, and muscles to move?

You're our final and greatest defense, kid. Show them what you're made of, Citadel of the Dead.

Xeile's eyes snapped open, and he lunged for the source of the voice just above him, but there was nothing but air. Instead, he saw that the flickering black substance around his body had somehow become more stable, with a patchwork of eighteen different pieces interlocking like a kind of strange plate armor across his chest. Is that what had caused his pain? As he moved about, he noticed that it didn't move so much like a piece of plate as it did a tightly woven mat.

Then, he realized the cold from his legs was gone. Completely.

The young man gasped, looking down at his feet, flexing his ankles, marveling at how easily they were able to move. Then, he saw Glenna staring at him through tears in front of him. Without a second thought, he got up and ran over to her, dropping to his knees, embracing her. "Hey, hey, calm down, what's wrong—" Xeile gasped and jumped away as he remembered his damaging touch, but Glenna didn't seem to have any reaction at all. She had just locked in place like a statue. Xeile hesitantly reached out and touched her shoulder again.

Nothing.

Tears formed in his eyes. "I can finally touch you…" he whispered. "I can actually touch people now…" He reached back out to Glenna, but his muscles seemed to fail him as he lurched forward. Glenna reached out and caught him.

"You're alive," Glenna whispered. "You're alive…"

"What else am I supposed to be?" Xeile asked, savoring the smell of her hair. It still smelled like wildflowers, even after all these years. "Don't you worry. I'm too stubborn to go down that easily."

Glenna let out a choked laugh and hit him on the shoulder repeatedly. "Don't you ever do that again! You realize how much I've worked so I can protect you, *idiot*? Three years! Three years of practicing so I can support you!"

"I'll be more careful." Xeile separated from her and gently cupped her face with one of his own hands. "I promise, okay?"

"No, you won't," Glenna said quietly. "You'll throw yourself in front of any danger to protect someone. Just like your damn mother." She put her head on his shoulder. Xeile reached up and cradled it, gently stroking her back as she gradually slowed her involuntary shaking. "You're not strong enough to do things like that, Xeile," she whispered.

"Just because I'm not strong enough to do the right thing and live doesn't excuse me from not doing the right thing," he responded softly. "You know that."

"Idiot," she said softly. "You'll get yourself killed."

"No, I won't," he said, kissing the top of her head. "Like you'll ever let that happen."

"Not while I draw breath," she said, wrapping her arms around him. "This is your only free one. You die again, I'll resurrect you so I can kick your ass. Are we clear?"

"Yes, ma'am," Xeile said with a smile.

Kelt let out a cough behind them. Xeile broke away and looked at him. "Are you okay?" Xeile said, hurrying over to him. "Did it touch you anywhere?" The weapons master just stared at him in mute horror. "What?" Xeile said. "Yes, I died for a little bit. Now, are you hurt?"

"He didn't bring you back."

Xeile turned to see Criske Val-Zhang staring at him with a similar expression. "What do you mean?" Xeile asked.

Criske frowned. "He didn't bring you back. You were dead for ten minutes. Then…a bunch of spirits came down and…well…I have no idea what happened. But they were there, and then they weren't. All of the sudden, you had a pulse and are alive again." He shook his head. "That shouldn't be possible. When you told me you were undead, I didn't believe you. Sorry I doubted."

Xeile let out an uneasy laugh. "Spirits don't just spontaneously help people like that. They don't have clear enough minds for that unless you bond and talk with them, from my experience anyway." Xeile suddenly felt a hand on his shoulder.

"Come with me," Kelt said quietly. "We need a place to talk in private." Kelt looked at Criske, Henrik, and Glenna. "You all come too. Follow me."

Unsure what else to do, Xeile followed him, keeping track of Kelt's frame as he moved through the headquarters with an efficiency only brought about by memory. The night was passing quickly, and it wouldn't be too long before the sun would arrive to shed light on the awful destruction that had taken place. "Don't you need to…like…take command here or something?" Xeile asked.

"No," Kelt said. "Even with all my experience, there are still people here that outrank me. They'll take command. Right now, this is more important."

He continued to lead them on a series of twists and turns that made Xeile lose track of where they were. The number of spirits that were present seemed to get fewer and fewer as they walked, until Kelt came to a sudden stop. "We're here," he said.

"Here" turned out to be a remote garden full of flowers Xeile couldn't identify, though the faint scent of lavender did cross his senses. Kelt was standing in front of a few stones that were arranged in some kind of pattern. Kelt reached down and looked over at the Dwarf. "Henrik," he said, "give me a hand with this."

Henrik hurried forward and grabbed the other side of the stone. "Lift," Kelt said. The two of them heaved upward in unison, and the stone gave way without complaint. Underneath the stone was a trapdoor, which Kelt lifted to reveal a hole large enough for a grown Human man to fit through. Kelt set the stone off to one side. "Inside," Kelt commanded.

One by one, Kelt helped lower them down into the opening, which turned out to be a seven-foot-deep hole. Kelt soon followed after them, then shut the trap door behind them.

"Sorry to be the gloomy cloud on a sunny day, but how can we tell where we're going?" Criske asked. "I can't see my hand in front of my face."

"Do not worry, *Khlanro*," Henrik said, his voice seeming to carry and echo around in the complete darkness. There was the sound of a hand slapping around on the nearby stone. "This tunnel has the geometry of a *Khlan*-made project in the second century After the First Trifecta. Which means…"

There were more echoes of a hand slapping on stone until there was a thunk of a hand colliding with something wooden. "Here we are!" he said. There was the sound of water, and then, an eruption of light that made Xeile wince. When the strain on his eyes finally lessened, Xeile saw Henrik in front of all of them holding a wooden lantern filled with some kind of strange, mucky water that was…glowing?

"*Akhqii*," Henrik said.

"Bless you," Criske said.

Henrik raised an eyebrow. "It is a *Khlannar* word. It means 'light,' but it also refers to this strange substance we've found underground in the mountains in our homelands. Our ancestors relied on this moss for light, as our miners still do. Do you wish to lead the way, Master Kelt?"

"Yes, but you hold the lantern. Damn glowing stuff puts me on edge." With Kelt as their guide, they walked down the tunnel and made a couple of turns. With each step, they seemed to be getting deeper underground. The air was colder. Xeile fought the sensation of rising panic in his chest, but he couldn't seem to force himself to take a full breath. Then, Glenna's hand slipped into his. "I'm here," she said quietly. Xeile felt the tightness in his chest loosen, and he kept walking, not letting go of her hand. Eventually, the room opened up, and Henrik veered off from the rest of the group, going around to various spots on the wall, pouring water from earthen jars into similar wooden lanterns.

The room was soon illuminated by a soft blue glow that gave everything a flat appearance and deep shadows. Xeile looked around and saw that the room was also full of strange, twisted crystals and runic writing. Some of the crystals were as tall as Kelt, spiraling up into the domed ceiling, acting like pillars. At the back of the room, there was a small altar that appeared to be made out of a white-and-black stone that Xeile didn't recognize. On the altar was a small bowl made of what appeared to be lead and it was full of what Xeile could only guess was salt. On each side of the bowl, however, was something Xeile recognized instantly: incense burners. His mother used something similar to burn sage and herb bundles all the time back home whenever he got sick.

"Where are we?" Xeile asked.

"This is a warding chamber," Glenna said softly. "I didn't think the Guardians would have one… Not here anyway."

Kelt looked at Glenna and raised an eyebrow. "I'm surprised you recognize it," he said. "Not many people have even heard of them, let alone seen them."

"I'm not exactly average," Glenna said wryly.

"Would you mind sharing so the rest of us don't gawk about like idiots?" Criske asked.

"A warding chamber is a space that repels malicious spirits," Glenna explained. "Necromancers use them as a fail-safe for when they try to summon something and it goes south. A lot of older structures had these too, from before the Trifecta, when necromancy was a larger threat. This one is a high-quality one, but you can improvise one with salt, incense, and lead. Incense is for purifying the air, lead is for binding the area to the earth, and salt is a purifier that acts like a binding agent for keeping the whole space tied to the natural world. Of course, this space has crystals here too, which tend to serve as a way to absorb aura energy and wild magic, both of which a spirit needs to function, and magicians too." Glenna looked around, coming to a conclusion. "This could be a prison as well, couldn't it?"

Kelt nodded. "Yes, but only in the rare cases where a person was possessed by something that wanted to harm them. The person's internal desire to push the spirit out, plus the room, would generally get the spirit out of their body. Right now, I'm using this for a different reason. Very few people actually know about this place, and we need a space where we won't be overheard or sensed. I don't want our horned friend paying us a visit again. Sit down. This might take a while."

The group had a seat, Xeile peering around the room, feeling a strange sense of nostalgia. But why? Then it occurred to him: His mother had kept a bowl of salt in their house too. It wasn't made of lead, but it was still there, next to their firepit. Xeile had always assumed it was for cooking. But was it?

Then, the more he stared at the crystals, the more familiar they seemed. He quickly pulled out his necklace and stared at it. The stone embedded in the filigree looked almost identical to the ones that filled the room.

"What's that?" Kelt asked.

"A necklace my mother gave me," Xeile explained. "Ever since I said I could see people that no one else could, she gave it to me, said it was hers from when she was an active Guardian before she retired. I just…thought it looked really similar to…these rocks."

"May I see it?"

Xeile looked at Kelt and then slowly handed it over. "I better get that back," Xeile warned him. "It's all I have left of her."

"You will," Kelt said. "If there's one thing I knew about Mathiene, it's that she didn't give arbitrarily." He held up the necklace in the light, looking it over with a critical eye. After a few silent minutes, he held it out to Xeile, who snatched it and put it back on. "It's not part of any uniform or any kind of merit badge I know of," Kelt said. "But I can tell you it is definitely of Guardian make. She could have had it privately ordered by one of our jewelry smiths, but it'd be an awfully strange order to make."

"Might I have a look?"

Xeile turned to see the Dwarf looking at him with a somber expression. "I am very familiar with the craftsmanship of metalwork. I might be able to identify the maker and region."

Xeile hesitantly handed the Dwarf the necklace. Henrik cradled the necklace and held it with reverence, easing the distrust Xeile felt. The Dwarf started whispering to himself as he peered at the necklace, turning it over in his hands, feeling the metal, holding it close to his eye, blowing on it, holding it up to a light source, tilting it back and forth, then handing it back to Xeile.

"My best guesses, as absurd as this might sound, is that this necklace was made by Khodan ibn Makiir, the master jewelry smith for the Ihvihlic family. It bears all the hallmarks of his work. Though, I'm not sure how your mother would have gotten permission to get a piece of work from him. Whoever ordered this would need the royal family's approval."

"Royalty?" Xeile asked, confused. He looked at the necklace and then back up at Kelt. "I figured my mother was good at what she did, but royalty? That seems"—his heart clenched in his chest—"a little absurd."

"Your mother was one of the best Guardians I've ever seen. She was a one-woman army," Kelt said. "There's record of her completely destroying a group of rogue magicians by herself. Some of the things she did were almost superhuman."

Xeile nodded, but there was still an uneasiness he couldn't identify running through him as he slid the necklace back on.

Kelt clapped his hands together, making everyone jump. "On to business. It's time everyone got up to speed on what we know about our murder case and, more importantly, that damn creature." He pointed at Criske and Henrik. "You two start, and we'll work our way around."

Over the course of the next hour, they all talked about what they knew, had seen, or heard related to the double murder and the strange monster that was wreaking havoc on the town. When they finished, Kelt appeared to be deep in thought, biting gently on his first knuckle as he untangled his mind.

Finally, he just looked at Xeile, got on his hands and knees, and bowed to him. Xeile recoiled. "What are you doing?" he asked.

"Apologizing. I know it probably means nothing to you, but I've hated myself for what I've done. Even though you said you've forgiven me, you still deserve an apology."

Xeile felt a swirl of emotions hit him. He reached forward and put a hand on Kelt's shoulder. "Look at me," he said quietly.

Kelt looked up, his blue eyes matching the ambient light of the room.

"If you're sorry," Xeile said quietly, "then find out why the Trifecta ordered you to kill my mother without a trial first. And don't you dare bow to me."

Xeile swallowed and forced the truth out of his mouth. "You're not the one who really needs to apologize, but I'm grateful you did." The moment he said those words, a fire started in the pit of his stomach, a new kind of drive that filled his entire body and rushed to his head.

"We're going to capture whoever has murdered these people in Trifectus. Then, we're going to find out who ordered my mother's death, and I don't care if I have to drag them to a trial by their teeth, I will hold them accountable for what they've done. To the both of us." Xeile raised an eyebrow, extending out a hand to Kelt. "Sound fair?"

Kelt sat upright and stared at Xeile for a long moment. "You know, Glenna was right. You are an idiot." Kelt smiled. "Just like me." He reached out and took Xeile's hand with a firm shake. "Pleasure to work with you…"

"Xeile. Xeile Taeris."

Kelt frowned. "Wait…zeal? As in 'with enthusiasm'?"

Xeile nodded. "Spelled differently, but yeah. My mom said it was one that my father picked before he passed away."

The weapons master seemed to focus in on Xeile with a new intensity. "Did you know your father very well?" he asked.

"No. He died before I was born, apparently. My mother said he died from some kind of chronic illness."

"Do you know his name?"

Xeile nodded. "Of course. His name was Xain Taeris."

Kelt leaned back and exhaled. "Oh, Great Answers… Xeile…I'm not sure how to put this any other way, but I think that horned monster is supposed to belong to you."

THE OUTCASTS

Criske was distinctly reminded of the time he had fallen off a roof and had the wind knocked out of him after landing on his back. Xeile wore a similar expression. It was hard to tell in the flat blue light, but he looked sick to his stomach, his black eyes widening. The shock on his face was obvious.

"What do you mean? Are you saying that thing is…after me? I've never seen it before I got to this city!" Xeile protested. "That doesn't make sense."

"I said it was 'supposed' to belong to you, not that it should. I came across some interesting documents in the library you might want to know about." Kelt then described what Criske could only define as a life of bad luck for one particular scholar, and a tale of unlikely heroism.

Xeile listened with intense focus, and Criske could practically see the gears turning in his head.

When Kelt finished, Xeile sat back and sighed. "Well…a lot of things make more sense now."

"How so?" Henrik asked. "I am personally just more confused. Who is this group of Nomads to try and bind a wild monster to one so young?" Xeile looked at Henrik and sighed. "Well, you have to understand Nomads first. Nomads aren't like the Humans in stationary living spaces. They constantly fight with each other on a smaller scale. But, the only way they maintain their independence from the barons of the Territories is how they fight: stealth raids, intimidation, mystery, and assassination. By taking Xain, poor Faralan essentially stole their greatest line of defense. Considering what we've seen that thing is capable of, would you even think about going near a group protected by that?"

Henrik shook his head. "Still…how could a child survive such a malicious presence? A spirit like that could easily overpower a man, let alone a young one."

"People will try anything if they're desperate, yeah?" Criske said. "Maybe these Nomads were on their last legs and went with the most radical solution they could think of?"

"They were trying to make a Deathrite Shaman," Glenna said quietly. Everyone in the group froze and looked at her. Glenna shrugged. "What? They were. Judging by the description Faralan wrote, that kid's aura was pitch black, and there are only two kinds of people that have that aura: dying people and Deathrite Shamans."

Kelt cursed. "No wonder Faralan ran." He scowled.

"What's a Deathrite Shaman?" Xeile asked.

"I'd assume a shaman that deals with dead things, yeah?" Criske quipped.

"Gathered as much. I suppose they'll handle rites too? Or maybe just wrongs?" Xeile quipped back. They exchanged a smile.

Kelt pinched the bridge of his nose as if he were fighting off a headache. He looked at Glenna. "Is he like this normally?" Glenna nodded and the weapons master sighed. "A Deathrite Shaman is kind of like a primitive necromancer. They interact with spirits and command them to gain intelligence and fight for them in battle."

The levity vanished from Xeile's face. "What? How?"

Kelt shrugged. "Generally they'll bond with a spirit, then take part of its energy before forcing it to physically materialize. That normally hurts the shaman more. Later necromancers figured out how to get around that issue, which has come to mean the creation of the modern wraith as we know it. No one has seen a proper Deathrite Shaman among the Nomads in at least seventy years. They're illegal according to the laws of the Trifecta."

Xeile looked positively sick now, or was that just the blue light? Criske wasn't sure. "And… do Deathrite Shamans make spirits remember more about themselves?" Xeile asked.

"No. That's not possible…" Kelt said, eyes wide and looking to Glenna. "At least, not to my knowledge?"

Glenna stared long and hard at Xeile. "You already did that to a spirit, didn't you?"

"I didn't mean to!" Xeile protested. "All we did was talk. I was trying to help the murder victim remember details so I could help Kelt. As time went on, she started talking more, and she started being empathetic. She actually willingly gave me energy, vanishing in the process so I could find Kelt, after I drove off the monster. I still don't get it. It wasn't intentional at all."

Kelt leaned against the wall, crossing his arms. Everyone fell silent for a moment.

"Well… It seems…like we know the reason your mother told you to stay away from Guardians. Abilities like that…would be very, very dangerous in the wrong hands," Kelt said distantly. His focus returned to the hodgepodge group in front of him. "We've been down here as long as I can spare. Xeile, you should probably stay here. I'll notify the head medic, but no one else can know that he's here. If anyone asks, he's been placed into special custody for medical reasons. Understand?"

They all nodded.

Kelt turned to Criske and Henrik. "We three need sleep, so our first priority will be to get a few hours." He looked at Glenna. "Can you find Usumi? We need her here."

Glenna nodded. "I have no idea where she went, but I'll drag her back here." She looked at the ground and frowned. "She should have been here, unless she was off researching something in private. That woman…" Glenna sighed. "Her head's in the clouds half the time."

The weapons master gave her statement a dismissive wave. "I don't care where her head is half the time, just as long as it's here the other half." He turned his attention to Xeile. "You stay here and rest, damn it. No heroics, no sneaking off to do battle with the beast. One of us will be back down with some food and drink shortly."

Xeile brightened considerably at that statement. "Food?"

Glenna let out a groan. "Why did you say the magic word? Do you even realize how much this boy will eat?"

"He looks like he needs it," Criske said quietly. He looked over Xeile, feeling a pang of sympathy for him. The boy had the look of the chronically hungry Criske had seen in so many other individuals. Sunken cheeks, easily visible collarbones, and a razor-sharp jawline. His arms looked like twigs, especially when he stood next to Henrik. Criske was amazed he even had the strength to run about and be as active as he was. "How long has it been since you've had consistent food in you?"

Xeile shrugged. "Oh, I guess around three months or so. I've kind of lost track and just taken food as it comes—no reason to be finicky—I would have spent more time snaring or fishing, but I was on the run. I didn't have much time to slow down."

"You can—"

"Stop," Kelt said. "We'll be here all night if you continue. Bed, you two."

"Yes, sir," Criske said with a sigh.

"Yes, *Vahndrii*," Henrik said offhandedly. He froze for a moment and looked like someone had clocked him over the head with a truncheon. Kelt recoiled as if someone had done the same to him. Without another word, Henrik stood up, saluted, and left. What was Henrik calling him "father" for? Sarcasm? Kelt shook his head and let it slide. There were more important things to worry about.

Criske looked at Kelt with a raised eyebrow. "You coming, sir?"

Kelt nodded, with Glenna getting to her feet as well. Xeile rose and embraced Glenna. "I'll be waiting for you," Xeile said, kissing the top of her forehead. "Don't go killing anyone out there, alright? Kelt doesn't need that kind of paperwork."

"You're no fun," Glenna said, her voice muffled in his shoulder. Criske smiled, noticing for the first time that Glenna was actually slightly taller than Xeile. They broke the embrace, and Glenna gently stroked his cheek. "Someone should be back soon. Stay out of trouble, okay?"

"I'm trying," Xeile said with a grin. "Should be a little easier now that I've got you back."

Glenna's face sobered. "Count on it."

She saluted Kelt and grabbed his arm. "Get it right this time," she said before leaving.

Kelt was silent the entire way back, his face flitting between somber and questioning.

When they emerged from the tunnel, the night sky looked strangely bright to Criske, who shortly realized that dawn was fast approaching. "I'll be back to get you and Henrik in a couple of hours," Kelt said. "Off to the barracks with you."

Criske didn't need telling twice. He gave Kelt a salute and quickly found his bed, sinking into it and immediately falling into the black of sleep.

It seemed like just a few seconds later when he felt Kelt grab his ankle. Criske sat up with a groan, rubbing his eyes. "Ah, damn it," he said. He looked over and saw Henrik in a similar state of hating the world for having time run by so quickly.

Kelt jerked his head toward the entrance. "Come on: breakfast and then we've got work to do."

"Yeah, sir," Criske said, rubbing his eyes with his fingertips. He stood up, already fully dressed. He tried to smooth some of the wrinkles out of his uniform without success and plodded his way toward the mess.

The mess was probably one of the oldest areas in the entirety of headquarters. It was still like the others, low and squat, but with many chimneys to let the smoke escape. However, the signs of multiple repairs over the years were clearly evident by the sight of resealed cracks, different colored roof tiles, and the signs of new and seasoned wood intermingled with each other. Criske looked over at Henrik, who under normal circumstances would probably be spouting facts about the place, staring at the building like it was his only reason for existence. Then again, Criske couldn't blame him. He felt about as tired as Henrik looked. The Dwarf's eyes had deep bags under them, and his normally rigid posture had a hunched look to it.

Criske couldn't help but notice the wondrous smell of cooking pottage. The cooks must have happened on some seasonings or maybe fresh ingredients, because the pungent smell seemed to invigorate him with new life.

When they entered the mess, it was actually fairly quiet for once. The morning rush that normally accompanied dawn had disappeared. The mess was generally open day-round, year-round, as so many patrolmen came and went with inconsistent schedules, though they stopped doing hot meals around midnight. It was part of the reason so few people volunteered to do night patrols. There was a high chance that you'd wind up without a hot meal at the end of your shift.

Fortunately, the stew was hot, and even somewhat good. It appeared to be some kind of barley mixture with potatoes and onions. There were even some carrots and herbs thrown in. Criske grabbed himself a bowlful, sat down, and began eating. Henrik did the same, drinking down the weak morning ale with grim determination. Kelt did much the same. Black tea from some far-flung Elven isle with a splash of cream was handed out to them afterward. "It's not coffee, but it's better than nothing," Kelt noted apologetically.

They had almost finished their cups of tea when Kelt began giving them instructions. "Criske, I need you to take a bowl to Xeile. Henrik, you're with me. The creature did a hell of a number on the library. I need to help with some records. Criske, you'll be joining us afterward. Clear?" Criske and Henrik agreed and they went their separate ways. Armed with a bowl of stew and a much better outlook on life—even without much sleep—Criske could feel the buzz of the tea seeping through his body. The summer sun shed light and warmth upon his skin, blowing away the fog of night. When he finally made his way to the concealed tunnel, Criske dropped down into the blue-lit lane, food in hand.

He entered the room, finding Xeile sitting cross-legged and staring into one of the crystals, the blue light from the watered moss filling the air with a flat, omnipresent glow. "Hey," Criske said.

Xeile jumped up, spinning around to locate the source of the voice. "Ah." Xeile relaxed his posture. "Hey," he said quietly.

"I brought some food."

"Thanks." He walked over, grabbing the bowl and eating it in a matter of just a few minutes. When he finished, he handed the bowl back to Criske without a word.

"How're things down here?" Criske asked.

"Blue and quiet," Xeile said, motioning vaguely. "Not much in here, really. But, Kelt says it's the best place for me, and I trust him, odd as that is." He sat back down in a cross-legged position, staring at the altar. "It's strange, though…I can't seem to sleep. I tried for hours last night when you all left, and it just didn't happen."

Criske looked around. "All this light, I imagine not. Have you considered covering your eyes with something?"

Xeile nodded. "Yep. It's just…it's like my body isn't tired anymore. I mean, I still feel some of that cold that I felt before…but the tiredness isn't there anymore. It's strange. I've never had problems sleeping before."

Criske shrugged. "Well…keep trying, I guess. Your body can't really heal without sleep." After a moment, the Half-Elf spoke again. "Thank you for saving my mother. I know that may not mean much, with you stuck down here, hunted by people, and—"

"No need to thank me," Xeile said with a smile. "I would never forgive myself if I didn't.

The last thing I want is to create a reflection of myself that has the power to actually hurt people."

Criske fell silent as Xeile's words hit him. The Half-Elf managed a jerky wave of farewell before walking back down the tunnel, exiting and replacing the stone that hid the entrance, the statement still rattling around in his skull. If Xeile was doing the right thing, what were they doing to him? Stuffing him in a corner until they could solve this later? Shaking his head to clear it, Criske hurried over to the library and let out a curse when he saw it.

The oak and metal front doors had been blown off, splitting in several places from the impact on the stairs leading to the building. The stone of the steps had actually cracked under the weight of the doors. From what little Criske could see of the inside, multiple bookcases had been knocked over, their content knocked onto the floor and scattered about. The scribes of the library had hung multiple pieces of what looked like tent canvas to try and shield the works from the elements, but he could still see that some of the writings were damaged beyond repair. It didn't take him long to find Kelt and Henrik, though. They were crouched over a body that was covered by what appeared to be frostbite. Henrik put his head in his hands and let out a similar, low-voiced prayer to the one Criske had heard before. Kelt looked at him with a tight mouth and a knitted brow. "Looks like our librarian here paid the price for trying to get me those records mentioning 'Harvest.' The creature must have found him when it entered the library."

Criske sighed and went to get a closer look. He saw the same kind of gouges in the nearby wall, and then looked over the body with a critical eye. "Well, all the symptoms seem to match. It's a pretty safe bet that we've found what's done the actual killing."

"Right," Kelt said. "But can that…thing make records disappear? Because all of the records of Guardians that start with the letter *H* are missing, and now we have no way of knowing where they went to."

Criske thought for a moment, frowning in concentration. The answer had to be here. They just weren't looking hard enough. He examined the scene. The boy died in the hallway that led from the back room where the archives were.

It went to the front of the library where Kelt would have been. There was no sign of forced entry from any other point, so the person who stole the archives would have likely gone in the same way as the apprentice. Or, they were already going back to get the records when the apprentice stumbled into them.

But how could they ambush Kelt and nearly kill him if the monster was summoned at the front of the building? It was not like the creature was quiet. And wouldn't someone else have heard it if it had come all the way from the front to back? "Hey, let me see the body again, yeah?" Kelt looked at him with a raised eyebrow, shooting a warning glance at the moving people at the scene around them. "May I see the body, sir," Criske corrected.

"Be my guest."

The Half-Elf leaned down and looked at the body again, this time paying closer attention. As he looked the victim over, more details started to reveal themselves. The frostbite was far more widespread and scattered. And…yes… bruises. Not from where he fell, though. They were in the wrong spot. Instead, they seemed focused around his lips, with one of them extending up the side of the apprentice's nose. A flash of inspiration came to Criske. "Hey, can we shift this guy?" Kelt looked at him in confusion. "Turn him over," Criske explained. No one moved, and Criske met Kelt's eyes. "Trust me on this one."

Henrik eyed Kelt, who gestured for him to get to work. Henrik gently rolled the body onto its side, shuddering when he had finished. Criske turned and looked at the back of the apprentice before running his hand down the spine. It wasn't long before he found what he was looking for. "Ah-ha. Got ya, bastard," Criske said. "Stab wound straight into the spine." He tapped the back on the body's upper spine. "You can kill someone immediately with that. The bruises on the front look like they clamped his mouth shut as he tried to run for help. Knife to the back, dead after a few minutes at most. But, that won't look consistent with the other bodies. So, a little trick or two to make the frostbite appear while he's just barely alive, and we have ourselves a nicely hidden shank job."

Henrik seemed to stare into the distance for a moment before sharing his own thoughts. "*Khlanro*, theoretically speaking…you'd generally want to do this kind of thing where the body was hidden for a while, yes? Until you were well away from it?"

Criske nodded. "Yeah. Generally, these can get messy, and trying to get away from them can draw a lot of attention if you're, you know, covered in blood or something."

"So the person in question could have used the monster as a distraction, no?"

The three of them studied each other. Criske felt a heavy weight sink to the bottom of his stomach.

"So, the creature was a distraction to allow them to get away in time," Criske said. "But if that's the case, the culprit would control the monster. Which means each time the monster was used, they'd have to be close by. That'd make things like the other murders incredibly hard. Wouldn't they have been spotted eventually?"

Henrik stood up, his entire body tense. "We are coming at this from the wrong angle." Confusion was etched on both his companions' faces. "We are making the assumption that the person must be close by," he clarified. "But we aren't specifying how close, or if they have to control it without any barriers between them.

They could have sequestered themselves in a building, hidden from sight, commanding it as they saw fit."

"'Could have,'" Criske said, a boiling pit in his stomach. "So many assumptions. We just don't know enough!"

"I'm inclined to agree." Kelt sighed. "But it's not like we can get answers from a dead person." He gestured to the scene before them.

The words bounced around in Criske's skull, but he couldn't figure out why. Then, something clicked inside his mind and he grabbed Kelt's arm.

"Wait a second. Maybe we can." He lowered his voice, leaning closer to both Kelt and Henrik. "Maybe we can see if Xeile can talk to him…or his ghost…or whatever you call it. I bet there's more than one spirit in this library too. The person probably wouldn't have hidden from a person they couldn't see, yeah?"

The other two fell silent as they considered the possibility of Xeile's assistance. After the silence continued to stretch on, Criske rolled his eyes impatiently. "Come on. Normally we'd leap at the chance to talk to an eyewitness! What's the holdup here?"

Kelt's expression darkened. "Criske, I had to execute his mother. He wouldn't lift a finger for anything I touch. He may have said some nice words back in that cave, but talk means nothing to reality. Would you help me if I killed your mother? Think on that for a moment."

"You didn't 'have to' execute anything," Criske snapped. "You could have refused the orders and been stripped of rank or whatever, yeah? That aside, he's not like you or me. For him, morals come first. He might be angry, but I think he'll know it's the right thing to do. Dragons and phoenixes, we could ask Glenna to request it. He'd go to the moon and back for her alone. It's not like you have to ask for his help directly. Just fill out the paperwork or whatever to bring him on board as an adviser or whatever. You don't have to do everything by yourself, you know! Now, are you gonna let your own guilt stop us from solving the case, or help us actually get somewhere?"

As soon as the words came out of Criske's mouth, he realized just how many rules he had broken. Not wanting to dig his grave any further, he just sat there, his mouth clamped shut. Henrik was looking back and forth between Kelt to Criske, his eyes wide and face pale.

Kelt stared at the body for a long moment, then nodded.

"You go talk to him this time," Kelt said to Henrik. "Don't promise any payment or things like that yet." He pivoted on Criske and pointed a finger at him. Criske felt his insides chill under the weapons master's icy blue gaze. "And you, don't you ever talk to me like that again. I could have you whipped or worse for language like that."

Criske thought for a moment about the dark-stained whipping post that was tucked away in the sparring equipment closet and shuddered. In his mind, he heard the terrible sound of the lash, a vicious crack as it sliced open his skin. No, he never wanted to hear that sound again. "Yes, sir," he whispered.

They all stood up, looking down at the dead body one last time for now. Kelt walked by Criske and grabbed his arm, leaning down. "Your words were crass and out of line," he whispered. "But thanks for keeping my head on straight."

The weapons master walked away, leaving Criske standing next to the body, unsure how to feel. He looked at Henrik. The Dwarf gave him a small smile. "You play dangerous games, *Khlanro*."

Criske looked around at the library, then down at the body once more. His words seemed to echo in the quiet of the hall. "Well, I've never been one to play it safe, have I?"

THE SOLDIER

Kelt pounded on the door to Usumi's office one more time. There was no answer. "Where is she?" he muttered. "What's the point of having a head magician if I can't find them to ask about magical things?" The door didn't have an answer for him. He shook his head and walked back into his office, annoyed. He needed coffee. Badly. That tea in the morning hadn't been nearly enough. As he set the water near his fireplace to heat up, Kelt found himself staring into the flames, his thoughts churning.

He had scolded Criske because he had to, but how much truth was there behind the boy's words? What would have been the consequences of refusing to take the order? It came from the actual Trifecta itself, with all three seals. No representatives were listed on the writ of execution, meaning they had all individually looked at the writ and approved it. Of course, he couldn't refute a unanimously decided writ by the Trifecta itself.

But why did the entire Trifecta personally want Mathiene to die? The more he thought about it, the worse a feeling Kelt got. He recalled Xeile mentioning that they'd find the actual culprit behind his mother's death, the one who put forth a demand for her to be executed in the first place. But what were they going to do against the actual Trifecta? If there was anything to do about it in the first place, that was.

The Trifecta, comprised of all three nations of Meraria, where matters of international impact were decided, headed by the three ruling representatives, had decided she was a threat so dangerous she needed to die. Even after a decade of doing absolutely nothing but hiding! No… hiding wasn't exactly right…

Mathiene didn't seem to want to hide herself or Xeile, if her son's stories and Glenna's descriptions were to be believed. If she had wanted that, a Nomad tribe or complete isolation would have been much better. Even if they had to stay in a village in the early years, they easily could have just dropped off the map when the child was older. With her skill, they probably could have evaded capture for at least another few years, enough years for Xeile to safely separate from her.

So why? Why didn't she? Was it just for her son's sake that she took the risk—no, the inevitability? If that were the case, why didn't she tell him anything to warn him ahead of time?

She hadn't made it a secret she was a Guardian to him. So why didn't she say anything else? He reasoned that she may not have wanted to tell him she was doing something treasonous—like abandoning her post—but she could have warned him that at least someone would likely be looking for her. It was entirely possible that she thought she was in the clear. Who would look for her after a decade and a half?

The question stopped Kelt so completely, it took the kettle whistling to bring him back to his senses. "Damn it!" he cried, pulling his kettle away from the fire to let the water cool. He decided to focus his attention on the mortar and pestle where he ground the coffee beans. He dumped in two handfuls and started grinding vigorously. Like his thoughts, the beans slowly turned from wholes to pieces, then fragments, then to powder, easily shifted and scattered.

He transferred the powder to the small cheesecloth he used for his coffee, then quickly knotted the top. Next, he took the kettle and poured the hot water into his glass before dropping the coffee bundle in to steep. Under normal circumstances, he would have taken the time to let the water percolate through the top, but today wasn't normal. He had his least favorite paperwork to do.

Death certificates.

Using a new sheet of parchment and his pen, Kelt set about the gruesome task of outlining the incident last night and the manner in which the Spell Breakers died. He left blanks for the names and final cause of death, which would be left to a medic for an official diagnosis. He then repeated this task until he had enough copies, occasionally sipping on the coffee that was getting stronger and more acrid with each passing minute. When he sat back from his writing, his hand had a cramp and his coffee was almost undrinkable. He forced the drink down with a grimace and stood up, exhaustion trying to push him back down. As he left his office, Kelt slammed into Glenna, feeling the wind leave his body as he gasped for air.

Staggering backward, he looked up. "Can I help you?" he asked. "Did you find Usumi?"

"No," Glenna said. There was a hard look on her face. She held a piece of paper out to Kelt. "I found this in her office."

"How did you get in?"

"Picked the lock. Read the note."

Kelt gave her a sideways glance, but took the note from her and flipped it open. The writing completed in a strange red ink that glistened and flickered in the light, but the script wasn't done in a hurried scrawl. The letters were clear and crisp. Kelt felt at the ink, lifting his finger. The ink was dry to the touch but still slightly tacky in texture. The weapons master turned his attention to the message itself:

The rightful king will rise once more. You will pay for what you've done, McNair. Your final defenses are stripped. Your Citadels are now all gone.

The tides of change are coming. Glory upon the baron of Idolon.

Kelt felt his stomach, already twisting under the strength of his coffee, give a particularly terrible heave. "Glenna," he said, looking up at her calmly. "I need you to signal for an emergency meeting for the leadership. Any head of a group. Put in a word with the bellman."

"Not until I find out what happened to my master," Glenna stated, planting her feet apart, folding her arms in defiance.

"The attacker wasn't after those other Elves, they were after Usumi. The whole attack at the library was so we would miss her getting abducted," Kelt said. "And it's likely the work of the Remnant."

"What would this 'Remnant' want with Usumi?"

Kelt looked at Glenna and put a hand on her shoulder. "I don't know, but I damn sure am going to find out."

THE CITADEL

Xeile stared at the ceiling and tried to suppress his mounting frustration. How much time had he wasted down here, in this place with nothing but blue light and strange crystals? His initial relief at finding out he wasn't going to be killed had quickly given way to boredom, and now, a primal fear.

Why couldn't he sleep?

He tried lying down, he had tried exercise until he was pouring sweat on the stone, but that just made him hungry. Nothing seemed to diminish his energy levels enough for him to close his eyes and drift off to that comforting black. After just a few minutes, his energy seemed to trickle back into him, pushing the omnipresent cold from his knees down to his ankles.

"What is with this place?" he whispered, the sound bouncing around the room. "What are you doing to me?"

He sat up when he heard the sound of footsteps. Without a moment of hesitation, he scurried and hid behind the altar as quietly as he could, not daring to even breathe.

"Xeile? Where might you be?"

Xeile looked over the altar and saw a very confused Dwarf looking around the room. "Oh, hey," he said, emerging from his hiding place. "Your name is... Henrik, right? You work for Kelt?"

The Dwarf nodded. "That is correct. I am one of his apprentices, in fact." He gave Xeile a small bow. "It is nice to finally meet you properly, under somewhat better circumstances."

"Indeed," Xeile agreed. "So...did you bring food or something?"

Henrik frowned, his face becoming somber. "I'm afraid not. I have a...request...or rather...a question from Kelt."

"Oh?" Xeile said, somewhat surprised. "I thought I was just going to be stuck in this hole for a while...until he figured out what to do with me." He saw Henrik look around as if he'd rather be anywhere else. That was probably not too far from the truth. This place was unsettling at best.

"Well, he wants you to…" Henrik sighed, looking at the ceiling. "*Khlaniik val draqiir nov*, ancestors save us…I can't believe I'm saying this." He looked at Xeile, his words tumbling out over themselves. "He wants you to talk to a murder victim."

Xeile took a step back. "Excuse me?"

"A person critical to our case has unfortunately perished, and we need to know if we can determine who his killer was. Or if his spirit is there at all."

Xeile swallowed. "If he died a violent, unexpected death, it's entirely possible. No guarantees on that, though. A spirit generally has an obsession that ties them to the world when their physical body dies. But…don't you have experts on this kind of thing? Magicians that are trained and whatnot?"

Henrik took a deep breath and looked around for a moment before grabbing Xeile's shoulders, staring at him with a magnified intensity, the odd shadows cast by the multiple blue crystals creating shadows and angles where there was normally friendliness. "Do you not realize how incredible your ability is?" Henrik asked quietly. "How rare it is?"

The young man shifted uncomfortably under the young Dwarf's grip. "I see dead people, it's not really that great. It's more of a pain than you'd think."

Henrik's grip tightened on his shoulders. "You don't just see spirits, though that would be rare enough. You can hear them, talk with them, and interact with them in a manner that they not only understand but can reply to."

Xeile tried to shift away again without success. Henrik continued speaking.

"Do you realize what you have? There are people in my homeland who would kill for your gift. Kill, Xeile. That is how powerful your ability is. And here, you have the chance to use it for the good of others. Please, I know you have difficulties with Kelt, to put it mildly. But the world has need of one with your talents."

Xeile shoved Henrik away, nausea rising in his stomach. "It's not good!" he said. "Nothing about what I have is good!" He pointed at Henrik. "Have you killed someone before?"

Henrik slowly shook his head.

"I have," Xeile whispered. "She just…died because I absorbed her energy." He crouched down on the ground, head in his hands, fighting the urge to scream. "I didn't even get to know her name. I never got to know anything about her. Just that she died. These powers made me into a murderer."

Henrik stepped forward and put a gentle hand on Xeile's head.

"You are not a murderer," he murmured. "You did everything you could to save Criske's mother. You saved Kelt when you could have easily done nothing. You're a good person."

"No," Xeile whispered. He looked up at Henrik. His vision was starting to blur, but he forced himself not to cry. "Of course I went out to save Kelt. He's the only family I have left, and even that's a stretch. He didn't even know I existed until a few days ago. And how could I just stand by and watch that woman die? I wouldn't be able to live with myself if I didn't do something."

Henrik exhaled, then sat down across from Xeile. "I was insensitive. Please forgive my harsh words. I have…difficulties when it comes to spirits." He paused for a moment, then nodded, as if he were coming to a decision. "How familiar are you with Dwarven religion?"

"I'm not," Xeile said. Where was he going with this?

Henrik nodded. "Fair enough. In our religion, our ancestors, our *Khlaniik*, are everything. They generally follow us around in the form of spirits, providing guidance to our decisions."

Xeile looked behind Henrik and noticed a distinct lack of spirits. "So…where's yours? If you don't mind me asking. Did they just figure that you had your life sorted out and pass on?"

Henrik forced a laugh, and Xeile shifted uncomfortably. "Not quite. You see, no *Khlaniik* came to me when I was born. I am one of the few *Khlaniik-Araq*. I have no ancestors to guide me." His voice went quiet. "And in my family… that wasn't exactly acceptable. So, I came to the Guardians, where I've been fortunate enough to find a new family. To see someone who is just able to…gather spirits to them so naturally…is rather difficult for me. I apologize."

Xeile felt guilt stab at his chest. "No, no, I'm sorry. I should have been more considerate of your position," he said. Silence fell between them again. "So, Kelt wants my help?"

Henrik nodded. "That's right."

Xeile stood up and flexed his neck. "Welp, nothing for it, then. I'll help him, but there are two things I'd like first."

Henrik looked up, his eyes flashing and a smile forming on his face. "And what might those be?"

"Guardian protection. I need to make sure no one kills me for trying to help you. Some kind of license or something to assist you. I figure you'd know what one of those might be?" Henrik nodded. Xeile swallowed and mustered up his courage for his second demand. "I want some actual clothes. Not Guardian ones, but some new clothes, new boots, and maybe a cloak. If I'm going to work with you and be seen by people, the last thing I want is to look like a beggar and embarrass the lot of you."

Henrik let out a laugh. "That's all? No other demands? Payment? Money? Favors?"

Xeile shrugged. "Isn't helping people enough? Doing the right thing is its own reward, don't you think?"

The Dwarf got to his feet and stopped laughing. He stared at Xeile for a moment, as if trying to figure something out, tilting his head to and fro. Finally, he shook his head. "I figured Criske would be right about you, but I had no idea…" Henrik turned around and started to walk away. "Watch yourself, Xeile. Men like you have a nasty habit of either saving or destroying the world."

As he watched Henrik leave, the last part of his statement rolled around in Xeile's mind.

Men like you have a nasty habit of either saving or destroying the world.

Men like you. Men like you.

What could he mean by that? A bit of time had passed with Xeile pacing around the dimly lit space until he noticed something else.

There was a chill in the air.

The Outcasts

The meeting chamber wasn't exactly a grand affair, very unlike the posh nobles' houses Criske had seen the inside of before, where gold and silver were basically mandatory parts of the decoration, with fine wood furniture, plush seating, and exotic foodstuffs on a plate for occasionally snacking.

The meeting chamber of the Guardian headquarters was clearly not a place where much was spent in pursuit of comfort. For one, the room was stuffed into the upper floors of the main citadel of the headquarters, where the armory and food stores were kept. In the summer heat, the air was stagnant and hot. Several of the small windows were thrown open in the hopes that a breeze might pass through. No such luck today.

The chairs were made of simple wood, square, and seemed deliberately crafted to cause back pain when sat in. At least, they were according to Kelt. Criske, being an apprentice, had been made to stand in a corner, with sweat dripping down his back, causing an infuriating itch that he longed to scratch but couldn't. His uniform clung to him with sweat, and he would have traded half of what little he owned for a damn drink of water.

The others sitting around the circular table didn't seem to be faring much better than Kelt, save for the single Elven woman, who was probably long since used to heat and worse in her homeland of the Tropiciea Archipelago.

The Dwarf in particular looked miserable, hunched in his leather apron with his long white beard and balding head. "Are we going to start, Keelt?" he asked, Kelt's name sounding odd in his thick accent. "This place is *nikav ahna voqdein.*"

Criske had no idea what those words translated to, but he could hazard a few guesses and agreed with them in uncomfortable silence.

"Soon. Our guest should be here soon."

Kelt's words filled the room with a sense of quiet anticipation, further augmented by the heat. Suddenly, the door opened, and Henrik stepped through. He quietly joined Criske in the corner. "Greetings, *Khlanro*," Henrik whispered. "Be prepared."

The Half-Elf was about to ask what to be prepared for, but Kelt stood up. "Before he arrives, I'm going to tell you all the entire situation. Usumi has disappeared, with a note left in her room. And it was likely left by the Remnant."

The words' effect on the council was almost instantaneous. They all looked around and at each other, overwhelmed and shocked, and clearly uncomfortable. The whole room was laced with something Criske didn't like to see in a superior's body language: fear. The balding Dwarf leaned forward. "I thought we stamped all those crazed folk out nearly eighteen years ago, Kelt. You saw to a good deal of it personally! How could they have returned? We executed anyone associated with the Remnant on the spot."

"The note left behind would suggest otherwise," Kelt said, handing it to the nearest person. She was an older Elf, but her age did little to mar her beauty, save for a few wrinkles around her eyes and faint laugh lines. Her black hair laced with silver strands was cropped short, and there was a Spell Breaker symbol on her uniform, along with two lines under it, marking her as a veteran. Retired from active Spell Breaking, but still capable of teaching. Criske couldn't help but admire the fact that after all this time, she stuck around to help out the younger folks. She looked the note over with a critical eye, then frowned. "This is rather vague, but definitely threatening. Do you think it could be an imitator?"

Kelt shrugged. "That possibility is still on the table, but as the rest of you have dealt with the Remnant, I wanted your opinion before I put the patrol into full mobilization and on high alert."

The Elf handed the note to the Dwarf, who pulled out a glass globe, which he then filled with water before peering down his hooked nose at the note. After a moment, he grunted. "It certainly looks like the type of ink they used. It's not dried blood, at least. Wrong shade. Even if it is an imitator, I'd agree with, at minimum, partial mobilization."

He handed the note to the woman on his left. It was the head medic, Nedra, who looked it over for a moment before nodding. "I'd say this would warrant it. Besides, with that boy in town, I'd rather not have him get killed when we could do something."

"Boy?" the Dwarf said sharply. He looked at Kelt. "What boy? One of these two?" the Dwarf said, pointing in the direction of Criske and Henrik.

Kelt sucked in a breath and exhaled, trying to lower his heartbeat. "No. There's a young man in our custody who has fought and driven off the monster before, but he is incredibly ill as it is."

"How could he fight off a creature like that single-handedly?" the Elf asked.

Kelt took a deep breath. "I don't know for sure, but it seems that the creature is after him, to some degree. I don't know why, and I don't think he knows himself. But I do know that he could be an incredible asset in helping us solve this case." He leaned forward, and Criske saw him proclaim the real reason the meeting was being held in the first place. "I want to bring him on as an independent aide. He can see and interact with spirits and whatever is terrorizing our city. Will you help vouch for me on this?"

"Spirits? See them? What kind of power is that? Is he some kind of medium?"

"More than a medium," Kelt said quietly. "He's…undead."

If the word "Remnant" was bad, then the word "undead" was even worse. The Dwarf actually was driven to his feet. "Undead? Are you *insane*, Kelt? There are no undead left in Meraria. It's…it's not even possible. No one has the skill to create such a being anymore. No one since Taron Idolon, the bastard himself!"

"That's why I asked you all here today," Kelt replied. "I want you to hear from eyewitness accounts, and decide for yourself, what he is."

Kelt nodded at Criske and Henrik. "Ladies and gentlemen, please welcome Mrs. Zhang to our meeting."

Criske felt his stomach flip. His mother was here? She was going to hear about the case for sure. What would she say? How much would she worry? Criske felt his anxiety rising and fought the urge to search for a nonexistent hiding place. Henrik put a hand on Criske's shoulder.

"Don't panic, *Khlanro*. Trust in her."

The Half-Elf tried to follow Henrik's advice, but his breath still caught in his throat when he saw his mother enter the room. She was wearing her best outfit, one of her dresses from older times, a brilliant red dress with a white sash at the waist. On her feet, however, was a pair of sandals favored by the Humans down south. Her hair was tied up in an elaborate braid down her back. Criske saw the handiwork of his grandfather in that. Blind he might have been, but his skills as a weaver and basket maker could still be seen in his clever fingers. She wore no makeup, but she didn't need it. He could still hear the men in the room suck in a collective breath at her beauty.

"Hello," she said with a polite bow. "I am here to tell my story." Her accent was heavy against Kelt's crisp words.

Kelt nodded politely to her. "Yes. Would you mind starting from the beginning when you first noticed the creature?"

Mrs. Zhang nodded. "Yes. I first notice the *ba-xi* when I was walking home from work at tavern. The air got cold. Not good, so I try to run. But pair of big red eyes chase me. I try to lose it, but got stopped in alley. Then, boy named Exile came out and drove it off with chain and black glow around his body. Hurt him a lot. Then, ghost come out and glow, give him power. After that, he tell me to go get help from Guardians and disappear. He in my tavern few days ago before that. Nice boy, but look very sick."

"How so?" the Dwarf asked.

Criske's mother tilted her head and looked at him, trying to figure out what the Dwarf meant. The Elf woman looked over and spoke quickly in High Elvish. "He wants you to describe what the boy looked like."

Mrs. Zhang's eyes widened in recognition, and she clapped her hands together. "Ah, okay! His skin very gray, unhealthy looking. His eyes all black with no color. He cough up blood too. In a lot of pain and limping."

The Dwarf nodded. "You said that he had a black glow around his body. Can you describe it in more detail?"

She thought for a moment. "It is like skin, but not. Around his body, but it has…cracks, like broken pot. When he attack creature, the black went up chain and seemed to hit creature. It was very big, like giant horse with antlers of deer."

The Dwarf stood, his eyes wide. Although it didn't mean much to Kelt or anyone else in the room, the Dwarf seemed to know what it was. "No…it can't be. An auramancer in this day and age?"

Mrs. Zhang give the Dwarf a confused look. Kelt stood, shaking Mrs. Zhang's hand and bowing to her slightly. "Thank you very much for your testimony, Mrs. Zhang."

Criske's mother bowed in response. "No, thank you. Guardians so nice taking care of my family. You watch my *Kiresu*, he find trouble if it not find him first." With that and a final bow to everyone else in the room, she left as though gliding away on a cloud. Not for the first time, Criske wondered how his father had ever been so fortunate to marry his mother.

The Dwarf looked at Kelt in dismay. "This undead is also an auramancer?"

Kelt frowned. "What do you mean?" he asked. "I've never encountered one of those. I said he was undead because his aura is broken, but his soul is still in his body. Does that make him an auramancer, Raqman?"

The Dwarf shook his head. "No, though the fact he's alive…I didn't think it possible. An auramancer…it is very old magic. Back when the Territories and *Khlaniikar* fought over resources up north, we outmatched them in every way.

Technology, tactics, even training. But, there was one group of magicians that made us stop."

"Idolon!" Henrik blurted.

All eyes turned to Henrik, who quickly looked at the floor.

"It was the Second Timber War, fought around nine centuries before the Trifecta was formed," he mumbled. "A magician named Vosh Idolon used necromancy and other magic to make the Dwarves pursue peace. The other Territory barons cast a vote and gave him his own fief as a result. He was Taron Idolon's ancestor."

Raqman nodded in approval. "You are correct. And some of those magicians were auramancers. The Trifecta has banned it, but there hasn't been a registered auramancer since well before the Trifecta was formed. As it requires your aura being broken, no one thought it was worth the risk. Without exception, auramancers live short lives because of wild magic poisoning. But…to be undead and an auramancer…" Raqman shuddered. "Would the Remnant create such a weapon?"

Criske thought for a moment. Something clicked inside his mind, a terrible picture weaving itself together for him in less than a moment. "I don't think the Remnant did," he said. "I think…I think the Guardians did."

The room went completely silent. All of the summer heat was ignored. Every single head turned toward Criske. Kelt's face darkened. "Would you mind explaining how you came to that conclusion, lad?"

"Xeile's mother was a Guardian who ran away," Criske clarified. "You don't do that lightly. She knew she could be executed for it. Why run away just because of pregnancy when you can retire for medical reasons, with all the honors and pay? Unless she knew there was something about her pregnancy she wanted to hide. I mean, shame could be a factor, sure. But to hide completely? For around fifteen years? No way. She knew he'd be different, and she knew that people would want him for some reason or another. So she hauled it, trying to hide him the best she could."

Raqman's face went red. "A bold claim you have no proof of! What use would the Guardians have for taking a *small child*?"

Criske looked at the Dwarf and shrugged. "I don't know. Fighting spirits used by the Remnant? He seems to do a pretty damn good job of it, yeah? I'm not saying we would, but his mom probably thought it was a possibility. Barring that, she probably thought it'd at least paint a massive target on his back, yeah? Even if the Guardians didn't use him in a battle, he'd always be wanted by bad people for something. No chance of a normal life for him, yeah?"

"That still doesn't explain how the Guardians are at fault for creating this undead abomination!" Raqman said.

The Half-Elf's temper rose. "Really? His mother was a Guardian. What one of us does, we all share the blame for. She didn't feel like she could trust her superiors. Whose fault is that? Ours. Maybe, if we had been more trustworthy, this wouldn't have happened. Honestly, we're damn lucky he hasn't used his abilities to hurt us yet…sirs and ma'am." Kelt gave him a stare that made it quite clear that he was to shut his mouth. Criske felt his face flush as he went silent.

"Considering I killed his mother, I'd say we're lucky indeed," Kelt agreed. "And furthermore, he's in our custody and willing to help us, if you'll sign off on it."

The weight of the proposal seemed to make the shoulders of everyone at the table sag.

To Criske, it wasn't something that needed a lot of thought. Then again, he had actually talked to Xeile. He had seen how strange Xeile was, how oddly powerful his sense of justice was, to the point where it overrode his sense of vengeance. The others in the room hadn't seen that.

"We have him in custody? Where?" Raqman said. "And you want to ask him for help? Despite all of the potential dangers?"

"He is currently in a safe location," Kelt explained. "He's already given me his word he'll help me with this case, so long as I investigate who ordered the execution of his mother. I just need to make it official with a writ of temporary employment. He'll be a mercenary to us."

Criske saw the trepidation on everyone's face, and Kelt's impatience starting to rise. "It's the easiest way for us to keep an eye on him to make sure he doesn't hurt anyone, and it could potentially help us catch who's behind this. I had four Spell Breakers die instantly when they tried to attack this thing." Dark silence filled the room. "He's fought it off twice now. I'm not going to throw my people into the jaws of death if there's another solution," Kelt added after no one made any movement.

"You didn't seem to have that problem six years ago," Raqman muttered.

Kelt stood up so quickly, his chair fell over, slamming to the ground with a loud bang. "What was that?" he grated.

Henrik stepped forward and grabbed Kelt's wrist. Kelt tried to pull out of it, glaring down at his apprentice. "*What?*"

"Does being angry now solve our problem?" Henrik asked. He looked at Raqman. "Does dredging up the past solve anything at the moment? We're here for solutions, not to jab at old wounds."

The young Dwarf's voice seemed to fill the room as he continued speaking, his words bouncing off the walls. "You are the leaders of the Guardians. You are to conduct yourselves as an example for others. Just as we give you our obedience, we expect integrity in return. That is the job of a superior to a junior. The Guardians have stood as a testament of unity among our three nations, a core that binds us together. How can we dare call ourselves that if we fight among ourselves? Now, having an undead and apparent auramancer with us does come with risks, but who are we to shrink from a challenge when we have the ability to save others? If we do not do something to save and protect, no matter the risk to ourselves, can we truly call ourselves protectors? No, we're little more than cowards!" Henrik brought his fist down on the table with a force that made Criske and the rest of the people flinch.

Criske saw Henrik's locked jaw, withering gaze, and flaring nostrils. He fought the desire to take a step backward. It was like staring down a man in a dark alley with not just a knife but a damn war hammer. "You know lives are at stake! But as we sit here, with each passing moment, Usumi could be dying or worse. There is a solution in front of you. Take it. If you don't, what good are you?"

Henrik let go of Kelt's wrist, and Criske already started to see the bruises forming on his skin. Henrik gave one last look around the room. "I thought we had more honor than this," he said flatly. "But I suppose not."

He walked out of the room without being dismissed, and no one stopped him.

Everyone was silent for a good two minutes before Kelt spoke. "You know…I never thought I'd have to be verbally lashed by my own apprentice."

"He should be facing the lash for insubordination," Raqman said. "He still had a point. We can't cower and chatter about like moles in a den. I approve the use of this…auramancer."

"As do I," said the Elf Spell Breaker. "The time for being overly cautious has long since passed at this point."

The head medic nodded twice. "The boy was already trying to solve the case when we found him. He'd keep trying even if we didn't use him. We can't have people thinking vigilante investigation is acceptable. It'd undermine trust in us and set a dangerous precedent."

Kelt nodded. "Then it's decided. We will employ Taeris as our first undead investigator."

The Soldier

Kelt strode out of the council and looked around for Henrik. He was nowhere to be seen.

"Sir!" Criske called. "Sir, should I go get Taeris?"

"No," Kelt said over his shoulder, "you're going to find me your fellow apprentice and drag him back here. I'm going to grab Glenna, and we're going to tell Xeile about his new employment."

"Why are you bringing Glenna?"

"Insurance that Xeile doesn't change his mind and try to murder me."

"And you think Glenna would stop him?"

Kelt sucked in a breath. "Good point. I'll try to win her over first, and then we can work together to convince him. Go find Henrik so I can have a word with him. We'll meet up at the library. Any luck, I'll have Xeile in tow, and we can finally get back on this case." Criske saluted and ran off, leaving Kelt to his own devices.

It was midafternoon, and an absolutely sweltering day. The sun seemed determined to force everyone to run for cover. Kelt trudged his way to the best place he could guess Glenna would be: Usumi's quarters. Sure enough, after a few knocks, Glenna called through the door in a groggy voice, "Yeah?"

Kelt immediately turned around. Glenna wasn't wearing her standard uniform. She was in her underthings and nothing else. Glenna's daze seemed to disappear in an instant. "Oh, damn it!" She slammed the door shut. Around five minutes later, she opened the door in full uniform.

"Sorry about that," she said. "I was up late last night doing some reading on magical creatures and shamans. Must've fallen asleep. What can I do for you…sir?"

The weapons master loosed a sigh. "I need your help with Xeile. I've managed to get the council here to approve of using his help. I'd like to bring you along when I go get him…and bring you onto the case… He needs someone he can trust. Right now, you're the only one he has. Do you understand where I am coming from? I could order you to help, but I really don't want to."

Glenna took a deep breath, rubbing her temples with her fingertips. "If it's for his sake, then yes. I will help you."

Kelt felt his heart leap. It was the first good news he had gotten all day. Now if he could get some sleep, he'd be in a really grand state.

Except there were murder victims. And a monster on the loose. And an undead who hated him for murdering his mother. And that mother's writ of execution was strange to start with.

Other than that, life would be grand.

Sighing, he set off with Glenna, and the two of them traveled in awkward silence. "So… are you and Xeile, an…item?"

Glenna looked up at him with slight disgust but answered anyway. "Yes. We happen to be engaged now." She held up her hand, showing a small wooden ring. "Though he coughed up blood as he proposed and asked if I wanted to leave him in the process." She looked at the ring, and a warm smile crossed her face. "Then again, we've never exactly been conventional."

Kelt scratched the back of his head. "Well… did you two fall in love immediately? I can't imagine Mathiene being too happy with Xeile hanging around you all the time."

Glenna snorted. "Actually, she was rather concerned I'd set him on fire, but she warmed up to me in time." She looked at Kelt, her deep-purple eyes echoing the frown she wore. "Did you happen to know Mathiene at all? You know…before you…"

"Some," Kelt murmured. "We worked together on several missions against the Remnant. She was a good fighter, but a bit…temperamental. And ridiculously strong. I've never met a stronger woman in my life. She picked up a Dwarf in full plate and threw him over a table with one arm."

"Why was she throwing a Dwarf over a table?"

"Tried to cheat her at cards," Kelt said, grinning at the memory. "It was a long night after that. I had to do a lot of paperwork."

Glenna stared at him for a moment as if she were trying to figure something out. Then, she shook her head and kept walking. Kelt would have asked her what she was thinking, but he wasn't sure he wanted to know the answer. They hurried over to the small garden that hid the underground chamber. Kelt immediately noticed that the air dropped in temperature. He looked over to see Glenna put her hands on her belt as if ready to draw a weapon, but he didn't see one readily available. Kelt drew his sword. "Be very careful about your magic," he said quietly. "Your aura can break from the slightest touch of this monster."

The magician's apprentice nodded.

Crouching and cautious, the two walked toward the stone that needed to be lifted upward. The temperature continued to drop to the point where Kelt could see his breath. "This isn't good," Glenna muttered.

At that moment, the cobblestones exploded outward, sending chunks of rock flying. "Get down!" Kelt screamed, tackling Glenna to the ground, shielding her with his body. Several fragments raked across his back, leaving bloody furrows that made him grunt in pain. He rolled over, sword at the ready.

A pair of malevolent eyes stared down at him, giant red spheres of wrath. He heard a terrible keening cry. There wasn't time to do anything else, so Kelt shoved Glenna as far away as he could so that the creature wouldn't hit her, and braced for pain.

"Stop!" The red eyes froze as a bloody figure emerged from the hole in the ground behind them. Xeile clambered out of the earth, clutching one arm, staggering. "Kelt, get Glenna out of here!" he yelled. "I'll hold it off."

Kelt didn't hesitate. He dropped his sword, scrambling to his feet, scooping a still-stunned Glenna up in his arms and carrying her away despite her protests. The creature tried to follow, but Xeile jumped in front of its path. As Kelt looked over his shoulder, he saw Xeile standing weaponless before a giant horse like beast with a colossal rack of antlers, each one ending in bulbs of black flames.

"You will not touch them!" Xeile declared. His voice seemed unnaturally loud, and not entirely his, as if he were a choir speaking in unison. "I will stop you every time. We are the Citadel, the greatest and final defense!"

The weapons master froze and whipped around. He had only heard that statement twice in his life. He turned back around and doubled his speed, sprinting with Glenna in tow. "Kelt, *what is going on?*"

"I don't know," he said, breathing hard. "But it's about to—"

There was a terrible screeching sound, and a bestial scream of pain. Kelt heard Xeile let out a cry. Then, a loud bang like a crack of thunder, followed by a deafening silence. A wave of cold hit Kelt's back, sharp enough to make him gasp. He rounded the corner and dropped Glenna off. "Stay here!" he commanded her. He turned back around the corner to find out what had happened.

It wasn't difficult to see.

The creature, apparently crazed with pain and desperate to get away from Xeile, had smashed a hole through the outer walls of headquarters before disappearing. Xeile was lying on the ground, covered in a layer of what looked like frost. Kelt hurried toward the boy, picking up his sword along the way, just in case. "Xeile, are you—"

"Don't get any closer!" Xeile shouted.

Kelt stopped immediately. Xeile put one hand on the ground, then another, forcing himself onto his hands and knees, his entire body shuddering. "I thought…you said…that chamber warded off spirits…" he said, his breath coming out as a light mist.

"It's supposed to," Kelt said. "I guess our monster isn't a spirit…"

"Get Criske, and some of those stones," Xeile said, his words labored. "Please…it's…it's the only thing…that helps…"

It was only through years of physical conditioning that Kelt was able to run as fast as he could to the medical bay, procure three resonance stones, and then immediately sprint to the library, where a very confused Criske and Henrik looked at him as he took the shallow stairs two at a time. "Xeile needs you," he said. "Come on!"

Criske immediately followed Kelt. A small crowd had started to form around the scene, talking quietly among themselves.

"Move!" Kelt commanded. The group immediately parted, allowing Criske and Kelt through. Kelt shoved a stone into Criske's hand. Glenna immediately snatched the other two away from Kelt and started filling the stones with energy from her aura, sweat forming on her brow under the strain of the task.

Though Criske could fill his with more energy, Glenna's training seemed to make her remarkably efficient. No, even with training, Kelt hadn't seen a magician fill a resonance stone so quickly. For every one transfer of energy that Criske used on Xeile, Glenna gave four. What was even more remarkable was how much energy Xeile's aura held, a black, ethereal crackling force that surrounded his skin and seemed to have no limit to the amount it could drink, a dark miasma that just refused to clear around his body.

Time passed in minutes, but Kelt felt like time had slowed to a crawl. He turned to the crowd that had gathered and was watching in silence. *I need Nedra,* he thought. *But I have to stay here to watch Criske…* An idea came to him. "One of you sorry lot go get the head medic!" Kelt pointed at a male Elf. "You! Go get her!"

The Elf nodded and ran away to find her.

Kelt pointed at a nearby Dwarf. "You! Go find out from our head administrator who the master mason is for repairs. Tell him Inquisitor Kelt McNair wants a work order put in." The Dwarf saluted and then ran off. "And the rest of you need to clear out," Kelt said. "This area is still potentially dangerous." Gradually, the gathering of people dispersed. Kelt turned his attention back to Criske and Glenna.

They were still feverishly working, Glenna showing signs of strain under the rapid turn-around she was producing with her crystals. Criske wasn't showing signs of strain, but an odd shimmer had encased his body as he worked, and he bit the inside of his cheek as he concentrated on the task at hand. His eyes were a strange pale color Kelt had seen before. Just one more question that he needed an answer to and didn't have enough time to investigate.

As Criske put another stone over Xeile and the energy was sucked out of it, the young man let out a gasp. Kelt recoiled. Looming over Xeile were eighteen figures in various stages of battle armor and…Guardian uniforms? They were all holding weapons, staring at Xeile with concerned expressions, seeming to kneel in midair. "Live, brother." Their whispered words reached Kelt, barely discernible from a spring breeze. "Fight on, brother. We are here. Fight on, brother…"

Xeile let out a gasp and sat up, letting out a cry of pain. "Thrice-damned evils! It's freezing!" he cried. He turned and saw Criske and Glenna, as if just suddenly being made aware of their presence. He hung his head, his shoulders hunched, and he drew his knees up to his chest, wrapping his arms around them. "I'm sorry," he said. "I couldn't even catch it." His arms tightened so hard around his legs, they began to shake.

Glenna sat back, looking like she was about to be sick. Criske shook his head. "No way. You prevented it from killing anyone else here. That's more than enough for now."

"It's not good enough," Xeile said, his jaw clenching with grim resolve. "I have to catch it. I'm the only one who can." Criske fell silent, unable to dispute the argument.

Glenna reached out and put a hand on Xeile's shoulder. "It isn't your fault. You'll get him next time, when we're better prepared. Now stop moping. Unless you want to see how good I am with fire again."

Xeile's head shot up and he shook his head. "I'm stopping," he said, holding up his hands quickly. "See, stopping. No moping about for me. I'm fit as can be." Despite his reassurance, Kelt could still see his hands were shaking.

"Can you stand?" Criske said, getting to his own feet before he offered his hand to Xeile.

The young man took the Half-Elf's hand, hauling himself shakily to his feet. He turned to Kelt. "So…where am I starting on your investigation?" Xeile said. "You needed my help, right? Considering a whole group of people saw me, I'm guessing the time for hiding is over?"

Kelt blinked a few times. "You're not helping with anything until you are medically cleared," he said firmly.

"But the case—"

Kelt held up a hand, cutting Xeile off. "You are more important than the case at the moment. I can't have you falling ill in the middle of the investigation. Guardians look after their own," he said. "And the last thing I need is Glenna distracted because you're unwell."

Xeile clamped his mouth shut and nodded. "Okay."

It didn't take long for Nedra to arrive, breathless and rather disgruntled. "Less than an hour!" she cried. "I leave you alone for less than an hour and you've already broken something, Kelt!" Despite all of her grumbling, she did give Xeile a full look over, checking his limbs, his black eyes, his heart, and his breathing before delivering her verdict.

"He's a little shaky," she said. "But he'll make it. I wouldn't do much physical activity over the next few days, and a resonance stone once or twice a day wouldn't hurt either. You've got plenty of signs of wild magic poisoning still in your system, but it seems to have lessened significantly. Still too high for my tastes, though."

Kelt nodded, taking the information into account. "I'll look after him, I promise."

Nedra squinted at him, disbelieving. "See that you do, Kelt." She walked away, leaving the four others standing in silence.

"Come on," Kelt said. "We should head to the library and at least see if the assistant left a spirit behind." He looked at Xeile. "Can you do that, or do you need to rest?"

Xeile nodded. "I can. It won't require any energy or exertion."

"Alright. Criske, you support Xeile if he needs it. Henrik, lead the way."

Criske walked side by side with Xeile while Glenna and Kelt followed up behind them. "Is he bluffing?" Kelt asked.

Glenna shook her head. "He's a terrible liar. If he says he'll be fine, then he'll be fine."

They continued walking in silence before a question entered Kelt's mind. "What did you do to him with fire?" he asked.

Glenna smiled at the memory. "Well, he wouldn't stop staring at me as I practiced. I was…having a bad day. I told him to stop, and he didn't. So I singed his eyebrows off. Took them weeks to grow back in."

Kelt let out a small laugh. "Remind me not to upset you too much. I'm not sure I could handle your wrath if that's someone you love."

Glenna looked at him with a carefully neutral expression, her deep-purple eyes unreadable. "Probably not. Let's just hope you never have to find out, for Xeile's sake. He may have forgiven you, but I'm not exactly the forgiving type…sir."

She sped up her walking so that she was beside with Xeile, grasping his hand firmly in hers, leaving Kelt to ponder whether he had just been threatened or given an objective answer. He wasn't sure which option made him more uncomfortable.

An attack, murder victims, with the criminal still on the loose, and now a mage that had bones to pick with him still.

Yes, besides all those, today was shaping up to be a grand day indeed.

THE CITADEL

Xeile held Glenna's hand and tried his best to look like he wasn't going to be sick. Fighting off that creature had made the painful cold surge back from his ankles straight into his upper abdomen and fingertips. He considered himself lucky that Criske and Glenna were nearby, though Glenna didn't look fantastic either. Her dark-brown hair was stuck to her head with sweat, and she did appear a little green around the face. Criske seemed none the worse for the wear, besides being a little out of breath from the running he had to do to get there. Xeile reached out and grabbed Glenna's hand. Her hand wrapped around his, interlocking their fingers in a tight grasp.

"You're cold," she murmured.

"Yeah, that happens," Xeile said. "I did ask Kelt if he could get me some clothes if I help him. I don't think Henrik's gotten the chance to tell him my demand for clothes yet."

"I don't think Henrik's gotten the chance to say anything to Kelt after roasting him over an open spit, with all of the other senior leadership," Criske said dryly. He shook his head. "I mean, I know I've got a bit of an attitude, but at least I have the common sense to not go off on people bigger than me…most of the time."

Xeile nodded. "Fair enough. So… you're Kelt's apprentice? How'd you manage to land that?"

Criske frowned and shrugged. "Just kinda happened. I went to report the first murder I found while out on patrol, and boom, I'm an apprentice and Henrik is too. Not complaining too much, just wish it would be a little safer. My parents are probably worried sick, though they would never say so to my face."

Parents. Xeile had difficulty remembering much. His mother really never seemed to worry, except when he wandered off when he was younger, but most parents did that, right? "Well, everyone's parents do that, I suppose," he reasoned. "Except maybe Glenna's. They were more worried about what she would do to others than the other way 'round."

"Valid fear," Criske said, grinning.

Glenna rolled her eyes but smiled nonetheless. "Just don't you forget, Val-Zhang: I'm the best damn magician in the Guardians. I have the power to give you a sudden and terrible haircut."

Criske's hands reflexively went to his golden locks, his brown eyes wide in mock terror. "Not my wondrous hair! Oh no!" He lowered his hands and raised an eyebrow. "I may be half Elf, but I don't care about my appearance that much. If I did, I probably wouldn't have joined the Guardians." He leaned into the other two. "The uniforms have no sense of poise. All that gray everywhere, yeah?"

Xeile and Glenna cracked smiles at that. Xeile's smile quickly faded as he saw the destruction of the library. They had managed to cover the entrance in some kind of sheet, but Xeile could still see the broken and chipped stone of the stairs. Henrik was standing there expectantly, his arms behind his back, staring intently at them as they moved forward. He had been quiet, and removed himself from the conversation with a grave expression.

"Hey," Criske said in greeting.

Henrik merely nodded at Criske in silence before turning to Xeile. "I have taken the liberty of getting you some new clothing. They are inside, and you've already got Kelt's protection." The Dwarf then turned his attention to Kelt, his face like the stones his people loved to work with.

"So, what is my punishment, sir?"

Kelt looked down at Henrik, his expression critical as he rubbed a hand over his face in frustration. "I do have to punish you," he agreed. He stood in silence and then seemed to reach a decision. "You have two options: ten lashes and discharge or twenty lashes and you stay enlisted."

"Twenty," Henrik said.

"I was hoping you'd say that," Kelt said with a grim smile. He put a hand on Henrik's shoulder. "It'll probably happen tomorrow. But I want you to know that just because you're being punished, that doesn't mean your words were wrong. I expect you to keep calling me out and holding me accountable. That is your right as an apprentice. But make sure it stays between us and Criske, are we clear? I'm not sure I could talk them down to so few lashes next time."

"Yes, sir," Henrik said, swallowing.

"We'll just have to work on your delivery when other people are involved. Inside. We have to keep an eye on Xeile, make sure he doesn't run off."

Xeile held up his hand that was grasping Glenna's. "I'm not going anywhere," he said firmly. "I gave you my word to help you. I intend to keep it."

Kelt looked at Xeile and had a strange expression on his face. Was it pain? "Well, good. Let's see you get to work. Any spirits here?"

That was a rather strange question. Of course there were spirits here. Most of them were busy walking up and down the stairs, muttering to themselves. A few were sitting there, immersed in deep thoughts about questions they probably didn't have answers to in life. Xeile wondered just how strong their curiosity had to be to keep them bound to this world of existence long after they had left their mortal bodies behind. "Yes," he said. "There's plenty. But…are any of these the one I need to talk to?"

"I'm not sure. Do you see hair color? Eye color?"

Xeile shook his head. "No. I don't think their eye color from the afterlife matches their real ones…" Xeile frowned and tried to think about a new problem. How would he be able to find a spirit that he'd never met before? A few ideas came to him. "Do you know where he died? Spirits tend to stay around those areas, unless somewhere else was incredibly important to them. And what was he last doing?"

Kelt frowned. "He was going to get me records related to anyone named 'Harvest' that was in Guardian service, I think. But then he was apparently stabbed in the back, if Criske's estimation is accurate. It probably is," he said with a nod in the Half-Elf's direction, who stood a little straighter at the acknowledgment.

The weapons master pulled back the tarp and led them inside. Two large Elven women in half-plate crossed their spears as Kelt went to enter a particular hallway. He looked at them in confusion. "I'm doing an investigation, stand aside, please."

"You cannot pass by order of the baron."

Kelt's eyes widened. "What? The baron? *Where are your papers for that?*" Even though the Territorial baronies elected a king from among themselves, in their own Territory, a baron's word was law. Besides running their own barony, the king only served as a diplomatic representative and head of the military in times of crisis.

The warden reached into her pocket and handed Kelt a note. Kelt opened the note and peered at it, then looked at the red wax seal at the bottom. "*What?*" He looked up. "We're finally making progress! I need to get through here!"

"The baron has deemed that you were moving insufficiently fast. He is now personally overseeing the investigation."

The weapons master took a deep breath and swallowed the fireball temper Xeile could see desperately wanted to escape. Kelt cleared his throat, and turned to Criske and Henrik. "Well, you two, looks like we're—"

"Might I see the paper?" Henrik asked. "If you please, sir."

Kelt handed him the slip. Henrik read it over carefully, and then a grin broke out over his face. He stepped up to the warden. "I notice that the baron neglected to mention independently employed investigators. He's not a Guardian, but he is working the case. Does that give him permission to pass through?" Henrik jerked his head toward Xeile. "If you try to stop him, that'd be a violation of article seventeen, section two, paragraph nine of the laws of the First Trifecta. Do you want that on your record? And I will happily report you to the administrator. As you're probably aware, he has a deep and abiding love for paperwork and following all of the rules."

The warden looked at Xeile and her eyes narrowed. "You're the independent investigator? Who are you?"

He looked at the wardens, both of whom were as pale as the moon. "If you don't step aside, do you want me to ask the council to pay you a visit, then? Or we can just go get Head Medic Nedra. I'm sure she'd love to hear why you are barring me from finding a murderer. Does that sound fair?" Xeile asked. He tried his best to make himself sound friendly and cooperative. The wardens essentially flattened themselves against the wall to let him in. Xeile pressed his lips against Glenna's quickly. "I'll be back soon. You have my word."

Glenna nodded and folded her arms expectantly, glaring at the wardens as Xeile continued down the hallway toward the records and the supposed spot of the murder.

Despite all of his fears of not being able to find the right spirit, he seemed to have worried unnecessarily. The hall reminded him a lot of the woods, calm, and with practically no spirits to speak of. Animals seldom left a spirit behind, as they rarely clung to pieces of their past that were unresolved. When they did, they were usually malevolent. Xeile shuddered as he thought of the spirit of a horse that was abused that chased him for miles as he made his way to Trifectus, confusing him with its previous owner. He kept a sharp eye out for any possible spirits. Some of them could be so faint that only their eyes would be visible. Those flat, disklike eyes made the hair on his neck rise.

The stones here didn't look like most of the building as he walked down the hallway. They looked older, darker, more filled with a history of wear and tear than the rest of the library. After a few moments of searching, he finally found a male spirit with sea-green eyes floating in the hallway, going back and forth in what seemed to be a panic.

Xeile sucked in a breath. "Hey," he called out. "What's wrong?"

The spirit ignored him, continuing to float back and forth for a little while, so Xeile sat himself down in the spirit's path and waited.

Eventually, the spirit came back and stopped short as if Xeile were some kind of door or fence. The spirit looked down. "Oh. Harvest…I have to get the records for Harvest…I can't find them…"

Xeile got to his feet. "No…not at the moment, but I need your help finding something. Inquisitor McNair asked me…to help him find…" Xeile wracked his brain for something official sounding. He needed to keep talking with the spirit if he was going to get any answers. But that would take days before the spirit really started to engage with him, if the experience with the spirit of the Elven woman was anything to go by. He felt a lance of pain in his chest and looked up at the spirit. "Can you help me find someone? I need to know her name. She was an Elf woman, with longer hair. About as tall as me… She lived and worked in this city, I think." The spirit gave him a blank stare. "She knew Harvest," Xeile continued. "You might be able to find records there."

The spirit's face lit up in a bright smile. "Oh. Records for Harvest…"

"Yes, records for Harvest," Xeile repeated gently. "Can you show me where the records are?"

The spirit looked farther down the hallway but made no motion to move. So, Xeile kept going down the hallway. The spirit followed him, a puzzled expression on its face, as if it was trying to remember something but couldn't quite get it to emerge.

The hallway now had an ominous feel to it. There were no windows farther back, and after Xeile stepped through a doorway that appeared out of place, there were no windows in the room. It was all lit by candlelight, and not beeswax candlelight either. No, this flame wasn't bright and clear. They were tallow candles, yellow and flickering, casting dim light upon the hallway, just enough to see where the hallway led but not enough to see everything. The air was dry here, and it made Xeile long for a cool drink of water. However, the summer heat didn't reach them here. Was it the thick stone walls that blocked the outside world? Or was something more arcane at work?

Even if there wasn't, this place's air seemed to tingle and crawl with some kind of energy that made Xeile shiver. "Hey," he said in a tentative whisper. "Is anyone else there?" His voice carried in an echo before fading into silence. If there were any other spirits, they didn't emerge at his words.

Checking behind him to see that the spirit was still there, Xeile continued down the hallway, his footsteps felt like a violation of a sacred order of silence. The loudness of his footfalls made a thought come to mind. No wonder the person who killed the assistant needed a distraction. Every single sound carried in this place. It reminded him of the wind on a moor. "Alright," he whispered. "Just get on with it." He picked up his walking speed and reached the end of the hallway, only to find a flight of stairs that spiraled downward. "Damn it," he whispered. "Why does everything have to be in dark and uncomfortable places?"

Still, he took a nearby candle and its holder from the wall before hurrying down the stairs. As soon as he reached the bottom, his foot made contact with something that crunched like a dead leaf from a tree in autumn. Xeile pulled his foot back and peered down at the ground to notice that it was actually a scroll of parchment. He then looked up to see that the thief had neither been gentle nor caring with the archive. Multiple books and scrolls had been rapidly thrown about the room in what looked like a frantic search.

Xeile looked around the room and quickly found that there were candles down here as well. Sharing the flame of his own, he quickly lit up the room with a dim glow, delighted to discover that they were the steady light from beeswax. He set his candle down on a nearby table and got to work, scanning the room, hoping partially that the assistant would give him some help. He hadn't read anything of substance in at least a few months, and his skills were far from stellar at this point, and he had no idea how to read Dwarf or Elvish either.

Still, he saw the section for all of the Guardians with the names that started with *H* was empty. "Hmm…so they made off with those," Xeile whispered. "But what about the people that worked under Harvest…"

He scanned through the racks and racks of documents, occasionally climbing up a nearby ladder to get a closer look. That was a tricky process, and several times, he nearly lost his footing and dropped his candle. After a particularly nasty attempt, he sucked in a deep breath and let out a low whistle, turning to the spirit. "Close one, eh? Could have set the whole place on fire…"

A question rammed forward into Xeile's mind. Why didn't the criminal set the entire archive on fire? It would have been the easiest way to cover up the tracks and their motives for sending the monster. They wouldn't have had to kill anyone either. Why would they get rid of the perfect chance to erase their presence? After all, there would have been no way to tell who started the fire in the first place. There was only one reason Xeile could think of that they wouldn't have burned this place to the ground: they would need to come back here for some reason.

But what reason would that be? Were they looking to steal all of the records? He frowned and shook his head. No. If they stole too many of them, it'd be watched day and night. There were too many records here to even consider that practical. Plus, they'd have to come back here, and that was risky in its own…right…

Xeile slid down the ladder and started looking around rapidly with his candle. The only reason he could think someone would want to come back here was either for information, which he had already ruled out, or it had another purpose that was well hidden, and the thief knew about it.

He kept searching the room, but try as he might, nothing seemed out of place beyond the scattered scrolls all over the ground. So, he set his candle aside on a nearby rickety table and got to work rolling up the scrolls and stacking them in a pile. As he was stacking, he was aware the spirit was watching him with the usual sort of detachment Xeile was used to. Then, as Xeile picked up a handful of scrolls, the spirit's eyes went wide and it stared at the ground.

"Harvest…" the spirit whispered. "I have to find Harvest…"

Xeile looked up at him and frowned. "I'm trying," Xeile said patiently, "but it's hard to do without your help. Do you know anything about Harvest?"

The spirit's eyes didn't move from a spot on the ground. Instead, it just clamped its hands over its ears and shook its head. Panic filled its expression. "No…no…no…it wasn't me. I didn't see anything…please…please don't…" The air noticeably dropped in temperature. Xeile reached out and grabbed the spirit by its shoulder. The chill left the air as the spirit looked up as if suddenly realizing he was there again.

"I'm here. I can help you," Xeile said. "It's okay. I'm here. You didn't see anything. I'm not going to hurt you."

The spirit slowly lowered its hands from its ears, and Xeile felt the cold rise slightly in his legs, biting, gnawing at him. The panic in the spirit's face faded and it looked at Xeile. "You… you saw it too?"

"Saw what?" Xeile asked gently, risking holding on to the spirit for longer. The cold was really starting to stab at him now. "What did you see?"

The spirit pointed at the ground. "She came from there. A woman…from the deep…" The spirit shuddered slightly. "She chased me when I went to get McNair…" The spirit looked up at Xeile. "I died…" it whispered. "I bled to death…" It started to shake, his face one of horror. "Oh, Great Answer…I'm dead! I died!"

Xeile let go of the spirit as a surge of painful cold went up his arm, sucking in air in between clenched teeth and fighting back tears. The spirit looked at him. "I'm dead…" it whispered. "But you can see me."

Xeile froze, looking at the spirit in mute surprise. He nodded a few times. The spirit floated toward him. "My name is Alvor. The person just came out of the ground. It wasn't my fault, I tried to get help so they wouldn't steal the records… I tried—"

The living young man held up two hands. "Relax," said Xeile. "I know you did. That was very brave of you. You don't have to worry anymore. Kelt and I are going to solve this, but I need your help. You said something about a woman from the deep?"

Alvor nodded. "She just came up from the ground, I didn't understand. She started ripping records off the walls…"

Xeile turned his attention to the floor, taking slow, tentative steps, feeling each stone under his foot. He wondered why they didn't smooth over the floor in this place, maybe add some rush mats to better preserve the scrolls that were on the ground. Then, he saw it. Almost seamless with the floor, there was a round tile made of what looked like a similar stone material. The only difference is that this seemed to have a small handle-like piece carved into a divot.

There was no way he could lift something that heavy on his own. Not without some leverage or way to make it easier on his back. He'd ask for help, but Kelt and the others weren't allowed back here. Looking down at the small handle, Xeile had an idea. Taking his shirt off, he quickly tore it into strips, tying the pieces together with sturdy knots. He threaded his improvised rope around the handle several times and grabbed both ends. His muscles screamed in protest as he walked backward, pulling with as much weight as he could muster. A few months ago, he'd probably have no issue with this, but that was then and this was now. Sweat started forming on his head, back, and legs. The stone started to lift, slowly, oh so slowly, out of its resting place on the ground. Just as he felt like his arms were going to give out, he felt a surge of warmth up his back that spread down into his legs.

He looked over his shoulders and saw Alvor grabbing him by the back and pulling as well. "Alvor, stop," he said. "You'll vanish if you do that!"

Alvor gave him a sad smile. "Hey…I'm already dead. So let me do this. Let me help you. Let my last act mean something more than an investigation."

Xeile felt his footing starting to slip as his worn-out boots began to slide against the floor. He had to make a decision. He looked over his shoulder to the spirit, weighing the choice, then nodding consent. His heart wouldn't forget this.

He felt a rush of energy surge through his body, and he regained his footing as he yanked the stone backward. The stone came clear with a sudden lack of resistance, flipping over and slamming onto the ground with an authoritative bang that echoed up through the archives and made Xeile's ears ring for a moment. He turned around just in time to see Alvor's eyes fade out of existence.

He felt himself go weak at the knees and slump to the ground, panting. A terrible fear rippled up his spine. He looked down at his arms. They were shaking. He tried to get them to stop, but they wouldn't. "No…" he whispered. "Stop…" He brought his arms close into his chest and doubled over as the warmth exploded out of his body, going from warm to hot. He felt like he had sunburn all over his body and a bobcat had raked its claws across his back. He bit off a strangled cry of pain. If the cold was terrible, the heat was nearly unbearable. Then, the heat faded. Xeile felt something he hadn't felt in a long, long time. Strength.

His limbs shaking, he brought himself to his feet, Alvor's words still crashing around in his mind. He looked at his hands, raw from pulling on his improvised rope. He clenched his unsteady hand into a fist and forced it to his side.

He hardly noticed the trample of boots down the stairs, and was dimly aware of the flickering tongues of what seemed like black smoke that surrounded his body. Xeile turned around to see the two Elven wardens staring at him as he stood before them, shirtless, with torn, stained pants and almost-destroyed boots. In such a dark space, he should have been cold, but he wasn't.

His blood felt like it was boiling. "Get me McNair and his team," Xeile said, his voice low. The Elves froze in place. "Please," Xeile added. The wardens still didn't move. They just stared at him, their eyes wide, their faces pale. Xeile took a step toward them. "Are you alright—"

The two wardens scrambled away from him. "Don't touch me, monster!" one screamed. She bounded up the stairs, and the other followed quickly after. Xeile lowered his hand

and clenched his fists again. The fire in his veins seemed to flicker and fade out. He wanted to go get Kelt, but he was afraid they wouldn't let him back into the archives if he left, so he just sat down, his knees drawn to his chest, his arms hugging his body as energy he didn't know how to expend coursed through him, energy he hadn't felt in months, no…years.

"Am I just going to keep murdering people that are already dead?" Xeile whispered to himself. "Am I just going to keep hurting people? I forgave Kelt…" He looked at the books and gritted his teeth. "I said I was sorry to my mother for getting her killed. I don't even know if I can hold my fiancée without her dying. At this point, all I'm doing is hurting people by staying alive. Why won't they just let me die?"

The archives of the Guardians held hundreds of names. They held years and generations of history, but they had no answer for him.

THE OUTCASTS

Henrik heard a colossal crash and nearly jumped out of his skin. Criske and Kelt immediately grabbed for their weapons, scanning for danger. Glenna raised one eyebrow, looking for a source of trouble, but remained leaning against the wall, arms folded across her chest.

The wardens immediately took off down the hallway. "Should we go after them?" Henrik asked.

Kelt slowly nodded, and the four of them cautiously made their way down the path. Eventually, when they got down the stairs, the sound carried up to them. "Get me McNair and his team," Xeile said, his voice resonating through the stairwell.

Silence. Kelt held a hand up to stop Henrik and the rest from moving any further.

Xeile's voice broke the silence again. "Please." Still no response. There was the sound of a few footsteps. Xeile's voice adopted a concerned tone. "Are you alright—"

There was the sound of metal hitting stone and the sound of boots thudding on the stairs as the wardens took flight. They skidded to a halt when they saw Kelt looking at them with a concerned expression. "Everything alright, wardens? Is he causing any trouble?"

"Get down there and fix your insane hire. He's ripping the damn place apart and threatened us."

Criske let out a snort he turned into a repressed cough. The Elves looked him up and down with obvious disdain. "Perhaps this one is being a bad influence," one of the Elves suggested politely while the other gave a cruel smile. Criske's smile faded immediately and his face darkened. Henrik opened his mouth to retaliate, but Glenna beat him to it.

"Better a bad influence than a coward," Glenna said brightly. "Fortunately there's no one in this room that's like that. Not at all. No running away from potential danger here." Glenna looked at the ceiling, gently stroking her chin. "Well…wait." Her purple eyes widened in mock horror. "Oh dear. I think I'm the bad influence." She turned to Kelt. "Inquisitor, *what should I do?*"

Kelt looked down at her, squinting like he was warding off a bright light. "I suppose we should hurry up and find out what happened to poor Usumi, considering she was your master and whatnot," he reasoned.

The name had an instant effect on the Elves, who both suddenly looked uncomfortable. "Just hurry down there and see to it that he doesn't break anything. We'll know if he does," one of them snapped. They shoved past Kelt and walked down the hallway in what Henrik presumed they thought was dignified silence.

Criske watched Glenna, a quizzical quirk in his brow, but said nothing. Glenna just stared back with a smile playing on her mouth. He eventually shook his head and returned to the matter at hand.

They slowly walked down the stairs. It was difficult, as it was only wide enough to fit one person at a time. Kelt took the lead, with Glenna just after him and the other two following suit. As Henrik made his way down, he heard a voice.

Xeile's. He was talking to himself, his words just barely audible as they echoed upward.

"Am I just going to keep murdering people that are already dead? Am I just going to keep hurting people? I forgave Kelt…I said I was sorry to my mother for getting her killed. I don't even know if I can hold my fiancée without her dying. All I'm doing is hurting people at this point by staying alive." The words made Henrik feel like he was a gross intruder on Xeile's privacy. "Why won't they just let me die?"

If he felt like an intruder before, now he felt vile, like someone had slammed a fist into his solar plexus. He looked at Criske, whose face was set in a grimace. He looked at Kelt. The weapons master's face was a neutral mask. Then, he looked at Glenna.

She was rooted to her spot on the stairs, staring straight ahead into nothing, her breaths deep. Her fists clenched at her sides and then splayed open. The motion repeated itself several times. Her eyes brimmed with tears, and she looked up at the ceiling to keep them at bay. Henrik fought against taking a reflexive step back as he saw her face. Her brow was knitted, her teeth bared, her eyes narrowed.

Kelt had the good sense to step aside and let Glenna through first. As they entered the room, she stood over Xeile. He looked up at her, fear clear on his face. She got down on one knee and held up a hand to his face. "I took this ring," she said quietly, "with the intent of us spending the rest of our lives together." She grabbed him by the shoulders and wrapped him in a tight embrace. Her dark-purple aura flared to life like a hazy bubble around her skin.

"No!" Xeile cried, trying to shove her away as the flickering black swirled and swam around his body. "It'll kill you!"

"Then I'm dying in your arms," Glenna snapped. "And I'm okay with that."

"Get. Off," Xeile said, grabbing her arms, finally wrenching her free. Glenna looked at him in shock as he physically lifted her off the ground and set her away from him. He took several deep breaths. "I'm not going to have your blood on my hands," Xeile said. "You can't think like that, Glenna. It's dangerous."

"Then why are you doing it for me?" Glenna retorted. "I'm not letting you give up on yourself, you self-destructive moron! That's why I'm not letting you die. No offense, but none of us here are going to let you keel over anytime soon from your own idiocy. Some people actually want you to live, Xeile. You've still got a job to do. Are you just going to leave me stuck here with a Half-Elf who doesn't wash half the time and a Dwarf who has an iron rod up his ass?"

Criske frowned and took a tentative sniff of his uniform and winced. Henrik frowned and looked at his patrol partner. "Do you think I have…"

"Sometimes," Criske said. He gave Henrik a reassuring pat on the shoulder. "Don't worry, it's one of your charms."

Glenna jerked a thumb at Kelt. "And do you really want to leave me with him to deal with?"

Xeile shook his head. "No," he said. His voice was dry and raspy. "I don't want you killing anyone anymore. You know that."

Henrik felt surprise course through him. He looked at Criske, who just shrugged in a silent response.

Kelt said nothing, his face impassive.

Xeile's eyes snapped to the side as if he'd heard a sudden sound. "What?" Glenna asked, looking in the same direction.

He looked back at his fiancée, then scrambled to his feet. "None of you said anything, right?" he asked. He looked at Kelt. "Are there any other parts of his archive where we'd overhear someone?"

The weapons master shook his head. "No. But…" He turned and saw the strange hole in the floor, with the stone moved aside. It didn't take Henrik long to see how such a feature had been hidden in the dim lighting of the space. And it also didn't take him long to identify what it was for.

"It's an escape tunnel," Henrik said.

The others turned to him, waiting for a moment. "And?" Glenna prompted.

"You've never seen one of these? Say you are in a mine," Henrik explained. "If the main entrance collapsed, you would obviously want an alternative exit. In Dwarven architecture starting in the first century after the formation of the First Trifecta, it became quite popular to apply this mining principle to surface dwellings as well, particularly if a room only had one entrance or possible exit. Say this room had a sudden cave-in and you could not access the stairs. A person could manage an escape by using this tunnel and get to safety. Even before the Trifecta was formed, it was very in vogue for wealthy families to have these escape tunnels in their home in case of a rival house attack or assassination attempt, so the family line would be safe from harm."

Kelt knelt down to examine the hole, tentatively holding a candle down into its mouth. Henrik could just make out a stone ladder that went downward, into darkness. He looked at Henrik. "Can you tell who made this?"

"Let me have a look." Henrik walked over and felt the stone circle, paying careful attention to the handle, running his fingers along the top of the stone and feeling it between his fingers before giving it a sniff. "Clay…" he murmured. "That makes no sense. Humans use lime plaster for most of their flooring. But this entire room uses hardened clay…" Henrik frowned, his mind working rapidly. "The handle is definitely of Dwarf craftsmanship, a very second-century style by how it is embedded into the setting. Earlier craftsmen would have had the handle protrude."

"Why embed it into the clay?" Criske said. "That's a pain in the ass to get out. And the handle is so small, there's no way you'd be able to get it out of that spot without a rope to drag it. It's way too heavy."

Henrik nodded. "You are correct." He bit his knuckle for a while, deep in thought. "This kind of embedded handle and weight would not be appropriate for an escape tunnel. It would take too long to move in an emergency. That kind of embedded handle generally takes a special lever to move…"

Xeile examined the handle for a moment, looking at it with a frown. "Would a lot of people have that lever?"

Henrik shook his head. "Certainly not. Too heavy to really carry around. The only ones who would have that would be servants or people who maintain…" The answer came to Henrik in a flash. "Construction!" He turned to Criske. "Criske! You are a genius!"

Criske looked around, trying to reconcile Henrik's words. "I didn't say anything, but okay?"

Henrik waved his words away. "You were right. It is far too heavy. But there is a reason for that! You want to keep what is down there good and sealed. Unable to be accidentally or purposefully explored. Why?"

"Smuggling," Criske suggested. "You don't want people boosting goods around the city without a trading license. It's why you can't go on the rooftops. It's too easy for people to get around illegally."

"Yeah, and they could die," Glenna piped up. Henrik grinned, nodding and giving Criske a pointed look.

"Yes, yes. Now…do you remember how I mentioned that the city has expanded multiple times?"

Criske nodded. "Yeah. What's that got to do with roofs and tunnels?"

"Well, what if I told you the buildings aboveground weren't the only things that were expanded upon? As you know, this was a trading land long before the Trifecta formed. Wealthy merchants would settle here. And would the wealthy want to bother with something like a shared washroom with commoners?"

Criske laughed. "Oh, dragons and phoenixes no." The merriment on his face faded. "Wait… Washroom… Are you…"

"I think we have an answer on how our criminal got away so quickly," Kelt said approvingly.

"How much do you want to bet if we checked the sites of our other murder victims, there will be a similar entrance to the sewer network." Henrik patted the top of the large round stone. "Like this one here?"

THE SOLDIER

Kelt felt his stomach lurch. "Would it be possible for them to use the tunnels? I mean, it's not like sewers are made to be…navigated or survivable. Wouldn't the miasma down there choke them to death?"

Criske lowered his head in thought for a moment. "Not necessarily. Depends on how the sewers are laid out and used." Kelt's focus shifted to Criske with a raised eyebrow. Criske shrugged. "Look, there could be sections of it that aren't used anymore, yeah? If smuggling or doing shade was my business, I'd figure out all of those spots as quickly as possible. And…would a magician be able to, like, filter the air down there or something?"

They all turned to Glenna. She pressed her lips together, her folded arms giving her an air of annoyance.

"Sure," she said after a moment. "I mean, it'd be really difficult, but you could do it if you were very careful, had the knowledge of what to filter, and a good amount of practice. That stone cover wouldn't be too hard to move either."

Henrik got to his feet and brushed his hands off on his pants. "Well, then, we have a hypothesis, now to see if it will withstand reality."

"How do you plan to check on that?" Kelt asked.

"Our fair city has plenty of maps, including maps of its construction. Along with some historical records, I should be able to find enough evidence. If I may be so bold, I would recommend you would use your experience to find some very brave Spell Breakers to explore the underground sewers. After you schedule my whipping, of course."

Kelt gave him a nod. "Good work, all of you. I recommend you all take a break. You won't be getting one for a while, come shortly. Criske, go see your family. I'm sure they'd like to see you. Xeile, go get yourself checked out at the medical bay, and, Henrik, go with him. We have to make sure that we won't kill you tomorrow." Kelt winced as he forced the command out of his mouth. That command never got easier, even after so many years.

Henrik gave him a very solemn salute. Xeile got to his feet and followed the Dwarf out, a small smile on his mouth when he looked at Glenna, until he disappeared out the door. Glenna smiled back, her purple eyes twinkling with emotion that vanished as soon as he left. She leaned unceremoniously against the wall, sizing up Kelt. "So, what am I doing?" she asked. "Standing around as decoration?"

The weapons master's eyes narrowed as he mentally weighed her back. "No. You're coming with me. I have to question you about Usumi anyway. Nothing like an interrogation, but you knew her best before she vanished. I have to get your testimony."

Glenna sighed. "Right, I can do that." She shook her head. "Some head magician she's been."

"She was a successful Spell Breaker for years," Kelt defended.

Glenna snorted. "Right. Didn't make her any more or less competent at her job. I knew more about most magical subjects than she did."

"Somehow I doubt that," Kelt said dryly.

"I can't change the truth." Glenna shrugged. "I'm more acquainted with the brutal side of magic than she'll ever be."

Kelt swallowed a cutting comment and simply walked up and out of the archives. When he and Glenna walked down the hall, he saw the two wardens. "Make sure no one passes through here without papers save for the five of us," he said. "Our independent investigator made a break in the case that the baron will want to know about."

"Good," said one of the wardens. "You can tell him yourself. He's in front of your office."

Kelt's eyes widened. "Pardon?"

"He's in front of your office. He came by a little while ago but didn't want to disturb you in the middle of your work. So, now he's standing in front of your office." The warden smiled knowingly, falsely. "You enjoy yourself now."

Glenna rolled her eyes as the pair of them walked toward the weapons master's office. "So… this baron is a good person?"

"I don't know," Kelt said grimly. "I've not met him before. He seems to be running a fairly decent fief around here. I can understand him getting impatient, but I don't understand why he wants to oversee the investigation himself all of the sudden. Stinks of nobility feeling pompous, if you ask me."

As they rounded the corner, they saw the baron of Fief Trifectus. He was a man of medium stature, just slightly taller than Glenna, half a head shorter than Kelt, with black hair and dark-brown eyes. His skin was tanned as if he spent a great deal of time out under the sun. He was in his forties or fifties by Kelt's guess. Still athletic enough to use a sword but experienced enough to try not to. His face was lined and weathered from the elements. What was most surprising to Kelt was his complete lack of a personal guard. Most of the barons elected to have a personal guard, and for good reason. Although the Trifecta had done a good job of fostering peace between the nations, personal rivalries between barons had resulted in more than one assassination.

"Hello, Kelt," he said. His voice was unexpectedly soft and low. He looked over to Glenna. "And good day to you as well, miss."

Kelt gave the baron a small bow. "Hello, sir. May I introduce you to Glenna Nall. She is the apprentice to the currently absent head magician."

Glenna copied Kelt's bow. "Hello, sir."

The baron smiled warmly. "Pleasure to meet you." He looked at them for a moment and froze. "Ah. I don't believe I have introduced myself. I am Rald Taeris-Marneaux. It's a pleasure to meet you both."

Kelt felt his stomach contract and a bolt of lightning go up his spine. He looked at Glenna, whose eyes were wide in horror and her face had paled. "Would you run that name by me again, sir?" she asked, her voice weak.

"Rald Taeris-Marneaux. At your service, I suppose," he added. His eyebrows knitted together after her face didn't regain color. "Are you feeling alright? You appear to be ill…"

"Lord Baron," Kelt said. "Please step inside my office. It…wouldn't be safe to discuss matters here…"

Rald gave Kelt a confused look, but stepped aside, allowing Kelt to unlock his door, and they all went inside. Kelt pulled up a chair for the baron to sit in. To help calm his mind, he immediately went about making tea for everyone. He noted Glenna opted to stand in the corner, surveying everything in the room.

His mind was clamoring. A coincidence was astronomically unlikely. But how would

Mathiene even come into contact with Rald if he were nobility? Was it an illicit love affair? Did he know and that was the reason she was forced to abandon her post, for fear of retaliation from him?

And was he taking over the case because he had heard of the monster that supposedly once belonged to him?

Kelt quickly dispersed the tea around and sat down at his desk, noticing suddenly that Glenna's eyes had not shifted off of Rald for one second. She seemed to be searching for something. Perhaps resemblance to Xeile? "So… Baron…I heard you are taking over the case and I am no longer allowed to access certain areas of the case?"

Rald's smile was without humor. "Entirely for your own safety, I assure you. I don't want to risk any more Guardian lives than the ones already lost to this problem."

"We take our oath knowing full well we can die in the line of duty at any time," Kelt said. "And we did just get a few recent developments in the case, including access to a medium who has enabled us to get more information than we thought possible."

"A medium?" Rald asked. He leaned in excitedly. "Truly? A medium? How fortunate! Are they a Nomad, perchance, or perhaps one of the Dwarven priests? Or could it be that the Guardians have their own mediums here?"

Kelt leaned back in his chair, wary of the sudden enthusiasm. "He is independently contracted by us, but no, he is not a Guardian. I take it you are interested in mediums?"

Rald nodded. "Most certainly! I happen to be one myself! That's why I wanted to take over the case, but I was afraid to keep you on as the lead. Your skepticism for the paranormal is… rather legendary."

Kelt and Glenna shared a look, and Glenna stepped forward, staring at Rald with unusual intensity, which made Kelt uncomfortable compared to the easy swagger she normally had. She was focused. "What color is your aura, sir?" she asked.

The baron looked at her and raised his eyebrow. "That is a rather personal inquiry, Nall. Why the sudden interest?" Glenna didn't respond, she just stood there, staring at him. The baron sighed. "Well, if you must know, it happens to be gray, believe it or not. But I'm afraid I cannot summon my aura on my own to prove it to you. Nor am I willing to have it forcibly activated, if that was your next question." He shrugged. "But, of course, you don't believe me—"

There was a knock on the door that resounded throughout the room. "Who is it?" Kelt called.

"It's Xeile!" the voice responded.

The baron stared at the door and gave a gesture of approval. "Enter!" Kelt called.

Xeile opened the door and stepped through, coughing. "I just had a thought about…" His words drifted off upon seeing the unfamiliar face. "Oh. Sorry. If I'm interrupting something, I'll just come back later…"

"Stay," said the baron. It wasn't a suggestion. Xeile looked at Kelt, who nodded, his lips a thin line to echo the stiff way he was standing. The young man closed the door behind him. He let out another round of coughing and doubled over, pulling a cloth back to reveal flecks of blood. The baron stood up and moved to the other side of the room.

"Don't worry," said Xeile. "It's not contagious. It's a chronic condition I have." He looked at Glenna. "I was wondering if you could charge these for me," he said. He proffered her two resonance stones. "The head medic said I should be using these on the regular. I couldn't think of who else to go to. I asked Criske, but he couldn't get it to happen reliably."

"Leave it to me," Glenna said, taking both of the stones in her hands. In an instant, her dark-purple aura flared to life, the flickering violet surrounding her body. The stones slowly changed color until they matched her aura. She then handed them back to Xeile, and the color immediately drained from them. Kelt saw for just the briefest of moments a black flickering swirl across Xeile's skin.

He smiled at Glenna. "Thank you." He reached his hand out as if he were going to stroke Glenna's cheek, but he froze, dropping his arm down to his side. "I'll talk to you later. I love you."

"Love you too."

He turned to leave and the baron's voice rang out. "You were not dismissed, young man."

Xeile looked the baron up and down. "I do not answer to your commands," he said flatly. "But as long as you don't treat me like a plague victim, I'd be happy to stay, sir."

"As a matter of fact, you do answer to my commands, considering you are in my city," Rald said firmly. "I am the baron, after all."

Xeile looked the baron square in the eye. "Oh? Where is the baron when my hometown got raided by Nomads? Or when a bad harvest happens? I don't see you paying out of pocket to keep your citizens from starving."

The baron took a deep breath and exhaled. "Boy, do not try me. I, unlike you, have many responsibilities that make it rather difficult to immediately immerse myself in a case. I understand we barons are far from perfect, but I do at least expect you to give me the respect my position deserves."

Xeile continued to stare at him. "And what have you done to earn that respect?" he asked. "You were born into the right family? Nothing but chance on that front."

"I am working this case now," the baron said, his voice low. "Try my patience again, and I might have you arrested for slander."

Xeile looked back at the baron and shrugged. "You deal with the monster and get all your men killed, then. I don't ever want to do it again. But right now, I'm the only one who can face that thing down. I don't much appreciate you getting in Kelt's way when he's made good progress, sir."

The baron's mouth tightened. "I can easily get that creature removed," he said. "My aim was to search for the spirits of victims and make sure they were undisturbed while I worked. But, as Kelt says that's no longer an issue, I will be removing said monster. And you will remove yourself from my presence before I have you caned like the child you are."

Xeile's eyes narrowed, and Kelt cleared his throat to remind Xeile what was at stake. "Yes, sir," Xeile finally said, his tone exasperated. "My apologies, Lord…?"

"Rald Taeris-Marneaux," the baron said curtly.

Xeile's eyes widened. "Wait…Taeris?"

"That's right. Now do you understand the gravity of your impropriety?"

Xeile stared at the baron. "I can't believe it," he whispered. "I can't even begin to believe I have a chance of being related to you…"

He backed away from the baron as if he were a rotting corpse.

Kelt sighed, putting his head in his hands. "Lord Taeris-Marneaux, this is the medium that I hired. His name is Xeile Taeris."

The baron's eyebrow rose. "Your last name shares a part of mine? A rather strange coincidence, but nothing more, I assure you. I wouldn't associate with someone of your ilk in that manner. Now, unless you give me a very good reason for your continued involvement with this case, I am having you removed from it. You clearly do not have the temperament for investigative work."

Xeile's jaw clenched and he looked at Kelt. Kelt stared back, wishing silently he could hit the baron over the head with a chair, but he was powerless. The baron did have the right to control any investigation within his city, unless it involved an international threat, which they couldn't prove at the moment. Between the laws laid, and Xeile's insubordination, he had no wiggle room for technicalities or favors.

"Xeile, tell them."

The command jolted everyone out of the fog of tension. Kelt turned and saw Glenna staring Xeile down. He looked back to see the young man staring back at her, anger on his face. "No, Glenna," he said. "We've talked about this. My mother—"

"Is dead and can't keep you safe anymore. That's my job," Glenna snapped. "If you won't tell them, I will."

Xeile's eyes widened. "Glenna, you can't. I told you that in confidence—"

Glenna turned to Kelt, cutting him off. "You want to know why he was so convinced the Guardians would kill him? It's his actual name." She turned to Xeile. "Isn't that right, Exile Idolon?"

THE CITADEL

Xeile stared at Glenna in disbelief. How could she? Now he was dead for sure. He had just barely managed to get himself a relatively safe position by Kelt's side. Even if he couldn't work on the case with the Guardians, that didn't mean he couldn't at least try on his own time. But now, she had just outed him. If this fop of a baron didn't kill him, then Kelt likely would.

He turned slowly to face Kelt and saw his blue eyes locked on him. "Is that true, Xeile?"

Xeile nodded slowly. "Yes," he choked out. "But I don't expect you to believe it for a moment. Taron Idolon has been dead three hundred years, and the last name went with him best I know. I don't know how my father got the last name. He could have easily just lied to my mother, but why would you want to associate yourself with the worst necromancer to ever plague Meraria? Especially when she was a Guardian?" He looked at the ground. "I always knew I was strange. But I didn't know why? At least…not until…" Xeile felt his throat tighten. "Until you came looking for my mother, Kelt."

Kelt just stared at him for a long time.

"Well," he finally said, "I can assure you that I knew nothing about it. Had we known about you, I likely would have gotten you placed into protective custody or some other alternative."

"I know," Xeile said. "Just because you didn't know about it, doesn't mean the rest of your squad didn't. I heard them. You were gathering firewood. They made all kinds of mentions about 'tying up loose ends' and 'making sure the program didn't get out.'" Xeile's hands tightened into fists. "It was…hard."

Kelt raised an eyebrow. "You overheard us? We camped at least a mile away from your village."

"I followed you," Xeile said. His voice sounded like it belonged to someone else entirely. "I was completely ready…" He looked away. "I was ready to kill all of you."

"Glad you didn't try," Kelt said softly. "You wouldn't have managed it."

"I might not have," Xeile agreed. "But my mother would have."

"She was dead by the time we got to camp."

"No. She wasn't."

Glenna's eyes widened instantly. It took longer for the baron and Kelt to fully understand the implications of what he'd just said. Kelt leaned back in his chair, staring at Xeile. The baron gaped at Xeile, his mouth opening and closing rapidly like a fish out of water, incapable of making sound.

Glenna put a hand to her mouth. "You… Xeile… You idiot…"

"I didn't mean to!" he shouted at her. "I didn't want to! I was desperate. I shoved her soul back into her body. I noticed that a piece of her aura was broken, so I…" He lowered his head. "I gave her some of mine," he said. He started shaking uncontrollably, as if the freezing rain from that night were still slamming into his skin, running down his back. "I had no idea she would try to… What it would be like…" He felt his knees start to tremble. "I just wanted my mother back."

The baron had turned a terrible green color, then a nasty pale white. He looked at Kelt. "What are you waiting for, man? Arrest him!

Do you not hear him confessing to *creating an undead?*"Kelt stared at the baron. "Just because he says he did something doesn't mean he did. I have no way of proving it. I can't just go around arresting people without probable cause. And as I didn't see anything, and my fellow Breakers didn't either, I can't lock him away. My sincerest apologies, Baron, but my hands are tied."

The baron got to his feet, looming over Xeile. "Mark my words, I will not have a necromancer in my fief. I will have you arrested and hanged, boy!"

Xeile looked up at him, calm washing over him where he should have been stormy.

"You seem to mistake me for someone who's afraid to die," he said. "I've done just about everything I can to die without regrets. You want to get me arrested and hanged? Sure, you can do that. Let me know how this case works out when we meet again in the afterlife." His voice was strong but soft.

The baron's left eye began to twitch. "You insolent little—" He brought his hand up and went to strike Xeile across the jaw. The baron's hand never reached its target. Glenna's hand had reached out and seized the baron's in an instant.

"Don't hit my fiancé," she said. Her voice was like iron being dragged across a grindstone. "Or you might die. He'll drain the life right out of you."

She let go of the baron's hand, who lowered his arm and looked at Xeile with a mixture of fear and loathing. "I'm going to write to the king," he said. "He will see reason and you will be put to death." He looked at Kelt. "And you…you are off this case for your clearly demonstrated lack of competence, trusting"—he looked Xeile up and down—"this thing." Rubbing his wrist, he exited Kelt's office in a huff.

The three of them were silent for a long while. Xeile wasn't sure what to say, or what to do. Part of him was livid with Glenna. No, most of him was angry with Glenna. The fury stoked higher and higher with each feeling of betrayal, making his gut writhe and a muscle in his cheek twitch.

Kelt was the one who spoke first. "Please tell me you didn't actually…do that to Mathiene…"

Xeile looked at Kelt and could only manage a small nod, fighting back the urge to yell at him, to say it wasn't his fault. Kelt's face fell. He put his head in his hands for a moment, took a deep breath, and recomposed himself.

"I can't arrest you," he said. "But that doesn't bode well. Neither does the baron kicking us all off the case. As great as he says he is, you're the only arrow in our quiver for that damn beast creature. I'll try talking to him and make him see reason. You two…well…Glenna, you go take him to the guest quarters. Xeile, you might be off the case, but I'm keeping you close by."

Glenna gave Kelt a casual salute. Xeile followed her in silence. It was heading toward evening at a rapid clip. Xeile chewed on his cheek and forced his frustration downward, trying to focus on only following Glenna. Eventually, they reached a squat building that was on the outer edges of headquarters. "These are the quarters," Glenna said. "Don't go wandering around without an escort or you might get arrested. And stop being peeved at me. I'm just doing what you should have done to start with."

Xeile's anger came to the surface. "Glenna, they tried to kill me. Telling them I might be connected to a terrible person in the past is not a great idea. It makes me go from an oddity to a threat. That baron is going to really put the screws to people to get me hanged, and you just spent the small amount of protection I had!"

"What? Protection from the people trying to kill you?" Glenna gave him a sour laugh. "Yeah. Great protection there."

"Then what did you give me, *exactly*?" Xeile yelled.

Glenna raised her eyebrows. "Excuse me? You know better than to—"

Xeile lifted his hand and slammed it into the wall, trying to channel his anger into motion. The shock ran up his arm, but there was no pain. So he swung again, and again, and again, a small seed of panic rolling around in the fiery anger. Flecks of blood appeared on the stone.

"Stop!" Glenna shouted. "You idiot! You'll hurt yourself!"

"It's better than hitting you, which I really, really want to do right now!" Xeile shouted at her. He swung his fist into the wall again. "I trusted you, damn it, and you threw my trust to the wolves! Do you even trust me?"

"I do!" Glenna shouted back. "Now stop being overly dramatic and—"

"Glenna, I can't feel this." He showed her the torn, bloody, and already-bruising knuckles on his hand. "I can't feel this at all. My body won't even let me sleep now. I had to set my damn mother on fire so she didn't kill people. The Guardian magicians made me chronically sick. I'm always dying. I have been for the past three months. Those little stones are basically just a bandage over a wound that isn't closing." He sucked in a deep breath.

"Well, crying about it isn't going to help you get better," Glenna said coolly. "Maybe you should trust me to help you—"

"Glenna, I don't want to be some invalid you tend to!" Xeile shouted. "I just want you to love me! To depend on me back! Sure, I may not be able to take care of everything myself, but I can at least stand by my own choices. I chose to not reveal my name because I don't like it. I chose to trust you with the knowledge of my last name, because I figured you would ask me if it was okay to share it with others first!"

"Can you blame me? Your choices have been pretty damn stupid!" Glenna countered. "You had to run all the way down here just to forgive a man? You should have told my parents. They'd have taken care of—"

"With my mother's blood on my hands? With Guardians raiding the village and killing me? I wasn't going to risk bringing that down on your family. Take it from me, it really hurts to lose parents."

"Fair, but when you got here, you should have gone straight to Kelt instead of traipsing about following ghosts. You're the one seeming so determined to just lie down and die. I'm just trying to keep you alive."

A terrible feeling of nausea rolled up in Xeile, and the words slipped past his throat and flew out of his mouth. "So are you trying to keep me alive for my sake or yours?"

Glenna opened her mouth, then closed it, and stared at him in shock. "What?"

"Do I have a choice on what I do with my life anymore? Or are you going to shove me into a corner, cutting off routes until I do what you want? You're helping me, but only in ways that you deem worth it."

"That's not true," Glenna protested.

"Really?" Xeile asked. "Because that's not what just happened. I gave you the choice to walk away, despite me having all of my problems, despite constantly being on death's door. Despite you knowing that I don't play it safe when other people are at risk. You chose to stay. You put the ring on. You trusted us to work as a team. To make an effort to fix this mess together. But you keep insisting on doing everything yourself without checking with me first! You refused to keep my secret. You've placed us both at risk because you couldn't resist trying to win an argument. You don't trust me to take care of myself anymore, because you know better than I do. You're treating me like your delicate little flower that can't be bruised, and that hurts me more than any broken aura."

"You're not being fair," Glenna said.

"Neither are you. I don't have any power over my life anymore, and you just made the one choice I had left. If we are going to be married, we have to trust each other and talk things through, like equals, before doing them. Do you want a partner to spend your life with, or do you want a child to take care of, Glenna? I still love you, but you need to think on that for a while."

Xeile turned and opened the door, entering his small guest room, and slammed the door behind him.

THE OUTCASTS

Criske could smell the food cooking before he even opened the door. It was a heady, herbaceous aroma that lifted his soul and made his stomach growl. When he entered the room, he heard a familiar cry. "*Who's there?* I'll kill ya!"

"It's just me, Grandfather," Criske said.

His grandfather, deprived of his usual rocking chair in the new accommodations, had taken up his post in a corner with a stool, leaning up against the stone wall for support, his milky eyes roving the room continuously for any signs of danger they couldn't see.

"*Kiresu*, how good to see you!" his mother said, clapping her hands together, then giving him a warm embrace, which he returned. She had stowed away her good dress and had returned to her simple working pants and shirt, though she still kept the braid in the glossy hair that ran down her back. "We were so worried you were never going to visit."

The Half-Elf felt a stab of guilt. "Well, I'm sorry. I've been very busy. I haven't really even had much time to sleep, let alone visit as much as I'd like. It's kind of stupid. You all are even closer, and I've gotten to see you less."

"Is the case really that brutal?" He turned to see his father, eyebrows crinkled in concern for his son. "I know that it's been dangerous, but I didn't think it was quite that bad."

"Well…" Criske frowned, wondering how he could phrase it and not make his parents more concerned than he knew they already were. Truth was, the case had just kept sliding from bad to worse the closer to the answer they got. "We're making progress, but it's proving to be really difficult, since the criminal doing all of this has some kind of magic on their side we haven't figured out yet. I'm sure we will, but it's pretty stressful for Kelt and the rest of us in the meantime." He didn't mention how multiple people had died in the middle of this case so far, nor the fact that the magic the criminal had been using could kill highly trained fighters on the spot. But, at least he had been truthful.

"Magic," his father said softly, shaking his head. "I'll never really understand magicians. What a pain."

"No kidding," Criske agreed. "Still, if they weren't magicians, we'd probably be having a much harder time catching them. The criminal would probably have been better off just doing what they want the old-fashioned way. I don't know why they keep using magic. It doesn't really make sense to me. They keep leaving a trail when they don't really need to, and I can't help but wonder why."

They all fell silent for a moment, and the only sound Criske heard was the clatter of a wooden spoon on the clay pot that was on the coals his mother was using to cook. He took another sniff of the air and smiled. "That…smells incredible. What kind of stew are you making?" he asked.

"Oh." His mother waved a hand at him. "It's just pea and onions. These Guardians are very nice. They let me work as laundry woman. And your dad can even work as a gardening hand."

Criske turned and looked at his father, raising his eyebrows. "Really?"

Ren gave him a beaming smile, standing a little taller. "Yep. Turns out you don't need two hands to pull weeds and the like. They even pay me half decently. Between your mother and I, we've been able to afford to eat regularly. You should have seen their faces when we came down there, looking for work. They seemed so surprised that their people in protective custody would want to do anything besides panic. I'm just hoping that after this case is over, we'll be able to work here. It's much better than what we were doing before."

The Half-Elf felt his throat tighten. "Yeah. I hope so." He made a mental note to ask Kelt about the possibility later. The more money his family could bring in, the more he could save up for a rainy day. It wasn't too long before the four of them were seated around the cramped table, eating a small but hearty meal of dark rye bread and peas with sorrel sauce in relative quiet. Just as Criske finished with his portion, he heard the shouting.

He couldn't quite make out the words, but he recognized the voice.

It was Xeile. And he was not happy in the slightest.

Then, there was the sound of a door opening and slamming shut, the force of which echoed through the wall and into their room with a muffled bang. Criske looked over at the wall and sighed. "I should go check on him," he told his family.

"Who, your friend?" Leeha asked. "Here, make sure to give him something." She hurried over and handed Criske a small portion of bread.

"Mom," he began to protest.

"No. You know you don't go empty-handed to friend's house," she said, pointing a long finger at him. "Now go."

"Yes, ma'am."

So, with the scraping sound of his chair echoing across the floor, rye bread in hand, he exited his family's living quarters. He froze as he nearly ran into Glenna, backing several steps away. "Sorry," he said quickly.

The last thing he wanted to do was make her mad, particularly since she seemed to be in a less-than-pleasant mood. Her jaw was clenching and relaxing, and she shot him a glare that could have withered a thornbush. "What?" she snapped.

"Nothing," Criske said hurriedly. "I didn't say anything."

"*Kiresu*, who's that?" his mother called.

Criske closed his eyes and took a breath, exhaling slowly. "Just a coworker!" he said over his shoulder.

"Is she pretty?" his mother asked.

Criske felt his face flush. "She's taken!" he shouted, fighting the urge to try and slam his head into the wall hard enough to forget his current situation.

His mother let out a disappointed sigh. "*Kiresu*, you need to hurry. A wife not happen without your help, *yeah*?" Criske quickly shut the door to his family's quarters with an authoritative clack.

He looked at Glenna. "I'm sorry," he muttered. "She's not going to give up on that one anytime soon."

Glenna's snarling expression lightened slightly. "What? She determined to marry you off? Got a dowry set aside for you?"

Criske gave her a pointed stare. "Yeah, like anyone is going to want to marry a Half-Elf that lives on Guardian pay with three other mouths to feed. Good luck with that one."

Glenna sighed. She cast a glance back at the door next to his, fiddling with the smooth wooden ring on her finger. She looked back at Criske. "Can you help?" she asked. She pulled a heavy crystal-like object out of her pocket and handed it to him. "He's being a bit of an ass right now. Probably doesn't want to see me at the moment."

Criske took the stone from her and stared at it, then identified it. "Dragons and phoenixes. This is a resonance stone? This thing's massive."

"It's the personal one I use for practice," Glenna said. "It holds a lot more than those puny ones down in the medical bay. I figured you could use it to practice and transfer energy to Ex…Xeile at the same time. His hand's also pretty beat up. If you could help with that…I'd appreciate it."

Criske could practically hear the metallic squeal of her pride unbending as she walked away, her heavy footfalls clacking against the stone walkway. He looked at the object in his hand, frowning. He had tried earlier that day to help Xeile, but he hadn't been able to. The Half-Elf looked at the door next to his family's and sighed. "Nothing for it, then." He hesitantly knocked on the door. The only response he got was silence. He coughed twice. "Uh… Xeile…it's me, Criske Val-Zhang. One of Kelt's apprentices."

More silence.

"Can I come in?" Criske ventured.

After another long pause, there was an answer. "Sure."

Criske opened the door to see Xeile standing in front of a washbasin pouring water over his hand. Criske let out a low whistle. Glenna certainly hadn't been exaggerating when she said Xeile had been hurt. He had completely skinned his knuckles and parts of his fingers as well."

"Oof. What happened there?" he asked.

Xeile shook his head. "Just getting a point across."

"Want some help cleaning that up?" Criske offered. "Can't have that getting infected."

Xeile turned around, looking at Criske with his eerie black eyes. It was amazing how hard his expression was to read when he didn't have an iris. "I'm not sure you can touch me," Xeile admitted. "I'd rather you not get hurt."

"Oh, well, I've got something that might help with that," Criske said, showing him the crystal. "I know I couldn't get it to work last time, but I figured it might be worth another shot, yeah?"

The young man gave him a small nod. Criske shut the door behind them and pulled up a nearby chair from the dining table, staring at the stone. He had said it'd be worth a shot, but he honestly had no idea how get it to work again.

He struggled to remember what Henrik had said before, but his memory wasn't clear enough. He had been so focused on other things, and then with all the panic that had ensued afterward, the memory of how he managed it had disappeared, same with his panic over Xeile the last time. He had charged it before, but slowly. He looked up to see Xeile sitting on the bed across from him, staring into the distance. "Sorry," Criske said quickly. "Haven't had much practice."

Xeile shrugged. "Not like I've got anywhere else to be."

Criske resumed his focus on the stone, struggling to recall the memory, but nothing came. Then, an idea struck him. The stone was like a conduit for energy he could give to Xeile from his aura. Best he could tell, the reason it was dangerous to touch him directly was that it took too much energy all at once. But the stone had a limited amount it could hold. "Hey, would you mind holding on to the other end of this? I want to try something."

Xeile gave him a look but extended his non-battered hand and grasped one end of the stone. Criske then changed the focus of his attention. Instead of trying to pour energy into the crystal, he imagined that strange sense of being alive that he had felt before, the heat, the energy that had swirled around him when he first put energy into the stone. He focused on that sensation, trying to bring the memory back. The smell, the sound, the feeling of his hair standing on end. Then, he felt it, a controlled stream of cold shooting up his arm and down his spine. It steadily drained the warmth away. When he couldn't take it anymore, Criske's eyes snapped open and he let go of the stone, leaving it in Xeile's hand, sucking in a shuddering breath. "So…you feel any—" Criske let out a gasp, feeling himself freeze to the spot in fear.

Behind Xeile was a very familiar-looking ghost.

It was the spirit of the dead library assistant. However, he wasn't exactly the same. The spirit gave him a small smile, and there was a thin strand of thread running from the center of his chest to Xeile's. A small, steady blue glow seemed to emanate from a shard under Xeile's heart as he was surrounded by what looked like flickering black smoke.

"What?" Xeile asked, his face lit with concern. "Are you—"

"Look behind you!" Criske shouted, pointing. The spirit started to fade. "Look behind you, quick!"

Xeile turned around just as the spirit faded into nothingness. He turned back around. "What? Did you see that spirit too?"

Criske nodded. "It was the ghost of the library assistant! I think you're taking them with you, kind of absorbing them, yeah?"

The young man's eyes widened. "Really? You saw the spirit of the assistant? He poured his energy into me earlier today." Xeile put his head in his hands. "I thought I killed him! Well, killed his spirit, anyway."

"No," Criske said. "I'm not sure how, but you seem to have taken a little piece of him with you or something. Some kind of blue…shard."

Xeile nodded. "All spirits have some kind of shard in them. I think that's what keeps them…" Xeile's eyes widened. "Criske. We have to go get the rest of the group. Now." His voice was strong, energy barely contained in his words.

"What? I mean, yeah. Obviously. We can possibly get more details out of the assistant, yeah?" Criske asked, feeling his heart race.

Xeile shook his head. "I can do you one better. If this can work for Alvor the assistant, I think I might be able to make the spirit of one of the original murder victims appear."

THE SOLDIER

It was a long time before Kelt could bring himself to move. After Glenna and Xeile left—no, Exile…if he even wanted to be called that—Kelt was bound to his chair with chains of thoughts, winding so tightly around his attention that it drove everything from his mind.

Xeile was apparently, in reality, named Exile Idolon. Judging from the look he gave Glenna, he'd obviously wanted to keep it a secret for fear that it'd bring the Guardians crashing down on him. Never mind that the Guardians couldn't do a thing to him, as they had no way to prove his lineage. He could see why he'd want to hide it from people, as the very name "Idolon" was one that everyone associated the Taron Idolon, the mad necromancer-king from three hundred years ago. With the thought of Taron, another idea struck Kelt.

The Guardians could do nothing to Xeile, but the Idolon Remnant would leap at the chance to bring him into their ranks. He'd be the ultimate status symbol, an ideal figurehead, even. An heir to Taron Idolon, restoring the "rightful line" back to the throne. The people that believed that madman necromancer deserved to be king, the Nomads turned into a corrupted barony, would adore having such a powerful figurehead. Moreover, a figurehead that distrusted Guardians and government. Getting to his feet, Kelt began pacing. Night was falling, but he only stopped to light a small fire in his hearth before he continued walking around his office, his head staring down at his feet. The motion was knocking things loose in his brain, pushing him to come to conclusions as the night air tried to chill his skin.

No matter how much he walked, his brain refused to concentrate. Eventually, he threw his hands up in the air and left his office, locking the door behind him. Time to go practice, or something. Anything to clear his mind again.

The training grounds were eerily quiet at night, the only sound the shuffle of beneath of soft sand beneath his feet. Kelt walked over to the practice weapons rack. They didn't have many nonconventional weapons. There were practice spears, swords, and staves. The bows were stored in a shed to protect them from rain. The summer night was relatively cool, but not the unnatural cold that came from the monster. Instead, it refreshed him, invigorated his senses. Kelt pondered over the weapons before eventually selecting a spear.

Going through the various drills he had practiced for nearly twenty years, Kelt stabbed at imaginary foes with vigor, using his restlessness as a grindstone for his deadly precision. In truth, he would have loved to use a glaive at the moment, but no person with common sense would let the average Guardian anywhere close to those. Getting them to be competent with the standard-issue short sword was hard enough as it was.

Eventually, he was lathered in sweat, his muscles aching with the exertion of close to thirty minutes of nonstop drill work. But with that exhaustion came clarity, his brain finally pulling itself from a fog to bring pieces together.

Xeile's last name was Idolon, which would mean his father's last name was Idolon. That didn't initially match what he gleaned from the documents at the library, but the Taeris boy in those journals had gotten his name changed after he was rescued from the Nomads that were trying to bond him with that terribly aggressive spirit in an act of necromancy. But there was an issue with all this: the last name Idolon was extinct. Taron Idolon killed his entire family, wiping out any potential way for the name to be passed on.

Or was that a lie? The Remnant certainly didn't think Taron was dead, but considering their obsessive reverence of him, they wouldn't dare take his name unless they had a legitimate claim to it. And if they found someone who belonged to the Idolon line, the Remnant would stop at nothing until they managed to kidnap him. All of their resources would be bent to capturing this one child. The only way Xeile would ever be safe was by becoming completely anonymous.

And in order to do that, Mathiene would have to disappear completely before giving birth. Had Xeile's lineage been discovered, forcing her to leave for the sake of her unborn child, even when facing the charge of abandoning her post? If so, she was a woman of remarkable character.

A Guardian in the truest sense of the word. So much self-sacrifice. Kelt felt a pang of longing in his chest that he shoved down. Now was not the time for sentimentality. There were other things he had to work through.

The weapons master stowed the practice weapon away and jogged slowly around the practice field to cool down and prevent cramps, the sand making the task twice as difficult. "What else did he say?" Kelt said to himself between gulps of air. "What else did he say?"

Xeile outright told him that he had resurrected Mathiene's body by giving her a piece of his aura, which struck Kelt as incredibly strange. When a necromancer brought a body back to life, it was usually a fresh body, but the spirit was hardly ever the person it belonged to. Most of the time, it was someone else or, worse, a collection of spirits shoved into one mortal coil. Most of Mathiene's personality would likely have disappeared, and she had apparently come back looking for vengeance. Xeile said he'd been forced to kill her to protect the Guardians that had taken her life.

The thought sent a shiver down Kelt's spine. He thought, really thought, for a moment. He didn't know many people who would be willing to go so far to protect complete strangers. It must have been devastating. Top that off with the fact he had to look at the Guardians and not take vengeance for fear of dropping more trouble and Spell Breakers on his head, and it was an absolute nightmare scenario.

And after all of that, Xeile had forgiven him. Worked with him to save others. Jumped into the fray to help complete strangers again, when he could have just run and hid, and been utterly blameless for it. The thought made Kelt stop jogging, taking a deep lungful of air as his mind then focused on another fact Xeile had shared with him.

Someone, Guardian or otherwise, had shattered Xeile's aura before he resurrected Mathiene. That ultimately was how Mathiene had died too. No one could touch her in combat. Even Kelt, as weapons master, could only hold his own against the unnatural crushing blows of her massive sword because of his years of constant training and instinct.

An image resurfaced of her grabbing a skull of a nearby Breaker, a Guardian named Vedri, and smashing him into a stone wall, leaving nothing but a bloody pulp… Then the image of Nodra from four years before getting an arrow in the heart, then the approaching knives of his Dwarven tormentor, heading to slice open the side of his face yet again—

Kelt doubled over, grabbing his head, taking quick, shallow breaths. "Damn it," he said through gritted teeth. "Now is not the time. Now is not the time. It will never be the time. You have to move on, lad," he muttered to himself. "You're safe in Trifecta. You're safe in Trifecta. You're safe…"

When his rapid, fluttering heartbeat had finally calmed down, Kelt looked up to see Henrik standing in front of him. His heart skipped a beat, and he straightened up, coughing twice.

"Ah, how can I help you, apprentice? Are you fit for your punishment tomorrow?"

"You don't have to act in front of me, sir," Henrik said. His face was hard to read by moon and torchlight, as most of his expression was hidden in shadow. "I understand. There are days when my past haunts me too. You were a Spell Breaker. Difficult memories are often part of the job, from what I have heard."

Kelt nodded, his insides relaxing slightly. "Fair. I just can't afford for people to see me have those difficult days. Part of being a leader."

Henrik nodded. "I know what you mean." He turned and Kelt could finally see his face. Henrik looked worn, beaten down by something he wanted to say but couldn't quite find the words for.

"You want to talk?" Kelt asked, gesturing to the sand around them. "There's plenty of sitting room."

Henrik seemed to think about it for a moment, then nodded once more, sitting down on the ground. Kelt sat next to him, waiting for him to speak. It took a while before words finally started coming out of Henrik's mouth. "I…initially joined the Guardians because I wanted to start over. I wanted to get rid of my old life, you see. My family and I did not…how do you say it…see each other face to face?"

"Do you mean 'eye to eye'?"

"Ah. That is the phrase. Well, yes. My family and I do not always get along. I came from…an elevated position at home. Being the second son, I was not going to inherit the *Khlaniik-Maqraj*, the responsibility of my lineage. It is tradition that the second son should join the military or find some similar venture to occupy their time with. I chose academics, which was respectable in my parent's eyes. What wasn't respectable was the kind of academics I chose."

"Why?"

Henrik stared straight ahead as he spoke, not meeting Kelt's gaze. "I became a *Dwaq Makraan*."

Kelt's eyes widened. *Dwaq Makraan*, or what the Humans called "Tunnelers," were the people who mapped out the miles and miles of tunnels that lay underneath the Khlaniik Mountains that the Dwarves used in older times before some kind of catastrophe had driven them to the surface world. Some tunnels were still in use, but it was a labyrinth underneath those mountains, with countless old cities and areas long abandoned and forgotten. It was dangerous and often lethal work. Often a job full of thrill-seekers and the desperate, the *Dwaq Makraan* had a reputation for short lifespans and crass incivility that was reviling to most others of their kind.

"I can't imagine them enjoying you risking your neck," Kelt admitted. "Still, you mapped those?"

"I more than mapped them," Henrik said. "I've been piecing their history together, trying to find out what drove my *Khlaniik* to the surface in the first place. The issue is…there was one time that my crew and I went too far. We ran into some kind of miasma. I was the only one to escape alive. The rest told me to run before they fell on the ground and died."

"I'm sorry to hear that," Kelt said quietly.

"After I found out it was an attempt to kill me and make it look like an accident, I was at a loss for what to do. So I came here."

Kelt swallowed a few times. He knew that Dwarven politics could get incredibly messy with their direct inheritance laws, but this was a different level of complicated. "Why would they try to kill you?" he asked. "You're the second son. And, forgive me for making assumptions, but you don't seem like the kind of lad who would assassinate others for gain."

Henrik laughed. "Oh no. I wouldn't dream of killing anyone in my family. It'd throw the *Khlannaran* into chaos. I found there was very little I could do to improve my situation or standing. In my family's eyes, I wasn't worth keeping."

The Dwarf drew his knees close to his chest, wrapping his arms around them, staring off into the distance. "I forsook my last name. I decided to change my identity and started over with the Guardians. I have no idea if my brother is the one who ordered me to be eliminated, and I honestly have no courage to ask. I have no *Khlaniik* to guide me in the matter, so I've largely been playing this by ear. I managed to escape the Dwarfdom intact and was able to sign up. Fortunately, my time as a *Dwaq Makraan* has come to be of great use."

Silence fell between them. Finally, Kelt looked over at Henrik. "Why are you telling me all this? There was no reason you had to."

"When I am rightfully punished for my wrongdoing, I wanted to prove that my intrusion on your privacy will stay between us."

Kelt let out a heavy sigh, an invisible weight pushing down on his shoulders. "Well, Henrik, I appreciate that. But it isn't something I'm too ashamed of. It frustrates me more than anything. Most people who are Spell Breakers are only in the position for a small amount of time, maybe five years or so, for good reason. Most of them have enough sense to stop after the first terrible experience. I didn't."

Silence visited them, like a blanket that wrapped around them in the summer to ward off the chill of bad memories. Kelt stood, brushing off his pants. "Well, we should be getting some sleep. It's going to be a rough day tomorrow." Henrik nodded, pushing himself off the ground. He saluted Kelt before walking off into the night.

The weapons master returned to his room, his mind much clearer now. Henrik's discussion on family had blown away the fog that had obscured his next task. Now, it seemed so simple. He may be off the case with the monster, but there was another very important investigation the baron had said nothing about.

It was time to get some answers on why a Guardian would try to kill Xeile Taeris when that wasn't part of their orders.

THE OUTCASTS

Henrik opened his eyes and stared at the barracks ceiling. It was plain pine wood, but the sturdy beams held up the ceiling well enough in a latticelike design that was very clearly first-century Trifecta. This was a Human design, no doubt about it. He saw many interlocking wooden joints, and very little in the way of nails, an elegant solution to having poor access to iron. The beams were barely visible in the predawn darkness, and with all of the windows still shuttered closed, the only source of light was the openings that allowed smoke to escape from the firepits in the barracks. The barracks didn't have a chimney, as they wanted the heat to radiate out, not up. In winter, shifts would have been assigned for fire duty, ensuring that they stayed lit and ready to provide much-needed warmth.

But right now, the two fires that had been built previously had burned down to weak coals and almost no light. The cockerel had yet to crow. He wasn't sure what shook him out of his dreams, but now he was up regardless. He doubted that he could fall back asleep, even if he wanted to.

Today was the day he was to be flogged.

The Dwarf thought about it as if it were just an item on his itinerary, a thing on his to-do list. It amazed him how detached he felt about the experience. He figured he was supposed to feel dread, a kind of anticipatory fear of the pain to come. But he felt nothing.

He rolled out of his bunk, dressed in his uniform, and mechanically made his way to the mess hall, being sure to take only a small amount of food. He didn't want too much in his stomach after all. The cooks seemed startled to have someone so early, but they served him a kind of weak beer that had little in terms of flavor, and some groats-bean mixture that offered even less. Not for the first time, he wished he had access to some of the spices or herbs from the mountains back home. The sting of the Nahdr peppers, the earthy flavors of *kuudmin* and *kadawiir*, and most of all, fish. Oh, how he missed fish! The lightness, the ease of eating, not so heavy and determined to sit like a rock in his stomach like the beef and mutton the Territories seemed to obsess over.

Henrik shook his head. This was his home now. He had to get used to that. The food stuck in his throat, requiring him to swallow twice before he could get it all down. After turning in his cookware, he hurried over to Kelt's office. He went to knock on the door and froze. Kelt probably wasn't up yet.

"Morning to you, lad."

Henrik turned around to see a bleary-eyed Kelt standing behind him with a mug of something hot, the steam coming off of it in delicate curls. "Care to join me?" he asked. "I still have some in a pot."

The Dwarf nodded silently.

Kelt gently opened his office door and stepped through. Was it just Henrik's memory, or was there even more paperwork on his desk than before? Regardless, there was a heady aroma that filled the room, enlivening his senses. It was a scent he knew well.

"*Kaifei*," he said, letting the Elvish word roll off his tongue in a sigh. "I thought you'd prefer tea."

"Tea is good to enjoy drinking," Kelt said. "But I view coffee more as a medical necessity at this point. Please, have a seat. I'll get you a cup."

Henrik sat down in the chair across from Kelt's desk, and the weapons master took a kettle from nearby the fire, pouring out a lightly colored liquid that then turned black as it filed a cup. He set it across from Henrik. "You might want it with some honey if you aren't used to it," Kelt advised. He reached into his desk for something Henrik couldn't see, then put it on the desk. It was a small jar of the golden liquid.

The Dwarf delicately put some into his cup and gave it a tentative stir before sipping on it. He felt the initial sting of bitterness that faded away to a unique sweetness that made his eyes widen with nostalgia. He set the mug down and stared at it.

"*Hahnrak-Nalaiir*," he said softly. He looked up at Kelt. "Where did you get this?"

Kelt smiled. "Well, being a Spell Breaker can actually win you a favor or two," he said. "One of the few perks of the job, if I'm honest. It was a gift from a nobleman for saving his son. He has a prize apiary and supplies me somewhat regularly with some of his product."

Henrik nodded. Honey was one of the Khlaniik Mountains' best exports, the unique wildflowers and plants giving the liquid a much-prized flavor. There were even apiaries that created specifically flavored honeys with strategically placed flowers. This particular type, *Hahnrak-Nalaiir*, could go for fifty Trifecs a pot, about three months' pay for a regular shepherd.

The Dwarf made sure to sip and savor the brew.

"Interesting you can tell what kind of honey this is," Kelt said offhandedly, not looking up as he signed another piece of paperwork. "Considering it is a honey that almost exclusively belongs to the royal household."

Henrik nearly choked on his coffee and forced himself to swallow more of the liquid than he intended, burning his throat and mouth in the process. "I suppose we all get lucky on occasion," he rasped. "The nobles I served were generous with me at one point."

The weapons master snorted, looking at Henrik from under his brow line. "I know I'm old, but I have yet to go senile, Henrik. I saw your signaling horn the night the monster attacked me at the library. It has the seal of the royal family of the Dwarfdom on it. You've served them directly at one point."

The Dwarf opened and shut his mouth, weighing what to say, settling on the explanation that was closest to the truth. "Even though I am connected to them in some manner, it has been almost a year since I've been back in the Dwarfdom. I did not consider myself favored by them. I do not know if they were the ones who ordered me dead or not. The simplest way to ensure that I stayed alive was to remove myself from the sphere of politics entirely, and that included the royal family. Forgive me for asking, but what does this have to do with today, sir?"

Kelt leaned back in his chair and pondered the question for a moment. "Nothing," he finally answered. "I desired to give you a taste of home. When you join the Guardians, your claims to all titles and nobility are suspended during your time of service. It is my duty to get to know my apprentice. You are getting severely punished today, I wanted to check on you."

"I do not feel much of anything," Henrik admitted. "It is very strange." Kelt leaned forward now, putting his arms on his desk and interlocking his fingers around his cup of coffee.

He took a swallow and sighed. "Well, I'm here to tell you that you will definitely be feeling something. I'm not going to lie to you, getting whipped hurts like nothing else I've felt. You'll likely be immobile for a day, maybe two if your injuries are severe. They won't give you anything to dull the pain, but the medical bay will at least try their best to keep it from getting infected. You'll have to take it easy for a while after that so your wounds don't open up."

Henrik felt his mouth go dry at the description of the whipping process. He knew he wasn't as worried as he should have been about the actual event, but the recovery afterward sounded terrible. Would he really be unable to do anything for days? What would Criske do? What if they missed something during the investigation because of his absence?

His spontaneous speech seemed to become a more terrible idea with each passing moment. There must have been some visible indication of his emotions on his face, because Kelt spoke again. "Looks like you understand how difficult it will be for everyone else without you in commission. That's good. It's about to get a lot harder. The baron of the fief will likely be delivering paperwork that gets me barred from working the case today as well."

The Dwarf's eyes widened. "No… how could he do such a thing? You're one of the best there is!"

"Pettiness knows no bounds," Kelt said grimly. "He wants to be able to step in and save the day, claim prestige for himself, I think. Problem is, we both know that will likely get him killed, and a lot of other people as well. As I won't be allowed to work the case, I'll be counting on you to take the lead."

Henrik's mind felt stretched, and there was a sudden ache in the back of his skull. "Me?" he sputtered. "Sir…that seems rather… unreasonable. There are many more qualified than myself."

Kelt shook his head. "I beg to differ. You have something that very few people will have, something instrumental to this case: Xeile's loyalty. He and the baron will get along about as well as horses and snakes. He may trust Criske too, but Criske doesn't have the same charisma to deal with the baron that you will. I expect that may come with age, and with you as his well-spoken partner. You're going to do your absolute best to ensure that idiot baron doesn't get my people killed until I get put back on the case. Are we clear, Patrolman? If we are, say so."

There it was, the inescapable order. Henrik bought himself a moment by sipping a small amount of coffee. His response was quiet, but he looked Kelt in the eye. "Yes, sir. We are clear."

Kelt beamed at him. "Good. Now, you got checked by the medics yesterday, right?"

"Yes, sir."

"Very well, now we—"

The door to the office flew open. Henrik instinctively dove out of his chair and onto the ground. Kelt was on his feet, his hand on his nearby sword in almost an instant. Kelt relaxed slightly.

"Damn it, lad," he said. "You nearly made my heart stop."

Henrik looked up to see Criske wheezing, doubled over. His face was flushed and covered in sweat. "Sorry," he said. "Just figured I'd tell you that…Xeile…" Criske held his sides and let out a hissing sound that reminded Henrik of an angry goose. "Ah, damn it…Xeile's…got another breakthrough for us. Did you know he can…bind himself"—Criske took another gulp of air—"to spirits?"

Kelt's eyes widened. "Gods no… He's bound himself to a spirit?"

"'A spirit'? Try Alvor, the library assistant that was murdered. What's more, he thinks he might be bound to one of the murder victims, as long as I charge his aura again, that is." Criske smiled, his breathing slowly steadying. "We can get information straight from the sources."

The implications mixed with Criske's excitement and hung in the air. The case could be blown wide open. It wouldn't solve everything, but it would definitely put them ahead. Alvor's murder was the most recent, and the one that was likely to have the murderer still trapped in the city since the lockdown was put into place. He turned, smiling to Kelt, but his face fell when he saw the thunderous expression on his master's face.

The weapons master reached out and grabbed Criske by the shoulders. Kelt's grip must have been more than firm, because Criske's face twisted to a cringe. "Look at me," Kelt said. Criske looked up, his confusion turning into fear. "Never. Ever. Do that again without experts nearby. Do you understand me?"

"S-sir, we just—"

"*Do you understand?*"

"I do," Criske said weakly. "Please let go. You're hurting me."

Kelt let go. His breathing was shallow. He took two steps back, and he was staring at—no, through—Criske, as though he was seeing something else an entire world away. He blinked and just as quickly seemed to return to the present. "Sorry. I just… I've…" He swallowed twice. "Other magicians have lost their lives to that kind of experimentation. Even with the best of intentions, I don't want to lose you to reckless folly."

"I'm not a magician…but I hear you…" Criske swallowed. Kelt raised an eyebrow. "Sir," he added hurriedly.

"And two left feet make for poor dancing," Henrik said. Kelt and Criske stared at him in confusion. The Dwarf's face flushed. "I take it that phrase does not exist in this language?"

"Um…kind of? I think?" Criske said. "Does it mean I said something obvious?"

"Yes and no," Henrik explained. "We use it the same way you use…a witticism. When you say one thing, but your tone means another… what is that word…"

"Sarcasm?" Criske offered.

Henrik snapped his fingers. "Yes! That is the one, *Khlanro*. You say you are not a magician, but I believe that your abilities will soon prove otherwise."

Criske started to argue, but pointed looks from both Henrik and Kelt made him press his lips together instead, reconsidering.

Henrik looked at Kelt. "Sir…I would like to go to the library to gather more information for the case."

Kelt stared at him for a long time and then sighed. "Very well, if you think it will help, permission granted. But you have your whipping at noon. Time is short." Henrik saluted them both and hurried off.

The request may have seemed like it was out of the blue to them, but not to Henrik. He was the only one who could really do this kind of digging with anything resembling proficiency, mostly because he would be the only one who would know what to look for in the first place.

The sun was making its ominous climb toward his fateful hour of punishment, blazing like an eye of judgment, raining heat down on his skin, making him quickly break into a sweat under his woolen uniform. Henrik made his way up the library steps, pushed past the canvas that was serving as a temporary door, and walked straight up to the desk, where a new library assistant was waiting. He put his hands down on the desk with enough force to make the assistant jump. "Hello," he said, trying to keep the urgency out of his voice. "I'd like to see city maps of Trifectus, both modern and historical. Do you happen to have any of those?"

The assistant nodded a few times. "We should have at least one or two," she said. "Follow me."

She guided him through the library, and Henrik couldn't help but see the swath of destruction the beast had cut through the building. Several shelves of books had toppled over and were currently being righted, with a few other assistants carefully cataloging and putting the books back in their rightful places. It looked like slow, meticulous work. Henrik wondered if several of them were doing it as a form of punishment. The other assistant quickly guided him to a room all the way in the back of the library, separate from the main shelves, guarded by a warden. She showed her badge, and after careful inspection, the warden let them pass.

Inside the room was a massive collection of scrolls, from floor to ceiling. The things that weren't scrolls were tubes of hardened leather, reinforced with wood. On one wall was a massive work in what seemed to be copper or bronze. It took Henrik a moment to realize what it was. When he finally made the connections, he gaped in wonder. It was an entire map of Meraria, engraved into a single sheet of metal. The number of hours artisans sank into it must have been monumental.

He turned to another wall to see a much more detailed map on white canvas, done in the flowing, dark lines that characterized the Elven artistic style, showing the expanse of the Tropiciea Archipelago, the domain of the Elves and their empress.

He turned to the other side, but saw that there were no maps of the Dwarfdom or Territories on the walls. The assistant must have noticed his confusion, because she explained as she wandered around the map room, scanning the walls, looking for the specific information Henrik requested. "Welcome to the Cartography Chamber," she said. "We have a huge collection of maps here. A few are originals, but most of them are copies that are sent to us by the three governments. If what you want exists, it'll be here…" She let out a whoop of triumph and pulled several tubes off the wall, taking a look at their labels before placing them on the large wooden table in the center of the room. "Here you are," she said. "The city of Trifectus, surveyed out to the first century of the Trifecta, including some of the initial plans, just in case you want them."

"Many thanks, miss," he said with a small bow. "I am in your debt."

"Sure," the young girl said, looking him up and down. "You stay out of trouble, and for the love of all that's good and gracious, don't damage anything in here. The head librarian will string us both up by our toes in the dungeons and leave us to rot."

Henrik raised his hands in surrender. "I would not dream of hurting a room this beautiful."

The assistant nodded and then left, leaving him alone with the maps and his thoughts.

Henrik clapped his hands together and immediately got to work. He was familiar with maps, particularly historical ones, but Trifectus proved to be a fascinatingly unique place. He could see various surges of development during prosperous times, and then sudden stagnation as money or resources ran dry, like a gradually expanding lake of water, the buildings and streets slowly took shape as the years passed by. There was a map for about every twenty to fifty years of development. Using the Guardian headquarters as his starting point, Henrik delved deep into the maps, combing them over for minute details. Eventually, he found what he was looking for: the Dwarven crafting of an underground sewer system, which worked up until partway through the second century of the Trifecta. There had been a plague that year that had cut the city population in half and stopped all construction for another thirty years. Being careful not to damage the maps, Henrik used a straight rod he found in the corner to check for straight tunnel lines.

Sure enough, there was development of the sewer system out into a city street, down across the city. The initial series of houses was later knocked down and moved over to accommodate the expanding headquarters. But those tunnels would still be there. He went back to the original development plan done by the engineers and noticed something unusual. There was a drainage reservoir that was never linked to an actual drainage system that reached aboveground, if this map was to be believed. In fact, all of it seemed to have never been connected.

"Found you," Henrik said in a vicious whisper.

Standing up and stretching from his work, he procured a spare piece of parchment and made a rough sketch he could pass off to Criske and Kelt. He had just stepped out of the library with his parchment in hand when he saw Kelt and Criske waiting for him at the bottom of the steps. The sun had reached its zenith. The hour had come.

"It's time," Kelt said.

Henrik nodded and handed the map to Criske. "Here. This is a rough makeup. That entrance we discovered shouldn't be the only one. I traced its route the best I could. If our theory is right, you should find other entrances along the path I've sketched. It's not much, but it's a start."

Then, with his head held high, knowing he had done what he could, Henrik let Kelt lead him away, toward the sparring grounds, and toward the whipping post.

THE CITADEL

Xeile tried to make the room stop spinning as his legs buckled. "Damn it," he whispered. He hadn't felt this weak in days. "No, not now. You're finally making progress." He sank to his knees, leaning against his bed. His shirt was soaked through with sweat. Despite the reassurances he had hurled at Criske, he could feel it in his bones: he'd gone too far.

With a groan, he forced his aching arms upward and took off his ratty, filth-caked shirt. What had ever happened to Henrik getting him a new set of clothes? He supposed the reappearance of the monster had driven everything but solving the case away from the Dwarf's mind. Xeile could hardly blame him, but he longed for the days when he could actually remember being well rested and clean at the same time. He tried his best to recall those times in Davadain, the crisp and clear spring, with the last vestiges of winter snow stubbornly clinging to the pines, dripping icy water down to the earth, soaking the ground and swelling the crystalline streams that were thawing back into life.

An ache formed in his chest, followed quickly by a sense of confinement. His heartbeat quickened, thunder boomed across his memories, the sound of a sword, slithering and clinking through damp earth—

Xeile forced himself to take deep, slow breaths. He was already seeing ghosts. He couldn't afford to be haunted by anything else.

He looked around at his quarters. They were simple in the extreme, with a cot, a chest for clothes, a small table with two chairs, and a washbasin. On the table was a set of new clothes, which made him feel better, even in his miserable state. The Dwarf had remembered after all. It was difficult, but he managed to pull himself up into a chair, sitting and panting with exertion as he stared at the new clothes, then down at his own. They were ripped and stained in multiple places. The few spots he'd patched were starting to wear down. No wonder people thought he was a homeless vagabond. He certainly looked the part. Gingerly taking off his undershirt, pants, and boots, he limped over to the washbasin and tried to clean himself up the best he could. It was difficult work, removing the layer upon layer of dirt he had plastered on himself over three months of constant travel and panic. It was like the dirt had ground itself into his skin, fusing to his body like a protective overcoat. But slowly, and with frequent breaks to catch his breath, Xeile managed to remove most of the dirt he could reach before finally washing his face and hair.

His hair was a nightmare. Tangled, matted, far longer than he was used to. "Come on," he said to a particularly vicious knot. "You damn thing." He let out a frustrated sigh. "If I had some soapwort, this wouldn't be a problem." But eventually, with a lot of water, his hair finally untangled itself. He was surprised by the sheer amount of hair he had. Three months without cutting it had made it long enough to go down to his shoulders. Despite that, not a single bit of hair graced his face. His mother always told him that it made him look graceful. He thought it made him look too young. Cleaned and somewhat steadied against the exhaustion he was feeling, Xeile took a deep breath and left his little room after donning his new clothes. No, not his room, and not his clothes. He didn't own his own room or clothes. Not yet, anyway. He'd have to earn that.

It was a bright day outside, overcast with clouds hung thick in the air in wavy white lines, breaking up the sheet of blue. He looked at it and frowned. Off-and-on rain was a distinct possibility. He used to hate days like that up in Davadain. It made travel in the woods and working outdoors so difficult. That far north, getting wet in any capacity was always risky. Wet meant a quick drop in body heat, which meant never getting warm again, which meant being frostbitten at best or killed at worst.

Unsure what to do, he meandered about a common area he didn't recognize before seeing a small, insignificant garden on a side path. Curious about the plants, he hurried over to stare at the beautiful blossoms. It took him a moment to recognize what they were, since he'd only seen them once or twice in his life. Pointy, tight groups of light-purple buds radiating out from a central cluster of greenery. Lavender. The smell was faint but enjoyable. He took a deep breath and felt muscles in his back loosen. Now if there was only the smell of woodsmoke, it'd be an excellent day. A thought occurred to him. "Hmm… Glenna likes lavender…" he muttered to himself. "I mean, she does, right?" His heart squeezed as he realized he couldn't remember. Still, he looked around to make sure no one was nearby before carefully selecting a few stalks before wandering around the garden to see what else he could acquire.

It wasn't long before he found more plants he could gather: hyssop, daisy, and what appeared to be some kind of marigold. Satisfied, Xeile decided to go find his fiancée. He froze when he saw a person he didn't recognize staring at him, arms folded, a scowl on his face. It was a large, barrel-chested man with massive arms that seemed determined to escape from the confines of his gray uniform. His head was shaven, with a faded Nomad tattoo pattern going from his forehead and up through his scalp. He had a large, rough gray-and-black beard that stood out against his broad, sun-beaten features. His eyes were a dark misty gray that reminded Xeile of snow that had been mixed with wood ash.

"Oh!" He tried to not look too guilty as he stood there with a fistful of flowers. "Hello… um… sir."

"I didn't expect you to be here," the man said. His voice was incredibly deep, and his tone was none too friendly. "But, this will do."

Xeile took a reflexive step back. Then, he felt an incredible pain in the back of his head.

The world went black, without sight or sound.

The world came back into focus slowly. It only took Xeile a few moments to realize he wasn't in the last location he could remember. It was too dark. There was no sun. There was only some kind of blue light that made everything slightly hazy and flat. A lantern. Like the one Henrik used in that small chamber.

Then, he realized just how much his head hurt. He let out a small groan of pain.

"Ah. You're awake."

The voice was…potent. It was like a strong pine-needle tea. Full of body, like an entire forest crammed itself into a small container. This had the same kind of feeling, but it wasn't like pine needles. It was more like a winter wind, a cold, seeping force. Powerful, but passively so.

Commanding and driving others away with sheer presence alone. The speaker had a strange accent he couldn't quite place. No rolling *r*'s of the Dwarves, no nasal twang of Criske's home, no staccato clipping like Glenna, and no lilting drawl that crept into Kelt's gravelly voice. Xeile slowly looked around, trying to keep his head from throbbing.

His eyes eventually fell upon a figure that looked vaguely familiar. He had very dark hair, black. His eyes were like bright, flat disks that seemed to change color, flickering with purples, reds, blues, and greens. He was of average build and appeared to be middle-aged. Ropes of muscle, but not the kind of muscle Xeile had seen from people back home, muscles from hard work and daily labor. No, this man's muscle looked like Kelt's. Broad shoulders, narrower waist.

The muscles of a soldier, or perhaps a fighter of some kind.

Xeile went to move, but then felt that his wrists and ankles were bound with something bitingly cold and very familiar. Metal. He was chained. Panic seeped into his bones. He swallowed the lump forming in his throat and gently tested his bonds. Moving too much would just make him chafe and get sores. That was the last thing he needed.

"You'll have to forgive me for restraining you," the warrior said, his voice still quiet. "Being cautious is a habit of mine. I want to talk to you."

Xeile took a deep breath and tried to sound braver than he felt. "I'm here, so talk."

The man gave him a knowing smile that made Xeile's stomach drop. Those ever-changing eyes seemed to pierce right through him. "Well, largely, I wanted to make sure that you were functional. A companion of mine was worried that you might be unwell and in need of some assistance."

The young man shifted in his chains as he let out a terrible, grim chuckle.

"Sorry to worry them, but the truth is, I'm not sure I'll ever be okay again. I was doing okay. Then I was chained to a wall."

The warrior's gaze hardened in annoyance, and then smoothed to neutrality. "You seem very unfazed by the fact you're suffering from consistent wild-magic poisoning."

Xeile sighed. "What am I supposed to do? Curl into a ball and weep? We all die. I refuse to spend the few days I have pining for something I can never have. I'm not going to wind up a ghost. I'll do what matters, and I refuse to pass leaving things unfinished."

"Oh, cease your dramatics. Why even bother finding significance?" the warrior asked. "If you're dying, shouldn't you be a little more selfish with the time you have left?"

Xeile shook his head and immediately regretted it. The throbbing pain upgraded itself to a pounding pain in the back of his skull. "I can't do that. I'd regret it if I walked by someone who needed help, and didn't even try."

The warrior laughed, the sound like iced water being poured down his back. That's when Xeile realized that it wasn't just a feeling. He was actually cold. The room itself was dropping in temperature.

He started struggling. "You need to run!" he said. "There's a monster coming! It'll gore you!"

The man raised an eyebrow. "A monster?"

"Yes! A huge horse with antlers and skulls! Please, just trust me! Run! Save yourself—"

A terrible neigh and the rumble of distant hooves filled the room.

Xeile's interrogator turned, his smirk fading before his head snapped back to look at Xeile, and he snapped his fingers. The manacles around Xeile's wrists shattered, freeing him, and he fell to the rough, wet stone on his hands and knees. The man reached to help him up. "Don't touch me," Xeile said, panting, trying to keep the room from spinning. "Just run… I have to stop this thing."

"Don't be a hero," the man said. "Come with me…" He extended a hand. Xeile shook his head.

"Just run. I have to stop this," he repeated.

"Even if it kills you?"

"I'm not letting this thing get away from me again!" He thought briefly of Glenna. "That bastard is mine. I won't die, trust me." The man and Xeile looked over toward the source of another thunderous neigh. Xeile felt his head throb and ears ring from the sound, the cold stone under his hands chilling further by the second. He began to shake. "Go!" he yelled at the warrior.

The kidnapper's colored, flat eyes looked down at his victim, with no panic on his face.

Instead, he gave Xeile a very solemn nod. "You're a man above others, Exile. Your grandfather would be proud, I think." And with that, he took off running at a speed Xeile didn't think possible, as if the air itself were pushing him forward.

There was another neigh. The hooves grew louder, and then thunderous. Xeile hauled himself off the floor, the room spinning. He tried desperately to maintain his balance. He had to. He couldn't let the creature chase after that man.

It was so hard to think, and his vision blurred from the intensity of the cold, his breath coming out in rapid puffs of fog. A distant memory surfaced in his mind, of a time that he'd intensely gotten into trouble.

He was lost in the woods in late autumn, and stumbled across an injured rabbit. A lynx was about to come in for the kill, but he had grabbed a stick and rushed in, spouting words of encouragement to himself that resonated in his mind now. Xeile thought of Glenna, of Criske, and Kelt, who would tear the world apart to find him. They'd find a way to put him back together. As long as he had them, he could do it. He could live after this. "You don't scare me anymore," he whispered. His hands curled into shaky fists.

His words were met by a sudden silence. Then, the hoofbeats resumed as the monster slowly clip-clopped its way into the room, the sound of hoof on stone enveloping him. It still looked like a horse with a shaggy mane and antlers with skulls hanging from it. Its body was still absolutely massive, seeming to fill the cavernous space in an instant. The cold was so intense, it hurt to breathe. Its eyes were otherworldly, red with animalistic fury.

Xeile felt his knees tremble with the rest of his body, but he set his jaw and raised his hands as if he were going to grapple the creature to the ground. "I am Exile Idolon, and I'm going to stop you."

The creature stared at him and let out a snort and a shake of the head, the skulls hanging from its antlers rattling and banging against each other as it did so. It reared back with a neigh that made Xeile's ears ring and brought its hooves crashing down on the floor.

The world erupted into cold and ice. Xeile staggered backward with a cry, and then planted his feet. He wasn't sure what made him do it, but he charged forward, hands outstretched. With a giant leap, he grabbed on to one of the skulls hanging off the creature's antlers. He ripped one off, then another. The cords came free with horrid, wet snaps. The creature stumbled backward, stunned. Hope soared in Xeile's rapidly beating heart, and despite the pain, he reached up and ripped off another skull, ignoring the terrible pain in his hands. Then another skull, then another. Finally, he managed to grab the last one and tore it off, staggering away, gripping it tightly with a sense of finality.

"Stop."

The voice was primal and powerful enough to make Xeile cease his desperate assault, sucking in shallow breaths, trying to fight through a daze of pain.

"I am trying to protect you, not harm you."

Xeile hung there, holding on to the skull, confused. He looked around for the source of the voice. "Who's there?" he asked.

The creature lowered its head and Xeile's feet hit the ground. Hesitantly, he let go of the skull.

The creature looked at him. Those red eyes full of fury had been replaced by an icy calm blue. "I am." That's when Xeile realized the source of the voice. The creature wasn't talking.

There was a rider on its back that had previously been obscured from his view, one that hadn't been there during previous encounters.

It was a ghost with the same icy-blue eyes as the beast. He was actually rather thin, his arms and legs wrapped in bindings and furs, with thick riding boots and heavy gloves. The ghost had a tattered cloak across his shoulders. His face was angular and hard, as if food was not a guarantee in his life before he died. "We have been trying to protect you since you arrived."

Xeile sucked in a shuddering breath that stung his lungs. "You've killed innocent people…" He was going to say more, but the pain in his throat and chest prevented him from speaking. It took all his concentration just to remain on his feet.

The man frowned. "They were far from innocent. All of them wanted you dead. And I cannot let you perish before your purpose is completed."

"My…purpose?" Xeile asked, still shuddering from the cold.

"Yes. We still have much to do if we are to conquer the rest of Meraria with the might of House Idolon, Lord Taron."

"'Lord who now?'" Xeile asked, swallowing. He knew perfectly well who the man was referring to. Taron Idolon, the necromancer-king who was so terrible, they created the Trifecta after he died. But he had to buy time. He walked slowly over to the man. Regardless of who this man was, or what he was doing on top of the creature, Xeile knew he had to stop them both. Anything related to Taron Idolon was not a good sign.

The man smiled at him, a smile so genuine, so kind, it gave Xeile pause. "Sorry, Taron. I forgot that you aren't one for rank."

"Yeah, that's me," Xeile said, walking closer. He gave the man a grin, his knees shaking. "Can't be too stiff with my own friends and forces. Makes me very untrustworthy."

"Well said," the man agreed, grinning. It felt as though he were greeting an old friend, and yet like he was intruding on something ancient and evil. Suddenly, his face darkened. "We'll save him, Taron. Your brother will be king yet. Mark my words, those damn Elves and Dwarves will get what's coming to them."

"Indeed," Xeile agreed quietly. He reached out a hand and grabbed hold of the creature's flank. A wild idea crossed his mind. He had forced the creature to run by pouring energy into it, shocking it. If he could pour energy into it, could he take energy away from it?

Xeile wrapped his arms around one of the creature's legs. It started to kick and thrash wildly, making his entire world a spinning blur of pain. But sure enough, his aura flared to life in a freezing, smoky black haze. And he felt energy surge into him.

When Criske had given him energy through a stone, it was like a steady stream. This, to Xeile, was like an overwhelming torrent, crashing over him in a deluge that threatened to break his will, his soul. And he felt something else, something he hadn't felt from touching any other spirit, not even his mother.

It was a mind. A powerful foreign mind with a will all its own. It didn't have any normal sense of logic. It slammed into Xeile's remaining consciousness with an animal fury that at first terrified him, but he steeled himself. He had dealt with this before. It was a horse that refused to be tamed. A wild stallion that was beholden to nothing.

His voice didn't feel like his own as he spoke. Was he actually speaking? Was it in his mind? He couldn't be sure. The entire room was still a blur, his ears were ringing again, and he had vomited while trying to hold on, but his mind was being wiped blank by this creature.

"I don't want to tame you. I just want you to stop killing people. Please. Don't. Please, just listen." The words were jagged and raw. Like the stubborn rocks that jutted out from the roaring rapids, refusing to give in. Then, to his shock, the fury started to decrease, and then a voice resonated in his ears, like a howling gale was compacted down and forced to whisper.

"*You…seek guidance…yet you do not have a bond.*"

The creature stopped thrashing. Xeile slid down on the floor. He was dimly aware that he was bleeding and that several people were shouting. He felt of some kind of cold breeze on his face, even though his entire body felt like it was on fire. A metallic taste flooded his mouth. "Please…don't hurt innocent people… anymore…"

The freezing wind intensified, coming in waves. "*You do not fear death. You are like him… I will show you…the soul you've made.*" The pain and heat intensified, then slackened. Xeile lay huddled on the ground, shaking as his body refused to return to a normal temperature. Was he going to be locked in a chilling and blazing vortex forever?

Then there was an incredible, steady heat in him. A hard, resolute feeling he couldn't shake. It was surrounded by flickers and sparks, but that steady sensation was still there. It was like a piece of metal that had been heated on the forge. Then the warmth cooled as if his very heart were an ironwork that was being quenched in a barrel of water.

The heat became a steady warmth. Xeile opened his eyes and something slowly came into view. It was the creature, its massive horse head looming over him, its eyes still an icy blue. That voice like the howling wind came into his ears once more. "*I have connected with another. The forging is done.*"

THE SOLDIER

Kelt sat in one corner of the room as Henrik let out a groan of pain, trying so hard not to move as they bandaged his torn and ragged flesh. Kelt bit down on his lower lip so hard it almost bled. This was an accurate and appropriate punishment, but despite all his years of working with the Guardians, floggings never got easier. In reality, it was almost less painful to be subject to one than witness one. Every single lash, Kelt was grateful he wasn't the one who had to do it. It was his apprentice, and technically his responsibility, after all. Guilt formed like a solid mass of burning coals in his chest, making him writhe and shift in his chair. *I should have reprimanded him immediately, or cut him off,* Kelt thought. *I have to do better.* He went to stand, but Henrik let out a moan.

"Don't leave…please… The map…read the map…"

His words shackled Kelt to the spot. Just before he had been whipped, Henrik had given Kelt a map, claiming it was a likely hiding spot for criminals and warranted investigating. Criske would likely be able to find his way around to the various locations. Kelt hadn't bothered to read it. He had been too occupied trying to prepare himself and Henrik for the event. Now, he had to give it a look.

"I'll read it," Kelt promised. "But I have to go get Criske and Xeile."

Henrik smiled at him, a weak, delirious grin. "Oh. Good." And then he promptly passed out.

Head medic Nedra checked him briefly, feeling his pulse. "Ah. He's passed out from the pain, but his pulse isn't weakened. We'll look after him. Go."

Kelt went, the guilt settling into his stomach. Two years ago, he probably wouldn't have minded as much. But now…just the thought of whipping someone made his stomach turn. What was wrong with him? He found Criske with his family for lunch, the group chatting casually among themselves. Criske, however, sat at the table, and it didn't look like any of his food had been touched. He was staring into the distance as if his mind were miles away. As soon as they noticed Kelt, everyone fell silent and stared.

"Who's there?" the old man yelled. "I'll kill ya!"

"Peace, sir. I need to discuss case matters with Criske."

"Bah!" The elder man started to stand. "You can see yourself—"

"It's fine," Criske interrupted. "He's my boss." He stood and followed Kelt out the door. When he shut the door behind him, Criske looked up at Kelt. "So, how is he?"

"He's...in a lot of pain," Kelt admitted. "But I have no doubt he'll pull through. Medic Nedra is seeing to him now. He gave me a map. Considering you patrolled so often...I am going to give this to you. I'm likely going to get a notice of being thrown off the case today."

Criske grimaced, but nodded. "Yeah. You're actually making progress. Heavens forbid something actually get done, right?" He took the map from Kelt and peered at it. After a moment, he nodded. "Yeah, I know where all these are. You want me to look into it? See if any of these have a port like the one you mentioned?" He continued to stare at the tunnels. "Wait…this is one street over from where we found our victim," he said, pointing at one of the streets on the sketch. "Hmm… We need to go explore these tunnels. Maybe get Xeile and Glenna first, along with a Spell Breaker crew, yeah?"

Kelt nodded. "I would start with Xeile. I have some other things I have to research, but gather everyone you can and fill them in. Then put in a formal request for a Spell Breaker squad. You shouldn't get too much protest for that. If anyone does, send them my way. I'll be in the archive in the library."

"The archive? What are you going to do there…sir?" he asked.

"I'm putting an old case of mine to rest. Or trying to. I told Xeile I'd look into his mother's sentencing."

Criske nodded. "Fair enough. I'm on it, Kelt." Kelt raised his eyebrow at the informality, but the weapons master didn't say anything. "Sir," Criske blurted, inwardly kicking himself. He gave Kelt a casual salute and hurried off.

It'll be in good hands, he told himself. *Criske is competent. He'll be okay.* He hurried over to the library, then to the archives, where the two wardens now let him pass by unopposed, staring at him like he was going to burst into flames. He hurried down the staircase, taking the steps two at a time. Then, he started the gruesome task of digging through writs of execution. Xeile's and Mathiene's orders would have been right next to each other if Xeile had one. So, Kelt dug through the records, organized by time of the writ being issued. Then he discovered something that made his stomach feel like it had dropped into his feet. There wasn't a writ of execution for Xeile at all.

But there wasn't one there for Mathiene either.

That can't be, Kelt thought, his nausea growing. He flipped back and forth between the two writs where Mathiene's should have been. *No. I held it. I held the writ in my hands. The seal wasn't fake. I checked it. Was it misplaced? It must have been.*

Kelt spent the next two hours going through the records, trying to find anything related to the writ of execution. No luck. His breathing quickened. Then, a slow fire started in his toes, spreading and flaring upward through his legs, then into his stomach, then his skull, causing his blood to pound and his ears to ring. Rage filled him.

It wasn't an execution for wrongdoing. It was an assassination.

He felt a sudden desire to find the nearest body of water and throw himself into it, to scrub his body, to rid himself of the sensation of filth that settled in him. He suppressed his anger, remembering Xeile's expression as the boy stared up at him, agreeing to help him.

He was right. He was right to be paranoid. The entire time.

Kelt shook his head. *No. It just likely isn't on file here.* Doubt snuffed that theory immediately. Upon being sealed, a writ of execution was immediately filed away in the archives for keeping within the law. A new thought occurred to him.

He searched for Mathiene's assignment record. It was there, her performance as a Spell Breaker was exemplary. Multiple rogue magicians stopped, several honors awarded to her. Then, roughly fifteen years ago, her records just ended. Nothing listed, not even her going missing. If Kelt didn't know better, he would have just assumed she was still at her post. No questions raised.

But Xeile is roughly sixteen or seventeen, he said…that means anyone on assignment with Mathiene would know she got pregnant while on assignment. This is before she went missing. He then looked at all of the other people on her final assignment, which was apparently to hunt down a possible rogue magician or group of magicians related to suspected necromancy. His heart skipped two beats when he saw an unexpected name: Harvest Zhong.

They knew each other. Is that…connected?

Then, he saw another name on the list: Usumi Watazashi.

The world seemed to tilt and spin under his feet, heaving up and down. Usumi knew Mathiene. That meant…she should have known Mathiene was pregnant. She should have known about Mathiene running. She might have even known about Xeile… Why wouldn't she have said anything? She knew Harvest too, and she still hadn't said anything…

A horrible chill went up his spine as he recalled Criske's words.

It could be a traitor…

Kelt took a deep breath. But the note… She was kidnapped. She couldn't be a traitor… But that didn't excuse the fact she knew about Mathiene and said nothing when Xeile came along. She even had Glenna as an apprentice. Glenna had to have mentioned him or Mathiene at some point over the years, right?

Despite all of the explanations he gave himself, his stomach still had an unsettled feeling, like a simmering cauldron that occasionally had a bubble popping on the surface. *I have to find Xeile and get more details,* he concluded. *As painful as that will be.* He gritted his teeth and turned to head upstairs when there was a great crash, the door to the archives flying open with a bang.

Criske was standing in front of him, wheezing. "Kelt, we have a problem," he gasped. "Xeile's… Xeile's disappeared."

"*What?*" Kelt snapped. "He just…ran off?"

"I don't know, but Glenna left a note saying she was going to go look for him. We have to find them before they get themselves killed."

"Assemble a search party, now, head up and get a dispatch ready. I'll be there in two minutes."

Criske nodded and hurried back up the stairs.

Kelt's hand drifted down and gripped the handle of his sword. *I just started figuring this all out,* he thought as he rushed after his apprentice. He had to get his armor on, and then they were going into those tunnels. *You survived for three months to get answers. Don't die on me now, Taeris.*

The Outcasts

Criske looked in awe at the eight men and women around him. He had seen some incredibly tough people before, warriors that could slit the throat of someone before they even blinked. He had been friends with some of them. But that was nothing compared to this lot. They all strapped on their swords and donned their chain shirts and helmets with an ease and speed he had never seen before. They all wore focused looks of confidence born from practice. Each of them had numerous scars on their hands, neck, and head, close calls on various assignments, or what his father liked to call "practical badges of service."

The eldest of the group appeared to be about a decade older than Kelt, a huge man, around six feet tall, with more muscle than Criske had ever seen before. His gray hair was a wild, ropy snare, his ebony skin marking him as one of the rare Human tribes of water Nomads. His beard was threaded and decorated with a series of brightly colored beads, and his face was covered in scars. From the interactions others had with him, Criske could tell, he was clearly the senior of the group, and they looked to him as their leader.

That's why when he walked over to Criske, the boy felt his heart fly into his throat. "So," the warrior said. His voice was a rich bass that seemed like it would carry at fifty paces, even if he whispered. "You're Kelt's apprentice, then?"

"One of them, yeah…I mean…yes, sir. Well, there's another named Henrik, but he's not here," Criske stammered.

The old man nodded. "Good. Good. Let's see if my student chose wisely."

"Your student?"

"Yes. I taught Kelt about weaponry when we were much younger. I was also one of his examiners when he tested for the title of weapons master."

"Ah," Criske said, unable to think of much else. He was too preoccupied by the man's weapon at his waist, a hammer that looked quite capable of cracking skulls open. "That's good. We'll need your experience to deal with that… thing."

The man's eyes darkened. "Yes. Yes, we will. I don't know much about this Exile fellow, but I have been filled in on the creature he's fighting against. Sounds like one of the nastiest wraiths I'll have ever dealt with."

Criske swallowed and nodded. "I've seen it in action. You can't even let it touch you."

The man smiled. "Don't worry. Even if it touches me, I won't keel over that easily." He patted Criske casually on the shoulder. The Half-Elf felt his knees buckle under the pressure of his hand. "Now, do you still have the map?" Criske handed it over. The man nodded. "Good. Any recommendations about which entrance we use?"

Criske pointed at a particular entrance, the same one that was near the murder victim he'd found on patrol. "My guess is that their lair, base, or whatever you call it is going to be closer to here. It's roughly in the middle, so quick travel all around. Near that deposit place right here."

The man nodded and smiled. "And you and Henrik found all this out on your own?"

The apprentice shrugged uneasily. "Well, not really all by ourselves. We did get some hints here and there. Some help from Kelt too… and we'd still be stuck without…Xeile…" The thought of Xeile made his heart squeeze. They had worked so hard to keep him safe, but he had disappeared without a trace. Criske just hoped that Xeile was going to be okay. He had set up a search party, just like Kelt ordered. The weapons master had gone with them, telling him to remain behind with the Spell Breakers until they got into the tunnels, then he was to go back to headquarters and wait with Henrik.

"Xeile?" the old man asked. "Who's that? Another apprentice?"

"No, Xeile Taeris…he's a medium that was helping us on the investigation…" Criske's words drifted off as the man visibly paled, his eyes going wide. "Have you heard of him before?"

The man shook his head. "No…it's just…a medium? An honest-to-Orithan'awun medium?"

Criske nodded. "Yeah. He drove off what we're hunting all by himself… Kind of…shoved, or shocked, it away…"

The man's eyes narrowed. He lowered his head, muttering to himself in High Elvish.

Criske was fairly sure he wasn't supposed to understand him. Few Half-Elves ever actually got the chance to learn Elvish of any kind, let alone the language reserved exclusively for female Elves. The fact this man knew it was even more exceptional. "It can't be…a Citadel?"

Criske didn't let on that he'd understood, making his face a careful mask. This man knew something, but Criske wasn't sure what it was, or what it pertained to. "So…are we set to go?" Criske asked.

The man looked up and looked at the rest of the Spell Breakers. They all stared back at him expectantly. "Orders, Breaker Gallrick?" one of them asked.

The tall man patted Criske on the shoulder. "He's going to lead us to the entry point. Standard procedures. This is a nasty wraith, at least in a confined space. Archers, you're going to do a lead, then fade. Two go and drop. Hold the bar until I hit point. Got it?"

Criske had no idea what that meant beyond the first sentence, but everyone else murmured their assent. Gallrick looked down at Criske. "Well, lad. Lead the way."

Criske felt incredibly out of place leading a group of eight heavily armed Guardians to the sewer passage. People immediately scrambled out of the way on sight of them. It was midafternoon, and plenty of people were out and about. But they didn't run into any traffic. Criske occasionally saw a Human Territories member of the Watch, in their red-and-tan uniforms, talking with locals, likely asking about the case.

Criske thought about those Territory soldiers with a grin as he walked toward a likely end to the whole affair. That'd teach them to not throw Kelt off a case next time around. When they turned the corner to reach the entrance, though, his smile faded. The seal to the unused sewer looked like someone had blasted it apart with a high-powered ballista or had taken hammers to it. "Looks like someone got here first," Gallrick said. Criske looked at the rubble, squinting. He saw something on it. A few bloody handprints, as if someone had cut their hand as they were trying to shift it. And if he was right, those handprints…

He grabbed Gallrick's arm. "Keep an eye out for anyone in a Guardian uniform down there. Head Magician Usumi has gone missing. She might be captive there. Her apprentice could be too."

"The apprentice have a name?" Gallrick asked.

"Glenna Nall," Criske said.

Gallrick nodded. "We'll keep an eye out, but that monster has to come first. Map?"

Criske handed the map over to Gallrick, who stared at it for a moment before pocketing it. "Alright. We'll try to be back as quickly as possible. Give Kelt my regards."

Criske stood and watched as the eight of them dropped through the hole and into the inky darkness. "Best of luck," he murmured softly. "I get the feeling you're going to need it."

34

THE CITADEL

Xeile continued to silently edge his way down the tunnel, glad that his soft-soled boots weren't making noise. Even so, every single sound carried and the echo made moving undetected incredibly difficult, making him far more nervous.

Matters were not helped by the massive horse creature that traveled quietly behind him. Its hooves didn't seem to make any noise at the moment, which was an improvement over the thunderous sounds of before. But it emitted a faint blue glow. Thanks to the fact he could see spirits, Xeile wasn't even sure if that glow was visible to anyone but him. He had been walking for what seemed like hours, but didn't have any accurate gauge on how long he had been down here.

He didn't speak at all, but he could feel a chill on the back of his neck, like the horse-creature was breathing winter wind onto him. He wasn't sure why it was following him, but it wasn't attacking. He'd take his victories one at a time.

Eventually, he heard a voice.

"Damn it. He better be here or I am going to burn off his eyebrows."

He recognized the threat instantly. "Gigi!" he whispered softly. "Gigi, is that you?"

The sound of running footsteps pounded closer and closer to him. Xeile readied himself to bolt, but a glowing purple light rounded around a corner and came charging toward him. In the middle of the purple light was Glenna, a scowl on her face. The purple light died as she came to a stop in front of him. "Found you!" she whispered triumphantly. "What the blazes are you doing down here?"

"What are you doing here?" Xeile countered.

"Looking for you. You weren't in your room, so I started searching. I figured you were looking at one of the crime scenes. I found a cracked cover on the ground, so I moved the pieces and investigated."

"Wait, you came here without help? We need to get out of here. Now."

"Are you being pursued?"

"Don't know. And I don't want to take any chances. I'll tell you the details later. Do you remember the way out?"

"I do. Come on." She concentrated, and her aura flared to life around her body, filling the area with purple light. "Just be careful not to touch me," Glenna commanded.

"Right."

The three of them walked down the strange sewers. They were completely devoid of smell, long abandoned, and dry, like a dark tomb forgotten in time by the world of the living above. Glenna led the way, Xeile staring at her back, the creature silently drifting behind him. Glenna had no reaction to the creature. Given that it was a ghost she couldn't see or hear, he wasn't surprised. But he'd have to tell her at some point. The only question was how.

After a period of time, Glenna froze so suddenly that Xeile nearly crashed into her. "What's wrong?" he asked.

"Down!" Glenna screamed.

She grabbed him and they collided with the stone floor. A solid object came soaring overhead and slammed into the rock, the sound of the collision making Xeile's ears ring.

Glenna immediately rolled off of Xeile, her aura flaring to life and stretching outward, then suddenly retracting, a blast of flame erupting where it had just been. Xeile flinched and squeezed his eyes shut against the sudden burst of light.

"Well, then…" a woman's voice said, calm and collected. "What are you doing here, my dear apprentice?"

Xeile heard footsteps. Then, he saw the lilac glow. He didn't immediately recognize who the woman was, but Glenna did.

"Usumi? What are you—"

Another object came rocketing forward, but now, with all the light about, Xeile saw the source that sent the projectile. As soon as Usumi's aura retracted, the rock flew at them. Glenna just barely dodged out of the way, sending off another blast of fire that blinded Xeile. He staggered back, letting out a cry of pain from the sudden brightness hitting his eyes. He heard a muffled thump and the sound of Glenna's body hitting the ground.

"No!" he cried. As his vision came back into focus, Glenna was on the ground, bleeding from a gash on the head, not moving. "No," he choked out, dropping to his knees and reaching for her without thinking. "No…no…stay with me, Gigi…" he said, his voice louder. She didn't respond.

Xeile put his head to her chest and was rewarded with the sound of a heartbeat. She was still alive. Relief coursed through him, then anger. He looked at Usumi as she stared down at them with her violet light swimming around her.

"Don't even think about trying to touch me," she said with a faint smile. "I'll drop a rock on that little girl's head and she'll be dead. If you want her to live, you'll cooperate and come with me."

Xeile looked at Glenna, then at Usumi. He tightened his embrace around Glenna. "No," he said firmly.

"What?"

"No. I'm not giving you what you want. If we die, then we die together."

"You'd have your own girl die with you?"

"No," Xeile admitted. "That's why this is such a stupid idea."

Xeile willed energy to flow from him into Glenna. His aura came to life, a dull gray that quickly turned into a black that matched the surrounding shadows.

Glenna's aura flared to life and she let out a cry of pain, her eyes flying open. She sat upright, pulling a dart from her collar and throwing it in one smooth motion. Usumi tried to react with some kind of magic, but she wasn't fast enough. Xeile knew that if Glenna were in peak condition, the dart probably would have hit something vital. As it was, the dart sank deep into Usumi's thigh. The magician let out a cry of pain, her aura flickering as her concentration broke. The head magician turned and fled, limping down the hallway.

Xeile tensed, about to pursue. He halted as he heard Glenna let out a pained moan. "Damn it," she mumbled. "Stupid woman. Got the drop on me…"

"It's okay," Xeile said gently. "I'm here. I'm here. Just hush. We'll get you out of here. Can you stand?"

"I think so."

Xeile gently put one of Glenna's arms around his shoulder. "Just lean on me," he said. "We'll get you looked at."

"Damn it…she's getting away…"

"Don't worry about that," Xeile said softly. "It's more important we get you to safety. Leave catching her to the other Guardians. Come on."

"I'm sorry I used you…" Glenna said, her words slurred.

"What? I think you've hit your head too hard. We'll get out of here. I promise."

"You can touch me…"

Xeile felt his face flush. "Um…as great as an offer as that is, now isn't the time, I think…"

"No, idiot," Glenna groaned. "You can touch me without draining my aura."

It took Xeile a moment to realize that Glenna was right. Even though he had poured energy into her, he didn't feel the same biting cold in his lower body. He didn't feel the power seeping into him. He didn't feel the pain either. It had been so consistent for the past three months that he hadn't even bothered to check if he hurt or not. Like it was white noise he could tune out, except for the occasional sudden attacks. "We'll deal with it later. We have to get you out of here."

It was slow going down the single hall. Glenna was having difficulty concentrating, making her physically manifested aura dim and flicker sporadically. Even though he could see thanks to the horse creature behind him, Glenna was both disoriented from the lack of light and her injury. It felt like it went on for miles, but Xeile wasn't sure. It wasn't until he actually felt his shoulder hit a ladder that he found a potential exit. After feeling around, he smiled. "Looks like we have a way out. I'm not sure I can move whatever is blocking the way." He gently set Glenna down, leaning her against a wall. "I'll be back quickly."

He climbed up the ladder, but when he went to push the cover of the exit away, it didn't budge. He tried shoving harder, but it still refused to move. Whatever this was, it was solid. Not metal. Stone maybe? He looked over in Glenna's direction. In better circumstances, he might've asked her to do magic. "What now?" he whispered to himself.

"I can show you."

Xeile startled and nearly fell off the ladder. He turned and saw the antlered horse walking over to him. "I can show you how to move it."

"Alright," Xeile said slowly. "How do I do it?"

"Close your eyes…and dream…"

Xeile closed his eyes. "Okay…I've got the first part down pretty well, but the second is a bit of a problem. How do I dream without going to sleep?"

"Touch the stone. And dream…as I do…"

Xeile gulped, reached out, and touched the stone. The horse-creature touched his nose to Xeile, and the young man gasped.

A torrent of energy and emotions thrashed and kicked around in him, threatening to tear free. A horrible icy chill filled him. He would have let go of the ladder and curled into a ball were his fingers not frozen stiff.

"Ice is a sister of water, the greatest knife of time."

He suddenly got a clear image in his mind, an image of water freezing in a crack of a cliff face by the sea, pushing and expanding gradually over time, over so many days, maybe even years, of winter. The ice finally dominated the rock, almost encapsulating it with icicles and frost. Eventually, there was a crack and the stone fell into the sea with a mighty crash. The image was vivid in Xeile's mind despite the pain that wracked his body. Then, just like that, the image and the pain were gone. He heard a thunderous crack above his head. He looked up and his hand was glowing a painfully bright teal blue. No, his entire body was encased in it. But above him, the cover was covered in veins of ice. He gave it another shove, and the cover split apart, falling on top of him, barely missing his head, nicking his ears and slamming into his shoulders, one of which let out a funny popping sound, followed by a wave of pain that nearly made him black out. He slipped off the ladder and landed hard on the ground, groaning in pain. All the energy in his body seemed to have drained out of him. All his sleepless nights hit him in an instant. He looked up to see the horse-creature standing over him. "What…what did you do to me?"

"I showed you the path. You provided the energy."

"But now I…can't…move…"

"You are weak. You must get stronger."

"Thanks…a lot." Xeile tried to get up and move, but he couldn't. "Glenna, are you there?" he called. His tongue felt like lead in his mouth.

Glenna let out a muffled sound that sounded like "yaks" but Xeile guessed was affirmation.

"I'll come get you…soon…" he said.

"I hear voices!"

Xeile turned to the sound of a new voice coming from the same hallway Usumi had fled down. He tried to will his body to move, but his arm and back muscles refused to cooperate.

Then they cramped and put the question of moving out of his mind entirely.

Soon, the new person came into view with more tagging along, holding torches. Xeile tried to move again, and managed to crawl over to Glenna, getting up to his knees, leaning on the wall. He pulled the knife from Glenna's sheathe, holding it shakily out in front of himself, still leaning on the wall for support. The group finally came into view. It was a squad of armed people with serious expressions and what looked like Guardian uniforms, but Xeile couldn't tell.

He staggered in front of Glenna, leaning against the wall. "No... You're not touching her," he said. "I'll rip you apart if you try..." He didn't know where those last words came from in his mind, but they at least sounded impressive. Or, at least they would have sounded impressive if he could put any energy behind them.

"Steady, lad," the man at the front of the group said. "You're bleeding. We're here to help."

"Oh..." Xeile murmured. He couldn't let go of the dagger. "I don't need help. I have Glenna. I will protect those who can't protect themselves. Till my last blood and breath. I'll kill all of you if I have to..."

Something passed across the group member's face. Pity? Revulsion? Xeile couldn't tell, nor did he have the energy to care. He sank to his knees. "Don't...touch..." The world went black as the remaining strength he had departed.

THE SOLDIER

Kelt returned to his office and slumped down in his desk chair, putting his head in his hands. Criske sat in the room with him in silence after shutting the door. Kelt was grateful Criske was smart enough to not ask how the search for Xeile went. They had spent hours combing all over the city, and it had been hours upon hours since the Spell Breakers went underground. The sun had long dipped over the horizon, and the moon made its pale-white appearance, heralded in by the drone of abundant summer insects and a reduction in temperature, though the air persisted on clinging to the skin. He watched Criske, who was staring into the fire. Judging by the Half-Elf's expression, his mind was miles away.

Kelt couldn't help but wonder how Criske could sit so still under pressure. Most young people he'd met were pacing by this point, frustrated with their own inability to do something. But Criske was motionless. "How is Henrik?" Kelt asked.

"He's managing. If we're lucky, he'll be fully functional in two weeks. If they stitched him, he might heal faster, but that can be dangerous with whippings. We'll see how it plays out. My hope is that he'll stay healthy." The Half-Elf fell back into silence, absently drumming his fingers on his leg, his eyes fixed on a single spot on the wall, like he was reading something with great intensity. Kelt fought his own restlessness by building up the fire again. Though the heat was entirely unnecessary, he added some green wood to better repel the insects coming through the window, thrown open in the hopes of catching some nonexistent breeze. "It makes no sense," Criske continued suddenly, causing Kelt to flinch, "why Xeile would suddenly run off like that. It's like he didn't trust us… I mean, you, I'd understand him wanting to run from, but Glenna is here, and I doubt he'd want to leave her alone. That leaves kidnapping."

"I know," Kelt agreed. "But I haven't found him. Not even the Watch or our hunting party turned up any results. Makes me worry that he's hidden away somewhere, being made into some kind of…idol."

"Idol?"

Kelt nodded. "The Idolon Remnant… people that still believe that Taron should be king and want to tear down the Trifecta, they need a new figurehead since the last one died. Someone like Xeile could be a real prize for them. If they convince him to join their side… it'd be a disaster. Add on to that disaster that he is afraid of most Guardians, and we'd be lucky not to lose a significant portion of our Spell Breakers in the process of trying to kill him."

"Xeile won't do that kind of thing," Criske protested. "Not how he operates, yeah? He's too honest, too straightforward. He ran for three months to forgive you. Plus, I doubt he'd ever put himself opposite Glenna. If they're as close as it seems."

"You think they aren't?"

Criske pressed his lips into a tight line, weighing how to answer. "They've got… It's like they're in a big storm and haven't figured their way out yet. We'll see if they sink or swim, yeah?"

Kelt nodded but couldn't think of what else to say. Eventually, he forced himself to move, pacing back and forth along the length of his office, his mind both abuzz with activity and utterly incapable of concentration. The fireplace had burnt low again when there was a knock on the door.

Kelt snatched up his sword. He cracked the door, a familiar set of eyes peering back at him. Grinning, he yanked the door the rest of the way open. "Gallrick? Well, looks like you're not quite retired yet. I thought they had you on that cushy village protection assignment down south!"

Gallrick didn't return the smile, but nodded. "Nope. I got pulled here. Requested as backup for the whole mess going on here in Trifectus. First day here, I'm doing some kind of mission in a tunnel, and then find two kids down there, one of which seemed to have partially frozen over and made a cover explode. What in the name of Whanri'i is going on, Kelt?"

Gallrick looked haggard about the face, more weathered down than when Kelt had seen him last. More gray hairs, and even some white ones in his beard. He was still incredibly fit for his age, with rippling muscle, but there was a slight stoop to his shoulders, as if the weight of his deeds, both good and ill, were pressing down on him, deepening the shadows around his eyes and the heightening intensity of his dark-brown eyes. And in those eyes was a gaze of something Kelt wasn't used to seeing. Fear?

"Come in and have a seat. I'll explain."

Gallrick stepped in, nodded at Criske, who immediately stood and saluted before being acknowledged by way of a nod and sitting back down. Gallrick lowered himself into a chair near the fire. "So…explain."

Kelt did, outlining the investigation, the clues, and all of the evidence he had found about the possible murderer.

"What about the boy? That one named Xeile? Can you tell me his story?"

Kelt frowned. "Alright."

The more Kelt explained about Xeile and the circumstances that led him to this point, the graver Gallrick's expression became. "You said he could see spirits? Beyond a doubt? And he could interact with them?"

Kelt nodded. "Yes…but he's also…sick. We think it's possibly from a broken aura. But for some reason, he's still able to survive… We haven't figured out all the details. I plan to as soon as this case wraps up."

"Well, we found the boy down in your suspicious tunnels. He was guarding a girl, like a last stand, ready to die for her. Guardian girl of some kind."

"Glenna," Criske blurted. "She's Head Magician Usumi's apprentice. She went missing today!"

Gallrick's brows rose and he shook his head. "Well, we found her, unconscious, bleeding, being protected by a boy who was on his last legs. I've seen a lot of things in my time, Kelt. But that boy's eyes… I didn't think people like that still existed."

"What do you mean?"

"The people willing to give everything they have, without a second thought. Complete selflessness, even though there's nothing left in them to give…then…he…" Gallrick's words faded and he shook his head. "He spoke part of the oath, Kelt."

"The Oath of the Guardians?"

"No. He spoke the Oath of Citadels. He has no reason to know those words. He wasn't old enough. Seven winds, you're not old enough either." Gallrick chuckled.

Kelt frowned. "Citadels… I'm not familiar with the term."

Gallrick nodded. "I wouldn't expect you to know them. They were Guardians, specialized to hunt for wraiths and spirits. Basically the power of a Spell Breaker team, but packed into one individual. The Trifecta employed them when the Remnant surged back into power around two decades ago. They were volunteer only. Their auras were broken for a split second, then put back together. The brief exposure to wild magic enabled them to handle wraiths and spirits with their bare hands, to siphon power from magicians…it filled them with strength beyond that of a normal person, in exchange for a shorter life span."

"Intentional… aura breaking…" Kelt repeated slowly. He shook his head, horror rising up in his stomach, clogging his throat, robbing him of words.

Criske recovered from the shock first. "That's…terrible. Isn't that illegal? Per, like…the First Trifecta or something? Can't the current Trifecta not even legalize that? I mean, I'm no expert, but that seems not allowed, yeah?"

Gallrick sighed. "People were terrified. The Trifecta was losing Spell Breakers left and right. People as strong as Kelt and I are rare, even among the Breakers. Wraiths were popping up everywhere, killing with a single touch. Entire towns were slaughtered or taken over.

So…the Trifecta had the Citadel project take place. Eighty volunteers underwent the process. Fifty died in service. Ten of natural causes after retiring. Another ten went missing in action. As for the rest, they continue to serve, though I have no idea where."

"How can you know all this?" Kelt asked. "There's got to be proof of some kind. Surely this can't just be swept into a corner and hidden?"

"I know this because I served with them, Kelt. Sure, they were called Spell Breakers, but all of us who served with them knew better. Someone would scout the area, finding targets, then a Citadel would show up like a wrecking crew."

"Someone who set up spies…like maybe Harvest Zhong?" Criske offered.

Gallrick nodded. "Possibly. I've never heard of Harvest Zhong besides tonight, though. What concerns me is that this Xeile boy exhibits a lot of traits similar to a Citadel. But I'm not sure how. The experiments were very clearly ended after just a year. Too dangerous. Too many dead, and too powerful to control."

"Hey, didn't Xeile mention his mother was a Guardian?" Criske asked. "And Glenna…she used to practice magic with her…because she was the only one strong enough to deal with Glenna's spells…"

Kelt looked at Criske. "That doesn't explain Xeile's aura. It was clearly broken to pieces when we met him. Last I checked, your aura strength doesn't depend on your parents."

"True." Criske sighed. "But can we at least ask him if his mother was ever resistant to magic, or perhaps another question?"

Kelt lowered his head. "You don't have to ask Xeile. I fought her myself." He shuddered as the image of one of his fellow Spell Breakers was smashed into the wall, skull caving in. "She was definitely strong. The only reason we won…" The details came back to him. He was on the ground, moments from dying, but one of the Spell Breakers—the magician—sprinted past her. She had let out a scream and went to run after him. Then Kelt stabbed her in the chest. "The only reason we won is because she was trying to get back to Xeile. To defend her son. He went for the kid as soon as she was occupied."

Something about the image clamored around in his head, and the details rearranged themselves into a horrible, sudden realization. Kelt stood so fast that his chair fell over with a bang. "That whole mission—I don't think it was to deal with Mathiene. I think they were targeting Xeile in particular."

"Why would they want to do that, though?" Criske asked. "That makes no sense."

"Unless he had something different about him," Gallrick offered. "Something that made him dangerous."

"Something like what?" Criske asked. "He's not…special. He was stuck in a dead-end village, working on various bits and pieces. They're lucky Glenna wasn't there, though. She probably would have fried them all."

Kelt's eyes widened. "Say that again?"

"I said they were lucky Glenna wasn't there…" Criske's words drifted off. His eyebrows shot into his hairline. "You think they were after Glenna! Then why would they kill Mathiene?"

"We've been assuming this entire time that Mathiene ran off because she was pregnant with Xeile. But what if that's not true? There'd be no reason for her to run away because she was pregnant. She could easily have given birth and returned to her duties. Elvish women do it all the time during their services. What if, instead, she'd found something so powerful she decided to keep it hidden from everyone? Someone so powerful that they needed to be isolated?"

Criske frowned, then his eyes widened. "Glenna's always going on about being the strongest magician, how nothing is hard for her. When she was old enough, she went and joined the Guardians. She was already strong enough with her magic to become Usumi's apprentice at age fourteen." He looked up at Kelt. "So Mathiene took her and hid her, trained her up to protect herself, to prevent her from being used or something?"

"Not something, someone," Kelt said. "Someone like the Idolon Remnant. Someone of Glenna's talent, if made into a figurehead, could easily become a rallying point, the next Taron Idolon."

"Okay, so Mathiene dies because that's what the writ says. She's a big scary Citadel, so that makes sense. But why shatter Xeile's aura? He doesn't have any outstanding talents or anything. You think they were just trying to tie up loose ends, get rid of witnesses?"

Kelt let out a growl of frustration. He slammed a hand down on his desk hard enough to make the shock travel up his shoulder. "I don't know," he said. "We need to find out what really happened that night, from his point of view."

"Well, you can ask him when he wakes up," Gallrick said. "He's in the medical bay. The new head medic recognized him instantly. Said something about him being an 'annoyingly frequent visitor.'"

The weapons master took a deep breath. "Well, let's go find out, then. Time for me to see why I had to kill a woman without a writ of execution who was protecting her only child."

36
THE OUTCASTS

Criske entered the medical bay with his heart in his throat. Glenna was the real target? Criske had no doubt that Glenna was strong and talented. She was definitely intimidating, but worth committing two murders over? He wasn't so sure about that. But Kelt had a look in his eye, a kind of fire that made Criske keep well away from his reach, just in case.

Gallrick wasn't as high strung, but Criske could see the knitted brow and tightened lips that betrayed his unease. It wasn't hard to find Xeile and Glenna. They weren't in the intensive-care section, which made Criske's shoulders sag with relief, but Glenna's head was bandaged and she was lolling her head from side to side sleeping fitfully. Xeile, on the other hand, was completely motionless. Criske could hardly tell he was breathing.

Kelt walked over and started asking questions to the annoyed medic, who gave him hurried answers. Criske sidled up to Xeile's bed and reflexively checked for a pulse. The moment his fingers touched Xeile's neck, Xeile's hand shot up and gripped Criske's arm like a vise. "No!" Xeile screamed. "I don't want to raise you anymore!" The manic tone in his voice disappeared as his eyes focused on Criske. That's when Criske saw the startling change in Xeile's eyes.

They had turned an icy teal-blue color. The splash of color in his eyes made Criske jerk away, but Xeile's grip rooted him to the spot.

"Oh…Criske," Xeile exhaled, his shoulders slumping as he let go of Criske's arm. "I didn't run off. Someone kidnapped me! Then I talked with this strange guy…then the monster showed up…and—"

Criske patted him on the shoulder. "Easy there, pal. Take a few deep breaths. Kelt is here. Let's wait until he comes over, then you can explain everything once, yeah?" Xeile nodded, looking numb to the universe for a few moments until Kelt walked over.

"Xeile, thank goodness you're alright. What happened to you, lad?"

Xeile took a shaky breath and described what had transpired since they had last seen each other, from his kidnapping to his strange encounter with the man to meeting the monster, then somehow taming it, and, after that, his moment fighting Usumi.

"If it hadn't been for Glenna, I would have died," Xeile said with a smile, running his hand through his black hair. "I don't know what I'd do without her."

Criske shrugged at Kelt, unsure what to say. Kelt looked at Xeile. "Well…" Kelt said. "It looks like you were right, Criske. Regardless of what she was doing down in those tunnels, Usumi attacked her own apprentice, which is treason." Kelt turned to Gallrick. "You need to get your team down there as quickly as you can."

Gallrick nodded and strode off without another word.

Kelt stared at Xeile, who looked back at him expectantly. "Xeile…you said you've…tamed the creature somehow?"

"Yeah. It talks and everything. It looks like whatever those skulls were on its antlers made it go violent. It said it was…bonded with me or something."

Kelt's eyes narrowed. "Are you sure? Are you sure that's what it said?"

Xeile nodded. "Yep. It even did some kind of strange magic on me." He then described how he had managed to break one of those covers with just his hands and some kind of ice. "It was unnatural."

Kelt sighed. "And does this creature have a name?"

Xeile frowned. "Believe it or not, I didn't ask." Xeile turned to look behind him. "You have a name I can call you?" His frown turned to an expression of shock. His face drained of color. He turned and looked at Kelt. "So…he does have a name… 'Idolon,' but it was a giant horse creature. I can't think why it would share a name with a noble family."

Kelt opened his mouth, then closed it. He shook his head. "The symbol of House Idolon."

Criske whipped around to see Henrik limping his way toward them, wincing with each step. His voice was raspy, like he needed a drink of water and smoked too much pipe tobacco. "The symbol of the Idolon barony…it was a horse of some kind, I think."

"Well, what is it, then? Does it even know?" Criske asked.

Xeile stared at the invisible creature next to him. After a moment's pause, Xeile turned and looked at the rest of them, his eyes dark and full of anguish. He seemed to swallow a sob. He put his hands on the side of his head. "No… no… I don't want to be one…"

"What's wrong?" Criske asked. "Xeile, talk to me."

"He's a stagmare!" Xeile wailed. "A herald of death and necromancers!"

"Well…you've been on death's doors quite a few times," Criske said, trying to make it sound reasonable. "Maybe it just got attracted to the fact you've cut it close a lot recently."

Xeile looked up and shook his head. "No… Criske… No… I've…" Xeile slumped forward, putting his head in his hands. He started shaking. "I'm not a good person… This is all my fault. I didn't mean to…" He bit down on his knuckle, shaking.

"Come on, Xeile," Criske said gently. "Talk to me."

"My mother… The reason I ran from Davadain to here… My mother didn't stay dead."

"What do you mean?" Criske asked.

"She got brought back to life…" Xeile sobbed. "And she tried to kill me. I had to…"

Xeile made a gesture of reaching out with his arm, grabbing something, and shoving it into his chest. He doubled over, rocking back and forth. "I had to eat what energy was left in my mother's soul to survive. All I did was take energy from her, over and over. If I hadn't taken her energy over the years, she would have been so much stronger. She could have survived. It's all my fault." He rocked back and forth. "It's all my fault."

Criske immediately reached out and embraced Xeile. "You're not a monster. You're a good person who got dealt a bad hand of cards. That's all, yeah? You're not a monster. And no matter what you did then, I'm still here for you now? And so is Glenna. She hasn't left you behind yet, has she?"

"No…"

"Then it's settled. It's time for you to stop blaming yourself for everything. Come on, deep breaths for me. I can't have you passing out from lack of air. Nedra will kick us all out."

Gradually, Xeile's emotions settled, and exhaustion took over him, carrying him into an uneasy sleep. Criske looked at Kelt, trying to keep himself composed. "Sir…maybe we should leave the questions until morning? Xeile looks tired, and Glenna's not in much of a state to answer anything. As much as we want answers, it wouldn't be right to push for them now, I think…sir…"

Kelt stared at Xeile, his lips pressed together in a grim line. Then, he took a breath. "You make a fair point. Henrik, get back into your bed. You shouldn't be up yet. And from the looks of it, we all could do with some sleep. Criske, hit your bunk and stay there till I come get you. It won't be long before we put the final nail in this. I can feel it."

"Let's hope that the nail is in the case's coffin and not one of ours, yeah?"

"You're a right bucket of cheer, lad."

"I get called that a lot."

"Really?"

"No, sir."

The Citadel

Xeile stirred to a brightening dawn with the feeling he had been beat repeatedly about the head and shoulders. He groaned, tentatively stretching muscles that ached in protest, observing that he was in the Guardian headquarters medical bay again. Really, he disliked the familiarity he was gaining with that location. Pressing his lips together, he sat up very slowly as he attempted to recall the day before, but couldn't remember anything past the encounter in the tunnel. They must have been Guardians after all. Fantastic.

Then, a detail bloomed in his mind. Usumi had been down there. She had attacked Glenna, injured her. Xeile forgot his pain and looked around for Glenna. She was in the bed next to him, her head bandaged and a sour expression on her face he knew intimately.

"Let me guess," he said in a scratchy voice. "Bed rest for a few days and no fun whatsoever."

Glenna turned and her expression lightening considerably. "Nope. No exercise, no reading, nothing. Head injury. And aura shock. Thanks for that, by the way, it was loads of fun." She shrugged. "I was able to stick a dart in her. The blood should give the Spell Breakers a head start."

"Sorry I hurt you," Xeile said. He hoped that behind his plain statement, she could see the larger apology—the one for everything. She seemed to understand, her expression softening. She blinked.

"I just… It's really frustrating to sit and be able to do nothing. You understand?"

"All too well," Xeile admitted. "That first month… I'm glad I couldn't go near a town. I'm not sure I wouldn't have been violent or worse."

"How did you learn to calm down?" Glenna asked. "What made you change how you felt?"

Xeile stared at the ceiling, unsure what to say for a long moment. "Well…I saw ghosts. I saw that, even if I was angry, it didn't really fix the problems that mattered. Being the best or the strongest never seemed to matter. It was always the people they left behind, or the things they didn't do. I met this one ghost…he went by the name Yonhan. He was a Nomad, I think. He was always saying, 'I should have…' over and over. It really brought my world into focus. So I decided to not be scared of dying, since it's going to happen sooner or later, and instead be scared of not doing things that matter." Xeile paused for a moment and let out a weak laugh. "But what do I know? I'm not a philosopher or a wise man."

The two of them stayed quiet, watching the sun play with the shadows on the ceiling, contorting them into unusual shapes and sizes. It was like watching a river that he couldn't touch. He wondered if the ocean was anything like it. Xeile turned to ask Glenna and realized that she had fallen back asleep, her brow line smooth and scowl gone.

He smiled as he recalled the first time he had lost his eyebrows to Glenna's flame. He'd picked some apples during an autumn harvest and had some extras after dispersing them to a few people. He'd figured she could use a snack after her hard training. She was fast asleep, leaning up against a tree, snoring loudly in its shade, the leaves rippling above her, rustling slightly in a light wind. It would have been picturesque if a line of drool hadn't trickled down from the corner of her mouth. He'd set aside the basket of apples and reflexively reached out to wipe her mouth, just as his mom had done to him a thousand times.

Glenna's eyes snapped open and a lash of flame had burst from her hand. Both eyebrows cooked, many apologies were made, a lot of terrible curse words were exchanged. It was the first time they had ever really interacted, as Xeile was normally too wary of her to get close, for fear of being hexed in the middle of the night. It turned out Glenna wasn't malicious, just overly ambitious a lot of the time.

He knew his mother had worked with her on a consistent basis, teaching her how to control her temper, and practice fighting. Xeile had found that riveting to watch; Glenna was a powerful fighter, tricky in her movements, with plenty of feints and footwork, like a blacksmith's tongs, able to twist a situation to a shape that suited her liking. His mother, by contrast, was like a two-handed heavy sledge. Any blow she landed could end the fight, and even with all the tricks and techniques in the world, Glenna had never been able to overpower Mathiene's lifetime of fighting, training, and raw athleticism.

In fact, the more he thought about it, the stranger it was. Xeile frowned. Sure, his mother was well trained, capable, and definitely strong, but she was still in her midforties when she was fighting Glenna. She shouldn't have been able to throw Glenna about like she was a sack of flour with just one hand…right?

Xeile shook his head to clear it and felt his neck cramp in response. "Gah," he said softly, trying to keep his voice down so he didn't wake Glenna up. That didn't keep the medic from coming over, though. With her bright and beaming grin.

"Well, good morning!" she said cheerfully. "How are we feeling today?"

"I've been better," Xeile admitted. "Can I go get breakfast now? I'm starving." His stomach felt like it was trying to eat itself.

"Not yet. We have to check you out first. Don't want that food all coming back up, do we?" She proceeded to put him through a litany of tests that involved movement, which hurt; reflex tests, which hurt less; and examining his various wounds for signs of infection, which hurt a lot. Finally, when she had finished, she made a grand sweeping gesture toward the exit. "Well, I suppose I can let you go. Have a great day, and I hope we don't see you anytime soon!"

"If you say another word in that grating voice, woman," Glenna said, "I may have to strangle you."

The medic turned her bright expression toward Glenna. "Oh nonsense! You're just injured in the head. Don't you worry, ma'am! It'll get better soon and you'll be out exploding yourself before you know it."

"That was one time," Glenna feebly protested. "One time."

Xeile knew it was probably the second or third, but decided that discretion was the best part of valor, and excused himself from the situation by giving Glenna a gentle kiss on the hand. "I'll check in on you this evening, okay? Don't cause too much trouble, Gigi."

"I could say the same to you, idiot. If you get yourself injured one more time, I'm going to break out of this hospital wing and remove your eyebrows again. Got it?"

"Yes, ma'am," Xeile said, offering her a salute. "I will be a model soldier."

She smiled. "Get out of here before you give me a worse headache."

Xeile gave her hand one last squeeze before leaving the medical bay and heading toward the mess hall.

The morning was bright and clear, although too warm for Xeile's taste. The air was thick with moisture, like it was trying to grab hold of his skin and refusing to let go. "Could cut it with a knife," he grumbled. He looked up to the sky. Late morning by the looks of it. Guardians on morning patrol and morning duties had likely already eaten and left. He could dine in peace, without fear of being attacked, seized, or arrested.

His pace picked up as he caught the smell of cooking food. Entering the hall, he was engulfed by the wondrous scent of fish, potatoes, and something he could only identify as stew of some variety, maybe a bean or pea mixture?

Xeile hurried up, grabbing a bowl, looking at the cooks plaintively. "Hi. May I have some?"

"You have the money?" the cook asked with a raised eyebrow. He looked Xeile's uniform up and down. Following the cook's gaze, Xeile inspected himself for the first time. He was still wearing the uniform he had been abducted in.

It was spattered in mud, dust, and what Xeile suspected was blood, both his and Glenna's. He felt around in his pockets and his heart sank.

Of course he didn't have money. He hadn't had money for almost two months. He looked at the pottage in its clay pot on the fire behind the cook. To the soldiers here, it was probably the least appetizing on the menu. Even that seemed to be beyond reach. He wished he could just hurry into the woods and snare something, maybe even go fishing, but that was probably illegal here for some reason or another. If he left the city while it was on lockdown, he'd probably never be able to get back in.

Suddenly an arm reached past him and dropped a few coins on the counter. "Get him a meal, yeah? He's on contract with us."

Xeile turned to see Criske looking at the cook. He flashed Xeile a smile. "I know, they're a bunch of misers here, but at least it's hot."

The cook scowled at them, but he put some food into a bowl and handed it to Xeile. "Bring it up to the front when you're done."

Xeile took the bowl and sat down with Criske. Without hesitating, he started devouring all of it. It took him a moment to realize that

Criske was staring at him in a bizarre fascination. "What?" Xeile asked. "What is it?"

"You eat like the bowl will make its great escape at any moment. You've got nothing to worry about here."

Xeile looked at his bowl and felt like a rabid animal. "Sorry," he mumbled.

Criske chuckled. "Don't worry, believe me, I understand. I act the same way unless I think about it. Never know when your next meal is going to be, yeah? Didn't have to tell me twice to eat up during basic training, though most of the time we wound up vomiting everywhere. You ever have to do some kind of training?"

Xeile frowned, thinking back on it. "Not really. I wanted to study to be a smith, but I haven't gotten much of a chance. Too busy hunting or gathering food for folks so we could get by. My mother didn't really work beyond some basic labor and gardening. Didn't really know how to do much besides being a fighter."

"So you can…what…go live in the woods for an eternity?" Criske asked.

The young man laughed at the idea. "No, not really. Some things are really hard to make in the wild. Blades, clothes, rope…things like that are tough to replicate. I'd probably have to go to a town at some point."

Criske nodded regardless. "Still, you could do some cool things with those skills. Not having to answer to anyone, being your own person…" He looked wistful. "Sorry."

They sat in silence for a little while. "So…" Xeile said. "You have any idea what's next for the case? Any news?"

The Half-Elf sighed, tracing a fingernail idly along the grain of the wooden table. "No such luck yet. We haven't seen or heard from Gallrick or any of his team since they went below. That's generally not a good sign. Kelt's trying to put on a brave face, but…he just got a notice from the baron that he's now officially off the case."

Xeile let out a groan. "Oh, damn it…and we were just making some progress too."

Criske shrugged. "You know them noble types: everyone else can take the blame." He leaned back and stretched. "They'll be lucky to ever flush out the criminals at this rate. Still, being back on patrol won't be too bad. It'll be nice to feel the open air."

A jolt ran up Xeile's spine. The woods, surviving in them, the city, the tunnels…an idea quickly assembled itself in his brain. "Say… Criske…those tunnels…were awfully dark. There was no fire in them at all. Not a torch, not even a lamp."

The Half-Elf nodded. "Well, obviously. The last thing you want is to be breathing… smoke…" Criske's words drifted off as his mind came to the same conclusion as Xeile's. "Wait… You think… we could…"

Xeile shrugged. "I have no idea. But it makes sense, right? Criminals or not, they still have to be able to eat, have a place to sleep, and most importantly, have a place to breathe. Could we potentially flush them out with smoke?"

Criske frowned. "I dunno." Then, the Half-Elf brightened, a mischievous grin formed on his face. "But I do know someone who would."

THE SOLDIER

Kelt hadn't had the most stellar of mornings. He had been woken early, only to be given a notice that he and his apprentices were officially off the double murder case. He couldn't claim innocence anymore now that it was in writing. To persist in investigating would be in direct violation of the law. Top that news off with the fact he had pulled his hamstring during his morning sword practice, developed a spasm in his back that refused to die down, plus a lackluster breakfast, and he was feeling downright old and, as Henrik put it, "cantankerous," whatever that was supposed to mean. He had just gotten to the medical bay to see that Glenna was gone, probably recovering in the relative quiet of her quarters. His own apprentice was making a swift, if pained, recovery from his punishment.

Henrik looked up and tried to greet him with a salute as the medic continued wrapping his torso in bandages. "At ease," Kelt said. "Just let the medic do what she needs to do."

There was a loud creak as the medical bay doors opened. Kelt saw Criske and Xeile enter, talking with each other in hushed tones with many hand gestures involved. That wasn't a good sign. Kelt turned and looked at his other apprentice, who was sitting upright, looking like he'd have to feel better to die. Every single movement he made caused him pain. The wounds from the flogging had all scabbed over, and even though they would scar, it didn't seem like there would be any lasting damage to his kidneys or his muscles. He looked up and the cloud of misery cleared slightly. "Ah, Criske," Henrik said. "Greetings, *Khlanro*."

"Hey," Criske said. "Sorry to sound unsympathetic, but I need some of your random Dwarf architecture knowledge."

Henrik brightened even more at the notion. He winced as the medic continued wrapping bandages around his torso. "Go on."

"Well, it's about those tunnels you found. How…airtight are they?"

"Very," Henrik said. "You can't have sewage smell reeking all over the streets. They'd have several escapes in case they need oxygen, every half a block or so, which was standard back then. Today, they have more, of course. Why?"

"Because we have an idea to make life difficult for the people holed up in those tunnels." Criske explained the plan.

Kelt shook his head when Criske finished. "That's not a bad idea," he said. "But too many things can go wrong with it. If those tunnels have any wood support or burnables, it could wind up setting the entire system on fire, collapse a street, or set a basement on fire. But…maybe we can salvage it into something similar."

"How?" Criske asked.

"We flush them out with people instead. Even if they are magicians, they can only do so much when in a confined space and cornered. Dwarven dart throwers could make them be pinned. We can also block off several of the tunnels by filling them with stones, making the search areas more contained."

"But how would we even be able to see if it's working?" Criske protested. "And it would be a major risk to send bodies down there, just to have them blasted away."

Kelt sighed. "I'm not sure. That may be a risk we'll just have to take. You and I are off the case anyway, so I'll put forth the idea to the baron and leave it up to him—"

"What if they didn't have bodies?"

Kelt and Criske looked at Xeile. Kelt could feel unease swelling in his stomach. "What do you mean?" Kelt asked. "Do you have some kind of magic tucked away in your pocket?"

Xeile shook his head. "No, but this city is full of ghosts… Headquarters alone has a ton of them. If I can convince them, we could wind up pinning down the people's location without them even knowing we were hunting them down." Xeile suddenly started, then squinted in annoyance. He stared over his left shoulder. "Could you not sneak up on me, Idolon?"

Criske just stood there awkwardly, rocking back and forth on his heels. Kelt took a deep breath and let it out slowly to steady his nerves. "Are you sure you'll be able to control that many spirits?" Kelt asked. "It'd be a big task. Even bigger than dealing with your mother. What if they get out of control?"

Xeile's face visibly drained of color. "W-what—"

"You explained what you had to do to survive Davadain last night, and why you decided to flee south. I'm not going to pass judgment on you, but do you think you can handle something like this? What if they all turn malicious?"

Xeile stared into the distance as if he were running scenarios in his head. Whether they concerned the future or the past, Kelt wasn't sure he wanted to know. Finally, Xeile looked at him. "It shouldn't be that hard. I just have to put it in a way they'd understand. Get them to follow me for a little bit. It's not like I can control a spirit like it's a puppet. They were people once. That'd be little more than slavery."

Kelt looked at Xeile in a kind of awe, then he smiled. "You know, Xeile…you should be proud of yourself. Few would remain as principled as you these past few months."

Xeile staggered slightly as if he'd been hit in the chest by a hammer. He looked at Kelt, unable to form words for a few moments. Finally, he managed a response. "Thanks. I'll start working on it, then." He turned around and looked for Glenna. "Where's Gi— I mean, where's Glenna?"

Kelt frowned. "Probably in her room, trying to recover as much as her impatience will allow."

Criske's eyebrows furrowed. "In her room? That doesn't make much sense. Generally, you don't leave people with head injuries without supervision."

"True…" Henrik said. "According to Guardian laws enacted after the delayed death of Vhod Ramaanaiid, any patient with a long-term recovery injury must be checked out by a person who will be responsible for supervising their recovery. Generally, that would be…" Henrik's eyes widened. He looked at the medic who was quietly humming as she finished securing his bandages. "Excuse me, Miss Medic, but do you recall who checked out the girl named Glenna Nall?"

The medic beamed at him. "Oh, of course! She was checked out by her master, Head Magician Usumi! She carried the sleeping Glenna out in her arms. It was very cute."

Kelt felt like his insides were being filled with lead and then set on fire. He glanced at his apprentices. Henrik looked slightly confused, since he hadn't been caught up on everything that had transpired in the tunnels. Kelt was planning to tell him, but then Criske and Xeile had arrived. Criske looked like he had been hit over the head with a hammer. Xeile's face, though, made Kelt worried.

He had seen that kind of gleam in a person's eyes before. The face of a person whose entire world narrowed to a single point of focus as they stared into the distance, seemingly at nothing in particular. In reality, he was staring at something only he could see, a future of unpleasant probabilities. Xeile's eyes rapidly widened, then narrowed. He tilted his head as if he were listening to something. His jaw set. He walked over to Kelt.

"I know you can't really help anymore with the case," he said quietly, "but I'm getting my future wife back, with or without your help. I'm going to give you two options: I go without your help and experience and likely wind up dead, or I go with your experience and have a chance at survival. We both know that an official team probably won't be able to get there on time. The team you sent down there still hasn't come back."

"Xeile," Kelt said with a sigh. "I can't just—"

"You. Owe. Me. This." Xeile said each word like he was a hammer pounding an ingot on an anvil. "After everything you've done, you owe me this."

Kelt swallowed a few times, guilt surging and smashing around in him. He lowered his head. "Xeile, if I could figure out a way to, I would—"

"Section thirty-eight."

Henrik's words cut through the tension like a brush knife clearing away foliage.

Xeile and Kelt looked at him. Henrik raised an eyebrow. "Section Thirty-Eight states that all outsiders employed by the Guardians must be accompanied by a Guardian escort at all times when on duty. While we aren't technically on the case anymore, Xeile's contract is not null and void. So…if he were to…say… wander down into a particularly dangerous tunnel…we, as upstanding holders of the law, would have no choice but to accompany him, correct?" A slight grin formed on the Dwarf's face.

Criske laughed. "You dirty rules abider, you."

Kelt looked at his two apprentices. "Gentlemen, I am going to escort Xeile. Time is of the essence on this mission. While you are my apprentices, I can't let you wander into this situation unprepared. This mission will likely be lethal. If you go, there's no way to guarantee your safety, and there's almost no chance that backup will arrive. With that in mind, I'll give you the choice on whether you want to come or stay behind."

"I'm going," Henrik said at once. "It is my duty."

Kelt turned to Criske, who stared at the ground for a moment. The Half-Elf looked up, his eyes grave, his tone forcefully light. "I gotta go with you, yeah? Have to stitch you two back together again."

"Even though you have a family to provide for?" Kelt said. "Our deaths always have consequences for those around us."

Criske took a shuddering breath. "I don't think I could live with it if I didn't go. And my parents didn't raise a coward. They may not like it, but they'd understand."

Kelt nodded at them, then looked at Xeile. "Xeile, with me to the weapons and armory. You two, gather your gear and meet me in front of the library in thirty minutes. We're going to be taking a trip to the archives."

THE OUTCASTS

The air was thick and oppressive as they gathered in front of the library. Criske felt conspicuously out of place. He was dressed up in his uniform, with a padded jacket on over it, something a patrolman would likely wear if he were going to a more dangerous part of town where knives and slashing were common. Most patrolmen didn't bother with them, but Criske didn't like taking chances in dark places. The sun had barely moved since he and Xeile arrived, and Xeile had departed to be outfitted, leaving Criske alone. Finally, Henrik showed up wearing a similar uniform, his standard-issue short sword, a flattened piece of metal with wheels on the tips he couldn't identify, some kind of tube, and a knife. He also had, Criske noted, a horn and what appeared to be an actual chain-mail shirt over his padded jacket. "Where'd you get the money to snag that?" Criske asked as the Dwarf stopped in front of him.

"What do you mean?" Henrik asked. Criske pointed to the chain mail and Henrik looked down. "Oh. This? It was a gift from a friend of mine before he passed away. In tunnels, it is better to have thicker armor and move a little slower."

Criske shrugged. "I'll take your word for it. Never been in a tunnel like this before." Unease brushed tendrils of cold chills up and down his spine. Even though it was summer, cold insisted on always creeping back in.

The two of them stood silently and peered in the direction of the armory, hoping to see Kelt. Henrik looked like he wanted to say something but thought the better of it. His eyes were fixed in the distance as if his mind were far away. Maybe on some kind of dig site?

Criske swallowed and figured he would try to lighten the mood. "So…do these tunnels tend to have traps built in, or are they just your normal sewers?"

"It is unlikely these will be trapped, as they were a public works tunnel. More private escape tunnels in the Dwarfdom tend to be armed at their entrances or exits, however. If Xeile did not activate any traps, it is unlikely that we will run into any. Traps are not my primary concern."

"What is, then?"

"Ambushes. Tunnels and narrow dark alleys have much in common, *Khlanro*."

Criske nodded sagely. "Of course. They are both narrow, dark, and generally smell bad, yeah?"

Henrik let out an exasperated sigh, and Criske clenched his fist in victory.

Then, Kelt rounded the corner and their conversation died immediately. Criske had seen Kelt in armor before, but it was nothing like this. His half-plate and chain-mail mixture gave him an intimidating air. It was unlike anything Criske had ever seen before. It wasn't quite plate steel, but it wasn't a hauberk of mail either. It was like someone had stacked ribbons of metal on top of each other to form protection for Kelt's upper body. On his head was a round helmet with a thick nose guard. His sword was strapped to his waist, a shield at his side. He looked ready to ride off to war.

Xeile, by contrast, was wearing practically no armor. He had a Guardian's gray uniform shirt, pants, worn-out boots, and a set of gloves.

He had a thick cloak and hood on. At his belt were various lengths of chain and hooks.

"Are you going climbing?" Criske asked as Xeile approached. Xeile shook his head but said nothing. Criske got the feeling Xeile's mind was deep beneath the earth, searching for the one person he still had left from his old life. Criske put a hand on Xeile's shoulder. "We'll find her."

Kelt looked at the two of them. He reached out and adjusted Criske's jacket so that it was a tighter fit. Then, he jerked his head up at the library. The four of them climbed the steps; walked past the two wardens, who gave them confused, nervous glances; and headed down the stairs. Another warden was there in the archive. Kelt spoke a few quiet words to the warden, who nodded and offered them a strange metal bar that looked like a bent wagon tongue with two prongs sticking out near the end. Kelt stuck the bar into a small slot on the plate. The weapons master looked over at his companions. "Help me out with this."

Criske and Xeile hurried forward and heaved with him until the stone plate lifted upward. Using the bend in the tongue as a pivot on the ground, they gently set it down next to the hole. "Easier than last time," Xeile muttered. "Idolon, can you scout ahead?"

There was a moment of silence and then Xeile nodded. "Right. Not too far." He looked at the rest of them with his intense blue eyes. They seemed to almost glow in the dim candlelight of the archives. "Idolon's scouting ahead. Which one of us is going first?"

"I will," Kelt said immediately. "Henrik, you follow up behind me, then Xeile. Criske, you'll bring up the rear. You're the fastest of everyone here. If the rest of us get caught in some kind of trap, do not hesitate. Run and get help. Immediately." Criske opened his mouth to protest. "That's an order," Kelt said firmly. Criske clamped his mouth shut. He looked at the three of them. "Remember, in real life, there are no victorious heroes and terrible villains. There is just us, and the people down there who don't want us to do our job. We go down there, we do our job, and we get out. Rescuing Glenna is the primary objective. We're not going on a crusade to kill every last wrongdoer. We get Glenna, we get out. Say that back to me."

The three young men repeated his words, halting and stumbling on occasion. Henrik looked like he would have an easier time pulling out his own teeth, particularly with the "not going on a crusade to kill every last wrongdoer" bit.

Kelt stared at all three of them. "Lastly, if I die, Henrik, you will assume command. You know tunnels better than anyone else here. Then, Criske. Xeile, I can't command you to do anything, but please, don't take unnecessary risks." Xeile nodded.

Criske stared at the tunnel and his heart started to pound. The reality of the situation began to sink in. He could die down there, snuffed out, beneath the earth. His parents would have no idea. They'd make a plate of dinner for him that he'd never eat. He was grateful he hadn't eaten anything. His stomach was churning and heaving like a storm-whipped ocean. He looked over and saw that Henrik seemed unfazed by it. How could he be so unbothered? Granted, Criske had been in some incredibly grim situations, but rarely did he have to worry about anyone besides himself in those situations.

Xeile's focus on the inky black pool of nothing in front of them was so intense, Criske expected it to burst into flames. He spoke, his voice like iron quietly being scraped by a whetstone. "Let's go."

Kelt nodded and climbed down, then Henrik. Xeile went to go after them, but Criske grabbed his arm. Xeile looked at him, surprised. Criske felt his heart rate increasing as he stared into the blackness. He had to calm down, he had to breathe. "Dinner," he blurted.

Xeile's eyebrows knitted. "What?"

"My parents wouldn't mind having you and Glenna over for dinner, once this is all over. What's your favorite?"

Xeile must've been so surprised by the question that he responded immediately. "Smoked trout. Glenna likes bread and cheese." After a moment, a new light entered his eyes. "She's picky, though, so we'll have to make sure we get it right. Promise me you will?"

Criske nodded. "Yeah. Promise."

A promise of a dinner after danger. A hidden promise of survival. Criske's heartbeat steadied as he watched Xeile drop into the darkness, not bothering to use the ladder like Henrik and Kelt. After a few moments, Criske followed him, swallowed by the black unknown.

THE CITADEL

Xeile landed in the darkness with a soft thump, flexing his knees to absorb the impact underfoot. He let out a hiss of pain. He looked up to see Idolon carefully trotting along, his massive antlered head moving from side to side. The creature's hooves echoed with an unnatural volume in the cavern, and Xeile suppressed a shush, reminding himself he was the only one who could hear the sound.

He hoped.

Kelt lit a lantern Xeile hadn't noticed him carrying. "Criske, Henrik, candles," Kelt ordered quietly. The two apprentices must have had small candle holders on their belts or in the small packs they carried. After a moment of hearing steel and flint, two candles weakly flickered to life, warding off the darkness, illuminating their silhouettes.

Henrik reached out and brushed his hand against the wall, searching for something with his fingertips. After a moment, he must have found it because he brought his candle over for a closer look. "This is the fourth entrance in this tunnel line. We're looking for somewhere around entrance two, provided these tunnel markers are up to date."

"Alright. Distance?" Kelt asked, his voice still hushed.

"About two miles," Henrik said, matching his tone. "One entrance per mile."

"Let's move out."

And so they walked. As the minutes passed by, Xeile would occasionally peek out from behind Kelt to check on Idolon. The spirit had said nothing to him at all. What concerned him more, however, was the total lack of spirits in these tunnels. He had become so used to avoiding their opaque silhouettes and subtly glowing eyes for months that the cavern felt barren of life, even with his companions next to him. In fact, it didn't make much sense to him how there could be no spirits at all. He wasn't exactly an expert, but he seriously doubted that no one, absolutely no one, had died down here within the centuries since it was constructed.

"There are no spirits here," Xeile said, his voice unnaturally loud and weak at the same time. "Something doesn't feel right…"

Kelt let out a small exhale. "I get that feeling too. No spirits at all?"

"Not one," Xeile said.

"Maybe no one died in construction?" Criske offered. "It was never used, sealed up, and forgotten, right?"

"No," Kelt said softly. "I have a theory about what happened to the spirits in these tunnels, I just hope I'm wrong. If you all hear a screech, everyone is on high alert for a wraith. They've proven they can use them. And remember, never let it touch you. One touch instantly breaks your aura and kills you."

The darkness seemed to cling to everything, licking the edges of the group with something sinister. Xeile swallowed, but his mouth was dry. He continued to walk, his pulse doing a rapid tap. Sweat trickled down his neck despite the tunnel actually being cold in comparison to the summer day above.

After an hour, Henrik said they had reached the second junction and that the entrances they were looking for were probably close. He hefted a metal bow off his shoulder and readied an arrow before grabbing his candle in its holder again.

"*There is power…to the left…*" Idolon said, coming to a stop. "*If I continue, I may be sensed.*"

Even without Idolon's warning, Xeile could feel the unnatural drop in temperature. "Get ready," Xeile whispered. "Something's up ahead to our left."

Kelt immediately drew his sword. Xeile was fairly certain he heard the scrape of a sword and a knife being drawn from Criske's general direction. His hand immediately went down and grabbed a short length of metal chain with a weight on one end. It was only about two feet long but perfect for tight spaces like this.

It didn't take long for the group to catch up with Idolon, even though the rest of the group couldn't see him. As he passed by, Idolon whispered to Xeile, as if they could be overheard, "*I sense a great gathering of enraged dead, Citadel. Walk lightly in this realm between.*"

Xeile nodded but said nothing in response. Every single shift, scrape of a boot, or footstep seemed to be ten times louder than before. There was an unnerving stillness to the air, like someone had forced it to stop in place, become literally frozen in time. He felt like if he ran down the corridor, he would carry a breeze behind him.

He turned to the left and saw a faint glow. It reminded him of the flat blue light of the strange room he had briefly taken refuge in before Idolon had attacked again. He still didn't know how the spirit had managed that, but he had. He saw Kelt stiffen in front of him.

"Trap," the older man muttered. "Trap written all over it."

"Here," Henrik said, gently pushing his way forward. He reached into a pouch at his side and pulled something out. It took Xeile a moment to identify what it was in the dim glow. It was a tiny metal sphere, faintly reflective in the light. He made some kind of hand signal that both Criske and Kelt seemed to understand. Both of them ducked around a corner at the edge of the new hallway. Xeile joined them. Henrik flicked the ball down the hallway. It clacked against the smooth stone ground, bouncing as it went.

There was a terrible whoosh and the chill suddenly vanished, replaced by an intense heat, and even though he wasn't staring down the hallway, the light made Xeile flinch and shut his eyes, blinking away white dots from his vision.

"Looks like someone planted *kashiiq-rahnask*," Henrik whispered.

"What's that?" Criske asked.

It was Kelt who answered. "It's a popular type of fire weapon. You stuff a small container full of rocks or anything that looks sharp, you fill it with that luminous moss, then set up a flint and steel inside the container to respond to pressure, movement, or a trip wire. Then you go up in flames. Popular among the Remnant."

Henrik grabbed more metal balls from his pouch and flicked them down the hallway in a wide spread, the metal clattering echoing and colliding with objects. More distant blasts of heat and light followed.

"Well, if they didn't know we were here before, they do now," Criske said grimly.

"Let's move," Kelt said.

They hurried down the hallway at a faster pace. The air got cooler with each step, the blue light becoming brighter as they approached. By the time they had reached the tunnel's end, Xeile could see everyone's breath rolling out of their mouths like fog. In front of them was a metal door made of black iron with a heavy ring for a handle. Criske reached out, but Xeile grabbed his hand. "Don't. I have an idea."

He grabbed another chain from his small collection. He just had one with a hook left. He looped the rope through the ring, careful to avoid pulling on it. He tied a knot, his fingers stiff from cold and occasionally slipping. When he finished the knot, he motioned for everyone to back up. Everyone backed away with Xeile as he pulled the rope out to its maximum length, about six yards. Taking a firm grip, he yanked sharply on the rope.

The door swung open silently, as if the hinges were recently oiled and well balanced. Nothing emerged or exploded. The tension in Xeile's shoulders slowly eased. Then, a terrible scream erupted from the hallway. There was a dragging, then a thump. Drag. Thump. Drag. Thump, and a figure came into view.

It was like a dark shadow of a man carrying a rusted blade in one hand. Its eyes glowed red with an all-too-familiar malice. In the center of the being was a skull with a separate pair of glowing purple eyes.

"Shoot the skull!" Xeile cried. "The weakness is the skull!"

Henrik responded immediately with an arrow flying toward the creature's chest, but the thing just smacked the arrow away with inhuman reflexes. Then, it started running toward them, covering ground so quickly Xeile barely had time to dodge out of the way. The rusted sword slammed into the ground with a sharp screech, sending a violent shiver down Xeile's spine. Kelt moved in one fluid motion, disarming the creature before dancing out of the way of a grasping, shadowy claw.

Criske lunged with a sword and hit the skull, but his blade skidded off its top. The creature reached out to grab Criske's wrist.

Xeile responded without thinking. He flung himself onto the creature, tackling it to the ground. A familiar icy agony gripped him as he held the monster. It was the same agony he had lived with for three months. But he couldn't curl into a ball this time. His friends needed him. Glenna needed him.

He fought past the daze of pain, reaching into the center of the shadowy creature, grabbing the skull. It was like running his hands through glacial melt. He closed his fingers around the smooth bone and heaved. The skull came free with a sickening, gelatinous pop. He immediately raised his arms and smashed the skull against the ground, the fragile bone shattering into tiny yellow-white shards.

The black shadow melted away into the darkness, leaving a single red pulsing crystal that dissolved into dust.

"What…was that?" Criske whispered.

"That was a specter," Kelt said, his voice level, controlled. "It is a spirit that has been forced to take physical shape. This is extremely painful and drives them berserk. They…are lethal to touch because they drain all the energy from your aura until it breaks."

Xeile gave them a bitter smile. His mouth tasted like he had just downed a cup of metal shavings. His legs were screaming, his ribs felt like they had all individually been filled with stinging hornets. "Well…joke is on them, I guess. Mine's already broken."

Sudden relief of pain made Xeile gasp, and the cold started rapidly vanishing, like someone was cleansing his body. His chest and head became warm. Idolon's voice whispered in his ear, "*You are not broken. You and I walk together. You will learn.*"

Xeile got to his feet, looking at his hands. "I can take them," he whispered. He looked up at

Kelt. "I'm taking the lead. You all watch my back. I'll handle the spirits. You handle the rescue."

Kelt gave him a long look. He opened his mouth, clearly to protest. Xeile locked eyes with him and stared. Xeile won the silent argument and Kelt sighed. "You really are something else," he muttered. "Lead the way."

So Xeile glanced back at Idolon. "Stay with me." He looked ahead at the blue lights, and stepped through the metal door.

THE SOLDIER

Kelt stared at Xeile, opening his ears to his surroundings for the slightest hint of noise. It shouldn't have been possible for him to grab the specter. Though they weren't as terrifying as wraiths, specters were still lethal. It was rare for a Spell Breaker squadron to escape unscathed by one, unless someone had exceptionally good archery skills.

But then there was Xeile. He had reached into the creature, ripped out the source of its power, and killed it in one swoop. Even in all his years of Spell Breaking, Kelt had never seen something like that. A memory clawed at the back of his mind. Something Gallrick had said… something about a fortress? No…a Citadel… Was Xeile a Citadel? No, that didn't make any sense. He was far too young. He had no training either, from what Kelt had seen. The boy was practically skin and bones, running on sheer force of will, not a soldier of any kind.

But in this dim blue light, with a cloak wrapped tightly around him, a length of chain in hand, Xeile did look like something else Kelt had seen before: a necromancer. He didn't think Xeile had been lying when he had said he didn't want to raise the dead, or hurt others. But could someone even become a necromancer without training? No. It was too dangerous, and Xeile didn't have that look about him. He wasn't a soldier or a necromancer. He was something else entirely, a strange creation, a mash of necromancer and Guardian.

And the thought sent chills down his spine.

It wasn't hard to see why the hallway was only guarded by one specter. It was only wide enough for one of them at a time. Henrik was occasionally flicking metal spheres to see if any traps could be preemptively set off, the occasional clack making Kelt's nerves fray.

Then, at the end of the hallway, there was another door made of the same metal, and the same design. It was swung open as if inviting them in. Xeile saw something Kelt didn't and took off running. "Xeile, no!" Kelt cried.

"Glenna!" Xeile exclaimed. "Glenna!"

Kelt and the rest jogged after him. Kelt refused to pick up the pace any further than that. He had seen what could happen if an entire group walked into an ambush. They could easily all die at once. It was far better, tactically, to try and rescue one or two injured than have all four be incapacitated.

Xeile came to a sudden stop. He was shaking. Kelt came up behind him, as did Criske and Henrik. The metal doorway had led to a narrow entrance that then exploded outward into a huge chamber full of crystals that jutted out at strange angles. They covered the walls, the ceilings, and even a large portion of the floor. In the center of the room was a stone slab with writing all around it in a language Kelt didn't recognize. Glenna was bound to the table, struggling fitfully, obviously in some kind of stupor. She was drugged. As magic required concentration and mental clarity, it was the easiest defense against enemy magicians. Sitting next to Glenna's prone frame was Usumi, head magician of the Guardians, her legs crossed. She was reading a book, seemingly oblivious to the moans and slurred insults being flung her way by her own apprentice.

She looked up from her reading and beamed at them. "Ah. Well, well! Evening, gentlemen. I'd hoped it would be you all. Gallrick and the rest weren't much fun, you see." She jerked a thumb toward a wall. Kelt looked over and his stomach twisted.

Gallrick and the other Breakers were bound against the wall, spread-eagle, hanging as if they were unconscious. Blood trickled from most of their heads, and one of them looked like they had their foot blown off.

"So…" Usumi said, gesturing to Glenna. "As I have something you want, I figured we could chat, hmm, Kelt?"

Kelt drew his sword. "Guardians don't negotiate with necromancers."

"Are you just going to let him kill Glenna?" Usumi asked the rest of the group. "How heartless, that he'd needlessly throw away the life of a comrade when—"

The temperature in the room dropped. It wasn't a subtle tingle, like the one Kelt had felt when examining the bodies of the dead. It was a stagnant, terrible, damp cold that sank into his bones. His breath started becoming visible again.

"Let her go."

Kelt looked at Xeile and his brain started working rapidly. He, Criske, and Henrik may have accepted Glenna's potential death by taking the Oath of Service to the Trifecta, but Xeile was another matter entirely. Xeile loved her. Who knew what he would accede to so he could save her?

Usumi stroked her delicate, pointed chin thoughtfully. "Well, I might just do that, if you take care of those friends of yours you brought with you."

Xeile turned and looked at Kelt. "McNair," he said slowly.

Kelt stared at Xeile, pointing his weapon at him. "Don't make me do it, Xeile," Kelt said slowly.

"McNair," Xeile repeated.

The two of them stared at each other for a long, tense moment. Xeile suddenly staggered, clutching his head, letting out a groan. When he turned back toward Usumi, a dart was sticking out of his neck.

"Ah, poison," Usumi said casually. "There's the problematic thorn out of the way. Now…"

Usumi's aura flared to life as she flourished her hand in a graceful arc skyward with a laugh that was like steel scraping on stone. "Shall we begin?"

THE OUTCASTS

"Get Xeile and find cover!" Kelt bellowed. Henrik immediately ducked behind a larger crystal, locking an arrow into his strange metallic bow. Criske sprinted forward, grabbing Xeile by the arms as he slumped backward, dragging him to cover. Kelt flicked his sword upward in an arc, knocking something metallic out of the air. The dull clink echoed around the cavern like an ominous bell, heralding the start of violence.

Criske knelt next to Xeile and immediately felt for his pulse. It was rapid, his breathing ragged. Criske quickly checked the eyes. Dilated. Whatever toxin Usumi had used, it was fast-acting. Flipping a groaning Xeile onto his back, Criske gritted his teeth and did something his father would have never approved of. He brought his lips to the entrance point and sucked in. The poison was bitter and metallic, hot as it mixed with Xeile's blood. He immediately spat it out and wiped his tongue on his sleeve before doing it again, and again.

He was dimly aware that Henrik was making incredible shots at Usumi from around the corner, barely sparing a second to look at where he was shooting. His fire was all that was keeping Kelt safe as the weapons master truly showed his prowess for the first time, knocking darts away and running toward the altar to engage Usumi up close. Criske wiped his tongue on his sleeve again, praying to whatever deities that might be listening that he didn't just accidentally poison himself in the process of trying to save his patient.

"Don't let me pass out," Xeile groaned. "Don't let me pass out. He'll come this time. He'll come this time for sure."

Criske put a hand on Xeile's shoulder. "Stay here," he said. "We'll go get your girl!" With that, he stood, drawing his sword into a shaky hand, looking for the nearest cover that he could rush to. He saw a crystal to his left, just a few feet away. He took off at a dead run, leaping into cover as he heard a dart screech off of the crystal.

His blood pounded in his ears. He heard a laugh, cold and cruel.

"You're out of darts, Usumi!" Kelt called over her hysterical merriment. "It's over."

"I think not!" There was a dull roar, and the smell of ozone.

Criske felt himself blasted off his feet, his ears ringing. He sat up, his vision fuzzy. He looked over to see that Henrik was slumped against a wall, not moving, but groaning in agony. "What was that…?" he said aloud. His tongue felt thick and clumsy, like he had a mouth full of cold, greasy butter.

Then, he heard Kelt crying out in pain.

The sound made Criske look over, his vision clearing with the help of adrenaline to reveal Kelt also lying on the ground, shaking. Usumi was standing over him, his sword in hand. "You know," she said, casually twirling his sword in her hands, "you've caused me nothing but trouble over the past few days. I think it's time for the Guardians to find a new weapons master." The sword came wishing down.

"No!" Criske screamed.

The temperature dropped so suddenly, Criske gasped as his muscles cramped.

Usumi froze as well. She looked up, her eyes alert.

A loud sigh echoed around the cavern. "Once again, you prove to be a colossal annoyance of the highest magnitude." The voice was formal, clipped, containing a cool disdain that made Criske reflexively want to flinch away. He looked around for the owner. Had other Guardians finally come to the rescue? Then, his eyes fell upon Xeile, who was standing up, stretching slightly, as if he were preparing to do a light bit of exercising. Xeile should've been shaky from the toxins. Yet there he was, standing tall, his shoulders pulled back. For the first time, Criske noticed that Xeile was actually much taller than he let on, as he hunched over when he stood or walked. Combined with the look of removed disgust on his face, it gave him an imperial air.

Xeile walked toward Usumi. The mage's aura flared to life once more, a dazzling purple hue. Xeile's eyebrows rose. "Now, now," he admonished. "None of that." Xeile's own aura came to life, a crackling, flickering cloak of black. He was shaking, though from the cold, the pain, or the strain of maintaining his aura,

Criske couldn't tell. Xeile extended a hand out to Usumi. "Now… I believe you are forgetting your manners." Usumi's aura shot forward and then retreated so quickly, it was barely more than a flash, her magic already taking effect. A fiery blast enveloped Xeile's frame. It flickered and died immediately, and Xeile let out a low laugh that made Criske's spine shudder and shift in his body.

"Yes, quite rude," Xeile said. "When facing royalty, one must kneel."

Xeile's aura lashed out again, smashing into Usumi. Her aura turned from purple to blue for a brief moment. She sank to the ground onto her knees, gasping for air, clutching at her chest. "Much. Better," Xeile said with a satisfied smile, continuing to walk toward her, his black aura snapping and crackling. "Was that so hard?" he shook his head in mock dismay. "What passes for manners these days. I must say, you've been most impolite." He spat the last word out like Criske had the venom from his neck moments ago. "Though I suppose I must thank you. That toxin you gave him was enough for him to go unconscious and allow me the chance to… correct your error."

Xeile's words came back to Criske.

Don't let me pass out. He'll come this time for sure.

Usumi swung Kelt's sword at this new threat. Her movements were shaky, but the blow could still be damaging. Xeile made no effort to dodge. He flicked a boot out and brought it crashing down on Usumi's wrists, driving it into the floor with a sickening, wet crack.

Usumi let out a bestial cry of pain and curled into a ball. Xeile crouched next to her, balancing on his toes while he whispered in her ear. His voice echoed around the cavern, filling with a calculated, slow-burning anger. "I worked for years upon years to get a body," he said. He reached forward and brushed a lock of Usumi's dark hair from her head, his aura draining energy away from hers for a brief moment, causing her to let out a choked gasp. "I had to set up so many pieces," Xeile continued to explain. No… not Xeile, Criske realized. Whoever this was, it wasn't Xeile. Xeile didn't act like this.

"I had a small pool of candidates picked out, all prepared to be my new vessels, easily dominated, so narrow-minded in following orders," Xeile went on. "And then… just when

I thought I had the ideal candidate, you damn fools killed her. Right in front of me, no less. Talk about the height of disrespect!" he shouted into her face.

Not-Xeile was breathing heavily now. Then, he reined in his anger and gave her a smile that didn't reach his pitiless blue eyes. "What did you leave me with? Nothing but this pathetic, cowering whelp who has no strength, no capabilities, no connections. All he has is stubbornness. I even tried to win him over by resurrecting his mother to take revenge on her killers. You know what this idiot did, this *simpleton* did? He squandered his chance. Ripped her aura apart to save those murderers."

He sighed. "No matter. You have inadvertently started to rectify your disgusting error. He has found a few powerful friends, it seems, that can protect him while I wait. It is just a shame you will not be around to see it."

Not-Xeile reached out a hand wreathed in the crackling black only to have it freeze. "You cannot be serious," he muttered. He raised his head and shouted up to the ceiling of the crystalline cave. "She kidnapped and threatened your wife-to-be! She killed innocent people!"

Not-Xeile's hand extinguished and he sank to the ground, groaning. He looked up at Usumi. "Know this well, your desire has been met, Mage, and you shall be its martyr." With a shudder, Xeile's body slumped to the floor.

"Xeile!" Criske said, staggering over to him. The entire room was spinning.

"Don't touch him." Kelt's words were strained and weak, but a command nevertheless. "Make the arrest."

Criske turned his attention to Usumi, who was lying on the ground, whimpering. He pulled the manacles from his belt, his shocked brain only remembering the words from constant repetition in basic training. "You are under arrest for violating the laws of peace established by the Trifecta. You will be judged according to its laws and an equal tribunal. You will have a speaker to defend you. Your silence is allowed and your words shall be writ for our records." He latched the manacles on with a sharp series of clacks.

"And so the mongrel catches its prey," Criske muttered to himself, sinking to the ground, exhaustion washing over him. "But what's a dog to do when they finally catch the cart?"

There were no intelligible answers to his question. There were only Henrik's groans, Usumi's blubbering whimpers, and the terrible, billowing silence in between them.

THE CITADEL

Xeile's eyes snapped open. His mouth tasted like blood, his head pounded, and a deep exhaustion filled him from head to toe. He felt his body being restrained, struggling against it and hearing metal chains clank against stone. He looked down to see that he was in some kind of cell. He wasn't in the cave. His emotions surged upward, bestial at being confined once more. "Glenna!" he yelled. "Kelt! Henrik! Criske!"

He tugged at his restraints again, but they didn't give. He called their names again, but no one came.

"They are safe."

Xeile whipped his head toward the cell door. The tall man with ever-shifting eyes stood in front of him, most of his features and body obscured by a hooded cloak. Xeile opened his mouth to say something, but the man held up a hand. "I don't have much time. Know that I'm on your side. You passed out in that cave, and he surged to the surface. You were seen by Criske, so they had you locked away until you came to your senses."

A feeling of icy water filled Xeile's stomach, causing it to clench and make him nauseous. "What did I do?" he whispered.

"You are not him, and you are not responsible for his actions," the man said firmly. "I know your secret, Xeile Taeris. Why you're so reckless, why you seem to be alright with your own death."

Xeile shuddered but found himself unable to say anything.

"You will be safe for now," the man warned. "But I am going to give you this warning once: Do not get stronger, do not learn to fight, and do not use that spirit that has attached itself to you. If you do, I will be forced to kill you."

Without further explanation, the man walked away.

Xeile felt the plunge in his stomach. Why was the man telling him to avoid getting stronger? And not use Idolon? He didn't even know where

Idolon was at the moment. He wasn't in his cell. As far as he knew, Idolon had only used his powers through Xeile once. He partially agreed with the man about getting stronger. He had blacked out before, and some ugly side of him had come forth, leaving his better self to deal with the aftermath.

"*It is not you.*"

Xeile turned to see Idolon walk through one of his cell walls. "Idolon," he whispered softly. "What are you doing here?"

"*We walk together.*"

"What do you mean 'it is not you'?"

"*The one who hurts and disturbs the dead. It is not you.*"

"How can it be anyone else?" Xeile asked. "Just because I don't remember using necromancy doesn't mean it didn't happen!"

"*You house another.*" Idolon's voice was a sharp, biting wind in his mind. "*And you are strong, to contain him. I will help you.*"

"I don't understand any of this," Xeile said, shaking his head. "I am myself. That's it. That's all."

"*You know this is untrue.*"

"No…" Xeile whispered, a sinking feeling in his stomach. "No, it's not true. I can't be."

"*You must tell them.*"

"No!" Xeile cried. "No one would believe me…" He looked at the cell floor, feeling like the walls and roof were closing in on him. "No one could believe me. Not even Glenna could… I don't even believe it myself."

"*You must stop running from the truth.*"

"No…" Xeile said weakly. "No, I can't do that. I've worked too hard for that. I've tried so hard to start over…to move on."

"*To move on, you must accept what you are so you can change what you will be.*"

Xeile looked up to see the stagmare was staring at him with glacial blue eyes. He lowered his head in defeat. "Fine. I was…I am…still possessed by something. It wants to take over my body."

"*And you must become stronger so that never happens.*"

Xeile looked at the stagmare. "I can't get stronger. I'll die… I don't know how!"

"*I can show you. Do you wish for Glenna to face the same fate as the others?*"

Xeile stared at the ground. A strange, dark peace settled over him that he couldn't quite place, a peace he had only felt one other time:

when he decided to find Kelt and forgive him, leaving Davadain behind, his life draining away from him.

Get strong, or die trying…

He looked at Idolon and nodded, managing a single raspy word: "Okay."

"*Rest for now. You must recover.*"

"But what—"

"*For now, we must wait. Rest.*"

Xeile nodded and slumped against the wall, drifting into an uneasy sleep as he closed his eyes.

THE SOLDIER

Kelt stared at the wall in his office, his brain going nowhere in particular, too numb to think. The past twelve hours felt completely surreal to him. The culprit had been captured, Glenna saved before being whisked away to the medics for treatment. Henrik and Criske were there as well. Criske had injured his head with a nasty gash, but still, he had made the arrest. Xeile was currently locked away, despite Kelt's protests. Gallrick and the other Guardians were getting similar treatment under confinement. Usumi was currently being treated in an isolated chamber under heavy guard.

He sighed and stood up. "Well, time to go check on my walking wounded," he muttered to himself. He looked at his desk and his heart sank. Even as he survived perils, dangerous magic, murderers, and potential death, the paperwork still piled ever higher, almost as sure as the sun roamed across the sky.

The day was painfully bright to his eyes. When they had emerged from the tunnels, it had been the dead of night. After making sure the young ones were stable, arguing against Xeile being locked away in a dungeon instead of a medical room, and returning to his office, Kelt hadn't seen his cot, or the sun, since. Fatigue gnawed at him, down into his bones, straight to his marrow. His normally rigid posture had a slight stoop, and his eyes felt like they were filled with grit, causing a throbbing headache that refused to go away.

"Check on my kids," Kelt muttered. "Then coffee."

As he entered the medical bay, he wasn't surprised to see it full of activity. Still, he made his way to the most critical of those under him. Henrik was suffering the worst damage out of all of them. Going from a whipping to getting tossed onto the floor and aura shocked, Kelt was amazed the Dwarf hadn't passed out. As it was, he was in severe pain, his bloody back being stitched and rewrapped. Through his pain, he saw Kelt and managed an awkward nod. "Sir," he said gritting his teeth.

Kelt gave Henrik a salute before kneeling down next to him. "How are you holding together, lad?"

"I have been better," Henrik managed. His voice was raspy and dry. Kelt grabbed a nearby waterskin, but Henrik refused it. "No, not yet. It will just come back up. I'm sorry I didn't do more—"

"You did well, Henrik," Kelt said. "Few could have fired a volley of arrows like that. You bought us the precious time that we needed. Don't discount yourself, lad." He stared at the Dwarf's eyes until he was sure that his message had been driven home before standing. "Keep me updated as he gets better," Kelt said to a nearby medic.

"Yes, sir."

Kelt turned to the next bed. Criske lay there in a half daze, covering his eyes with one arm. His blow to the head had made him sensitive to light and sound. Kelt spoke as softly as he could. "Criske, lad," he called.

Criske moved his arm to get a quick glimpse of the speaker. Then, he slowly sat himself up in his bed. "Hey, Kelt…I mean, sir."

"Easy there," Kelt said. "You're the only one who could pay a damn bit of attention after that aura shock Usumi gave. Don't push yourself too hard. I'll need your memory for my report," he smiled to let Criske know he was half joking.

Criske reached out and clutched Kelt's arm. "Kelt…Xeile…"

"Xeile is okay, but—"

"Is he himself?"

The urgency in Criske's voice made Kelt feel a slight chill down his spine. "Yes? Best I know. Why?"

"Because for a moment there in the chamber…he wasn't."

"What do you mean?" Kelt asked.

"It was Xeile's body doing the action, his voice doing the talking…but it wasn't him. I don't know how to describe it… He was cold, cruel. He was talking about himself like he was another person, mentioning bodies and resurrecting people… He crushed Usumi's hand. No worries or qualms about it. He wasn't even angry about Glenna… The… He…was angry about something else. Then…he froze and passed out before he could kill Usumi, like his body was fighting itself, yeah?"

Kelt took a deep breath. "And you believe Xeile wasn't in control of his own actions?"

Criske swallowed. "No. No way. He was suddenly throwing his aura around, draining energy from Usumi like it was nothing… I mean, Xeile can do that if he touches things or connects to them somehow. But I've never seen him…deliberately do things like that. Say things like that. It just…wasn't him. I know it."

Kelt frowned. People often snapped under the pressure of sudden, deadly combat. Perhaps Xeile had finally done the same? "Criske, lad, you don't think that he—"

"No, sir," Criske said. He sighed. "Gah… I'm so bad at explaining. He passed out, and then this happened. He begged not to pass out because 'he' would come out."

"Did this…persona say anything distinguishing?" Kelt asked, trying to keep the skepticism out of his voice.

"Something about being 'royalty.' That's the only thing I can really remember clearly at the moment…"

Kelt's brain slowly chewed through the statement while he sat on Criske's bed. The Remnant had come to Trifectus and kidnapped

Glenna. He'd presumed they wanted the incredibly powerful magician apprentice. Before that, he'd believed they wanted Xeile. He considered why they would be so determined to kill Mathiene, going as far to assassinate her, but then break Xeile's aura. Then, he thought about how Xeile could have possibly survived his aura initially being shattered. Such a feat should have been impossible. Even being given energy was a temporary measure. There was no effective way to permanently repair a broken aura.

But spirits had a shard of their old aura attached to them, and if they used some other energy source, such as a host…

Kelt stood. "No," he whispered. "No…it can't be…"

He turned to Criske. "Tell no one else about this," he said softly. "No one. Not even Henrik. Not yet. That's an order."

Criske gave him a concerned and confused look but nodded, wincing as he did so.

Kelt left his apprentice and immediately made his way to the secure treatment room.

He pounded on the door. The head medic, Nedra, opened it. She looked at Kelt with surprise.

"Weapons Master, what's wrong?"

"I need to speak with your patient."

The head medic grimaced. "Well, that's going to be difficult. She hasn't opened her mouth since we've treated her for her hand. We had to amputate. I think she might be in shock over it."

"I don't give a damn," Kelt growled. "This is a matter of life and death, head medic."

She frowned, but nodded and let him through.

Usumi was sitting on her bed, mutely staring at her heavily bandaged stump that had been her arm. Her dark hair obscured her face from view.

"Usumi," he said.

Usumi turned to look at him briefly, then back at her stump. "You'll get no answers from me, Kelt. What I say is of no consequence now."

Kelt walked over, a fire filling him from head to toe. "That's a lie," he said. "And you know it. What was your Remnant really after?"

Usumi just turned and stared at him with deadened eyes. "It does not matter. I am to be executed. You cannot torture me." She gave him a small smile. "And we have already won. With the stagmare, I have given him the start of the power he needs. I will face my death with pride, knowing I have served the true ruler of Meraria."

Kelt felt his stomach heave. His worst fears had become reality. Fears that should have only existed in nightmares, myths, and legends. He left Usumi's chamber without another word, walking as fast as he could down through the medical bay to head to the prison. He would check on Glenna later. He had to make sure Xeile was safe and, more importantly, secure.

The headquarters prison was one of the most secure buildings in Trifectus. Capable of holding even the most powerful magicians, it was a square, squat building, just as unassuming as the rest of the structure around it. What wasn't immediately visible, however, were the two squadrons of wardens on duty and their series of complex repeated magical incantations that made it difficult for anyone to get in or out without permission.

When Kelt approached the prison door, an older Dwarf with a carefully styled beard and a heavy shield barred his path. "Halt," the Dwarf commanded. Kelt saluted and waited to be allowed to get closer. "Approach," said the

Dwarf. His Dwarf accent was thick, causing his *o* and *a* to be stretched out when he spoke in Territory. "And state your reasons."

Kelt spoke in a clear, loud voice. "I, Kelt McNair, weapons master of the Guardians, need to visit the prisoner Xeile Taeris to question him about the case of murders that have occurred for a fortnight."

"Present to me your orders of merits and rank."

Kelt took the series of badges off his left breast and left shoulder, presenting them to the Dwarf one at a time. The Dwarf looked them over with a critical eye, trying to detect forgeries. Finding none, he nodded. "You may pass, Kelt McNair."

Kelt entered through the heavy metal door and walked into the dimly lit corridor of the prison. It wasn't long before he came to the cell all the way at the end, the one that was built to house the strongest of magicians. He opened another door, closing it behind him with an ominous clank. Inside the room was a cell with bars, with Xeile chained to the wall, one arm uncomfortably raised over his own head.

"Xeile," Kelt said softly.

Xeile looked up, hope and fear in his eyes. "Glenna, Criske, Henrik, the others, are they—"

"Peace, lad. They are well for now."

"Is Usumi still alive?" Xeile asked.

Kelt's expression darkened. "She is, for now. Though I don't imagine she will survive for long past her trial. She'll likely be hanged."

Xeile let out a sigh of relief. "I didn't kill her, then. Thank all the gods…"

Kelt fought to keep his voice steady. "No, you didn't kill her. But someone maimed her significantly. And if Criske is to be believed, which I believe he is, it both was and wasn't you."

The look of terror on Xeile's face was unmistakable.

"So you know, then," Kelt said. "You know that you have another spirit inside of you."

Xeile's throat bobbed as he tried to swallow several times. "I didn't think it mattered. I thought it would just die with me…as long as I kept it from doing horrible things—"

Kelt sighed. "Xeile…it matters a great deal. And there are a great many people who would give their lives to make sure you survive." He bolstered his courage and delivered the terrible, gut-wrenching news. It felt like a hammer blow came from his mouth, striking with a terrible, unavoidable finality. "Xeile, your mother didn't abandon her post because she was pregnant with you. She ran from her post to make sure you were never used by the Remnant. But I'm afraid…she failed. We all failed. Now…you are possessed by the spirit of the Scourge of the North, the Spear of Ice and Death."

"Who's that?" Xeile asked.

"Taron Idolon."

THE APPRENTICE

Glenna stared at the ceiling, hating the lethargic feeling that ran through her limbs, the last vestiges of the drug Usumi had given her still in her system. As the sun's rays played across the ceiling, she thought about the past few days and just how much had occurred. She shook her head. It didn't do well to dwell on the past. All that mattered was the present. Things hadn't exactly worked out the way she had intended, but the end result was still the same. He was finally starting to show signs of being able to take control. She was running out of time.

I will get my old master out of you, Xeile, she thought to herself. *I promise.* Her silent promise drifted skyward, surrounded by unwitting witnesses and the dangers of an uncertain future.

It took her a moment to realize that Kelt was standing beside her. She started, struggling in her sheets. "Dragons and phoenixes, you could have said something."

Kelt looked down at her, and Glenna didn't like his expression one bit. "I'm…not sure where to begin, lass."

"Well, don't loom over me, for starters. Sit down." Kelt did so, not even commenting about rank or propriety. That wasn't a good sign at all. "What's the matter? You look like you've killed someone."

She saw him flinch at the words, and she felt a small amount of satisfaction from it. He took a deep breath. "It's about Xeile," he said.

Glenna's stomach plummeted, but she kept her face a neutral mask. "What about Xeile? Has he gotten into trouble again? The Guardians hired him as a mercenary, so his actions in saving me are legal, right?"

Kelt shook his head. "This isn't about that. That's fine. What isn't fine is how he rescued you. He crushed your old master's hand. Brutally. That was after draining her aura. He also says that he's possessed." Glenna felt her mask slip as her words froze in her throat. Kelt's eyebrows rose. "So you knew?"

"Well," Glenna said, "I guessed from the stories his mother had told me…him running off into the forest with a sword and whatnot… that he could be possessed, but I didn't notice anything strange when I lived close to him in Davadain."

The weapons master rubbed both hands across his face from forehead to chin before dropping his arms to hang limply at his sides. He had dark circles under his eyes, a stark testament to days of little to no sleep. There were lines around his eyes and mouth she had never noticed before. He looked at her.

"How much do you love him?"

"Until the ends of the earth and time itself," Glenna responded instantly.

"How far are you willing to go to keep him safe?"

"As far as I need to."

Kelt nodded but said nothing for a long while. Eventually, he looked at her again. "You better keep to your words, Patrolman Nall. He's going to need it in the coming weeks and months. You have to make sure to ground him in the here and now, not with spirits long dead. Do you understand?"

Glenna nodded. She understood all too well. "Yes, sir. But it's hard to protect him when the Guardians wanted to kill him, as did the Remnant. There's no place we can keep him safe. He doesn't trust anyone, Kelt. At this point, I'd be amazed if he even trusted me."

The weapons master heard her voice catch on the last phrase. "He charged toward certain death, knowing he could never come back," he said quietly. "He had just gotten to relative safety. And the first thing he did was run to you, because he loves you." Kelt put a gentle hand on her arm. "You don't find people with his level of conviction often, Patrolman Nall. He doesn't want to be safe, he wants to be by your side."

Glenna felt a hard lump form in her throat. When she could finally swallow past it, she spoke again. "But he can't stay by my side, Kelt. I still have four years left with the Guardians, probably longer. I can't marry him because we don't even have a place to live." Fury mounted in her chest and she gritted her teeth. "He's locked away in some hole, and I can't do anything about it."

Kelt took a deep breath. His face darkened. "There might be a way out of this yet. But Xeile's not going to like it." He looked at Glenna. "We have to tell the Guardians in command who he is."

Glenna's eyes widened. "What do you mean?" *Please no, please no. They'd kill him on the spot if they knew what he could do.*

"We have to tell the higher-ups that he's a shaman."

Glenna relaxed a little. "How would that help?"

"Shamans can't be arrested for practicing their religion. All of Xeile's actions could be spun as him following his beliefs to defend and save others."

The apprentice frowned. "There are a lot of holes in that plan. Xeile's not a Nomad. He doesn't have a band that he travels with. He doesn't even have Nomad blood in him."

"Have you ever met his father?" Kelt asked.

She considered the question, mulling it over. Xeile always assumed that his father was dead. Glenna always thought that he was dead as well, but should she reconsider that? During her many practice sessions with his mother, she would say that he was gone. Mathiene had just arrived in the village pregnant, if the locals were to be believed. No other explanation about the father, other than he wasn't around, if he even was her husband. Gossip had abounded, of course, though no one had teased Xeile. His mother was far too an intimidating presence for the other kids to consider trying her patience.

"No," Glenna said. "But I don't think we'll be able to get a hold of him either."

"Don't have to," Kelt said. "There's a set of journals in the library that will help me make a strong case for him being a Nomad in blood at least."

"But what band would he even be a part of?" Glenna asked. "There are no bands near Davadain. They won't come close to the Northern Forests because they think they're cursed."

Kelt leaned back, sucking air in through his teeth. "This…is the part you're not going to like. There is a particular kind of shaman that never belongs to a band."

Glenna's mind raced as she realized where Kelt was going. Bile rose up in her throat. "You can't be serious." She tried to sit up to further protest, but the world spun before her, and Kelt gently laid her back down.

"Calling him a Deathrite Shaman would almost be as bad as a necromancer," Glenna protested. "They're banned from practicing anything, Kelt. There's two, maybe three, of them in the whole of the Human Territories, and none of them could exactly be called a masterful magician."

Kelt took a deep breath. "True. They can't practice, but they are allowed to know, to research. More importantly, it helps explain Xeile's abilities to interact with spirits. He can talk to them, Glenna."

"I know," she said. "It's not exactly a common ability."

"No, but it is a useful one. It doesn't require magic of any kind, since it's something he can always do. He doesn't force the spirit to do anything either. But, with the ability being as rare as it is, we could convince the Guardians to hire him as an independent mercenary, like I managed to do with this case."

Glenna took a deep breath, then exhaled. *You have no idea how dangerous that could be,* she thought. There were too many ways that her old master could abuse that situation for her liking. On the other hand, keeping him surrounded by highly trained fighters could be a major benefit. No matter the outcome, Xeile couldn't be left alone.

"If that's our only out," Glenna said slowly, "then I suppose we'd be stupid not to take it. How can I help?"

Kelt put a hand on her leg. "You, lass, need to rest and recover. Do you understand? Xeile won't do anything I ask him to if you aren't on the mend."

Glenna grumbled something mutinous, but nodded.

The weapons master smiled. "Good. Now, if you don't mind, I'm going to go set up an argument for Xeile's release with a few people who know the law better than myself." In a moment, he was gone, already walking at a quick pace down a hallway.

So Glenna lay there, waiting, resting, and planning out her next moves in the days to come.

THE OUTCASTS

Criske sat in the courtroom fighting an instinctive urge to bolt for the door. Henrik appeared undisturbed, seemingly engrossed in the architecture of the Hall of Justice.

If Criske hadn't known what the building was ahead of time, he could have easily mistaken it for a cathedral. A soaring series of stone archways supported the vaulted wooden ceiling. The inside was lit by a dizzying series of shutters that could be opened or closed by using long iron poles. Just looking upward made Criske feel nauseous. Running on top of buildings was one thing, but he couldn't even gauge how many feet tall this might be.

"This building is a whole history to itself," Henrik murmured softly, looking at the walls and ceiling.

"Why?" Criske asked, trying to keep himself distracted.

"All three centuries of the Trifecta's building styles are here. Elven arches, Dwarven columns, and the shutter work is from the Territories. That and there are several smaller touches that can clearly mark the time in which different architects—"

A loud bang resonated through the hall, and the room fell silent. Criske felt his heart begin to race. A small, reedy-looking man spoke in a voice that resounded around them like a divine proclamation. In fact, he probably could have whispered and everyone still would have been able to hear him.

"So the trials shall begin!" the man said, his voice high and clear. "Our venerable justices, one from each of Meraria's races, shall preside over these affairs. Riinhan ibn Maqrok, of the Dwarves; Zhang Tu Wan, of the Elves; and Rend Valoris, of the Human Territories!"

Three figures in long gray robes entered the room, their hoods drawn over their faces so that all but their mouths were plunged into murky shadow. Their footsteps were heavy, ominous, as they climbed their way into the three chairs at the front of the hall. Before them sat a single iron chair tucked under a stone table. Heavy shackles were mounted onto the surface.

The reedy man spoke again. "We shall first begin with the trial of the former head magician known as Usumi!" He turned toward a side entrance. "Bring forth the prisoner!"

The side door opened and there stood Usumi, clad in a simple spun cloth dress, her dark hair hanging in fresh waves around her shoulders. Criske realized that even though she was missing one hand, she still possessed an air of superiority. Something clenched in his stomach. He turned to Henrik. "Hey, I've got a bad feeling about this. She's too confident."

Usumi was escorted by her four guards, pushed into the iron chair, and her forearms manacled to the stone table.

"Usumi," Rend Valoris said, his voice low and neutral. "You are accused of multiple counts of murder, improper use of magic, kidnapping, attempted murder, arson, and abuse of your position of authority. How do you respond to these charges?"

"I am guilty of nothing but doing what was necessary to bring back the true ruler of this land," Usumi said.

"Do you accept these charges?" Rend asked.

"I do. But know this: Our plan has been years in the making, Guardian, and I have already fulfilled my mission. I have succeeded. You may kill me, but it will not break me. We have already won," Usumi said defiantly. "Lord Taron has returned with a body to call his own."

The court burst into a frenzied babble. A few bangs of the gavel from the Dwarven justice quieted the room almost immediately.

"If you do not deny your charges," Riinhan said, "we will find you guilty and, according to the law, must sentence you to death by hanging."

Usumi sat up straighter in her chair. "I know the charges and have accepted my fate. But what are you going to do with Xeile Taeris?"

"Who?" Wan asked.

Usumi smiled and Criske saw her trap the moment before she sprang it. He swore under his breath.

"Xeile Taeris, also known as Exile. He currently is in your dungeon. He committed crimes against me, including crushing my hand, draining my aura, and using magic without being registered, as a mercenary in Guardian service, no less. He also holds the spirit of Lord Taron

Idolon, true king of the Human Territories and the rest of Meraria."

Criske expected the court to erupt in shouts and snapping; instead, there was dead silence, oppressive and thick as the summer air in the court. Sweat trickled down Criske's neck. Eventually, Rend spoke. "We will verify your claim. As for you, you are sentenced to death by hanging, according to the law of the First Trifecta. Your execution will be carried out at sundown." Riinhan brought his gavel down on the metal block again, causing a mighty echoing peal. A death toll. Usumi didn't resist as the guards escorted her away. She laughed, her voice high, clear, and cold. The side door shut behind her and her entourage with a bang.

After almost half a minute of silence, Zhang Tu Wan spoke, her voice clear and crisp. "What is our next case, announcer?"

The announcer coughed twice. "It is the case for…Xeile Taeris, for acting against the wishes of the local barony and continuing to work on the case, though he was ordered not to."

Criske's eyes widened. He looked at Henrik. "Can he be charged for that?" he asked quietly.

Henrik's eyes darkened and he nodded. "Yes. If he was employed by the Guardians, the same restrictions could apply to him if the orders were written in such a manner."

The side door opened, and there was an uneasy murmur throughout the hall. Xeile was standing there with shackles on both his arms and around his ankles. His guards guided him to the iron chair and roughly sat him down into it. His hands weren't removed from the manacles, rather he was locked to the stone by having the irons clamped around his forearms, hunching him over. Criske could see Xeile's skin was a grayish hue, and he seemed to have lost what little weight he had gained, plus a few pounds he couldn't afford to spare.

Anger welled up inside Criske, but he tamped it down. Now wasn't the time.

Wan spoke to Xeile. "You have been charged with vigilantism and violation of your mercenary contract with the Guardians of the Trifecta. What say you to these charges?"

Criske felt a sudden chill in the air. It cut through the stifling summer heat like a knife through a coin purse. Xeile looked up at the judge and said nothing.

"Very well," Zhang said. "We shall proceed with the trial. We have your document of hire before us, and it clearly states that you are to not be involved with the case should Kelt McNair be removed from heading the investigation, which he was. This would put you in violation of the law, unless you are willing to explain extenuating circumstances."

"They had my fiancée." Xeile's words were a quiet whisper. "If you think I'm going to sit by and hope someone else will go get her, you're mistaken." He stared at the stone table. "Just let me go, please."

"You are under accusation of breaking the law, you are not allowed to leave this court until the appropriate action has been decided upon," Rend said firmly.

Criske saw Xeile's shoulders tense and felt another stab of anger. Unfair. This was so unfair. How could Xeile even handle being talked to like this?

"Then…if you're going to charge me… what about you?" Xeile asked.

"Pardon?" Riinhan asked.

Criske felt it now. The temperature in the air was dropping. Others were shifting in their seats, looking uncomfortable. Every eye in the hall was focused on the scrawny boy chained to the stone table. "What about you?" Xeile asked again, his voice quiet.

"Explain your statement," Riinhan ordered him.

"You know, I had a pretty solid life up north in Davadain. It wasn't anything special, but I had my mother, I had Glenna, I had my craftwork, some nature. I was happy." Xeile looked up and the temperature dropped a little more. Criske felt his own sweat starting to sting on his body.

"Then, the Guardians showed up. You had a writ of execution for my mother. Your Spell Breakers killed her in front of me. Did you know that?" The question went unanswered, so Xeile continued. "But I swore I wouldn't take vengeance. I prevented the spirit inside of me, which resurrected my mother's corpse against my will, using my body, my blood. She almost went to attack them. I tracked her down to just outside the Guardian camp. I managed to stop her. Did you know that a resurrected corpse's soul can only really be free if you tear out its heart? I had to use an axe—well, more of a hatchet. Do you know how many swings it took? Thirty-two, before I could reach her heart. Resurrected corpses don't scream when you hit them, did you know that?"

Criske thought he was going to be sick. He saw the rest of the hall, save the judges, recoil away from Xeile, the color draining from their faces.

"This was after your Guardians tried to kill me," Xeile explained, his voice still quiet. "A magician broke my aura to pieces. That's where the spirit came from. I resurrected a corpse, because the Guardians of the Trifecta tried to kill me. Did you know that?"

The judges provided no answer. Xeile went on, and the temperature continued to fall. "I wanted to kill people, so badly then. That first week, I was so angry, I could hardly think. I buried my mother in the woods, taking her necklace as the only inheritance I'd ever live long enough to make use of. It was then I had my first attack of cold and coughed up blood. Didn't take me long to realize I was dying. You can die from having a broken aura, apparently. I didn't know that, but I could feel it, creeping up my toes, toward my heart, like it's doing right now, at this moment, tracking how many times I'll get to see the sun. There wasn't a lot of time left, so I made an absolutely insane plan."

He looked at the judges. "I'm not strong enough to get revenge on you all. What good would it do? It won't get the nightmares to leave me. It won't bring back my life. It won't make me healthier. So, I made the journey to Trifectus, so I could forgive Kelt, get word to Glenna that I love her, and die in peace in a back alley somewhere. That way, I wouldn't be too much of a bother or make much of a scene. Do you know what it's like, to truly understand what it means to have your days be numbered?"

There was no answer. Criske was starting to shiver.

"But then, I find you have a problem with a spirit," Xeile said. "A murder. I figured it could be my last act, my revenge, to prove that you murderers can't corrupt me…that I'll stand for what's good and right until my end, caused by 'justice.'" Xeile looked around. "You can see how well that turned out. I stopped the spirit that was murdering people left and right. I helped stop an evil magician, who the Trifecta made head magician, by the way, and saved a group of your Spell Breakers."

The temperature was so low in the giant hall that Criske was starting to see his own breath. His teeth chattered.

"You had no right to my help," Xeile said. "But I gave it to you anyway. I could've murdered people with a touch, but I didn't. The Guardians took away my family, my future, my work, and my home." Xeile looked at the judges. "You shouldn't charge me for a damn thing. You should be apologizing. But you don't care, do you? You're just a bunch of cowards hiding behind the fact you don't want to take responsibility for your own ignorant choices—"

A guard slammed a fist into Xeile's jaw. "You will either speak respectfully," Wan said, "or you will not speak at all."

Xeile's head hung there, motionless for a moment. "Did they knock him out?" Henrik asked. "He looks like he is unconscious."

Fear gripped Criske's insides. "No!" he shouted. "Get away from him! He's dangerous! Get away—"

"Peace, Half-Elf. I will not risk my vessel so easily." The cold command came from Xeile's lips, but were again not his words.

Xeile's head went erect. He looked down at his manacles as if noticing his situation for the first time. "Oh. How unfortunate. How does he get into these situations?" He looked up at the judges. "You must be presiding over his trials, yes?"

The judges whispered quietly to each other before Zhang responded. "Are you the spirit that possesses Xeile Taeris?"

Xeile let out a terrible laugh that didn't belong to him. Criske felt a chill in his spine that wasn't from the cold.

"Well, wouldn't you like to know?" he asked with a small smile. He looked at the chains on his wrists. "I could break these in an instant. I could kill about half this room, I think. One big go. It would be quite the show." He sounded delighted by the concept. "But Exile won't let me. He won't let me kill people. Not even the people that murdered his mother! Can you believe the spinelessness of the youths these days? At least Caragan had the grit to square up and look me in the eye before running me through."

"There is no way to prove that you are a spirit," Riinhan said shortly. "This could be an act. If so, I suggest you stop, lest you face further punishment."

Xeile spat out a tirade in a foreign language, his voice so loud and fierce that Criske almost couldn't register it was from his friend's mouth. But it wasn't any language he recognized. He looked over at Henrik. The Dwarf was gaping at the chained figure.

"What?" Criske asked. "What is he saying? I can't understand? Is it some kind of dialect?"

Henrik swallowed and nodded. "It is a very outdated dialect of Dwarf from up north, used roughly three hundred years ago. Only a few even study it. Fluent speakers are limited to a handful of academics."

"What makes it so rare?" Criske asked.

"Everyone who spoke it was on the fringe of the Idolon Barony," Henrik said. "An isolated group of Dwarves. The first victims Taron slaughtered and then resurrected when he began his campaign for dominance."

Criske returned his attention to Riinhan. The judge's face was obscured, but the Half-Elf could tell from his tone, the Dwarf was shaken.

"Such a language proves nothing—"

"Do you wish for me to tell you how I resurrected the dead?" Taron asked amiably. "It's really no trouble. Sadly, the children weren't strong enough to handle the process, but the adults managed just fine, if you care to know. It's all in the angle at which you break the aura. If you do it right, you can have them dead in just a few seconds. If you're efficient, you can get access to around fifty bodies in the span of around an hour—"

"Silence," Rend said.

Taron ignored him. "But personally, I preferred to take my time, as it were. I gave them a chance to join my cause, you know. They were on my lands, so therefore my subjects. But they insisted on following the Dwarfdom laws." Taron shook his head in disappointment, Xeile's black hair swishing to and fro. "So I dealt with them as invaders. Quite tragic, really. I have tremendous respect for the Dwarves."

"Silence!" Riinhan said, getting to his feet. "You will be silent, or you will be punished."

"You touch Xeile's body, and I'll kill you where you stand, runt," Taron said coolly. "For all of his flaws and idiocy, Xeile's body is also mine, which makes me its caretaker. I'll not have you harming him. He may let you scum trample all over him, but I won't stand for it, Guardian. And to be honest, at the moment, you are wearing my patience oh so desperately thin."

It hurt to breathe now. Criske coughed, shaking. "Taron," he said through chattering teeth. "Taron…stop. You can't kill using him." He took a step forward. "I won't let you."

Taron turned and looked Criske up and down before nodding in approval. "Ah, well, at least there's one person with some courage around here. But try as you might, I don't think you could kill me, boy."

Criske privately didn't think so either, but he wasn't going to let Taron know that.

Glenna now stood from her seat from behind Xeile and rushed over to within the chained figure's field of view. Taron's head snapped in her direction.

The room's temperature dropped even further. Xeile's aura flared to life, black, crackling, flickering in and out like hungry tongues, desperately seeking energy. Pain blossomed on Xeile's expression. He let out a breathless gasp, and then a single tendril of black reached out and touched a point in the air.

A translucent smoky figure took form, the outline of a giant horse with a rack of horns with icy blue eyes.

Criske recoiled in fear.

The smoky outline then changed into the towering shape of a man with a sword stuck into one shoulder and several arrows out of his back. The figure walked over to Xeile, who was shaking and writhing against his bonds in pain.

The voice that came from the shadow was faint, as if from far away on a northern wind.

"My bond is not with you. Return my shaman." There was a sudden cracking sound, and Xeile let out a terrible howl before slumping forward in his seat. The shadowy figure stepped back and turned to face the judges, disappearing into nothingness.

Xeile looked up, and glanced around, panic and confusion on his face. "What…what happened?" He looked at the judges. "Am I going to die?" Rend leaned over and whispered to the other judges. They had a quick conversation back and forth. Wan then stood, extending out a hand. "You will return to your cell while we deliberate. Three days from now, you will return. You will be placed under guard. Should you wish to study the laws surrounding your case, you are allowed access to a librarian who will obtain the information for you. For the record on this day, the court has adjourned until we reconvene in three days."

Riinhan slammed his gavel down on the metal block. The guards, now much more cautious, unshackled Xeile and led him from the courtroom. The side entrance shut, and the temperature in the room slowly began to rise as the rays of the summer sun penetrated the graceful stonework and wooden benches.

"Hang in there," Criske whispered after his friend. "Just three days. You can do it." He meant the words to be for just himself, but Henrik responded anyway.

"He better endure," Henrik said, his voice almost lost in the din of people getting up to leave the hall. "If not for his sake, then for our safety. I do not think three hundred years of ghosthood has made Taron Idolon any less dangerous."

Criske didn't want to say it aloud, but he couldn't decide which was actually more frightening: Taron Idolon or Xeile's questions the judges left unanswered.

THE CITADEL

Xeile sat in the dungeon for three days, readying himself for a death sentence. It was amazing how hard it was to do. He had always known his time was limited, especially when showing up to Trifectus. Honestly, he hadn't even expected himself to survive as long as he had. But now he had no loose ends. Glenna loved him, he had stopped the crime, forgiven Kelt.

So why was it so hard to accept his death?

He was chained to the wall, staring at the ceiling, sitting with his arms above his head, talking to Idolon. The giant stagmare was looming nearby, filling the air with a chill of a normally unseen origin. He was talking into the air, to no one in particular. Mostly because if he didn't talk, his mind turned to the gallows, and that was enough to drive anyone mad.

"Well, I mean, Glenna is highly capable. Of course I want to be with her. That's not exactly a possibility at the moment, and likely won't be given the circumstances. She's strong though. I bet she'll move on." He tried to say the words with optimism, but they caught in his throat. He pushed himself onward anyway. "And Kelt will be just fine. I mean, he hunted necromancers and other terrible things for years. My mother can't be the only thing he thinks about, right? He's got two apprentices now, and they look like they'll be great Guardians. Everyone will be just fine…without…me…" He tried to force more words out, but they just kept jamming in his throat as if he had just eaten a bag of raw flour. The words clung to his insides, making his mouth go dry and his throat itch. A fit of coughing and tears ensued. Dread chewed away at his stomach, and he looked at the well-swept but uncomfortable stone ground.

"Idolon…if Taron…tries to take me again…when they go to kill me…could you finish me?"

The question hurt to ask, and the reality of the situation pressed down on his shoulders, like the crushing weight of the ceiling above him.

"He will not control you while I am here."

"But when I go to get executed—"

"I will not let you die so easily. We are bonded."

"What are you going to *do?*" Xeile yelled, his frustration boiling over. "Gnaw on them with your ghostly teeth? Or are you going to possess me too?"

"I cannot own you. You cannot own me. We are one and the same."

Xeile rolled his eyes. "Behold!" he shouted to whatever deity was watching—and surely laughing at—him. "The horse of useless answers! He possesses the greatest magic power of all: being vague!" He looked at Idolon, his jaw working silently for a moment. "I'm going to die today," he said, his voice unexpectedly becoming quiet. The energy seemed to rush out of him. "The least you can do is give me the courtesy of honesty before I walk toward my grave."

"You do not understand. If you die, I will die as well."

Xeile looked at the stagmare. "Wait… what?"

"My aura is tied to yours."

Idolon's shape began to morph and change, rippling like water until in front of Xeile was a large barrel-chested man, tall and imposing. His hair reminded Xeile of the stagmare's mane, thick and knotted like ropes. He had a spear shaft sticking out of his chest and several arrows sprouting from his back. His face looked rough and scarred, much like the rocky shores of the rivers Xeile had spent so much time next to during his younger years.

"*Look at me*," Idolon said. His voice was much unlike the one that had whispered to Xeile's mind. It was deep but contained that same slight lilt that marked him as a man of the northern Territories, much like his own voice.

Xeile looked into those ghostly glacial blue eyes. Idolon's face was the clearest Xeile had ever seen of a ghost's. Every detail down to the delicate strands of his eyelashes was clear as a spring-fed pool. Idolon looked down at him and kept talking. "*I bonded us together. I will not let it be broken apart.*"

Xeile let out a small snort. "Yeah, because you could feel Taron. I'm 'like him,' right?"

Idolon knelt down so that Xeile was unable to look away from him. The spirit stared him in the eye. "*No. I bonded with you because of what you are.*"

Xeile rolled his eyes. "Oh right. The vessel of a mad necromancer. Next, you'll be saying I was chosen for some great quest. Am I going to fetch the sword of Josah before single-handedly destroying the Remnant to assist you in your final act of revenge?" Xeile looked at his cuffed hands. "Sorry, but I'm no fighter, and I'm not some chosen hero of destiny." He looked down at the ground again. "I'm just a wreck who learned the hard way that everything you have isn't always enough. I can't even kill an evil person."

Idolon reached out, and Xeile was shocked to feel Idolon's hand on his chin, lifting it so they were eye to eye once more. "*Never be ashamed that you cannot let others die by your hand. There is great courage in fighting evil, but there is even greater courage in allowing it to live, knowing you will have to fight it again. Your suffering is merely the cost of preserving the most precious thing you have: empathy.*" He reached out and touched Xeile's chest. The young man froze on the spot, rooted not by ice but by the ghost's words. "*I didn't bond with you because of birthright, prophecy, or the person you were. I bonded with you because of the person you chose to be.*"

Xeile was silent for a long time, his brain struggling to wrap his mind around the concept of not being special through powers but somehow being valuable all the same to this spirit he had no previous connection with before three months ago. "Well, it doesn't matter," Xeile muttered. "I'm going to be executed."

"*Then why not end your life here?*" Idolon asked gently. They fell silent for a moment while Xeile considered his question.

"I…I can't do it…" Xeile concluded. "I don't know why…but I just can't do it."

Idolon took a deep breath and exhaled. "*Because those you carry with you wish you to live.*"

Xeile looked up. "Obviously Taron wants me to live, but that's all the more reason to die."

"*What about the others?*"

Xeile frowned. "What others?"

"*The spirits whose aura fragments you've absorbed, they haven't disappeared. They've taken refuge inside you.*"

The young man recoiled away from Idolon. "No…It can't be…I'm possessed by three spirits?"

"*You are possessed by roughly seventeen others. They are different than Taron. They are not strong enough to control you, but they can lend their strength to your aura, to help keep wild magic from claiming your life. In return, you have become their Citadel, their greatest and final defense.*"

Something about Idolon's statement rang true in Xeile's bones. The words were the hammer, his body the anvil, his mind the heated metal between them. He couldn't even find the words to voice the shock. So he stared at Idolon in silence, trying to detect any hint of a lie in the ghost's face. There was none. He wanted to curl up in a corner and scream.

Suddenly, there was a banging on his cell door. Idolon looked over, then back at Xeile. "*You are a Citadel, Exile. Do not forget that.*" With that, the spirit stood and left, vanishing through a nearby wall.

The door opened, and in stepped three wardens in full plate, armed with spears. Xeile took a deep breath and looked up at them. "Make it quick," he said.

The wardens looked at each other in confusion. The one in the middle made a few hand signals to the other two. Xeile quickly found his vision obscured by a leather hood that shut out all light. He was dragged to his feet, his ankles bound by manacles joined with a short chain. It was long enough to allow him to shuffle but not to run. His wrists were secured in irons as well before he was dragged along a series of twists and turns.

Xeile's initial confusion of not getting stabbed to death faded as he came to another conclusion: maybe they wanted to execute him in public. He could feel the outside air, warm against his skin but cool enough for it to be nighttime in the summer.

His confusion returned as he felt himself being led up a long set of stairs, then stopped and pushed through a door that shut behind him. His hood came off and he blinked slowly. The room he was in was filled with candlelight, with a figure sitting before him in a heavy traveling cloak of high quality. His face was weather-beaten, his eyes sunk deep into their sockets. Despite that, his posture wasn't stooped with age. "Leave us," the man said. The wardens hesitated, then exited the doors behind them.

The man stared at Xeile for a long moment in silence. Xeile, shifted from foot to foot.

"Xeile Taeris," the man said. "It is good to see you."

Xeile tried to take a reflexive step back, but the manacles on his ankles prevented it. "Who are you? What do you want?"

The man nodded. "Both of these are very good questions. My name is Fenn Enran. I wish to procure your services."

Xeile frowned. "I don't think I offer any of those."

"Can you no longer see spirits?"

The young man nodded. "I can. What of it?"

"Excellent. You see, Xeile, I have a particularly painful problem. I am in need of a new agent."

"What are you talking about?" Xeile asked.

The man held up a finger. "Wait until I finish speaking. You, Xeile, have placed the entire Trifecta into a very tense situation. You are a rogue magician who helped us of your own accord. You've toed the lines of using necromancy. You've interacted with the dead, and if my sources are correct, you currently house the spirit of the most dangerous magician Meraria has seen in recent memory. According to Kelt McNair, you are a Deathrite Shaman, one in a group of magicians so rare I can count them comfortably on one hand. By all accounts, you should be executed."

Xeile nodded. He had accepted that as the likely outcome a long time ago.

"But," the man said, "I want to…cut you a deal. Your life and freedom in exchange for your help."

Xeile looked at the man and felt his heart rate increase. Was that even possible? Who was this man that could secure the freedom of a person suspected of necromancy?

"You will become, for the first time in three hundred years, the king's agent."

"The what?" Xeile asked.

"The king's agent. If you've never heard of it, that is for good reason. Despite the Trifecta being in place, each nation in Meraria possesses a network of spies, Master Taeris. The Guardians, as you have no doubt seen, can be manipulated, infiltrated, and twisted. Former Head Magician Usumi is but one example. In order for her to be elected, a majority of the Trifecta must agree on the position. I voted against her, the other two supported her. As a result, a significant number of people died, including one of my oldest informants, Harvest Zhong."

Xeile felt a sharp pain in his chest. "Harvest..." he said quietly. Another thought occurred to him as the words sank in. "You! You're the king of the Human Territories!"

Fenn rewarded him with a smile. "Correct. The technical term is 'king-elect.' The Territories do not have dynasties like the Dwarves or Elves. I came to the throne rather recently, nigh on four months ago."

"Four months..." Xeile said slowly.

"Yes. And simply put, I believe that for some reason, the other two nations are trying to blind me to the current state of Meraria. It is always difficult for the Territories, as we must elect a new baron to take the throne of king-elect every time the previous one passes away. The Dwarves have superior metals and engineering. The Elves dominate the sea with a breathtakingly powerful military. The Territories, as a result, have had to rely on different resources to keep the balance of the Trifecta: the acquisition of knowledge and exceptional people."

Fenn took a deep breath before concluding. "Someone, be they the Idolon Remnant or one of the other two nations, is trying to destroy this balance. They are trying to provoke disaster and, through disaster, war. Unsolved incidents are easy sparks to fan into flames of conflict." Xeile wasn't sure what to make of those statements. But Fenn had asked him to remain quiet. He shifted uneasily.

"The easiest ways to cause panic, of course, are murders and assassinations. They quickly become personal, and with well-done magic, they can be virtually impossible to identify with little in the way of evidence or witnesses. Unless someone could ask the victim themselves. That is an impossibility, given that necromancy or summoning spirits is illegal."

Xeile suddenly understood. "Unless you have a medium of some kind."

Fenn nodded. "Even then, spirits are seldom cooperative, being just a fragment of their former selves. Except for you. If I read Kelt McNair's report correctly, you have demonstrated that spirits open up to you, gain some part of their former selves."

Xeile frowned. "I don't know about gain… I think…they just remember things that were less important before I started talking to them. Most spirits focus on one thing, something that completely dominated their thoughts when they died." His throat tightened. "Most of the time, it isn't a pleasant thought."

"But you can do it—make them recall?"

Xeile nodded. "At least some…if previous experience is anything to judge by."

Fenn gave him a genuine smile of relief that made Xeile uneasy. "Xeile, I need dead men to tell tales. Without resolution, these smaller crimes will grow into something much worse. I need a man who can stop that. I need a man who will be—"

"A light in the darkness, a Citadel, the greatest and final defense." Xeile clamped his mouth shut. Where had those words come from?

Fenn's eyes brightened and his smile widened. "You really are full of surprises."

Xeile thought about it. Whatever it meant to be an agent, it sounded dangerous in the extreme. He could be gone for long stretches of time at a moment's notice. What would that do to Glenna? At the same time, what choice did he have? It was either the axe, or being able to only sporadically see Glenna even though it might possibly drag her into even more danger than she was already in as a Guardian. To see her for only a few moments, or never again. It wasn't a debate.

"I'll do it. You secure my freedom, I'll do it."

Fenn stood, beaming. "Master Taeris, you have made my evening. I will document your release as soon as possible, along with a few other things you'll need to start your duties properly. One last bit of housekeeping, you'll need a cover name for any documentation I have to record. Do you have any preferences?"

"Exile," Xeile said.

Fenn nodded, his face turning somber. "Very well, Exile. I shall begin work at once while you are escorted back to your cell." He started walking toward the door. He leaned over and spoke quietly into Xeile's ear as he passed by.

"I'm glad to see that the son follows the path of his mother."

Xeile whipped around, gaping at the king. "What?"

Fenn turned back, his face serious. "I will find the one who executed my finest hidden among the Guardians, Xeile. You may not want to seek revenge, but I will have it on your behalf. That, I promise you." The king exited the room.

Xeile didn't resist or do much of anything as the wardens came to take him back to his cell. His mother hadn't been a Guardian, and he wasn't a dead man. He was now a servant of a man he knew nothing about. He recalled his rage toward Glenna revealing his name, his actual name, to the baron, about not having freedom.

Now, as the wardens led him away, a terrible vise gripped his chest as a single word revolved around in his head: *Trapped.*

THE SOLDIER

Kelt sat at the table across from Criske and Henrik, mindlessly picking at his food and pushing it around on the plate. As Criske had promised before their daring rescue effort, they were having dinner with his parents. True to Criske's assurances, his mother was an excellent cook. Under better circumstances, Kelt would have called her food artful, the fish done to the perfect temperature, served perfectly seasoned with herbs and butter. But nothing really seemed to have flavor. It was the night of the third day, the day when Xeile was scheduled to be sentenced, quite possibly to imprisonment or death. The hall wouldn't reconvene until tomorrow, which made Kelt uneasy. Sentencing at sunrise was rarely a good thing in his past experiences.

In the worst mood of all was Glenna. She sat apart from the table, not even bothering to pretend she was eating. Instead, she just stared at the wall, her violet eyes hiding and barely containing what Kelt was sure was a roaring cavalcade of thoughts. Henrik and Criske weren't much better. Both of them looked like they were slightly sickened, anticipation probably causing their stomachs to heave.

A sudden sharp knock on the door made everyone jump. Kelt immediately reached for the sword that he had kept in arm's reach. Criske pulled a knife. Henrik tensed, ready to roll out of his chair if needed. Glenna stared at the door, her gaze so intense, Kelt wouldn't have been surprised if it caught flame. Then, the door swung slowly open.

In front of them stood Xeile in a plain red tunic, tan pants held around his too-thin waist by a thick black leather belt. Down his arms to his wrists from under the tunic were wrappings common among the northern Nomadic peoples, covered in symbols Kelt couldn't recognize. Xeile's ragged long hair had been roughly chopped to a close-to-even length, stopping at his earlobes in wavy strands. So much like his mother, yet his own person.

He gave them all a hesitant smile. "Hey… mind if I join?"

Glenna flew out of her chair and into Xeile's arms, nearly knocking him over with the impact. "Easy there," he groaned. "You're going to squeeze me to pieces." He returned her embrace. They stayed together for a long moment before Glenna broke the embrace and Xeile pulled her down to his height to kiss her on the nose. She smiled and gestured to the table.

"She makes excellent fish, you know." Glenna bowed her head toward Criske's mother, who bowed in return with a small smile.

Xeile looked at the table. Kelt saw his eyes shine for a moment, and then the reflection off the firelight in the fireplace was gone. "Great," he said, pulling up a nearby chair from the table.

"*Do I need to kill him?*" Criske's grandfather shouted.

"No," Criske replied loudly. "Friend of mine."

The old man nodded at his grandson. "Good enough." Within moments, he was snoring in his rocker again.

Kelt wondered for a moment how Xeile had managed to secure his release, or what fate awaited the boy now. He pushed the thought aside as he ate a spoonful of fish. The details could finally wait for once. Right now, there was good food and even better company to be had.

The King

Fenn had just made his way out of Guardian headquarters, surrounded by his guard, when he spotted a single figure in a giant heavy cloak with the hood pulled up. He was leaning against the wall with a sturdy-looking sword strapped to his waist. The king recognized him at once.

He turned to his guards. "Leave me for a moment. I have private business with this man. Make sure we are not disturbed."

His entourage obeyed immediately, covering him as he walked over to the man, who nodded toward an open door in a nearby building. The two entered, and the hooded figure led the way upstairs to a sparsely decorated room lit only by a few flickering candles. This was probably one of the man's many hideouts he had scattered across Meraria, no doubt bought with a false name and very real large quantities of money.

Finally, they reached the top room, which only possessed a few pieces of furniture. There was a small round table in the center of the room, two chairs, and a bedroll thrown in one corner. Beside the bedroll was a heavy and well-laden pack. The man took a seat in one of the chairs, and the king took the other, staring at him across the table.

The man threw his hood back, revealing a close-cropped head of hair and eyes that changed color in the dim light. "So," he said, "I take it he accepted your offer?"

The king nodded. "Of course he did. It was either that, or death."

The man nodded. "Good. That will give us more chances to get Taron out of him."

Fenn nodded. "Naturally. Though, do you think it wise to place Taron in such a potentially powerful position? Whether he likes it or not, Exile will have to become stronger or die. Such an atmosphere could be extremely dangerous. I'll not have him threatening my entire kingdom."

"I have been pursuing Taron for three hundred years. I can assure you that he won't act. At least, not yet. Xeile was far from his ideal target to possess. Even though I used Project

Citadel to lure him out of hiding, things still didn't go according to plan."

"I know," Fenn said. "The Territories lost one of their best informants in that mistake."

"We thought Taron had possessed her. We couldn't afford to hesitate if that was the case. That's why we used McNair. I didn't anticipate her having a child that could fulfill the conditions. My operative saw the chance and took it."

Fenn let out an impatient sigh. "At the expense of nearly killing him," he said. "And now we have a far worse situation. If my sources are correct, Taron gained complete control of him at one point during that fight with Usumi, then again at the courthouse. He doesn't have the willpower to resist Taron the way the Citadels would have."

"That's where the stagmare comes in," the swordsman stated. "He can control Taron easily."

"And rip Xeile apart in the process," the king hissed. "You've made a shaman! A genuine Deathrite Shaman, Dascke! If you think Taron is dangerous now, imagine what he could do with the ability to convince spirits to serve him of their own free will!"

"I don't have to consider," Dascke said quietly. "I've seen what a Deathrite Shaman can do. One of them is a close friend of mine. He's been opposing the Remnant for years. Without him, Taron would already possess the Idolon Barony lands again. I am aware of the danger, king." He spat the final word out like it was a piece of fruit that had gone bad. "Just continue to work with me, and we might be able to get out of this alive, with Meraria still intact."

Fenn sighed and lowered his head, then raised it as an idea struck him. "What of your friend? Could we possibly get him to train Xeile, or at least ask him how to separate the two?"

Dascke's ferocity broke for just a moment, showing actual pain as his eyes changed from red to blue. "If I could, I would. He left, said he was looking for someone precious to him. We didn't exactly part on positive terms."

The king let out a sharp breath and stood. "Well, then, I suppose we'll have to find another way. I'll make sure McNair stays close to Xeile. He's probably the only person capable of killing him, besides yourself, that is." Dascke nodded.

"Good. Whenever you can, make sure to put the people important to Xeile close to him. It will help him fight against Taron, at least for now."

"Let us hope he continues to hold on," Fenn said, walking toward the door. "For all of our sakes." He slammed the door behind him, quickly exiting the building and vanishing into the warm summer night with his guards.

THE SHAMAN

The sun was setting as the shaman came into the village, knowing he was attracting stares, if not for his appearance, than for the appearance of his horse, whose mane was woven with the strips of knotted cloth that told the stories of all its ancestors, not unlike the ones the shaman wore on his own arms. The stories of his family, passed down through generations of tales, all the way back to Taeris, the Redeemer of Men, Stagmare of the North. They were tales and legends that a person should always carry with them, of heritage, caution, triumph, and tragedy. Now, with a desperate fire in his heart, he hoped he could add one more to his wraps.

He galloped through the city, his focus entirely on a small road that led to the edge of the woods, only a mile away. His heart began to clench as the ruined shell of the small house came into clear view. Blackened wood and crumbling stone were collapsed in a heap on themselves.

Only the stone firepit in the center of the building remained, and even that was overgrown with weeds.

Dismounting from his horse, the shaman rushed toward the remnants, desperate for any sign of attempts to rebuild, but there were none. The home had been destroyed, and the only one to stake a claim on it was a nest of small birds that took flight when they heard his approach, letting out warning cries to their fellow brethren roosting in the dark pines behind the ruins.

The shaman stared at the ashes of the home and felt his stomach clench. "No…" he whispered. "No… Not now. Not after all this time…" He felt his knees gave and he sank to the ground.

"You alright there, sir?"

The shaman looked up to see a friendly faced, swarthy man in a heavy cloak looking down on him. The man got closer to him and knelt down, concerned. "You okay?"

"What happened here?" The shaman could barely make the words audible.

The man looked at the ruins and let out a heavy sigh. "Tragedy. Guardians came and burned the place down. Executed the mother on the spot, if her son's to be believed. He fell ill and left."

The shaman grabbed the man's arm. "'Son'? What do you mean?" The man frowned.

"Mathiene and her boy lived here for nigh on seventeen years or so. He was a good lad, always building stuff and helping. Then, he fell in love with this strange girl, Glenna, a while back. She went off to join the Guardians. She was a magician of some kind."

"Violet eyes? Straight brown hair? Slightly husky voice?" the shaman asked quickly. He stood to his feet, fear causing a roar in his ears.

"That's the one," the man said with a curious gaze. "Why, you know her?"

"Not well," the shaman said. "But we have crossed paths before." The shaman's mind was reeling. How? Was it a coincidence that Mathiene had been found by the Indigo Witch? No, it couldn't be. Then, his mind refocused on the subject that mattered.

"The boy…is he dead too?"

The man shrugged. "I dunno… He just left one day, said he had to get to Trifectus, meet some fellow named 'Kelt McNair.' Odd name, if you ask me."

The anguish in the shaman's stomach transformed into a caldera of fury. The Butcher of Mages… Anyone without training would be dead within five minutes. And here he was, this boy, going to face his death alone, while sick, under the influence of the Indigo Witch. The shaman stood.

He nodded politely to the man. "Do you know if he made it to Trifectus?" His voice was quiet, a calm that hid the rising storm inside him. "Xeile?" The man gave him a wry smile. "Well, I don't know. One thing's for sure, though, he either got there or died trying. Boy was stubborn as a mule and as unyielding as iron. Took after his mother that way. Is that what brought you to Davadain?"

"Xeile," the shaman repeated. He turned and started walking away.

"Wait! *Where are you going?*" The shaman said nothing and mounted his horse.

"*Where are you going?*" the man repeated. "It's late at night. You should at least stay for an evening meal, sir! My wife and I will help you, if you need it. Even during the summer, the northern lands kill without hesitation."

The shaman looked at the man and flashed him a smile, a glimpse of white through a sun-beaten face and bright-teal eyes. "You are generous, but I lost the fear of my own death long ago. I must depart." He reached into a pouch on his rune-pocked saddlebag and flipped the man a whole Trifec. The man's eyes widened as the shaman turned his sturdy, muscular horse around to face the lone road that led back to the main village of Davadain and, eventually, toward the south.

"What are you going to do when you find him?" said the old man, looking at the coin, then back at this strange traveler.

"I'm going to keep him safe," the shaman said. "I've already lost my love. I'm not going to lose the only child I have left."

The man knocked his heels into the horse's side, and it obeyed instantly, taking off down the road, leaving dusty clouds to dance in the setting sun, and the old man to ponder the traveler's words.